# SHIMURA TROUBLE

A Rei Shimura Mystery

## Sujata Massey

**severn House**

This first world edition published in Great Britain 2008 by
SEVERN HOUSE PUBLISHERS LTD of
9–15 High Street, Sutton, Surrey SM1 1DF.
This first world edition published in the USA 2008 by
SEVERN HOUSE PUBLISHERS INC of
595 Madison Avenue, New York, N.Y. 10022.

British Library Cataloguing in Publication Data

Massey, Sujata
  Shimura trouble
  1. Shimura, Rei (Fictitious character) - Fiction 2. Women
  private investigators - Japan - Tokyo - Fiction 3. Arson
  investigation - Hawaii - Fiction 4. Genealogy - Fiction
  5. Detective and mystery stories
  I. Title
  813.5'4[F]


ISBN-13:  978-0-7278-6601-1   (cased)
ISBN-13:  978-1-84751-054-9  (trade paper)

*All Severn House titles are printed on acid-free paper.*


Typeset by Palimpsest Book Production Ltd.,
Grangemouth, Stirlingshire, Scotland.
Printed and bound in Great Britain by
MPG Books Ltd., Bodmin, Cornwall.

# Acknowledgments

This book was awhile in the making, and I wish I could prepare a luau to have room enough to thank all the people who helped create it.

I'll start with Maeona Mendelson, who opened her little black book, and thus opened Hawaii for me. I am grateful for what I learned from Honolulu lawyer and activist Bill Kaneko about the loss of Japanese-American civil rights during wartime. Another friend of Mae's, University of Hawaii religion professor George Tanabe, offered great insights into many topics ranging from aquaculture to O-bon. Finally, thanks to June Shimokawa, who shared her memories of her father's wartime internment.

Another new and dear friend is Liz Tajima, who did everything from introduce me to Hawaii Japanese to help with this manuscript. I'm also glad to have interviewed Professor Ginny Tanji of the University of Hawaii and her focus group: Andy Tanji, Richard, Emily and Philip Tanimura, Jean Toyama, Ginine Castillo and Colleen Kimura. Great information on Leeward Side life came from Betty Shimabukuro, features editor at the *Star-Bulletin*, who also introduced me to librarian Cynthia Chow of Kailua. Through Cindy I made friends with the terrific Hawaii writer Deborah Atkinson, who I thank for her insights on water sports and Hawaii schools. I learned so much about real estate from Cori Meyers of Kapolei Realty, and Patrick M. Cummins, a partner in Hawaii Land Consultants and an expert in the intricacies of land ownership in Hawaii.

The Kapolei Police were so helpful regarding my questions, and the entire staff of the archives department of the Japanese Museum of Hawaii were extremely gracious to an unknown drop-in scholar, sharing documentation of the immigration experience and connecting me with community member Sidney Kashiwabara. I'd also like to thank Marji

Hankins for introducing the idea of Transpac, and the Transpac Foundation's Press Officer, Rich Roberts, for explaining more, and Ray Pendleton at the Waikiki Yacht Club for making it possible for me to greet the boats as they arrived. In the Kapolei area, my home base for both summers, I am grateful to Retired Officer Kane from the Honolulu Police Department for sharing his knowledge of native plants, and Kevin Won of the Honolulu Fire Department. Management at the Halekulani and Hale Koa hotels in Waikiki were very kind to answer many questions and check out the rooms. Doctors Nancy Withers and Ken Hirsh, thanks for the introduction to Tamashiro Market, and more. Kyoko, Gary and Brian Vogel, Mark and Julie Decascas, and Vanessa MacDonald and her friends made me and my children feel like *kama'aina* living in the neighborhood rather than tourists.

In the US, I thank my new writers' group in Minneapolis, Judy Yates Borger, Maureen Fischer, Stan Trollip and Gary Bush for their uncomplaining help with this manuscript and its revisions. In New York, I am indebted to my agent Vicky Bijur for finding a happy home for this book with editor Amanda Stewart and publisher Edwin Buckhalter at Severn House. It's taken a long time to get Rei to England, but she's there now! And I close as always with many hugs and kisses to Tony, Pia and Neel Massey, who were with me all the way from the shave ice stands and plantation villages to the less obvious thrills of writing and proofreading.

If I left anyone out, please accept my apology for the oversight. I owe you a plate of tofu-scallion pot-stickers at the Little Village Noodle House.

*Aloha.*

Sujata Massey

# Cast of Characters

Rei Shimura – part-time antiques dealer and part-time spy, at a loose end once again

Toshiro Shimura and his wife Catherine – Rei's parents

Hiroshi Shimura and his son Tsutomu (Tom) Shimura – Toshiro's only brother and nephew from Yokohama; Rei's closest Japanese relatives

Michael Hendricks – a spy who loves Rei but can't quite come in from the cold

Yoshitsune Shimura – a first-generation American of Japanese ancestry born in Hawaii; the son of Keijin Watanabe Shimura and Harue Shimura, Toshiro and Hiroshi Shimura's long-lost aunt

Edwin Shimura – Yoshitsune's son, who is married to Margaret, and father to the teenagers Braden and Courtney

Kainoa Stevens – owner of the Aloha Morning coffee shop

Charisse Delacruz – coffee shop barista

Calvin Morita – Japanese-American psychiatrist

Albert Rivera – land manager and 'luna' of Pierce Holdings

Mitsuo Kikuchi and his son Jiro – a Japanese developer and son

Josiah Pierce II – the oldest living member of the Pierce land-owning family

Kurt Schaefer, Parker and Karen Drummond, and Eric and Jody Levine – Michael's old school friends from the Naval Academy, and their wives

Hugh Glendenning – Rei's former Scottish lawyer boyfriend

# About Japanese Family Names

In the Shimura family, several variations of family titles are used to express relationships such as grandfather, grandmother and uncle. Respect to elders is shown by incorporating the prefix '*o*' and the suffix '-*san*' into most family titles. However, Japanese people who settled in Hawaii mostly spoke peasant dialects, and their descendents still carry on with more casual titles.

*Ojiisan*: Most typical way of addressing a grandfather. Variations are *ojii-sama* (super polite) and *jii-chan* (most informal)
*Ojisan* (with a short 'i' sound): Uncle
*Okaasan*: Mother. A variation used in this book is the more casual *kaa-chan*
*Otoosan*: Father

First names are often followed by the suffix '-*chan*', meaning 'little one', or '-*kun*' ('guy'). This affectionate suffix is widely used for children, teenagers, and now between friends in their twenties and thirties. Thus, Rei Shimura is called Rei-chan by all family members older than she is, and she sometimes addresses her male cousin Tsutomu as Tom-kun.

# One

When my father almost died, I made a deal with God. If he improved, so would I.

Deals are what I know; in the beginning, they were just for Japanese antiques. More recently I've dealt with international secrets, but I'm trying to keep that a part-time affair. This particular deal didn't have a great chance of succeeding, given my father's prognosis, and my own status as a lapsed Buddhist-Episcopalian-whatever. Still, I would give it my all.

If my father lived, I would stop being such a run-around. I wouldn't drink too much, overspend on clothes or pine after men who would never be mine. I already had a guy in my life: Otoosan, my very own Honorable Mister Father.

My father had been out of San Francisco General Hospital for a few days, and I'd been granted leave to nurse him at home, when the letter came. Despite the circumstances, in a strange way it was good to be back at my childhood home on Octavia Street – the renovated Edwardian house that always seemed to smell of furniture polish and narcissi. The only kitchen smell missing was soy sauce. Because of its high sodium content, it was banned from my father forever.

We'd been talking about giving up things we loved, my psychiatrist father and I, during our daily constitutional – a mid-afternoon walk through Pacific Heights. It was slower for my father now, and we skipped the hills altogether. When we arrived home, a sheaf of mail lay on the Tibetan rug in the entry hall. My father started to stoop to pick it up.

'No sudden up and down movements!' I said as I dove down smoothly before him. My father had suffered a cerebral hemorrhage, and the new precautions he would follow for the rest of his life were varied. My father grumbled lightly, then settled himself on a carved Chinese elm bench to switch his walking shoes for house slippers while I sorted the mail. A bill from Neiman Marcus: I wouldn't let him see it. Less problematic was the bill from Pacific Gas and Electric, and the San Francisco Opera circular. As I was starting to discard junk mail, a slim letter fell out of the pages of the neighborhood's advertising mailer.

The handwriting was unfamiliar, as were the foreign-sounding street, Laaloa, and town, Kapolei. Still, it bore a US stamp. When I scrutinized the postmark, though, it all made sense. Honolulu, HI.

I had been to Honolulu once, for a study-abroad botany course at the end of my high school career. That summer spent traveling through parks and gardens, with a bit of Waikiki bar hopping, was one of my best ever, although my father had grumbled that after earning my certificate, I still couldn't tell the difference between plumeria and the Tahitian gardenia.

'Otoosan, you have a letter from Hawaii.' I handed over the letter with a flourish. I was dying for him to rip it open on the spot.

'*Honto?*' Truly? my father asked, turning it over slowly. He'd been in the US for over thirty years, and while he was fluent in English, he persisted in speaking Japanese with me during the times we were alone together. I thought about answering in Japanese, but decided to stick with English because I was feeling distracted.

'Probably it's a time share offer or something. These marketers have gotten quite skilled at making their envelopes look personal.'

'But the name on the envelope is Shimura. What a coincidence.'

'Why don't you sit down at the table to properly examine everything?' I suggested. 'I'll make you a cup of green tea.'

While I waited for the water to boil, I heated the teapot and thought about how slow my life had become. I'd never thought the arrival of a handwritten letter could be the most intriguing part of my day. A few months earlier I'd fought for my boss's life and my own in a dank Tokyo garage, as part of my occasional work as an informant for the Organization for Cultural Intelligence, a secret American government spy agency. The woman I'd been, dressed in a winter-white Yves Saint Laurent trench coat and patent-leather boots, was a far cry from the current me slouching around in a Japan-America Society T-shirt and yoga pants. Now I had plenty of exercise, and time to sleep and read. I was only slightly bored.

I set a tray with the tea, a strainer, and my favorite *cha-wan*, a rough teacup made by a famous Japanese potter. When I went out to the dining room, my father had clearly finished the letter, and had set it in my place.

'This letter . . . it's remarkable. It's made me feel better than anything since my surgery.' My father looked at me eagerly. 'Please, take a look.'

'Thanks, Otoosan.' When I read the first line in the letter, I suddenly recognized why the envelope had looked so alien. My father's name, Toshiro, was spelled with a short line over the first 'o' in my father's name, a symbol sometimes used to signify a long, double vowel. My father didn't write his name this way, because there wasn't a double 'o' sound in Toshiro.

> *Aloha*, Toshiro!
>
> Let me introduce myself. I am the son of Yoshitsune Shimura, who was born 88 years ago and is blessed to be celebrating *beiju* on July 6 of this year. Our families are linked because my father's mother was the late Harue Shimura, who arrived in Oahu in 1918 to marry.
>
> After almost a century apart, it's time for our families to get acquainted. And most folks are happy to learn they have kin in Hawaii! If you like, I will help you find suitable accommodations. I recommend you stay at least a month for the birthday celebration, because there will be lots of family events to fill up your time. Please bring your eldest son, if he can make it too, and call me as soon as you get this letter so we can make arrangements.
>
> Your cousin,
>
> Edwin Shimura

I raised my eyebrows at my father when I'd finished reading. 'This is a big surprise.'

'What wonderful news that we have more family. Thank goodness I lived for this news.'

'Yes, but . . .' I paused, not knowing how to express what was dogging me. 'When I traced our family history a couple of years ago, I didn't recall your grandfather having any siblings other than his brother Koizumi – the one who moved to Kyoto and entered a monastery.'

'Actually, there always were some whisperings about a younger sister in my grandfather's family, who was no longer part of the family, when my father was a child.'

'Whisperings?' Now this was something I was interested in.

'I once asked my grandfather, but he became upset with me, so I never dared speak of it again.'

'So if this lost great-aunt of yours existed, why would she go to Hawaii?' I thought my father was too quickly jumping to conclusions.

'I imagine she was a picture bride. Thousands of Japanese women were exported to marry Japanese expatriates working on sugar plantations. It was a social phenomenon in the first quarter of the twentieth century. I believe there were Korean picture brides as well . . .'

'Oh, right. I saw a movie about that years ago.'

'Harue Shimura – my great aunt, now deceased.' My father's voice was sober. 'And now we have learned that another branch of our small family exists, in Hawaii.'

'But then, why – if Harue Shimura married and had a son – why would their name still be Shimura?'

'As you know, Japanese men do take women's names in marriage, if it's the only way to keep a clan name alive.'

'But there were two brothers to carry on the family name – your grandfather and your great-uncle Koizumi, although he of course had no children. Maybe Harue remained a Shimura because she didn't actually get married.'

'Why be so negative? I'll find out the facts when we arrive there, I'm certain.'

'You can't seriously be planning to go.' I caught my breath. 'This is the first we've ever heard of these people, and you're still in recovery.' I didn't add that his chances of suffering a stroke within the month were about thirty per cent.

'But it's for *beiju*. A very important birthday. Do you know its meaning?'

'Double luck,' I answered. 'If one turns the *kanji* character for the number eight upside down, it looks just like the *kanji* for luck. So if two eights are rotated, it's twice as lucky.'

My father nodded. 'Eighty-eight is a marvelous birthday – I can't wait to celebrate mine – and Hawaii is a lovely destination. I see you shaking your head, but please remember how Dr Chin told you I needed time to relax.'

The neurologist had spoken about relaxation when we were reviewing my father's release. But as I'd understood it, relaxation meant eating right, walking, and mild weightbearing exercise. 'It's a six-hour flight. What if you have medical trouble on the plane?'

'Usually there's a physician on the plane who can help with those matters.'

'You're the one who always helps. Remember?' Even though my father's medical specialty was psychiatry, he was often the only physician aboard when the occasional in-flight emergency occurred. At least, the only one who volunteered.

'Very well. I shall ask Dr Chin his advice before deciding when to go.'

# Two

My parents had no idea that I had spy training, which at this moment seemed advantageous. I intended to start simply, but would go to whatever lengths were needed to trace the backgrounds of Yoshitsune and Edwin Shimura, to make sure this letter that had fallen into our house came from true relatives, and not hucksters.

That evening, after delivering a steaming cup of chamomile tea to my father's bedside, I made a second cup for myself and went online.

Yoshitsune Shimura's name didn't surface anywhere in my preliminary search, although it didn't surprise me that a man of eighty-eight wasn't a blogger or MySpace member. But

Edwin Shimura, the cousin who'd written the letter, was a quick and plentiful hit on Google. Once I'd screened out a seven-year-old chess whiz at the Mid-Pacific Institute and a twenty-five-year-old Nickelback fan, I located our very own Edwin Shimura, a fifty-five-year-old man with a residence on Laaloa Street.

*So this is my second cousin*, I thought, studying a picture of a man holding a sign over his head that read RETURN OUR LAND! He looked a little like my father around the eyes; but the face was longer, no doubt the influence of whatever other genes had entered our family during the course of almost one hundred years in Hawaii.

I marveled at another picture of Edwin Shimura marching with Polynesian-looking men, holding a sign declaring MY LAND STOLEN TOO.

So Edwin was an activist for Hawaiian land rights. I'd taken a history elective during my long-ago botany program, and I'd learned that foreign missionaries and their descendents living in Hawaii had pressured King Kamehameha III into dividing up land that had previously been held by the crown. The Great Mahele allegedly led to the American overturn of the Hawaiian monarchy and the establishment of Hawaii as a US territory.

As I read on, however, I discovered that Edwin's interest in gaining land was not an issue of righting past wrongs. I followed a trail of articles in the two Honolulu papers, the *Star-Bulletin* and the *Advertiser*, describing how Edwin Shimura was going to court over rights to a prime parcel of waterfront property on the Leeward Side of Oahu. The land was owned by Pierce Holdings, a company founded by early sugar planters who came to Hawaii from New England in the mid-nineteenth century. Edwin argued that his grandmother, who had once worked on a sugar plantation owned by Pierce Holdings, had been given the property by the Pierce Estate's patriarch, Josiah Pierce, shortly before World War II. But no legal record of such a sale existed, and in the end, Judge David Namioka had ordered Edwin to pay court costs of $20,000 to Pierce Holdings.

In the late 1990s, Edwin was in the news again. He had declared his travel agency bankrupt, which he blamed on decreased Japanese tourism. Eighty-five Hawaii and mainland clients who'd bought air and hotel packages had lost their money.

By 2005, Edwin had reinvented himself. He was running a telesales company offering green-tea-based cleaning products. No news stories covered this venture, but he had various sales pages sprinkled throughout the Internet that led to the same, zero-security payment page.

As bad as this all looked, I craved more. And I'd stayed up long enough for it to be early morning in Northern Virginia, prime time for reaching Michael Hendricks, my good friend-boss-whatever, at home.

'Sis,' Michael said, picking up after the second ring. He didn't need to use my old code name, but old habits died hard. 'So, how's your father?'

As Michael spoke, I could picture him rubbing his ice-blue eyes to clear the remnants of sleep. Then I imagined the rest of him: the square jaw and prematurely silvering dark brown hair cut short with a razor, even though he'd been out of the Navy for years. He had a lean body that was more like that of a man in his early twenties than thirty-nine, something I knew from a few platonic – and frustrating – evenings we'd spent together.

'My father's OK, but itching to travel,' I said.

'So am I. The streets of San Francisco beckon, but travel doesn't seem to be in my cards right now.'

Michael and I had become attached during our time working on our last Tokyo assignment – so closely attached, in fact, that Michael had felt duty-bound to report his feelings to our superiors at Langley. The result had been private conversations with a CIA psychiatrist for both of us. According to the psychiatrist, Michael and I shared an almost telepathic bond that had sprung out of our work. Relationships like these were common among soldiers and police; people who worked closely with a partner in dangerous situations. He thought we were no danger to anyone, especially not to each other.

'Well, what's the problem?' Michael asked. 'You don't usually call this early.'

'I know. I've been up all night. My dad's been out of the hospital a few days and suddenly he wants to fly to Hawaii.'

'That doesn't sound like a problem to me.' Michael snorted.

'I'd go to Hawaii with him in a flash. Did I ever tell you that I lived there when my father was stationed at Pearl?'

'No, you didn't. And let me finish, please.' I elaborated about the letter, the newfound family, the eighty-eighth birthday, and Edwin's legal and financial history.

'I could run his name through a few databases for you – but Rei, I don't think having a bad businessman for an uncle should be a deal-breaker. Hawaii's gorgeous in July. As well as every other month in the year . . .'

'I like Hawaii too. But I'm not willing to go there if it means getting mixed up with a bad character.'

'It's an old man's birthday party.' Michael sounded reasonable. 'Go to the party, get together a few times, and spend the rest of the time relaxing. You deserve the trip to Hawaii as much as your father.'

'All I've been doing here is relaxing. I'm bored out of my mind.'

'You told me that your father said the letter raised his spirits! You know, there's supposed to be a link between mood and recovery from illnesses. I can email you a study proving it.'

'Hmm,' I said. 'I'm more interested in proof that Edwin Shimura's ancestor, this picture bride called Harue Shimura, was in fact the girl who left my family. That's the gist of it, Michael. We don't even *know* if we're related.'

'Well, that's research you can do yourself, if you're so bored.' Now Michael sounded amused.

'Well, I've already emailed a historical society in Honolulu that might have records for Japanese immigrants. And I'll phone my Uncle Hiroshi in Japan, just in case he remembers more about the so-called whisperings.'

'Don't forget to check birth records with the state of Hawaii.'

'But she was born in Japan—' I interrupted myself. 'You probably mean I should check the birth certificate of Yoshitsune Shimura in order to reference the names of his parents?'

'That's exactly what I was thinking. You do your thing, and I'll do my part for you – when I can. I'm afraid that for the most part of this week I'm swamped.'

'What's going on?'

'If I told you, I'd have to kill you.'

'Very original. I do miss you, Brooks.' I used his code name, holding on to the last bit of intimacy, before the call ended.

'Don't change that feeling.'

'What?' I was momentarily confused, especially when Michael made the sound of a kiss and hung up. I had a feeling that the CIA would not approve.

My Uncle Hiroshi had never heard anything about a missing great-aunt. He'd also received a letter from Edwin Shimura, though, and as a result he and his son, my cousin Tom, were already condo-hunting for the visit.

'If you and your father meet us there, it will be wonderful. When's the last time we've all been together?' Uncle Hiroshi asked over the phone.

Frankly, I would have been reassured if my beloved Aunt Norie was coming along, but apparently she was teaching a month of *ikebana* classes at the Kayama School right at the time of the *beiju*. And Chika, my younger cousin, was involved in her first job. She was as busy as my mother, who couldn't come because the grand opening of the boutique hotel she was decorating was in mid-June. Tearfully, we spent many late nights together, talking about the past, her fears for my father, and how she felt duty-bound to work harder than she ever had in the event my father couldn't resume his medical school professorship.

I had work to do, too. I exchanged several emails with researchers at the Japanese Cultural Center in Honolulu, who confirmed the existence of a Harue Shimura who'd emigrated from Yokohama in 1919 , at the age of twenty. She was married at the dock by a judge who also recorded the changing of name by her husband from Keijin Watanabe to Ken Shimura. The Territory of Hawaii had a birth record for a child born to her and Ken: Yoshitsune Shimura, eleven months later.

So my father's guess was right, that Harue's husband had taken her name. But according to the record, Yoshitsune was older than eighty-eight. I showed the birth certificate copy to my father, who assured me that in old Japan, *in utero* time was counted in a person's age. Thus, my father was really sixty-four, not sixty-three. He went on to tell me I was actually thirty-one and not thirty, which really made me crazy.

'It's still wrong,' I said to my father. 'If you count in an extra year according to Japanese custom, Yoshitsune Shimura should have celebrated his *beiju* two years ago.'

'I'm sure we'll learn their family customs when we arrive.' My father's voice was placid.

'I've lost the battle,' I reported to Michael the next time we talked on the phone. 'We're definitely going.'

'Well, don't worry too much about it. I ran the FBI check and neither your Uncle Edwin nor his wife Margaret nor the great-uncle have robbed banks or murdered anyone.'

'Great.' But I didn't mean it. I'd been hoping for a last-minute reprieve.

'And I have something even better for you. A surprise.'

'What?' I asked dubiously.

'I'll see you in Hawaii a week and a half after you get in. If the winds are with me.'

I was surprised – and elated. 'If the winds are with you? Is that something for me to decode?'

Michael laughed. 'I'm talking about the Transpac.'

'What the hell is that? It sounds like a military exercise.'

'It's the longest sailing race in the world: two thousand five hundred and ten miles, to be exact. One of my old Naval Academy classmates has been trying to rustle up an extra crew member, and after squaring things here at Langley, I can actually sail with them.'

'Super. So are you leaving from Annapolis?'

'No, there's a staggered start for the various classes of yachts in Southern California. My buddy Parker Drummond, who's based in LA, splurged a few years ago on a forty-foot schooner. It should be able to make the trip in under two weeks if the winds are with us and we push ourselves.'

'Where in Hawaii does the race end?'

'The finish line is when you pass that huge old volcano, Diamond Head. We'll dock at the Waikiki Yacht Club, and another guy on the crew, my friend Kurt, has squared away rooms for us at the Hale Koa, which is the military hotel right in the heart of everything.'

'So you're staying in Hawaii just a week,' I thought aloud. 'That means you'll be at sea longer than on land.'

'Yes, that's the way it works. I wish I had more time to

spend on land with you, Rei, but getting these three weeks together is kind of a miracle. I gave Len the full sob story, how Kurt survived three tours in Afghanistan and Iraq and it was a dream for us all – Eric, Parker, Kurt and me – to sail together once again just like we did in Annapolis.'

'It'll be a great bonding experience,' I said, trying not to feel jealous that most of Michael's vacation would be with three men, and not me. 'I hope you have a wonderful time out in the Pacific.'

'Well, it's not like it's going to be a two-week party,' Michael said. 'It's doubtful we'll get more than four hours' sleep per twenty-four period.'

Trying to sound casual, I said, 'If you get a chance, call me from your cell when you're pulling into port. I'd like to greet you.'

'I hope to be able to reach you using the boat's satellite phone even earlier than that. I'd love you to meet my boat – it's been a long time since anyone's done that.' Michael's voice was wistful, and I knew without asking who this must have been – Jennifer, Michael's young wife who'd been killed in an airplane bombing in the late 1990s. Jennifer was the chief reason he still didn't have a girlfriend – and also the reason I'd been sitting on my hands whenever we'd been together. Who could compete with a ghost?

Trying to shake my morbid mood, I asked, 'So when does the race start?'

'Three weeks. We'll actually be leaving before you.'

'That's weird, isn't it? That I might be passing over you in a Hawaiian Airlines plane?'

'I think it's great. Send me your itinerary and that day, I'll just keep my eye out for planes with purple tails, and I'll toast each one that flies over me.'

# Three

When I fly for work with Michael's group, OCI, it's usually in business class. I've become accustomed to free drinks and semi-decent food, and kind attentions from flight attendants. But this time my father was paying. The flight was economy, and the rear cabin where my father and I sat was freezing cold. I demanded extra blankets, but there was only one, so I gave it to my father. The only perk was free guava juice, canned.

'Just wait till we can make our own fresh guava juice in Hawaii,' I told my father. 'Not to mention that passion fruit and mangoes are going to be in season.'

'I don't believe you packed a juicer,' my father said.

He was right. I'd packed many things, but not the giant juicer that sat in state in our San Francisco kitchen. 'The townhouse is supposed to be fully furnished, and that means kitchen utensils. If there isn't a mechanical juicer, maybe I can buy a wooden hand tool.'

'I don't need pampering,' my father said. 'I hear that everything in Hawaii is expensive. Canned juice is fine.'

'But not as rich in fiber and anti-oxidants,' I pointed out.

'Are you going to talk about health the whole trip?' my father grumbled. 'If so, I want those headphones of yours. I see the flight magazine lists a channel for traditional Japanese music.'

'Here.' I handed over my noise-reducing headphones and showed him how to turn them on. After a few seconds, a look of wonder spread over his face.

'These are very nice.' My father sighed, then closed his eyes and leaned his head against the window.

The Bose headphones had been given to me by Michael, a gift before my last trip to Japan. I paid $5 to rent cheapies from the flight attendant and plugged into the same Japanese station that my father was listening to. Then I buried myself in a mystery set in 1940s Hawaii, *The Mamo Murders*, which kept my attention all the way until we landed.

My father survived the flight without a second stroke, but I practically had my own upon arrival in Honolulu. I'd advised Uncle Hiroshi and my cousin Tom, who were scheduled to arrive four hours earlier, to get their baggage, have a snack, and meet us at our gate. But nobody was there, and my calls to Tom's cell phone went unanswered. Had they made it after all? I finally learned that a separate terminal existed for flights to and from Japan. Adding to the confusion, all passengers – Japanese or not – collected baggage in a third terminal a shuttle-bus ride away.

'Uncle Hiroshi and Tom might never find us,' I fretted as my father and I sat sandwiched together in the steamy little bus. 'I had no idea this airport had so many terminals! It wasn't like this the last time I was here.'

'Oh, I'm sure we'll hear from them.' My father seemed relaxed and happy as we shuffled off the hot bus and joined a massive wave going into a building, and then down an escalator to a series of baggage carousels. My father called out, waving, and then I too saw Uncle Hiroshi, short and solid like my father, in a green polo shirt and khakis, and my cousin Tom, taller and handsome in his crisp blue jeans and a yellow polo. Hanging from their necks were leis made of tropical flowers and seedpods. When my father, uncle and cousin met, all bowed – an underwhelming reaction for brothers who'd not been together for three years, but one that was completely in keeping with family tradition. Greetings were exchanged in Japanese, and I looked around for Edwin Shimura. He must have already met Hiroshi and Tom, since they were wearing leis, but where was he now?

'You must be very tired, waiting for us,' I said to my uncle in Japanese, because he wasn't much of an English speaker.

'Not at all,' Hiroshi demurred. 'We have been visiting with Edwin-san. He's just gone off briefly to check on the rental car.'

'That's nice of him,' I said. 'By the way, does he speak Japanese?'

'Yes,' Tom replied. 'But it's a *strange* Japanese.'

'It's a bit like the way peasants speak,' Hiroshi explained.
'I mean *inaka* Japanese, from the nineteenth-century countryside. At times, I thought I was hearing a film.'

I laughed and said, 'Well, the countryside is where most
of the original Japanese emigrants to Hawaii have their roots.
Perhaps the Japanese language in Hawaii has retained this bit
of old Japan.'

Not Japanese personal style, though. Five minutes later,
Edwin Shimura bustled into the terminal, two more leis
outstretched toward us – a jumble of pink, red, purple and
white flowers in one hand, yellow carnations and black seed
pods in the other.

'*Aloha, irasshaimase*! Welcome! So happy to meet you
guys!' He plopped the lei over my head and then crushed me
into a hug that smelled of orchids, perspiration and cologne.
He bowed to my father, bestowed him with the lei, and said
warmly, 'At last. My cousin, I thrilled to meet you.'

Cousin Edwin was speaking the Hawaii-style English I
remembered from my school trip. It was softer than mainland
American English, with extended vowel sounds, and ds that
sounded like soft ts, and plenty of dropped prepositions. I
could understand him perfectly, but I wasn't sure how the
others were faring.

'How was the flight?' Edwin asked, grinning as if he anticipated a rapturous reply.

'It was fine,' I answered for both my father and myself.
'Thank you so much for staying to meet us. I know you must
have been waiting for a while.'

'No sweat,' said Edwin, whose forehead told me otherwise.
'I chance going to the car rental and get a better car for you
this whole trip.'

'The sedan with GPS that I reserved was not available,'
Tom said in his impeccable English. 'So Edwin-san did some
research and found there was a car available at one of his
friend's lots.'

'I used to work in travel, so I have lots of friends working
in and near the airport. I got you guys a minivan with a handheld GPS! And of course, a minivan has much more room
than a full-size sedan. I figured you'd have lots of luggage,
once I heard you were bringing a daughter along!'

I was sorely tempted to snap at him, but instead I walked

off to the luggage carousel, which had finally creaked into action.

'Ojisan, you stay with the others. I'll help Rei-chan,' Tom said to my father. As we waited at the carousel together, he asked, 'What do you think of him?'

'I haven't known him long enough to make a judgment,' I answered carefully. 'But you've been together a few hours. What's your opinion?'

'I'm concerned about the change in car companies,' Tom said. 'I think they might have given us an upgrade since the car we reserved was gone, if we had stayed to talk. Uncle Edwin insisted on our leaving the place, because he said that his friend's rental car agency would have the car we wanted. The minivan we've got is $5 more expensive than the car we reserved at Hertz.'

'Well, I'm sorry about the change, but $5 more isn't that bad, at last minute. Though I guess I'm a little worried, since Edwin did all this re-arranging before I arrived, that I'm not going to be permitted as the third driver of that car . . .'

'It's five dollars more per *day*,' Tom said. 'And we're here for a month, which means $150 more. And as far as your driving goes, the agency owner said that he listed you, providing that you telephone him with driver's license information. And there was an extra three dollars a day to allow you to drive!'

'At least the doctor refused to let Dad drive,' I said. 'If we had to add him on to the contract, we might as well buy a car, instead of rent one.'

'And don't expect much comfort,' Tom said. 'It's not so clean, and it makes loud noises. I don't mean to be rude, but . . .'

I watched Edwin, who was having an animated conversation with my father. I decided that his red and purple aloha shirt suited him perfectly; it was as loud as everything else about him.

Edwin caught my gaze.

His mouth still formed a smile, but he looked as if he sensed what I was thinking. This was not a comfortable situation at all.

# Four

No one protested when I offered to take the wheel for our drive to the resort where we had rented the house. Perhaps it was because everyone was tired, or because the minivan was such a rat-trap. There appeared to be taco or cracker crumbs all over the front seat, and some kind of unknown sticky substance in the driver's side cup-holder. It was the worst spot in a vehicle with stained upholstery, air-conditioning that blew in hot air, and a very loud engine.

'Now, Rei, you can just follow my car out H-1 West as I drive straight home and we'll start the reunion! Margaret's working today, but I can stop off and get a nice *pupu* platter somewhere,' Edwin said after we'd all settled ourselves, more or less, in the minivan.

In the rear-view mirror, I caught Hiroshi and Tom exchanging anxious glances. I didn't need to look at my father, in the seat next to mine, to know that he was also too fatigued to eat Hawaiian hors d'oeuvres at Edwin's house. 'I'm so sorry, but I wonder if we could come to visit tomorrow? We are all a bit tired right now.'

'Yes, I apologize, but I would really like to get to the resort, unpack and lie down,' my father said.

'For health reasons,' Uncle Hiroshi added.

'What health reason?' Edwin looked at my father curiously, and I realized then that my father must not have communicated anything about the stroke.

'My father's recovering from surgery,' I volunteered.

Edwin blinked. 'For what?'

'Nothing serious,' my father said shortly, and Edwin nodded.

'OK, OK! You come by when you ready. I gotta advise you that this place you thinking of staying, Kainani, is not a place where you can experience what it's really like living in Hawaii. You gonna be cooped up in a time-share tower with a lot of mainlanders. My buddy Irwin's got some rental cottages up the coast at Makaha Point you wouldn't believe, and there's a three bedroom available—'

'Thank you so much, Cousin Edwin, but the non-refundable deposit has been made,' I said firmly. 'And we're renting a whole house that we selected because it's just a mile from your home!'

'Call me Uncle, and it's closer than this.' Edwin pinched his left thumb and middle finger together. 'I can lead you out there. The problem is, it's a gated resort. They might not let a local guy like me drive on the premises.'

'Oh, dear. If you could lead us out to the freeway, that would be very nice,' I said, thinking that while Edwin was no doubt exaggerating, if we got off on the wrong foot with him, the whole month would be spoiled. And if things were spoiled, my father would be anxious – and that anxiety could lead to a stroke.

'OK then. Follow me.' Edwin slammed the minivan's door closed and then climbed into a silver Toyota Tacoma truck streaked with red mud, parked a few spaces away. He pulled out into the parking lot aisle, and I hurried to keep up.

'Well done, Rei-chan,' Uncle Hiroshi said from the back-seat.

'Don't say that until Rei's gotten us there safely,' my father cautioned from his perch beside me.

'I'm referring to the way your daughter handled Edwin-san,' Hiroshi said. 'It's a good thing she stopped him from taking us to the other house.'

'What do you think of Edwin?' I asked the rear-seat passengers.

'What do you think?' Hiroshi turned the question round with perfect Japanese etiquette that made me want to shriek.

'He wants to organize everything for us,' my father murmured. 'It's quite natural, I suppose, since we've come from far away.'

'I'm so glad you didn't agree to change resorts,' I said to my father. We'd stopped at the parking attendant's booth, and I suddenly realized I needed to pay. I turned to my cousin and Uncle Hiroshi in the rear passenger seats and asked for a parking ticket.

'Oh, no! Edwin has the ticket,' Tom said.

My heart sunk. There was no way I'd be able to flag down
Edwin, since his vehicle had already cleared the traffic gate.

'No need pay,' said the parking lot attendant, a middle-
aged Hawaiian woman with a small white flower tucked
behind one ear; a blossom that looked like one of the flowers
in my lei.

'I'm sorry,' I said. 'I don't have a ticket.'

'No, no. The guy in the truck before you, he pay for everything. He say tell you *aloha* and welcome to Hawaii.'

After we passed through the gate and on to the freeway,
following Edwin's silver truck, I thought about things. Maybe
I'd judged my new uncle too quickly. Paying for our parking
had been a kind thing to do. My father said as much as we
rode along past a landscape that no longer seemed tropical;
dry hills scattered with housing estates and big box stores like
Old Navy and OfficeMax. H-1 suddenly seemed like a typical
traffic-choked freeway in Southern California. Only the
shifting gray and white clouds overhead, the soaring mountains and occasional flashes of blue ocean gave me hope that
something different might be ahead.

By the time we'd passed the exit for Pearl City, Edwin's
silver truck was three cars ahead of us, and I tried to keep
it in sight, but there were plenty of distractions: vans decorated with Japanese company names, city buses, and cars
towing other vehicles with only a few feet of rope connecting
them. My father tutted in disapproval at the sight of young
men sitting atop steel trunks in the open backs of pick-up
trucks.

'Get around that truck before someone flies off and lands
in front of our van,' my father advised. 'Can we get into the
HOV lane?'

We could, I decided after reading a sign that defined a
high occupancy vehicle as one containing two people. Now
that was different from California – not to mention the fact
that the other cars here easily made way for us to merge
into the diamond-marked lane. I was almost shocked by the
courtesy. Perhaps this was an example of 'Drive with Aloha',
a message I had seen on an electronic traffic message board
a few miles back.

After passing the town of Waipahu, speed picked up. Most
of the cars had defected to a north-bound freeway. The traffic

jam was over, and there were fewer stores and houses along the freeway, just dry brown land marked with sparse trees, rocks, and the occasional large burnt-black expanse. There must have been some brush fires here, I thought, and then yearned a bit for the lush green north-east section of Oahu where most of my botany course had taken place. Uncle Hiroshi had been kind enough to undertake the search for our housing, but obviously he didn't know that he was booking on the non-tropical side.

H-1 West ended, and I was now driving a one-lane road called Farrington Highway. Farrington was a big name on the island, that of one of the most influential governors of Oahu, and founder of the *Honolulu Star-Bulletin* newspaper. My reverie was broken by a hand-lettered sign propped on the right side of the road. It read, FRESH COLD LYCHEE. Twenty feet later, a second sign entreated, YOU WANT? followed by the final enticement: SO SWEET! I slowed slightly to get a look at a man hunched in the payload of a dusty truck sorting fruit.

The next signs I saw were official ones: Kainani, 7 miles. And on the left, there was a sign for Laaloa Street, and a postage-stamp-sized neighborhood of older, unmatched houses, the antithesis of the large, sterile housing developments we'd passed between Honolulu and Waipahu. As Edwin turned off to his neighborhood he stuck a fist out the window and wagged it, his pinkie and thumb skyward.

'What does he mean?' Hiroshi wondered aloud. 'Are we doing something wrong?'

'Not at all Ojisan.' I explained to him that the *shaka* sign was a greeting that supposedly originated with a plantation laborer who'd lost some fingers in the line of work. People waved back to him making their own hand signals two-fingered ones, as a show of respect. Now the *shaka* sign was the standard wave used everywhere in Hawaii.

The exit to Kainani was hard to miss: a hibiscus-edged, Japanese-style arched bridge. As I slowly took the exit, which crossed back over the highway to the ocean, the yellow-brown landscape dissolved into a Technicolor golf course. To my left was a large pond where lazy black swans pecked around the edge; to the right was a gated community of grand, 1920s-modeled villas the color of orange sherbet.

We'd all rolled down our windows long ago, a reaction to the car's non-functioning air-conditioning, and now trade winds gently rippled through the minivan. Trade winds, one of the prettiest phrases I knew.

'This place was built by a Japanese developer,' Uncle Hiroshi said. 'It's as pretty as in the internet photographs, I think. Is it all right for you?'

'It's lovely,' I said. Despite my belief in supporting native plant landscaping, I was secretly relieved that we wouldn't be staying in the middle of a brown field. 'You can't always believe what you see or read on the internet, but this looks postcard perfect.'

'Check out the golf course,' Tom said. 'Eighteen holes, and the golf club is supposed to have one of the island's top Japanese restaurants.'

'Top Japanese restaurants are expensive,' my father said. 'Rei will be happy to cook; why, she's been cooking for me this last month and I've lost five pounds.'

'That's not much of an argument for my cooking,' I said, thinking that what had seemed like an act of love, feeding my father, might feel a little different if I were doing it non-stop for three men. 'I just hope the kitchen has some pots and pans.'

'The kitchen is quite luxurious, I think. Would you care to see the photographs?' Tom started rummaging in his carry-on bag.

'Not now, thanks. Security's ready to talk to us,' I said, because the cars ahead of us had all been cleared and now it was my turn to introduce myself at Kainani's gatehouse.

After I'd given our name and the street address of the house we were renting, a handsome young man in a green-and-gold aloha shirt and trim khaki shorts handed me directions and an envelope with keys to our house on Plumeria Place. Plumeria was the name of the particular flower in the parking attendant's hair, I remembered. Hawaii was coming back to me, fast.

I drove a half-mile farther, passing the Kainani Inn, a sprawling modern hotel on the beach side of the road. On the left was the fabled golf course, where a cluster of golfers had gathered to watch someone swing.

'Michelle Wie!' Uncle Hiroshi started thumping on his

window, as if the star teenage golfer might wave. She didn't notice, so I was forced to stop the car in order that Tom and Uncle Hiroshi could run to the golf course with a digital camera.

After ten minutes Hiroshi and Tom returned to the minivan, full of bubbly excitement over the young star. Finally we turned left at the small road cutting through the golf course that led to an elaborate iron gate with fancy pineapple designs and the name of the housing area, Pineapple Plantation. As the Aloha team member who'd given me the key had instructed, I waved the house key over a sensor and the gates parted to reveal a neighborhood of simple gray clapboard houses, each with a wraparound white wooden porch called a *lanai*. Another gorgeous word that had returned to my memory. Despite my intentions, I was happy to be in Hawaii.

'Well done, Rei-chan!' Tom said, practically jumping out of the car when I'd pulled into the driveway. I slowly got out of the car, still studying the house. It was clearly part of a mass development, but its simple, well-balanced design was architecturally pleasing, albeit American. The only factor that made these homes feel Polynesian was the landscaping: vigorous shrubs like ginger, breadfruit trees, and several species of palm. Thick banks of orange-spotted lauae ferns lined the walkway to the house, not quite covering the sprinkler heads set into the ground. I smelled plumeria everywhere, its dainty white blooms on small trees that looked as if they'd been planted only recently.

Inside, the house plan was modern. The heart of the home was a high-ceilinged kitchen with granite counters and stainless-steel appliances including a professional-looking juicer. As my father exclaimed over it, I looked past the pot rack hanging with anodized aluminum pans and across the neutrally furnished living room to huge windows showing views of the beautiful green lawns. So this is what you could get on the Leeward Side of Oahu for four thousand dollars a month – not bad, if you compared it to the cost of a month in a single hotel room.

Two bedrooms and baths were upstairs, one of which would be for Hiroshi and my father, and the other for Tom. I would sleep downstairs in my own bedroom, which was delightful because the room had its own *lanai*. Instead of using the downstairs air-conditioner, I could turn on the fan over my bed and open the sliding *lanai* door to the trade winds.

I lay down on my bed, intending to close my eyes only briefly. The ceiling fan whirred lazily overhead, and trade winds came through the sliding doors I'd opened to the garden. I heard the sound of a strange bird singing its evening song, and the laughter of children somewhere farther away.

Through my slightly opened bedroom door, I overheard my father speaking Japanese on the telephone, probably to someone at the hotel's Japanese restaurant. Yes, he was ordering sashimi, rice, and of course, miso soup. In some corner of my consciousness, I remembered that my father shouldn't eat miso because of the sodium levels. But I was too tired to intervene, too tired to do anything but lose myself in the soft purple twilight.

# Five

It was five thirty when I woke – eight thirty in the morning, California time – and I felt marvelous. I'd slept through dinner, and apparently everything else. And now, as soon as it was light, I would get to run.

I pulled on melon-colored shorts and a red running tank and my socks, and walked out to the empty, dark kitchen. After swigging two glasses of water and brushing my teeth, I went through my running stretches. I tucked a house key and a ten-dollar bill into the ankle-strap wallet I used for running, and then I was off.

The sun was rising, and already the pretty boulevards of Kainani were filling up. Elderly couples power-walked, young singles jogged, and fathers and mothers pushed strollers. Asian and Caucasian golfers cruised along in their carts; the resort's gardeners, their faces hidden by cloth-draped hats, were just getting set up to work.

I ran south along Kainani Boulevard, passing the timeshare

high-rise Edwin had decried, then condominiums, and a series of swimming lagoons. Toward the ocean loomed a large white house, about a story higher than the others, and set apart from them by tall green conifers clipped to perfect uniformity, like hedges were in Japan. I ran a little closer and looked through the copper gate decorated with jumping dolphins. A rock column was inset with the blinking eye of a security camera, an electric doorbell, and a name in copper *kanji* characters. It took me a minute to read the Japanese name, Kikuchi, but no extra time to understand the English underneath. PRIVATE PROPERTY – TRESPASSERS FORBIDDEN.

I jogged off, thinking about how the security camera must have caught me studying the house. Well, I thought defensively to myself, there had to be a lot of tourists staying at Kainani who would gawk at such a large place, especially since it had the water right behind it – unlike the townhouses, which all backed on to pleasant shared gardens. Only the Kainani Inn, the timeshare tower and the Kikuchi house had direct beach access.

Because of the pleasant breeze, I decided to run farther, even as I approached a wire fence marking the resort's border. A person-sized gap in the tall wire fence separated the green resort from a dry, rocky brown field that stretched to infinity. Obviously, this was an informal network of paths for workers coming and going from Kainani.

I squeezed through the gap and ran on, enjoying the feeling of being almost off the beaten track. It was an interesting place, with the sparkling ocean and a small industrial harbor on one side, and the towering mountains on the other. In the field, small herds of horses had their heads down, eating up seed pods that had dropped from the lacy kiawe trees growing profusely through the landscape. Kiawe was the same as mesquite; it had been introduced to the island to feed horses brought by settlers. Now I imagined that animal-grazing was one of the few things that could be done with fallow land that had once held fields of sugar cane.

Two more miles, and the dirt path ran straight into a cluster of small weathered cottages. Each one had a tiny *lanai*, and while the white paint had almost completely worn off the houses, a few rusty mailboxes still had painted names on them: Fuji, Narita, Ota. All around me, short paths stretched out with vacant cottages that looked identical. I was probably standing on the grounds of the old plantation laborers' village, perhaps where my great great aunt had lived.

I walked through the village, my pulse slowing as I searched for our family name. I didn't see anything, but Harue Shimura was on my mind, a woman barely out of her teens, rising to prepare breakfast and lunch for a husband and the single male laborers in the community. She would have had barely enough time to wash the dishes in the cold water she'd carried herself from a well, and then she'd be hurrying off behind the men to work stripping the husks of the cane in the fields. She'd work all day with barely a break, and when she came home after ten hours' hard labor, she'd take her bath along with other women in the communal *furo*, which would be dirty and lukewarm after the men had used it. She'd quickly ready dinner, clean up the dishes, and then involve herself with laundry and mending.

I would ask Yoshitsune Shimura about this place, I thought as I picked up my pace at the end of the village. I'd spotted a pitted asphalt road and, alongside it, a long barn-like wooden structure with a *lanai* running around three sides. The building was definitely of the same vintage as the houses I'd seen, but unlike them this was freshly painted bright green with rainbow-colored letters above the *lanai* that read ALOHA MORNING. Even better was the neon sign in the window: OPEN.

The old plantation store – which is what I guessed it had been – was now a coffee shop, judging from the looks of a small crowd of locals sitting on the *lanai* with paper cups in hand. The array of trucks and vans parked alongside probably meant the coffee was good.

I opened the screen door to the coffee house, which seemed very dark after the brightness of the morning sun. I stepped on to a rough, wide-planked wooden floor and made out glass-fronted wooden cases holding breads, buns and fruit preserves. The store seemed all-purpose, I realized, as my eyes continued to adjust. Now I saw racks holding fishing supplies, beach toys and swimwear, and some tables and chairs sat across from a coffee-service counter.

I waited my turn at the counter, where a pretty girl in her twenties with long black pigtails was drawing coffee from gleaming brass and stainless steel machinery.

'I'm getting this newspaper, and I'd also like a large bottled water and a small skinny latte, please,' I said when it was my turn.

'Water's in the fridge case, over by the door.' As the barista spoke she smiled, revealing a cute gap between her teeth. 'What kind of latte did you say again?'

'Skinny. With skim milk,' I clarified, just in case the coffee shop lingo was different on Oahu.

'Can't do that. Two per cent okay?' She leaned down to open a small refrigerator, her low-cut T-shirt gaping to reveal a healthy bosom.

'Fine.' I politely looked away, aware that the workmen behind me were taking advantage of the view. I wondered about her – did she really not mind being ogled, or was she actually clueless about what she seemed to be offering? It was a relief when she stood up and moved away to draw the espresso and heat the milk for my drink. She took a while doing it, but returned with a perfect cup.

I commented on the foam heart she'd made, and she beamed and extended a hand with chipped pink polish on the nails. 'I haven't seen you in here before. I'm Charisse.'

'My name is Rei,' I said, trying to remember the last time anyone in a coffee shop had taken the time to introduce herself. 'I'm staying at Kainani, so I'm sure I'll be seeing a lot of you in the next month.'

There were some chuckles from behind me, and I guessed that I'd provided the guys with an unintended double-entendre to brighten their wait.

'Nice place! I've been there a few times to visit a friend.' Charisse dimpled at me. 'Anyway, welcome to Hawaii.'

Someone behind me was making impatient grunts so I got out of the way with my goods and found a seat at a sugar-dusted table just vacated by a mother and two kids.

The coffee was good, but not quite as full-bodied as I liked. I sipped anyway, and opened the *Star-Bulletin*. I glanced at a main section full of national wire stories, then started in on the second section devoted to local news. I read about how a private school founded by a Hawaiian princess was struggling to maintain a rule that its students have Hawaiian ancestry. What did that mean, exactly? I wondered, looking around me at the mosaic of mixed features and warm skin tones. Who was Hawaiian here, and hadn't the Hawaiians themselves emigrated from other Polynesian islands?

I had much to learn, I thought, as I moved on to a picture of an adorable sea turtle and the accompanying soft-news story about how tourists on North Shore beaches were teasing them. When I turned the page, I spotted a story about the place where we were staying. Kainani's developer, Mitsuo Kikuchi, sought to develop adjacent lands where existing derelict plantation housing remained. The land was owned by Pierce Holdings, which was considering either a lease or outright sale to Kikuchi's Tokyo-based company.

Kikuchi had to be owner of the grand house I'd seen, I guessed, reading on. Pierce Holdings' spokesman said that Kikuchi's planned new restaurant and amusement park would bring a new road and several hundred new jobs for leeward Hawaii residents. However, a preservation group leader argued that the plantation village should be a registered historic landmark, and a group of Hawaiian activists had already filed papers asserting that the fields contained a sacred worship site.

Suddenly, I had the sensation that I was not reading alone. I looked behind me and, sure enough, someone was standing over my shoulder.

# Six

'Howzit?' asked the spy, who was an undeniable hunk – well over six feet and at least two-fifty, with shoulder-length black hair and skin as brown as cocoa. His sleeveless T-shirt and baggy, knee-length shorts revealed geometric blue-green tattoos on muscular arms and calves.

He laughed slightly, as if noticing my covert inspection. Embarrassed, I tried to remember what he'd asked me about. 'Well, I'm used to very strong Tanzanian coffee, so Kona's a bit mild for my taste.'

He looked at me for a second and I had the sense I'd said something very wrong. Then he burst out laughing – a deep, merry laugh that seemed to boom around the store.

'What's funny?' I asked cautiously.

'You a tourist, huh? I didn't realize at first, 'cause when I saw you talking to Charisse, I thought you just another *hapa* chick.'

'Well, I am *hapa*,' I said, recalling that this was the common term in Hawaii for a person of mixed ancestry. In Japan, the same expression existed, but it was said slightly differently: *hafu*. In English, it meant half. Half a person, not the real thing. *Hapa* was better; it almost sounded hip.

The hunk interrupted my linguistic analysis. 'Yeah, but I asked you *howzit*, which means, how are you? I wasn't asking for an opinion on my coffee.'

'*Your* coffee?' I asked. He wasn't wearing an apron at his waist like Charisse had. He certainly didn't look like an employee.

The man laughed again. 'I'm Kainoa Stevens, and that cup you're drinking comes from my cousin's coffee plantation on the Big Island. I own this place.'

I shook hands reluctantly, because I expected a man who looked part-Samoan to have a crusher grip. But the handshake was just firm enough, and he followed it up by pulling a business card out of his baggy shorts pocket. The card, still warm from his body heat, was decorated with twin palms, his name, and the phrase 'Coffee and Construction'. At the bottom were four phone numbers. Out of habit, I held the card the way one does in Japan, reading everything carefully before putting it down. Now, I was obligated to introduce myself, and since I wasn't carrying a card, I told him my name.

'Charisse said you staying at Kainani. How did you ever find your way here?'

'I chanced upon it, when I was jogging through the wilderness area.'

Kainoa laughed. 'Had to be something like that, because the road here is pretty indirect. But you gotta understand that it wasn't wilderness you crossed. It's all part of the Pierce Holdings, and if you trespass again, you better watch out that the *luna* don't catch you.'

'I had no idea I was trespassing. I didn't see any keep-out signs.'

'That's probably because you ran through the middle of the fields. There are warning signs on the fence along Farrington Highway.'

'So, what's a *luna*?' I asked.

'In plantation time, it was the guy who oversaw the workers. No sugar workers anymore, so Albert Rivera just oversees the security of the land. People around here call him the *luna* because that's the job his father worked, and his grandfather, too.'

'Hmm. I guess I'll have to put together a nice apology for him in advance, because I don't know how to return to Kainani any other way.'

'That regular route here is via Farrington Highway, but it's probably four miles longer than the route you took. I'd say, take a chance if you want to run over for coffee again – which I'm not even sure you do.' He smiled at me, but I sensed a challenge behind the straight, shining white teeth.

'It's *good* coffee, Kainoa, just not as strong as I normally drink it. I probably should just order a double shot in my latte.'

'At my cousin's plantation, he experiments with new varieties all the time. I think I'm gonna tell him, grow me a super-strong bean for strong mainland chicks.'

'Really, don't go to the trouble!' I suddenly had a sense he was flirting with me, and I didn't want to encourage him. Kainoa was not only half a decade younger than me, he was not Michael.

'Or better yet, I could sell this place to Mitsuo Kikuchi and make my own coffee plantation on the Big Island. What you think of that?'

'I was reading about Kikuchi's plans in the paper, as you probably noticed. Are you actually in favor of the development?'

'Sure.' Kainoa's tone was casual. 'I have a construction sideline business, you know, so I'm for most kinds of development. And as far as this business goes, hell, I'd much rather have two roads that come to my shop than a bunch of old shacks going to waste. When I was a kid growing up, sure I liked to hang out there, smoking *pakolo* with the mokes. Now that I'm a property owner, I don't want that kind of stuff over here.'

'But you wouldn't be a property owner with anything to gain if you sold to Kikuchi.'

Kainoa leaned so close that I edged back slightly. 'Hey, I'd love to stay where I am. But the thing about Kikuchi is, if he has an idea, he gets what he wants. You know the true reason that he built Kainani?'

'To make money?' I hazarded.

'More than that. He built it to have a hiding place for his *lolo* son. People in Japan or Honolulu ask what the son's doing, and he likes to say Jiro's running the resort. In reality, this do-nothing Jiro lives in a townhouse with a round-the-clock head shrink supposed to keep him out of trouble. I know because I see the two of them together constantly – at the movie theater, the Safeway, in bars. Jiro even comes in here couple of afternoons a week, trying to pick up Charisse, who's so simple and friendly she don't understand.'

'What do you mean about Charisse?'

'She's a great kid, but a chatterbox! She'll talk to anybody, go with anyone. Even a creep.'

If Jiro was getting around as much as he did, he sounded as if he was doing pretty well. I said, 'So you're telling me that Mitsuo Kikuchi is making sure his son gets good care within the grounds of a beautiful place, and he doesn't want people to know he doesn't have a job? That doesn't sound so terrible, especially if you look at the norms of Japanese behavior.'

'Well, to build this pretty holding place for his son, he screwed everybody,' Kainoa said fiercely. 'There was a local community there, about sixty or seventy homes. I grew up in that place.'

'Is leasehold like renting?'

'Not exactly. It was something the *kama'aina* landowners use to profit from selling their land repeatedly.'

*Kama'aina*, I recalled, meant child of the land. It generally meant local and Hawaiian, with the exception of the Hawaii-born descendents of the British and American missionaries, many of whom mixed their bloodlines with daughters of the Hawaiian chief class: strategic marriages that resulted in the acquisition of more land.

'Our parents and grandparents helped each other buy homes as early as they could, and in those days they only had the right to be on the land for a period of time. Usually, the lease-hold had a time period that sounded long – sometimes fifty, eighty years, like that.' Kainoa looked down for a minute. 'When my daddy turned seventy, he had twenty years left to live on the property. He was anxious about whether anyone would want to buy the place, with twenty years or less left on the lease before re-negotiation. He'd have to sell for almost nothing, to get someone to take it.'

'That's awful.'

'Yeah. So here comes Kikuchi, and he offers everyone on-the-spot money for their homes, but that's if they *all* agree to leave. And at the same time, Pierce Holdings leaks the information that they may be shortening the lifespan of the leaseholds.'

'But how could they back out on a lease, legally?'

'Pierce Holdings is the second largest landholder on the Leeward Side. Its CEO can force the state government to cooperate with them because if they don't cooperate, the company won't build a school, or a police station, or a road.'

'You mean the Pierces actually pay for government build-ings?'

'Sure. For the tax credit, and the power it gives them. If the government here wants to add a road they have to get permission from the big landholders or the military, who own the land where the road would pass.'

'How did you become owner of this coffee shop, since all the surrounding land belongs to the Pierces?' I asked.

Kainoa gazed around with an almost wistful expression. 'I took over this building after my father died. He bought it from the Pierces back when Ewa Sugar shut down. The sale was a kind of favor, because my grandfather ran the general store for over forty years, which is why my family would look like stink at me if I sold it.'

Again, a kind of paternalism from the Pierces, but at least the store had stayed in working people's hands. I said, 'Your store is the last living part of the old plantation village. I understand why you wouldn't want to sell off part of our heritage.'

'*Our* heritage? I thought you were a *malihini* from the mainland.'

*Malihini* was a pretty-sounding word, but I knew it meant newcomer, which wasn't the best thing to be in Hawaii. I said, 'Actually, my great-great-aunt came here in the twenties.'

'For real? Shimura's not a common name on this island,' Kainoa said. 'The only one I know of is one *lolo* dude who couldn't possibly be related to you.'

'I think you're talking about my cousin Edwin – but what does *lolo* mean?'

'Crazy. And hey, I'm sorry. But he's full of it, when he talks about discrimination against the Japanese. After the war, they took over politics, law, and real estate. The real Hawaiians are the only ones with a right to complain about losing land.'

'So, may I ask if you're a real Hawaiian?'

'A quarter, which was good enough for the Kamehamema Schools. The rest of me is Samoan and Filipino.'

So I'd been right about the Samoan part, although I didn't yet understand Kainoa's inner self. I didn't care for his playful, insulting behavior, a technique that big, good-looking men like him employed a bit too often.

As if sensing my thoughts, Kainoa smiled, his teeth sharp and white. 'I'd like to shoot the breeze all morning with you, Rei, but I gotta convince Charisse to stop yapping and make more coffee. You try come back here?'

'Probably,' I said, glancing over my shoulder at the counter. There was indeed a long line, but Charisse seemed oblivious, lost in yet another conversation.

'Well, next time you try a cuppa green tea. You might like it better.'

# Seven

I made it back across the Pierce fields unmolested except by a few knobby passion fruits, which dropped from an old, twisted tree on my head and on the path in front of me. When I entered the townhouse, however, carrying two handfuls of tiny fruit, trouble was waiting.

My father, Tom and Uncle Hiroshi were all seated at the dining table, with full glasses of water. There were empty plates, and knives and forks and spoons were all laid in the proper places. They looked as if they were waiting for someone to serve them. But what? I knew there was nothing in the fridge except for ketchup and sugar left by the previous renters.

Trying to ignore the accusatory expressions, I put the fruit on the table, and then stooped to unlace my shoes. 'Good morning, everyone, I've brought you some passion fruits – which I believe are called *lilikoi* here.'

'Where were you, Rei?' my father asked sternly.

'I went for a run, got a coffee, and came back.'

'You went to drink coffee by yourself? I'd been hoping you'd gone to shop for food for our breakfast,' my father said.

I glanced at my watch; it was eight o'clock. 'I imagine the stores are opening right now. Dad, did you take your pills? There's that one you need to take on an empty stomach, remember?'

'Safeway in Kapolei opened at seven,' Tom said. 'We wanted to go, but we didn't want to leave without you, because of course you'd want to choose what you need for cooking.'

The sinking feeling I'd had about doing the cooking and cleaning for everyone returned. If I didn't want to wind up like an overworked picture bride, I would have to subtly resist. I smiled and said, 'Yes, I'd like to help you go shopping,' before disappearing into my bathroom to shower off all the red field dust. After that, I hustled past them with the towel wrapped around me, into my room, where I unpacked khaki shorts, a black tank top, and sandals. I went out with wet hair, because the warm Hawaiian air would probably give me a natural blow-dry within a half-hour.

Tom took the wheel, in order to practice driving on the right side of the road, and I navigated. Safeway was easy to find, smack in the middle of a strip mall anchored by two mainland chains: Blockbuster Video and RadioShack. Inside Safeway, however, I was pleased to find two long aisles devoted exclusively to Asian foods, ranging from umpteen kinds of sweet bean cakes to *sembei* crackers and dozens of different instant noodle brands with instructions only in Japanese, Chinese and Tagalog.

Local pineapple and papaya was plentiful, but it was harder to find locally grown vegetables. I did the best I could, searching out island-hatched eggs and local lettuce and tomatoes, and then dealing with my father's shock at the prices when it was time to pay.

Even with the added weight of a dozen grocery bags, the minivan made it back to Kainani, where I prepared a large breakfast of scallion-and-tomato omelettes for everyone – two whites and no yolk for my father – plus toasted slices of a sweet white bread. Tom performed surgery on a Maui pineapple, cutting its flesh into perfect triangles. I cut into the passion fruit I'd picked up on my run, and scooped its runny yellowish interior into a small bowl.

When I tasted the passion fruit, I almost swooned. It was sweet-sour, fragrant, and the perfect complement to the excellent pineapple, which was not just sweet but complex, with almost a hint of coconut flavor.

Once we all had food in our stomachs, the mood around the table improved. I found myself enjoying a conversation with my uncle and Tom about what was happening in Japan.

'Rei-chan, I think you're ready to become a wife,' Uncle Hiroshi said, wiping his mouth with satisfaction on one of the decorative paper napkins I'd bought. 'I wonder what kind of dinner Edwin's wife will make for us?'

'Margaret?' I asked, resenting the easy sexism my uncle

displayed. 'Who knows if she's the family cook? It could be Edwin, or maybe the children, Courtney and Braden, if they're old enough.'

'They all have Western names,' Tom mused.

'That seems to be the pattern of most Japanese-Americans,' my father said. 'It probably has something to do with not wanting to be noticeably foreign, after what happened during the Second World War.'

'Yes, we cannot expect them to be Japanese at all,' Uncle Hiroshi said. 'It's been a century, almost, since our great-great-aunt arrived. It's only natural they are more American than Japanese.'

I thought about my uncle's words that night as we drove the minivan into the neighborhood where Edwin and his family lived. I'd expected it to be similar to the sterile new developments I'd seen along the freeway – and in Japan, as well – but Honokai Hale turned out to be an older community, a hodge-podge of modest homes that seemed to have followed no architectural master plan such as I'd seen in the town of Kapolei. Chain link fences, monster trucks, and barking dogs greeted us as we parked on Laaoloa Street in front of an asphalt-shingled two-story house with rusted air-conditioners fixed in the windows. Because of the elevation of the neighborhood, it offered a magnificent view of the Pacific Ocean shipyards.

'My goodness,' my father said, interrupting my contemplation. 'Could that be our Edwin's father – our *ojisan* Yoshitsune?'

Startled, I looked at an elderly man coming around the side of the house, dragging a hose. He wore knee-length rubber boots, dirty khaki pants and a white undershirt. With a complexion like keyaki wood, squint lines around the eyes, and a shock of white hair, he looked like an aged Japanese peasant.

My father bowed deeply and murmured a traditional Japanese greeting, but the man frowned as if puzzled, and asked in a heavy pidgin accent, 'You the one from Yokohama?'

'No, I am he.' Uncle Hiroshi came forward, bowing, and introduced himself in very formal Japanese, not the usual way a banker would speak to an old man in a dirty undershirt and fisherman's boots. Tom joined him, bowing and introducing himself.

Still the man wouldn't give his name, so I decided to speak to him in English. 'My name is Rei Shimura. May I ask if you are Mr Yoshitsune Shimura?'

'Nobody talk that formal out here. You can call me Uncle Yosh,' the man said, looking me over rather critically. 'You came for my birthday, yah?'

'Yes, we did,' Tom answered in English, as if he'd finally realized that was our great-uncle's preferred language. 'I'm Tsutomu, but please call me Tom. Like you, I prefer a nick-name!'

'You all a little late.'

'Uncle Yosh, I'm sorry. I must not have driven quickly enough.' I glanced at my watch, which read five to six.

'I mean that I made eighty-eight last year! Why you not come then?'

'I'm sorry,' I said, shooting a significant look at my father. 'I believe our families found each other a month ago.'

'Yes, Oji-sama, I regret we have come a year late to supper!' my father valiantly chimed in. 'We feel so lucky to finally meet you and to learn about the life of your mother, who must have been a very brave, strong, character.'

'My *kaa-san*?' Yoshitsune asked. I almost didn't understand him, because he was using the word for mother without the honorific 'o' in front that was customary in Japan.

'Your *okaasan*, Shimura Harue-sama,' my father answered politely, still in Japanese. 'She apparently left our family when she was quite young. We are eager to learn about her.'

'Surprise to hear that. She didn't choose to leave Japan.' Yoshitsune's voice was cool, and as he evaluated us, I felt a rush of shame, followed by curiosity that got the better of me.

'We want to know why,' I said. 'My father said he heard whisperings there had been a sister to his grandfather, but nothing more than that.'

'She didn't want to get married to some old fool they picked for her husband,' Yosh said, grinning slightly. 'So they said you don't want to marry, you gotta leave the house. She was thinking that meant she'd find a job somewhere in Tokyo, but she had no clue about the real, hard world!'

'This is fascinating,' my father said. 'What happened next?'

'Your great-grandpa bought her a one-way ticket to Honolulu and also some false papers saying that she had relatives sponsoring her. She told me she thought it was going to be a great adventure. She only got scared once she was on the boat, when the other passengers, all of them rough, poor people from the countryside, insisted she would have to be married for anyone to hire her or give housing. And that's how she came to meet and marry my fadduh, a few days after she arrived . . .'

'Good, you found us!' Edwin said as he opened the front door and broke into the story. 'But, Dad, look at yourself! I told you to get dressed hours ago; this is your birthday party!'

Yoshitsune waggled the hose at him. 'The koi need something to swim in. I gotta fill the pool again, there must be a leak.'

'Do you keep koi?' I asked, looking around the garden. Then I saw it, a small ornamental fishpond occupying pride of place in the center of a dry-grass yard. I followed Yoshitsune over to the pond and stayed, looking at the fish, as he stuck the hose in the pool, then ambled back over to the side of the house to turn on the water. I'd assumed only specially treated water went into these ponds, but the half-dozen long gold, orange and cream fish looked healthy. Whatever Uncle Yosh was doing, it worked.

'Come in, come in,' Edwin urged, and obediently, I followed everyone up a cracked cement path and left my sandals at the doorway. The shoes-off tradition was part of Japanese culture that had endured.

Inside, I was zealously hugged by Edwin, and then by a small, sun-browned woman with short black hair attractively streaked with silver, who introduced herself to me as Auntie Margaret.

'When we learned about you and your family, we were so excited.' Margaret spoke with a melodious lilt that so many people in Hawaii had, to some degree – perhaps vestiges of their grandparents' home languages. 'But you came by yourself! Where's your husband?'

'I don't know. I'm not married yet.' I smiled at her, thinking again that Hawaii wasn't so different from Japan, if a thirty-year-old was automatically expected to be married.

'Oh, still not yet!' Margaret laughed. 'We heard about your big-shot lawyer fiancé. He won a class action suit, yah?'

Now I flushed red and understood who the 'son' was that Edwin had referred to in his letter to my father. 'It's true that Hugh Glendenning did work with many other lawyers on a class action suit representing comfort women and forced laborers who suffered during World War Two. We're really not in contact with each other anymore, though.'

'What do you mean?' Edwin asked. 'I can help you find him; I'm good at tracking people down . . .'

'No. I mean, I don't want to find him. We're not engaged anymore.'

'Oh, sorry to hear that!' Edwin said, and Margaret looked at me with sympathy.

'Please take this small, unworthy token. It's not very good, but all we could find.' Tom blessedly interrupted the situation by offering Edwin a gift bag containing a bottle of California chardonnay we'd chosen at the Safeway.

'Very kind. Thank you!' Edwin waved us all to follow him into the tidy living room, which looked as if it had been decorated in the early eighties, with floral-chintz sofas, and lots of rattan. A young girl, her face hidden in a thick copy of Modern Bride, was lying on the carpet close to the air-conditioner. I sat down on a floral-patterned sofa with my father. Edwin put the bottle of wine into a cabinet which I saw already held many bottles of wine and hard liquor, some still in the boxes. So it seemed he rarely drank.

'Courtney!' Edwin called to the girl on the floor. 'I told you before, when the guests come in, serve the *pupus*.'

Before I could greet her, Courtney had shot up and gone through the kitchen door. Moments later, she returned precariously carrying a tray of deep-fried hors d'oeuvres. While everyone oohed and ahhed over the golden brown minced shrimp balls and oversized potato and eggplant tempura, I looked anxiously at my father. Fried foods were highest on his list of banned foods. Now temptation was staring at him from a blue and white platter, and he was stretching out a hand.

'Otoosan!' I whispered loudly.

'I cannot refuse. That would be rude,' my father said in a low voice before popping a shrimp ball in his mouth.

Tentatively I took a shrimp ball, biting through the crisp, golden brown crust to taste the freshest, sweetest shrimp I'd ever eaten, finely minced and exuberantly seasoned with biting, fresh scallions and cilantro leaves.

'This is delicious!' I said after I'd swallowed it. 'Who made them?'

'It's from a little *okazu-ya* in Waipahu. If you like *okazu* snack foods, I can tell you all the best places,' Margaret said.

'Please do,' I said, wondering how, if the food was take-out, it was so very hot and crisp. The answer came when I glanced at the stove and saw a deep pan of oil. The snacks had been refried at home, making them even unhealthier.

'Eat more!' Margaret urged. 'I'm sorry to say that I don't cook much since the kids got big and I started working.'

'Ah! Do you work nearby?' Uncle Hiroshi asked, smiling.

'Quite near. I'm director of housekeeping at the hotel.'

The smile on Uncle Hiroshi's face froze, and I imagined the calculator in his banker's brain had made a judgment on the family. And I too was recalling all the Japanese maids in the old novels I was reading about Hawaii, and how in the newspaper article I'd read, activists had rued that the proposed new jobs in the area would be mostly in the service industry.

'I'm too tired after work to do much cleaning around here – and I have to admit that I'm not much of a cook, especially of complicated Japanese dishes. I'm not full Japanese like you; I'm *hapa*, mixed with Hawaiian. Edwin calls me mixed plate.'

'I guess Rei is mixed plate, too. Her mother is American,' Tom volunteered.

'Never would have guessed it! Toshiro, did you marry a *haole* girl?' Uncle Edwin asked in a tone that I wasn't entirely sure was friendly teasing.

My father looked blank, and I quietly said that yes, my mother was Caucasian. *Haole* was a Hawaiian term that originally referred to anything foreign, one example being a tree, the koa haole, which resembled a native koa, but was widely regarded as an invasive pest.

Great-Uncle Yoshitsune joined us wearing a short-sleeved blue aloha shirt, his face and hands freshly scrubbed. Even in proper dress, he still resembled a garden gnome.

'Jii-chan used to do a lot of cooking when he was a young man,' Margaret said, nodding her head at Uncle Yosh. 'For a while he lived in Honolulu, so he knew the best butchers and fishmongers. He used to take my mother-in-law until she passed away ten years ago, may she rest in peace. Now the only one likely to do any cooking is Courtney, and that's just because she is so obsessed with planning her own bridal reception.'

'Are you really doing that?' I asked.

'Am not! I just like the pictures, the clothes, the . . . stuff,' Courtney said with a sigh.

'Between Harry Potter and those bridal magazines, my kid lives in a fantasy world,' Edwin said. 'Thank goodness you gotta be twenty-one to get married here – otherwise, she'd be picking out a husband when she start her senior year!'

'Daddy, please!' Courtney was bright red by now, tears starting in her eyes.

'Tell me about where to shop for fish, Uncle Yosh,' I said quickly, to change the subject.

'Tamashiro's on North King Street, in Palama. I don't drive no more so Margaret, you should go there,' Uncle Yoshitsune chided. 'I hear they sometimes still get *opihi*.'

'Too far, too much trouble,' Margaret said, smiling easily.

'What are *opihi*?' I asked.

'A small type of shellfish that clings to rocks. Harvesting it is quite dangerous,' Margaret said. 'What they call it in English, Edwin?'

'Limpet,' Edwin said. 'It's scarce, but it sure makes tasty *poke*.'

*Poke*, pronounced po-kay, was Hawaii's version of ceviche; I'd had it with tuna or octopus many times. Suddenly I had a yearning for it. This trip still had potential, at least from a gastronomic perspective.

'We have some things for you.' My father gestured toward the dozen or so gift bags we had brought with us. According to Japanese tradition, I had carefully wrapped each gift, and then put each box in an individual shopping bag.

'Oh, I don't need nothing,' Uncle Yosh said.

'Presents? Thanks!' Courtney seemed to wake up as she reached for a bag containing her gift certificate to Delia's, and her parents eagerly leafed through the bags, looking for

the ones labeled with their names. Aunt Norie had bought
Margaret a beautiful silk scarf, and I'd found a book on new
uses for green tea for Edwin.

'Where's Braden? We have something for him,' I said. Tom
had chosen the gift, the very latest Nintendo game from
Tokyo's Akihabara electronics district.

'The boy suppose to be here, but running late. We should
go ahead,' Edwin said.

Everyone seemed pleased with the gifts my father and I
had chosen, and Norie had sent over with Tom and Uncle
Hiroshi. The reaction I cared about was Uncle Yosh's to the
album I'd made. He sat himself on the sofa, turning pages
slowly as I stayed nearby, ready to answer questions. A strange
expression came over his face after a few minutes of studying
the album.

At last he spoke. 'I heard a lot about these people. But why
don't you have any pictures of Kaa-chan?'

I felt bad about Harue having been disowned. 'It was the
turn of the century, and perhaps any family pictures of her
didn't survive, or if they did, weren't recognized as such by
us. I'm so sorry; I want to go back and look again . . .'

'I have an idea,' Tom said brightly. 'Perhaps we shall learn
the name of her old schools in Japan, and get childhood photographs that way. We were able to find such photographs for
the males in the family.'

'She didn't go to school.'

'What?' I exclaimed, shocked because the Shimuras were
an intellectual family.

'She had a governess, she told me. Learned all these fancy
ways of talking – guess it was good over there, but hard here.
People laughed at her Japanese,' Uncle Yosh said, shaking his
head. 'Sorry to say, I was embarrassed many times.'

'Really,' I said. This corroborated everything I knew about
the folkways of the Shimura family. I wanted to continue, but
Edwin cut in.

'It's time for eat. Our dining table isn't so big, so we serving
food in the kitchen, and you can bring it out here. Please,
come try.'

My father had been ushered to the front of the buffet line,
so he was well away from my gaze. I couldn't possibly cut

in front of everyone to supervise his food choices; I could only worry.

An hour later, I realized that my father's decision to eat barbecued pork, sticky rice and deep-fried vegetable tempura was the least of my problems. As Margaret sliced a coconut cake, Edwin started in on his agenda, and almost everything I had feared about the trip came to pass.

# Eight

'Let's talk about the meaning of family.' Edwin canvassed the table. 'Jii-chan, tell everybody how it feels to suddenly realize you have two nephews and their families to celebrate your birthday? Good feeling, yah?'

There were polite murmurings from everyone.

'I got a whole lot of family history to teach you guys.' Edwin seemed to be pointing his chopstick directly at me. 'Things that happened here to us – to this family – you need to know!'

I sat numbly as Edwin narrated the story I'd gleaned from internet news sites: that in the 1930s Harue Shimura owned a small house on one and a half acres of land near Barbers Point, the old naval station. Harue had lived there after she'd retired from work on the plantation, around the time Yosh was starting his first job with the post office in Honolulu. Then, after Pearl Harbor was bombed and Yoshitsune was sent to an internment camp for Japanese-Americans in Idaho, Harue died of a stroke. When Yoshitsune returned in late 1946, the land and cottage had been taken over.

I interrupted, because Uncle Edwin had casually dropped in some information I hadn't heard before. 'Uncle Yosh, were you interned in a camp for Japanese-Americans?'

Yoshitsune only nodded, and I looked expectantly at him, wanting more. This was a stunning bit of family history, because very few Japanese born in Hawaii had been interned. The plantation owners had convinced the US government that their workers were loyal, and that the sugar industry would collapse if Japanese in Hawaii were taken away.

'I heard some first generation and *nisei* Japanese from Hawaii were sent to the camps on the mainland, but they were rare cases, weren't they?' I said, choosing my words carefully. 'How unlucky that you were among the few taken away.'

'Jii-chan worked at the post office.' Courtney spoke up, surprising me. 'The boss thought he was trying to look into military mail.'

'Yes, a complete set-up, if you ask me. They just wanted him to be gone.' Edwin sounded bitter. 'And we had the waterfront property, which they thought would allow him or my grandmother to send signals to the enemy.'

My father, Tom and Uncle Hiroshi had grown as still and quiet as Yoshitsune. I imagined our group was contemplating our own family history: how Harue Shimura's older brother became a right-wing historian who'd tutored the emperor, and the other brother had been an officer in the Imperial Army. *We* were the enemy, as far as anyone outside of Japan was concerned.

'Please, will you tell us about the internment camp? If it's not too difficult,' my father said after a pause.

'It was called Minidoka, in Idaho. A small place, with barbed-wire fence and around that, mountains,' Uncle Yoshitsune answered in a flat voice. 'We had no idea how long we'd be there. I felt I had to escape.'

'Jii-chan was smart. He found the way,' Courtney said. I smiled at my young cousin, thinking that her interest in family history reminded me of my own, when I was her age.

'One day some army officers came to visit,' Yoshitsune said, interrupting my thoughts. 'They were recruiting guys who could speak and read Japanese to work in intelligence. I volunteered. I did interrogations for the American and British military.'

'It's a great story, Dad. You some hero!' Edwin's words were quick; clearly, he wanted to return to his agenda.

Yoshitsune seemed to shrink into himself then. While I longed to keep the conversation going about intelligence, I knew it was probably better to do it later, when fewer people were around.

Edwin took over again. 'You heard the terrible thing that happened to my Dad? Think of how it was for him, when he came home, a free man who served this country in the war. He find his mama gone for ever, and all of a sudden Chinese people living in the house. They say the Pierces leased it to them.'

'Ah, yes, Rei thought that was what happened,' my father said, nodding.

'Internet search engines are useful, aren't they?' I said, in response to Edwin's injured look.

'The papers don't tell the real story. Because the old man was dead, my father asked Mrs Pierce what happened to his mother's house. Mrs Pierce said there was never a fee-simple sale to my mother – always just leasehold, and that had expired. That Pierce woman said the land couldn't remain idle, so she rented it to Winston Liang and his wife.'

'Well, since you don't have a deed of sale, do you think it's possible that your mother might have actually had a lease?' I turned to Yoshitsune, because I wanted to hear the story from him directly.

'I once saw a letter,' Yoshitsune said in a low voice. 'I found it sometime, must have been the mid-thirties, in her bedroom dresser. The letter said that Harue Shimura was granted this land in exchange for faithful service. It was signed by Josiah Pierce.'

'A letter,' I repeated, thinking that it didn't sound anything like an official, legal deed at all – but who knew how things operated in prewar Hawaii?

'The letter's gone,' Yoshitsune said, dashing my hopes. 'Everything was gone when I came back from the mainland.'

As if to put an exclamation mark on the disappointment, there was a bang at the front door, and after a moment, a teenage boy stuck his head around the corner of the dining room. He had the same attractively tilted dark brown eyes as his sister, but wore his black hair shaved close to his head. *A Hawaiian skinhead*, I thought, taking in the ripped T-shirt with its Quiksilver logo and way-too-long board shorts.

'Braden, you get your sorry self in here!' Edwin roared. 'Where you been so long?'

'Nowhere you need to know about.' Braden scraped his

chair loudly as he sat down with a plate containing nothing but pork.

'Braden, please. It's Jii-chan's belated birthday celebration,' Margaret said. 'Your cousins have been waiting to meet you!'

The boy glanced at each of us as his mother made the introductions. Tom and Hiroshi made slight bows from their positions at the table, but I didn't bother. I had a feeling that Braden would mock anything Japanese about us. His sister was watching him too, as if she expected something to happen.

Edwin picked up the conversation we'd been having before the sullen teenager's arrival. 'Now, like I was saying, this land, it was very nice because it's waterfront. Even on the Leeward Side of Oahu, waterfront property is worth a lot of money. The Japanese developer who built Kainani wants to buy twenty acres, of which our land is a small part – but probably worth five or six million.'

'Are you talking about the developer called Mitsuo Kikuchi?' I asked, glad for something to distract me from Braden. He was chewing with his mouth slightly open, a disgusting sight.

'Yes indeed,' Edwin answered me. 'Mitsuo Kikuchi wants to buy all that land from the Pierces to make a restaurant development.'

'That's a tough situation for you, isn't it?' my father said. 'If you want to get the land back, for nostalgic and emotional reasons.'

Edwin looked as if he thought my father was deranged. 'Of course I want to sell to him. I want to get the property, and then sell it. I mean, that's what my fadduh wants to do. Right?' He shot a look at Uncle Yoshitsune, who only raised his white eyebrows.

'It would be good for your whole family, economically,' Uncle Hiroshi pronounced. Money was the one thing he understood.

'Uncle Edwin, how will it be possible to sell the land if your father doesn't have a title?'

'We can prove it other ways. The evidence is all around.' Edwin waved his hand around as if the proof was floating somewhere above the dining table. 'You see that I'm a simple

working man; I never had the funds to hire a lawyer. A good
lawyer would have won the case.' Edwin looked at me again.
'Your ex-fiancé, he went and helped complete strangers for
free! He could still help us.'

'I don't think it's appropriate,' I said tightly, and noticed
both my father and Aunt Margaret look at me with concern.

'We must bring out the truth, quick as possible. And I'm
willing to make it worth everyone's while,' Edwin rasped.
'Since Rei won't talk to Hugh, we'll have to hire a real-estate
lawyer from one of the good Queen Street firms. Somebody
better than the last guy, Bobby Yamaguchi. I'll need you guys
to help me with the retainer; they charge you thousands, just
to get started. Whaddya think, Hiroshi? You a money guy,
right?'

Uncle Hiroshi nodded, and after looking at him, I saw my
own father and Tom nod as well. The family wouldn't let each
other down, even if it were heading straight for disaster.

Taking a deep breath, I spoke. 'Uncle Edwin, I'm deeply
sympathetic, but I'm concerned that this might actually be
a personal matter handled better, fully, by you and your
father.'

'I give you this promise.' Edwin was looking at the men in
my family, as if I hadn't even spoken. 'You get me the legal
help to fix this situation and then I'll flip that land to Mitsuo
Kikuchi for a price even more than it's worth – you know
me, I can be persuasive. And we'll split the proceeds three
ways – my family, yours –' he nodded at my father – 'And
yours.' A final nod to Hiroshi and Tom.

'This could be a lot of effort and expenditure for . . .' I cut
myself off, not wanting to be rude enough to say 'nothing'.
Instead I continued, 'How do you know the property's value?'

'I ordered a commercial appraisal earlier this year. You can
see the paperwork, if you like.'

'Yes, please,' Tom and Uncle Hiroshi said, almost in unison.
Margaret jumped up and hurried into another room, coming
back with a small sheaf of papers. After Tom and Uncle
Hiroshi studied it, they passed it to my father, and then it was
mine.

I scanned the appraisal. 1 Kalama Street was a ratty-looking
shack in the midst of weeds, and a line of type below listed it
as a rental property owned by Pierce Holdings. The appraised

value was five million dollars, which the appraiser had calculated based on the prospect of selling the cottage as a tear-down
property.

'You can go out there, see it yourself. Me, I got a court
order to stay away from the place, so I can't go there anymore.'
Edwin turned to look directly at the men at the table. 'So how
about it? Do you want to help us? If I'm being too pushy, let
me know. We're family.'

To my surprise my father said, 'I think we'd like to think
about this . . . challenge you have presented. May we give you
our answer in a few days?'

'Of course!' Edwin sounded aggressively jovial. 'I didn't
mean to surprise you with too much news at one time, but
you are just here for just a month. We got to use our time
well.'

*No*, I thought to myself. *It's not about using our time well.
It's about using us, period.*

# Nine

I broke the law right away the next morning by heading
across the Pierce fields for my run. Everything I'd learned
about Pierce Holdings in the last day had predisposed me to
dislike, and I seriously doubted the lands manager would shoot
a small woman in a red running bra and purple shorts, if he
came across me. I prepared an innocent response, in case I
was confronted, but I was not. I saw nobody there, nor in the
plantation village, and I fairly swaggered into Aloha Morning
and downed a bottle of ice-cold Fiji water while I waited for
my latte, feeling the sweat cooling against my almost-bare
back. It had been a wonderful run, largely because of the
absence of traffic. The only car I'd had to watch out for had
been a speeding Mercedes driving through Kainani, and I'd
just let it pass.

On this, my second full day on the island, I felt myself

falling into a routine. At the coffee shop I'd exchanged the *shaka* sign with Kainoa when I'd walked in; he'd grinned but remained in leisurely conversation with customers lounging on the *lanai*. While I waited for my coffee order to be made by a young, bleached-blond Asian surfer boy, I ambled around the shop, looking at the various things for sale. In addition to surfboards and macadamia nuts, there was a clothing section selling Hawaii-themed T-shirts, sarongs, board shorts and swimwear.

'You plan to swim home?'

I jumped at the sound of Kainoa's voice. He was right behind me, with a paper cup in one hand. 'Here's your latte. I had Joe make it with a double shot, no extra charge.'

'Thanks.' I saw his eyes go to the small crocheted bikini in my hand. 'Don't tell me you've got nuns in a convent going blind making these?'

Kainoa laughed. 'My cousin Leila crochets them, hanging out in her backyard while the kids play. They sell here and on the beach at Haleiwa, where of course the price is twenty per cent higher.'

'Cute, but a bit too young for me.' I put the bikini down, glad that my three-year-old Speedo was still serviceable. 'So, where's Charisse?'

'Didn't show up.' Kainoa shrugged. 'Second morning this week it's happened. If she gets in, I'm going to have her give the espresso machine a good cleaning – I can't handle this place all on my own, you know? And about the bikini, just take it home, yah? Forget your age, which is what, twenty-six?'

'Thirty. You're a very good salesman,' I said, smiling despite myself.

'It's not the only thing I'm good at.' His eyes held mine for a moment. 'What are you doing tonight? I'm going over to a club on the North Shore, nice little hangout where Jack Johnson used to play. I hear he's back on the island, which means he might even stop in and jam.'

'What a nice invitation.' I paused, thinking how I could rebuff him without causing offense. 'I'm sorry, but I can't go. Family obligations.'

'You got kids?' His thick eyebrows rose.

'No, but I'm caring for my father. He had a stroke recently, so I'm working on his physical therapy and diet every day, and I don't like to leave him alone at night.' I'd poured it on a little heavy, but I didn't want Kainoa to ask me out for another night. 'My morning run is the one thing I do for myself, and I treasure it.'

Kainoa followed me over to the bar, where I decided to use a squeeze bottle of local honey instead of my usual sugar. He said, 'All right then, I can take a hint. So how you getting along with your Hawaii relatives? Is your uncle still chasing waterfront property dreams?'

'He is – and no matter how *lolo* or annoying he may be, I'm sympathetic. So many Japanese-Americans lost property during the war. There are heartbreaking stories throughout California, where I grew up.'

'Hawaii's totally different,' Kainoa said. 'People here weren't put in the camps. Nobody stole their land—'

'That's not exactly true. If you look at the whole chain of islands in Hawaii, about twenty thousand were taken to camps on the mainland. In our case, Uncle Yosh worked at the post office, so he was accused of reading classified military mail.'

'Yosh Shimura – you talking 'bout the old buggah who raises koi? I didn't know he was interned.'

'Yes, he's the one.' I took a sip of coffee. 'Hey, this latte is perfect. Maybe it was the double shot.'

'I'd think you would have ruined it with the honey you added,' Kainoa said.

'It's my new habit; I'm trying to cut down on refined sugar.'

'Whatever,' Kainoa said. 'And regarding your crazy family business, don't even think about it no more. You got enough going on with your father. You don't need more life troubles.'

'What do you mean by that?' His tone had startled me.

Kainoa looked at me. 'You want to stay in good health, keep up your running, go swimming, try the honey in your latte. Where you might get hurt is going somewhere you shouldn't, especially on this side of the island.'

'Are you talking about the Pierce lands?'

'No, I'm not.' Kainoa looked at me levelly. 'I'm talking about the past. And it's just a tip, because I'd hate to see a nice girl like you get hurt.'

\*   \*   \*

Had Kainoa been threatening me? I wondered as I lounged in the pool with my father a few hours later. No, I decided. It was just the language gap between us. All of a sudden, I wished I really was a *kamaaina,* and not just another *hapa-haole* stumbling her way through misunderstandings.

The sun had warmed the pool to the most amazingly pleasant temperature, and the sky was beautiful and cloudless. The sun was high, but gentle trade winds kept me from overheating. From my supine position, I heard rumbling. Someone was talking; my father, no doubt. He was the only other person in the pool with me, and he'd been talking almost nonstop, all through the morning's workout of exercises taken from my new bible, *Move and Groove Past Your Stroke!*

I felt a hand slide under my back, and I jerked upright to find myself looking not at my father, but a much younger Asian man with spiky, gangster-style hair and small eyes with a strange glint in them. His upper body was typically hairless, but it was puffy with flab, atypical for any Japanese man, especially one in his twenties. And, unbelievably, he kept his hands under my back.

'Need help float?' he said in a heavy accent – not pidgin, but Japanese.

'Get away!' I twisted away, sputtering, because I'd swallowed a bit of water at the shock of the touch.

'*Wakarimasen,*' he said, and lounged on a blue Styrofoam noodle, the kind of water toy children were more likely to play with.

So he definitely was Japanese, and he was pleading that he didn't understand English. I didn't bother continuing the conversation in either language, but splashed back to my father, who was lounging against the pool wall, reading.

'Did you see the Japanese guy with the noodle? He just touched me!'

'Oh really? That's Jiro Kikuchi,' said Uncle Hiroshi, who had been lounging in a chair wearing a sun-shielding visor that covered almost his whole face. 'If he likes you, maybe that's a good thing!'

'*What?*' I was incensed.

'He's the developer's son, Rei,' my father said. 'We met earlier when you went into the restroom. I was just talking with him in Japanese, and then for a few minutes with his roommate.'

Now I remembered what Kainoa had said about the younger Kikuchi and his caregiver. I followed my uncle's gaze to a short, bronzed man in his thirties with thick black razor-cut hair wearing a Speedo suit and reading *The Annals of Psychiatry* behind a pair of dark sunglasses.

'Did the roommate mention that he's a psychiatrist?' I asked, recalling Kainoa's information.

'Yes, how did you guess?' my father answered. 'His name is Calvin Morita, and he's just like you, Rei, partly Japanese and partly American. He went to Yale for his undergraduate and medical degrees. Since you didn't care for Kikuchi-san, shall we introduce you to Dr Morita?'

'No!' I got out of the pool and found a chair far away from the matchmaking brothers, where I buried myself in *The Waikiki Widow*, the Juanita Sheridan novel that was the final book in the series I'd started on the plane. I hadn't finished two pages before Calvin Morita strolled over.

'Are you Doctor Shimura's daughter?' he asked with the long vowel sounds of the Midwest. I nodded warily.

He crouched down close to me. 'I'm Calvin Morita, and I live in the house over there.' He waved his arm in the direction of the end of the cul-de-sac, where the Kikuchi mansion lay. 'I was wondering if something happened in the pool.'

'Yes. Jiro Kikuchi just came up and grabbed me when I was swimming.'

'I'm so sorry. He's got some psychological issues.'

'Perhaps he does, but he still should be kept from touching women like that.'

'It's called schizoaffective disorder.' Calvin gave me a penetrating look. 'He's fine most of the time, but sometimes he expresses himself in a way that we would consider . . . boisterous. I know it's hard for a layperson to understand. I take care of him, so please accept my apology for not doing a very good job.'

I examined Calvin, who was neither good- nor bad-looking, just completely average, except for his physique. Such blown-up muscles on a man who was barely five foot six inches tall was ridiculous. And what kind of a doctor had so much time in his day that he could pump iron?

'You might want to stay very close to him, or avoid public

swimming areas.' I glanced over at Kikuchi, who seemed to be focused on rubbing himself against a noodle.

'Oh, he's fine, just a bit frustrated at times. And regarding supervision, it doesn't work well when I'm in the water with him. He feels as if he's being babied.'

'Well, you're doing splendidly at not hurting his feelings then.' I stood up, because I noticed that Jiro was getting out of the water. It was time for me to jump back in. I waved at Calvin and without another word dove smoothly under the surface. This time, when I came up, my father was beside me.

'Are you feeling better now?' he asked.

'Not really.' I was treading water, and my father joined me.

'Well, let's take your mind off the present and talk about the situation with Edwin,' my father said. 'I want to explain why Hiroshi and I are so concerned about it.'

'Hey, I'm concerned too, but that doesn't mean I want you to throw a lot of money into paying a lawyer to chase a dubious proposition.'

'I'm not happy to become involved in Edwin's personal life either, but Hiroshi and I must do something to amend for what our great-grandparents did to Harue Shimura by sending her to become a laborer in Hawaii.'

'But you can't apologize to her. She's dead.' As we talked, I kept my eye on Jiro Kikuchi, who was watching us, but seemed content to be poolside, for the moment, with Calvin.

'I received a telephone call from Edwin this morning, while you were running,' my father continued. 'He pressed me for an answer, and I have delayed until dinner tomorrow evening.'

'Where? At their place again?'

'No, ours. I would have asked you first, but you were gone. We can all cook together . . .'

The last time my father cooked, he'd started a fire. Hastily, I said, 'I'll cook the meal like I'm doing all the others. The only catch is I don't have a really good cookbook with me – I'll have to think up some impromptu things, I suppose'

'There will be nine of us, since Hiroshi invited Calvin Morita. I hope that isn't a bad surprise?' he added, when he saw my face.

'How could you? What's he going to do, bring along Jiro?'

'No, no, Calvin explained that he expects Jiro's father to be in town, which means he can come alone.'

'Just my luck,' I said grimly.

'Thank you for understanding, Rei. Also, I wanted to ask if you had time to drive me to my first appointment at the Queen's Medical Center today?'

'Yes, of course. What time?' I was in the mood to get away from Kainani.

'It's at two, but I thought we could go in earlier, and I'd take you to lunch at Chinatown first. Then, during my appointment, you could start researching legal documents that pertain to the cottage situation.'

'But we already know there was no real estate transaction. If there was a deed giving the Shimuras claim to the land, Edwin would have been able to use it for his earlier lawsuit.'

'You've said from the start that you don't trust Edwin,' my father said. 'So it's better for us to verify all the facts personally.'

'But you're supposed to be relaxing, not running around doing research.'

'It won't be so bad for me, if you help out. Hiroshi and Tsutomu are helping, too.'

'How?'

'My brother agreed to talk to a realtor about land values, and Tsutomu is going to try to reach the lawyer Edwin worked with before.'

I blinked water out of my eyes, thinking that my father had done more groundwork than I thought him capable of. Still, I doubted a land records search would turn up anything more than we had already learned from the appraiser's report we'd seen the evening before. I said, 'We must find a way to speak with Uncle Yosh privately. He probably could tell us some things that would make the situation clear. But do you want to do that, Dad? I mean, you're closer in age to him, and a man.'

'I don't think so. Yesterday when we met, he refused to speak Japanese. He's deeply conflicted about his identity. You have more of a . . . colloquial way about you than I do. You're the American. I believe you'll be more successful.'

'We'll see,' I said. 'But I hardly know how to bring it up, with Edwin always hovering and interrupting.'

'You might ask Great-Uncle Yoshitsune to take you shopping

before you prepare the meal. That will give you some privacy.'

As my father and I climbed out of the pool, I shot a glance over my shoulder. Jiro and Calvin were together on lounge chairs on the other side of the pool, far enough that they couldn't overhear us – or so I hoped.

# Ten

After phoning Uncle Yosh to set up our next-day shopping trip, my father and I set off for Honolulu. It was midday, so there was little traffic, and I had a chance to enjoy the massive mountains on the north side of the highway, and the sparkling sea on the south, although I knew I should ban those words from my vocabulary; in Hawaii, north and south were replaced by *mauka*, meaning 'mountainside', and *makai*, which meant 'toward the sea'.

That morning at the coffee shop, I'd learned the terms while reading both the *Advertiser* and *Star-Bulletin* newspapers. There had been articles about a series of fires on the Leeward Side. The scrubby, dry fields and mountains were perfect fodder for errant fireworks and sparks coming from electrical lines – and the region was also full of arsonists. Adding to the trouble was the scarcity of roads on the Leeward Side, and the challenge of fighting fires that often started high in the mountains. As I drove, I saw the same blackened field that I'd noticed when we'd driven in from the airport. The field had burned all the way up to the edge of Farrington Highway, making me realize that the highway had another role: firebreak.

I was starting to spook myself, so it was a relief to see regular, paved roads spreading out on either side of the freeway as we neared Honolulu. After we passed the exits for Pearl Harbor, it was time to jump on to Nimitz Highway. The route was straightforward but tedious, full of trucks, buses and traffic lights, and it was only when we finally turned right on King Street and began to see shop signs in Chinese that I relaxed. This was Chinatown on a small scale, graceful early twentieth-century buildings with curved facades and faded business names like Liang and Sons and Kowloon Traders. Mahogany-colored ducks hung in windows, and storefronts were cluttered with bins of glorious tropical fruit and vegetables.

I was excited about the shopping, and also wondered if Liang and Sons might be connected to the Liangs who'd taken over the Shimura family house. Perhaps, but I wasn't about to stop in and ask, as the building appeared vacant.

My father raised a hand in triumph as he spotted Little Village Noodle House. We were seated just before a deluge of office workers snapped up all the remaining tables, and were soon feasting on tofu-scallion potstickers, spicy stir-fried green beans and slow-cooked eggplant. This was the best Chinatown food I'd had since Yokohama.

'How did you ever hear about this place?' I asked my father between bites, as I inspected the packed, clearly local crowd.

'I was given the suggestion by one of the Chinese groundskeepers at Kainani. He also told me where to find property records, in an office called the Bureau of Conveyances, which is on Punchbowl, practically across the street from Queen's.'

'Judging from this restaurant, your friend is a good source. And speaking of property, I saw the name Liang on a building around the corner from where we parked. I wonder if it's the same family.'

'I saw it too,' my father said, 'but Liang is a common enough name. You need to look for a Winston Liang when you're checking records at the Bureau of Conveyances.'

My father had a lot of expectations, I thought, watching him pay the bill a few minutes later.

We still had time before my father's appointment, so we walked a few blocks to Chinatown's food market area. Unable to resist the boxes of lush produce piled up outside the stores, I filled a shopping basket with crisp mustard greens, two-foot long scallions, pale pink ginger, and heavenly smelling golden mangoes. Then my eye was caught by a fish market, and before I knew it I'd purchased a five-pound local *ahi* tuna.

It would make a fantastic dinner for our family tonight. I convinced the fish market to give me a bag of ice, and I bought a cheap Styrofoam cooler from a souvenir shop that fronted the shopping plaza.

After I'd loaded up the car, the parking attendant at the municipal garage gave us directions for the short trip to the medical center. There, I parked in the covered hospital garage, deciding it would help keep the food cool. I saw my father to the neurology clinic and left the building to walk along Punchbowl Street, a grand boulevard lined with palm and rainbow shower trees. The buildings I passed were imposing; some made of an older, pale yellow rock, and others in sherbet-colored stucco. The Kalanimoku Building, which housed the Bureau of Conveyances, was right in between eras: the long gray rectangular office building had a mid-century modern sensibility that stood out from the other, mostly twenties and thirties buildings nearby.

Inside, I followed a narrow corridor to a dreary records room packed with industrial gray file cabinets and bookcases. Straight away I went to the clerk's desk, and asked the fifty-ish Asian man sitting there how I could find records pertaining to the old Shimura address.

'I haven't heard of any Kalama Street in Leeward Oahu. Even if it exists, finding records isn't that straightforward.' He studied me with something of a challenge behind his wire-rimmed glasses. 'You see, our records are organized by the date of transaction, not address. Do you have that information?'

'I don't know the exact date, but the house I'm interested in may have been sold or rented in the 1930s,' I said.

'You have nothing more than that?' He sounded incredulous. 'I suggest you go ahead and search the ledgers each year, then, looking for that address and the buyer's name . . . which is?'

'Shimura.' I decided not to bring up the Pierce name, lest he ask me more about my interest in them.

'Ah, that's your family name?' He looked at me searchingly, and I nodded. 'It's not a common name on the island. That will make it easier for you.'

A real-estate agent needed assistance, so I moved off and picked out two heavy books, one which included the end of 1929 and part of 1930. It was not going to be remotely easy, especially since I doubted Harue Shimura's name was going to be found anywhere. *The things I do to please my father*, I thought, as I unloaded a heavy book bound in worn green cotton. I scrutinized the old typewritten ledger, trying to see any mention of names like Shimura, Liang and Pierce.

Pierce came up numerous times, and I made a careful record of each transaction's date, buyer, price, and address. I had reached the early 1940s, and my eyes were very tired, when my cell phone vibrated. As expected, it was my father. He'd passed his appointment with flying colors, and wanted to hear what I'd learned.

'Nothing so far,' I said. 'It's a lot of work, going through these books. Shall I put the search aside and just return to the hospital to take you home?'

'Actually, I hope to join you.'

I acquiesced, and a few minutes later my father walked in the door. Surprisingly, with my father around, the clerk became more interested and even went so far as to carry a few books to the table for him. Respect for age seemed to be as alive and well in Hawaii as it was in Japan, I thought, nodding my thanks at the clerk. Although my father was a pretty youthful sixty-three, he had sharp eyes, and seemed to be making faster work of the books than I had.

'Look at this,' my father said to me after forty-five minutes or so.

I was seated on the opposite side of the table, so I came around to look at the page he was studying. He pointed his finger to a line recording a sale of a building on Smith Street owned by Josiah Pierce to Clara Liang in 1945. It was not a fee-simple sale, but a sale with terms of seventy-five years, the kind of deal that Kainoa's family and neighbors had received.

'So now we know that the Liangs have a continuing business relationship with the Pierces,' my father said.

'I've been looking at other Pierce transactions. They sold land to many people.' I pointed my father to the handwritten accounting I'd done of twenty-five transactions, dating from the thirties to the early sixties. I'd come across plenty of names, mostly Anglo-Saxon but also a sprinkling of Chinese,

Japanese and Filipino. The amounts paid for properties ranged from figures as low as four thousand dollars to as high as twenty-five thousand, in the early sixties.

'*Ah so desu ka,*' my father said after a minute. 'There are many names, with many different national origins. It's like a microcosm of the old plantation populations.'

I'd been studying the names my father had pulled out, and the ones I'd come across. Then I saw something that made my skin prickle.

'Otoosan, all the Asian buyers have something in common. Do you see?'

My father looked at the names, and then at me. 'I'm afraid I don't. What is it?'

'Look at the names again – the first names. It looks as if all the Asians to whom Josiah Pierce was selling, during this pre-war period, were women.'

# Eleven

Was there some significance in the discovery that Josiah Pierce had sold property to women? On the long, traffic-clogged ride home, my father pointed out that perhaps the women were widowed or elderly, and had been sold the houses because they could no longer work the fields and live in free plantation housing. I countered that while this was a definite possibility, we had no information about the ages of the women he'd sold to. I didn't add the secret thought I had – that perhaps these women had been his mistresses. It was a horrible way to think about women, but the situation of a landowner taking advantage of a worker's wife or daughter was a sad reality, wherever in the world one looked.

Now I was wondering about Harue. My father and Uncle Hiroshi didn't know why she'd been sent away, but Uncle Yosh had hinted that he knew a lot about it. I knew from personal experience that only children were sometimes treated like confidantes by their parents.

'We didn't hear much about Harue's husband Ken from Yosh,' I said. 'It's so unusual that he took her name. We now understand that she was cast out of her own birth family – so why would they allow a laborer to be added to the family registry?'

My father didn't answer my question, but said, 'Take a look to the right.'

I followed his line of vision to a tall plume of smoke ahead. A helicopter carrying a water bucket was heading from the ocean toward it. One of the Leeward Side fires; I wondered if this one was accidental or arson. The traffic was slow, and became a crawl as we approached the old sugar mill town of Waipahu, where orange flames blazed across the hills. *Not in my backyard*, I thought to myself with relief, and the traffic picked up after we passed the scene.

The security guards at Kainani seemed to know us now, because they waved the car through with a smile and a *shaka* sign, but there was a short line at the gates to our housing area. As we idled, I noticed that most cars were driven by military, something I deduced from both the drivers' micro-short haircuts and the Department of Defense stickers on windshields. My attention was distracted briefly by the sight of a chubby young Japanese man walking slowly along the golf course. It was Jiro Kikuchi, and he had something with him – a golf club, which he was dragging along the grass.

'Where's Calvin?' I asked aloud.

'Calvin's coming tomorrow,' my father said, missing the point.

'No, I mean that Jiro just walked past and Calvin's supposed to be monitoring him because of his disorder. Did you see him?'

'No, I didn't, but what's this about a disorder? Did Calvin Morita reveal medical information about his patient?' My father sounded aghast.

It was my turn at the gate, so I swiped the fob and was admitted to MacCottage Land, as I'd begun to think of our pretty replica plantation village. After doing so, I replied, 'Calvin said something about schizoaffective disorder when he was attempting to explain what Jiro did in the pool. What do you know about this condition? Is it like Tourette's syndrome, where you can't control what you say?'

'It's not remotely like Tourette's syndrome, but I don't care to discuss anything that might seem like a comment on a patient's condition. And Calvin shouldn't have done that either.' My father frowned.

'So I don't have to be fixed up with him, then?' I asked while pulling into our driveway.

Uncle Hiroshi and Tsutomu were relaxing at the teak table on the *lanai* with frosty bottles of Asahi Super-Dry beer before them. The two of them had the unmistakable redness of a long day in the sun. The Hawaiian sun was too much for all of us – even though I'd slathered myself with sunscreen before running, I knew I had acquired a reddish tinge.

'You two are starting to look Hawaiian Japanese,' I greeted them cheerfully. When they appeared mystified, I added, 'You're getting a local person's tan.'

'Really?' Tom said, looking pleased. 'We were only on the golf course two hours today. The realtor picked us up, and then we were quite busy doing research in Kapolei the rest of the time!'

'Tell me while I cook,' I said, starting to take the cooler out of the car. Tom gallantly took it from my arms and I followed him into the kitchen, as did Uncle Hiroshi, who gave my father a glass of water and settled down with him in the living room.

'So, I learned about real estate today,' Uncle Hiroshi said. 'Prices here are great!'

'Ah, but you're biased. Hawaii's frequently labeled as the first or second highest priced housing market in the US,' I said.

'Actually, the realtor explained that the Leeward Side is a bargain,' Hiroshi said. 'Here there is more sun, and with it dry, good weather, for a better price, because of the distance from Honolulu.'

'I don't think this is far at all,' Tom said. 'Of course, this area would be more convenient if a train service existed. I wonder about the old days, because I saw old train tracks running through the golf course.'

'I saw them, too. My guess is they were used by the plantations for moving products rather than people,' I said.

'This is not about trains!' Uncle Hiroshi said. 'I'm teaching you about real estate. Apparently, Kikuchi Mitsuo, the developer of this resort and father of Jiro-san, who we met yesterday, has bought many small packages of land over the last few years.'

I nodded, thinking this was perhaps a tedious way to put together enough land for a resort, but perhaps the only way. I asked, 'Why was the realtor so forthcoming with you?'

'He has a colleague in the office who knows one of the holding-out people, a young Hawaiian who believes some things are worth more than money.'

'Kainoa!' I said aloud, and everyone looked at me. 'Kainoa is the owner of the coffee shop where I go during my morning run.'

'*Ah so desu ka.*' Tom looked thoughtful. 'Now I finally understand why you enjoy getting up so early in the morning.'

'Hey, stop it!' I made a punching gesture in Tom's direction.

'Rei can't seem to be without a boyfriend for even a day,' my father said dryly.

'It's a shame, because Calvin Morita seems like he won't have a chance. He might be . . . how do you say . . . Mr Right?' Uncle Hiroshi asked.

'Dr Right,' Tom corrected. 'Or should I say Dr Muscles? Otoosan and I saw him outside the golf club restaurant at lunchtime. He drives a Mercedes S Class.'

'I'm interested to hear what you learned from the lawyer.' I looked pointedly at my cousin. 'What was his name? Yamaguchi?'

'Bobby Yamaguchi,' my cousin answered, his lips curling around the incongruous first name. 'Our conversation was by telephone, and he didn't have much time, but Yamaguchi-san told me he was sorry he even agreed to help Edwin.'

'Why?' I asked. 'Was it because he thought Edwin's case had no merit?'

'I think so. All he could do was suggest that the letter proving ownership might have been intentionally destroyed, but the judge wasn't sympathetic. Yamaguchi-san also didn't care for Edwin's personality. He found him hard to work with.'

We all exchanged glances then, but didn't say anything. I guess family loyalty was silencing us even within our small unit.

'We have something to report from our own research today,' my father said as I put the fish in the fridge and began unloading the vegetables and fruit on to the kitchen counter. 'Things are looking quite interesting.'

My father explained that while we hadn't found any record of a sale from the Pierces to Harue Shimura, there had been a sale by the Pierces of a property in Chinatown to Clara Liang during the war years. I added in the bit about Josiah Pierce selling land to various Asian women, whom we imagined were former plantation workers.

'What if . . .' Tom began, then stopped. We all looked at him expectantly. 'What if Josiah Pierce wrote the letter to Harue and meant to formalize the sale with a regular transaction, but something happened to interrupt that?'

'Such as?' I asked, not following his train of thought.

'The war. It could have been seen as very bad to sell any land, especially waterfront, to someone born in Japan. Therefore, Mr. Pierce let her stay in the house until she died, but never actually sold it."

'That's a possibility,' I admitted. "But there was a long time in between the letter – which Yoshitsune claims he saw in the 1930s – and 1945, when the Liangs moved in. And why would a smart, powerful landowner just give away waterfront property? He sold to other Asian women for sums ranging from a few hundred to ten thousand dollars. Why would he give our great-great-aunt land without the deed of sale the other ladies received, and filed with the state?'

'Everything is a mystery to you, Rei-chan,' Uncle Hiroshi said.

'It's worth understanding everything before we make any commitments.' My father spoke directly to his brother. 'If we help Edwin attempt to regain the property, we will surely pay high legal fees. It's a stretch for me, especially if I have to retire because of my health.'

'Oh, we will help with the expenses! Don't worry about that. Please take care of your health,' Uncle Hiroshi said, and I looked away to hide my smirk; my father was playing up his health condition, just to suit his purposes.

'I almost forgot, Rei-chan, you had a telephone call today,' Tom said.

'Oh?'

'A woman from the Waikiki Yacht Club named Georgina asked for you. She said she'd been instructed to telephone you about four fellows?'

'*Four Guys on the Edge*?' I caught my breath, thinking about the oddly named boat on which Michael was crewing. Had something happened at sea, and that was why a stranger was telephoning me about the boat?

'Yes, that was it. The yacht is arriving sometime tomorrow afternoon at the Waikiki Yacht Club.'

'But are you sure? Mich . . . My friend told me he thought it would take just under two weeks.' I wasn't ready to introduce the topic of Michael Hendricks with anyone.

'Georgina said it will be coming in on its tenth day, and is apparently the first to arrive in its class. She also said that you may attend the boat's greeting tomorrow afternoon.'

'Tomorrow night is the big family dinner,' Uncle Hiroshi reminded me.

'That shouldn't be a problem,' I said, unable to hide my happiness. Michael was arriving, and soon I'd be swept away, temporarily, from the trials of family life. 'I'm doing the grocery shopping for the party in the morning with Uncle Yosh, so I can prepare most of what we'll eat before I leave. And we're doing seafood, remember? It rarely takes more than twenty minutes to cook a fish. I mean, your dinner's practically ready now.'

'Heh?' Hiroshi said.

All the while we'd been talking, I'd been chopping and sautéing. The *ahi* tuna was under the broiler, giving off delicious, hissing sounds.

'Given the topic we'll be discussing tomorrow evening, I don't think it's appropriate to bring four strangers,' Uncle Hiroshi said stiffly.

'Oh, I'm not bringing anyone. And *Four Guys on the Edge* is a boat name; it's not like four boyfriends.'

'My daughter has many talents,' said my father. 'I think we can spare her for a few hours, if seeing the end of this boat race is so important.'

'Thank you,' I said, relieved and slightly surprised to have my father as the ally in my corner.

'Not at all.' My father's eyes remained on me, as if he could see straight through to what really was important, even though he'd never heard Michael's name before.

# Twelve

I was as good as my word, and got up before six the next morning. I even skipped my run in order to cook. Spinach was washed three times, shaken and tied up in kitchen towels to dry. I put together a trifle from ladyfingers, rum, the whipped soymilk and an assortment of ripe mangoes, pineapple and bananas. When the rest of the family came down, I served a breakfast of pineapple, low-sodium miso soup, rice, and a bit of pickled daikon radish and then persuaded everyone to make a part of dinner. For my father, it was mincing scallions to use as a garnish and in multiple dishes; for Tom, it was chopping long green beans for me to stir-fry later with a ginger sesame glaze. Uncle Hiroshi seemed too shell-shocked to do anything but set the table, for which I complimented him lavishly.

Everyone was having fun by the end, and my father had to remind me it was time for my appointment with Uncle Yosh. I arrived at his door five minutes from the time I left Kainani.

Braden answered the door, looking sullen in just a pair of yellow and orange shorts. He rubbed his eyes; it was nine o'clock, apparently quite early. 'Jii-chan!' he hollered, and stalked off.

Uncle Yosh emerged, dressed in a faded but clean T-shirt and wrinkled pants. He looked surprised to see the van, and kicked its tire. 'This thing safe to travel?'

'So far, so good.'

'Where we going?'

'You mentioned a fishmonger on North King Street in Honolulu. I hope that's not too far . . .'

'No, no, it be worth it. But tell me the truth – your fadduh gonna let you drive this wreck all the way to Honolulu?'

'Yes, of course. I drove it downtown yesterday.' As we started off, I got right down to business, asking Uncle Yosh if he thought it was a good idea for us to pursue the land claim one more time. He shrugged, saying nothing.

'It's really your house, not Edwin's. I mean, it's your house if there ever really was a letter or deed—'

'It was ours in writing, for sure. I remember Josiah Pierce coming to our house one evening when I was a kid, Kaa-san sending me out. That musta been when the papers were done.'

The papers, or something else? I eyed my great-uncle, and struggled for the right words. 'Did you see Josiah Pierce at your home again after that?'

'No, never.'

'And your father? How did he fit into all this? Where was he during this talk?'

'He got transferred to work at a plantation in Maui, around the time I was two. Never saw him after that, 'cause he died in an accident there.'

'Why didn't you and your mother go with him?'

'The school. She was teaching here, and got paid for that. She wouldn't have such an easy job if she went to Maui.'

'I'm sorry that you grew up without a father. That must have been very hard.' As I murmured the apology, my thoughts were spinning. It seemed more and more likely that Harue had had a secret relationship with Josiah Pierce.

'Truth is, you don't miss what you don't know. Lot of men around the plantation seemed too angry. The men in those times drank a lot, and the wives hated it. That's why no drinking in my house, ever.'

'I apologize for bringing wine the other evening; I just didn't know.' I tried to refocus the conversation. 'If you were to revisit the day that you found the Liangs in your house, could you tell everything that happened?'

Yoshitsune was silent for a minute, and when his voice returned, it came in fits and starts. 'I never forget that day, March seventeen, 1942. The day I touched Hawaiian ground again, when I decided go for broke, I thought might as well return home right away, even though my mother had passed. I got the bus from Honolulu out to Waipahu, and a Filipino guy I knew since small kid time rode me out on his pickup the last few miles to the house.'

'Was the house located in the plantation village?' I asked.

'No, it was *makai*, near the water, nobody around and real peaceful. We had no friends nearby. That's why nobody wrote me to say the Liangs had taken the house.'

'What did Mr Liang say to you, when you tried to come home?'

'He wasn't there, when I went calling. Never saw the buggah. He probably down in Chinatown, running his store. The wife was the one who came to the door.'

'Clara Liang?'

'That's right.' He looked surprised that I knew her name, but I didn't elaborate. I didn't want to interrupt the flow. 'Clara Liang said to me, "What you want?" I stared at her and said, "Lady, you in my house." Then she laugh like crazy and say the house belong to her and her husband. They buy from Mr Pierce one year previously. While she talking, I kept looking over her shoulder to see inside. See a lot of strange furniture, but a few of our things, like the old *tansu* chest and some lamp that was my mother's. I said, "My name Yoshitsune Shimura, and I see you took my household goods, too."'

I was so caught up in the story that I'd inadvertently slowed to just less than fifty miles per hour, I realized after a lumbering truck passed us up. Not good highway behavior, so I sped up. 'What did she say when you confronted her like that?'

Yosh shook his head, remaining silent.

'I'm sorry if I'm being too nosy.' I shot a glance at him, and saw that the craggy-faced man looked close to tears. 'I don't mean to force bad memories. I was just hoping that some information from that encounter could help me understand what happened with the land.'

'Got nothing to do with land,' he said roughly. 'You want know what she said? I remember every word. She said, "You go away, dirty Jap, I know what you did at the post office. I will remind everyone, now that you're back." I didn't know what to reply, so I just started walking.'

'But you . . . you were a war hero,' I said. 'You worked with the OSS! How could she dare label you a traitor?'

'Not many know what I did. The family know, sure, but it's not something to show off about. And like I say, it counts nothing for getting the land back,' Yosh said. 'After I left the house, I thought about things. I had a buddy whose cousin was at Honolulu PD. I talked story with him, about my house. He said, only way you can prove your story is by showing the deed. Well, I don't know if there ever was a deed; if there had been any deed in the house, like the letter, you better believe the Liangs destroyed it. And there was nothing to prove ownership at the Bureau of Conveyances, as you learn yourself.'

'Who told you that we went to the land records office?'

'I heard it on the coconut wireless.' Yoshitsune smiled, and added, 'My old friend's brother, he work there. He told me there was a girl in, claiming to be family.'

So much for the helpful clerk and his questions about my name. 'Uncle Yosh, we found a record of Josiah Pierce selling another property to Clara Liang for a really low price, on Smith Street in Chinatown.'

'Yeah, maybe that's their old company building. I don't know.'

'Well, do you think there might be something odd about him selling to her rather than the husband?'

Yoshitsune shrugged again. 'Why you think that?'

'I . . . well . . . he sold mostly to Asian women. I was wondering if any funny business might have been going on.'

Instead of answering me, Yosh said, 'Watch it, we're at King Street now. Left turn, and better start look parking.'

Signs all over the interior of the Tamashiro Fish Market declared NO EATING ALLOWED, though it seemed like the antithesis of fine dining. Walls were covered by the darkness of time, lights were dim, and we had to jostle through a crowd of customers to look at the fish. Yoshitsune taught me the names as we walked along. Thin, silvery butterfish, best under a miso glaze; opah, with a body as round as a full moon; and opakapaka, the best pink snapper. A large, flame-colored fish with whiskers looked especially enticing; Uncle Yoshitsune explained that it was called *weke ula* and was quite delicious.

I took three and had the counterman clean and scale them. Ten minutes later the complicated business was done and paid for, and I loaded my icy cooler with what seemed like an aquarium's worth of sea life, because Yoshitsune had gone back to the prepared-dish counter for marinated sea urchins.

My great-uncle showed me an alternate route to the freeway on North School Street, which was dotted with *okazu-ya* open to the street where people were eating their lunches off paper plates. He persuaded me to stop, and pretty soon we were standing on the street, tasting poi-flavored Okinawan-style doughnuts and the crispest sweet potato tempura I'd ever eaten. Uncle Yosh, who'd added chicken yakitori to his order, ate quietly and fast, with obvious pleasure. In the silence, I pondered his story of the lost father, internment in a prison camp, and finally his mother's death. After he came back, life couldn't have been much better because he'd raised someone as unhappy and irresponsible as Edwin. My father said he wanted to help, out of guilt for what had happened to Harue. I thought if any help should be given, it should be to Yoshitsune.

'Did you ever receive reparations from the government for the internment?' I asked after we'd cleaned the oil from our hands, swigged down some water, and gotten back into the minivan, heading west.

'Yes. Twenty thousand dollah. I used the money to buy our house, and it was a good thing, because when Edwin had his financial trouble a few years back, he moved the family in.'

'Life has been hard for you,' I said, thinking of all the losses. He'd lost his father during childhood, he'd lost his happy youth during internment, plus his mother. And though he'd eventually married, his wife was gone, leaving Yosh in his old age with Edwin controlling him.

'Oh, not so bad. There was plenty of hardness to go around. The muddahs use to sing about it, I remember.'

'Your mother?'

'The other mothers had to teach mine the songs, you know, while they stripped the leaves from the cane in the fields. The plantation songs had a special name, *hole hole bushi*.'

'Women rice farmers sing *hole hole bushi* in Japan,' I said. 'Women are known for these songs, not men. I wonder why.'

''Cause it's about complaining, that's why!' Uncle Yosh then sang in a wavering voice, 'My man is always drinking . . . no more money . . . where shall I go?'

I laughed, enjoying the sound of my great-uncle finally expressing himself in Japanese. 'I guess there aren't many people who remember the words anymore.'

'You'd be surprised. Most people your age had either parents or grandparents on the plantation.'

'Uncle Yosh, I was wondering. I've seen the plantation village, but I would really like to see your mother's cottage.'

'You saw the photograph at dinner the other night.'

'Yes, but the picture didn't give a sense of the landscape or scale of things.' I shot a glance at my uncle, who was staring rigidly ahead.

'Things ain't like before, when the plantation was open for business. It's way down on the water, through five miles or so of Pierce land. Can't enter it that way, and on the other side the land's military, closed to people like us.'

'I'd be willing to risk traveling through Pierce land. I run there almost every morning and haven't been bothered.'

'Well, we can't go now. What's the point of drive all the way to Tamashiro's and spoil the fish driving round?'

'OK, Uncle Yosh. You've got a good point,' I said, thinking there was no reason to force the point any further. He didn't want to go. I was going to have to make the trip on my own, perhaps following tips from Kainoa, or – the thought struck me suddenly – going via the military side with Michael.

Despite the bit of awkwardness at the end, my trip out with my uncle had been a success, I thought as I dropped him back off at his house with his sea urchins before returning to Kainani. As I put the three fish in the coldest part of the fridge and programmed the rice cooker to switch on at five, I thought about what I'd learned. There was more he had to say, I was sure, but I'd learned the virtues of patience at my father's knee. The truth would come out in time. And now it was time to see Michael, so I could stop thinking about family business for a while. I changed my clothes, swept up the minivan keys, and left.

# Thirteen

The Waikiki Yacht Club was situated on the fringe of Ala Moana Park, the beach known as Honolulu's safest place for children to swim. I puttered along the parking driveway that edged the beach park, looking in vain for a spot large enough for my vehicle. As I drove, I couldn't help noticing how many of the mothers holding children's hands shot untrusting glances toward my Odyssey, as if the vehicle's rust, dirt and pure ugliness indicated a thug was at the wheel.

I gave up on finding a parking spot near the water, and as I returned to Ala Moana Boulevard, I decided to leave the minivan in the large parking garage attached to the Ala Moana Center. I backed easily into a generous space near Macy's, locked up and emerged from the shadowy garage into bright sun, and waited for the light to change so I could walk across the busy boulevard to the yacht club.

Entering the low white stucco building made me slightly anxious, as entering members-only places sometimes did. When I'd called Georgina back for more information on the timing of the boat's arrival, I'd thought about asking her what to wear, but decided against it for fear of being gauche. Now I wished I had. The halter back of my clingy orange and turquoise striped silk sundress, and my high-heeled turquoise-studded sandals seemed too feminine against the backdrop of club members wearing either polo shirts and shorts or bright cotton shift dresses. But that wasn't the biggest difference between the club members and me; as Edwin would have said, it was a *haole* place. I was the only Asian, *hapa* or otherwise.

I walked around the pleasant, teak-ceilinged rooms decorated with hundreds of nautical flags, choosing to linger in the trophy room, where there were almost a century's worth of cups, statues and plaques celebrating feats of sailing and

surfing. I did a double take at a series of trophies engraved
with the name of Duke Kahanamoku, the world's fastest
swimmer and most famous surfer during the first part of the
twentieth century. If Duke, who was indisputably Hawaiian,
was a member of this club in the old days, that was a good
sign. And then I saw another name that made my skin prickle:
Pierce. Someone called Lindsay Pierce, a big handsome blond
man photographed in 1968 holding a mammoth trophy. If
Lindsay was in his thirties in 1968, the date of the picture,
he'd have been too young to remember real-estate transactions taking place in the thirties. But the sight of him
reminded me of how badly I wanted to talk to someone in
the Pierce family. Now I'd found a connection.

I asked around until I was directed to Georgina Dobbs, the
woman who'd telephoned me about the boat's arrival. She
turned out to be a graceful woman with a mahogany tan and
helmet of silver hair. Her trim figure was flattered by her slim-
fitting floral cotton sheath dress, just like the others but
somehow more Hawaiian in appearance.

'Why, hello, Rei!' she said warmly when I greeted her.
'Funny, I thought you'd be Japanese, because of your cousin
who answered the phone – what good English he speaks!'

I eyed her more cautiously. 'I'm half-Japanese.'

'Oh, *hapa-haole*, just like my grandkids. My daughter
married a Hawaiian, so the children, good Lord, are they
gorgeous! Now I'm so glad that you're here, because the gal
I'd been counting on to help me carry mai tais had to take
the shuttle over to the Honolulu Yacht Club for some reason
or other . . .'

'Any update of when *Four Guys on the Edge* is arriving?'
I asked.

'Maybe an hour or two away. Can't tell for sure, but don't
leave.' She smiled at me. 'You could kill the time with a few
drinks in the bar. Our mai tais are infamous.'

The characters in Juanita Sheridan novels were always
sipping mai tais, but I couldn't risk getting tipsy when I had
to drive back to Kainani and serve dinner to nine people.
'Maybe later. By the way, I noticed a picture in the trophy
room – a man called Lindsay Pierce. Is he involved with Pierce
Holdings?'

'Hmmm. Lindsay is the younger son, and he left fifteen or

twenty years ago for California. As far as I know, he's retired.
Pierce Holdings isn't actively run by the family anymore, just
its corporate people.'

'Is there an older son?'

'Yes, Josiah Pierce, or JP Junior, as people used to call him
in my parents' day, when his father was still living. He retired
back in the 1970s, but I believe he lives up on Tantalus at the
old family house.'

'Well, that's convenient,' I said. 'There's a little real-estate
deal I'm looking into, with a Pierce connection. I'd love to
talk to him directly.'

Georgina raised her eyebrows, as if measuring me in a new
way. 'Like I said, JP's still in Tantalus, but I'm sure he's
unlisted. And . . . I really shouldn't do this, but . . . there's got
to be an old club directory lying around somewhere.' She said
a few words to the bartender, who produced one from under
the counter.

'Let me mark this down for you,' Georgina said, writing
on the back of a bill.

'Thank you.' I chatted a while longer with Georgina, and
when she was called away to the telephone, I took advantage of the break to step outside of the building toward the
water and tried the number she'd given me. It rang almost
ten times, an unusual occurrence in a world now filled with
answering machines, but at last an aged-sounding male voice
answered.

'My name is Rei Shimura,' I said, after I'd ascertained I
was speaking with Josiah Pierce the Second. 'Actually, I'm a
friend of a friend – Georgina Dobbs.'

'Oh, from the yacht club. You're calling to try to get me to
contribute to a fundraiser?' His voice sounded dismissive.

'No. I'm trying to put together an accurate historical record.
I hope to interview you about something relating to the plantation.'

'You shouldn't disturb me at home about that kind of thing.
It's all handled out of our offices in Kapolei.'

'I'm afraid the officers of Pierce Holdings may be too young
to help me. They weren't around sixty-some years ago.'

He paused. 'Who did you say you were? And what's your
company – or is it a magazine?'

'My name is Rei Shimura,' I repeated. 'And I'm actually

just visiting from the mainland. I know it sounds forward, but I would very much like to talk to you, face to face.'

'Well, then.' He paused, as if making a decision. 'Can you come to me?'

'I'd be very happy to do that.'

'How about tomorrow, say one o'clock?'

'Yes, thank you.'

'My house is close to the top of the road in the last stretch of houses before the parkland at the top.'

'Is there a number?'

'Yes, twenty-seven. But you'll know it because of the roses.'

More than an hour passed, during which I consumed two virgin mai tais and kept consulting my watch, wondering how late I could get away with leaving Honolulu for the Leeward Side. But my patience was rewarded as, finally, a ripple went through the yacht club's bar. *Four Guys on the Edge* had passed Diamond Head and would be at the dock within a half-hour.

'You must be happy to see your friend,' Georgina said as we left the building and walked along the dock, where most of the slips were filled with yachts, large and small, that belonged to the local crowd. 'And it looks like his boat will be finishing first in its class. Has that happened before?'

'He's never sailed this race, although the man who owns the boat is pretty seasoned. But Michael said something about there being a staggered start, which would put the boat's finishing rank into question still, wouldn't it?'

'That's right. The boats leaving Newport Beach don't all depart at the same time; there are so many of them, it could cause accidents. Instead, the boats follow a staggered schedule, and we record their total elapsed time, and subtract or add their handicap. The goal is for all the boats to get here around the same time, so we can celebrate together at the awards dinner – you'll be going, I assume?'

'I'm not sure. Hey, is that the boat coming in?'

'No, dear, that's just the shuttle taking people back and forth between the yacht clubs. But out on the horizon, I think I see something.'

The speck of something dark in the water became larger, and indeed it was a sailboat – a handsome, sleek hull. Four

men were aboard, busily rolling down sails and guiding the
boat into place. They all wore navy-blue polo shirts and ball
caps obstructing their bearded faces. Michael hadn't had a
beard before, so I was having trouble recognizing him. I bided
my time, making guesses. Michael might have been the wiry
man pulling down the front sail . . . or was he the one at the
wheel?

Even after *Four Guys on the Edge* had docked, I couldn't
discern Michael from the others. Then I noticed that one of
the men had a bit of silver hair showing from under a Naval
Academy cap, and was waving frantically at me. We made
eye contact, and my stomach made the funny little skip that
it had been doing for the last few months.

'Welcome to Hawaii,' I called out to Michael, whose eyes
were bluer than I remembered, set against the deep tan he'd
developed. The sea life clearly had agreed with him, I thought,
as he took off his cap and ran his fingers through his closely
cropped, salt-and-pepper hair. He was making no effort to
disembark after the boat was tied up and, as if sensing my
disappointment, Georgina explained that they couldn't set foot
on Hawaiian soil until the customs agent had thoroughly
inspected the boat for contraband.

The crowd around us was growing – after all, these were
the first to arrive in the fifty-foot class, which was worthy of
a big celebration. Georgina and I handed up the drinks, and
each man took one and also bent his head to receive a lei
made of yellow and white flowers and kukui nuts, the fruit
from Hawaii's state tree. But when it was Michael's turn to
take the lei, his arms were suddenly around me and, before I
realized it, I'd been pulled up the rigging and on to the boat.

'I missed you too much to wait a moment longer,' Michael
said as he embraced me in a classic friendly hug, perfect for
public observation. This close, I smelled something slightly
astringent about him – the seawater, and something else.

'What am I smelling on you – cologne?' I teased as we
separated.

'No. It's joy.'

What a romantic. 'I'm happy too, but I smell something –
a kind of citrus aroma.'

'No, it's Joy. You know, the dishwashing soap? We mix it
with seawater to clean ourselves.' Michael laughed. 'Speaking

of cleaning up, I can't wait to get off this boat and get a real shower, not to mention shave this thing off.' Michael rubbed at his chin.

'Sure,' I said rashly, since the family dinner was still two and a half hours away. 'I'd be happy to drive all of you to the hotel.'

That opened the floodgates for his three crewmates, all of whom had been quietly watching and smiling. I could understand the interest: their good friend had been without female companionship for years, so the appearance of a real woman was a curiosity. Michael introduced me to the Afghanistan and Iraq returnee, Kurt Schaefer, a deeply tanned, muscular man with white-blond hair cut military-short like Michael's, and green eyes that looked as if they'd seen too much. It was easier for me to connect with the softer-faced crew captain, Parker Drummond, who was a real-estate investor in Southern California. Finally, I met the fourth man in the group: Eric Levine, an engineer at Goddard Space Center, who had terrible sunburn. He didn't say more than a quick hello, because he was on his cell phone trying to help his wife, who was lost somewhere in Los Angeles trying to meet Parker's wife, Karen, for the next flight to Honolulu.

The customs inspector arrived and Michael and Parker followed him as he went below deck looking for contraband. Kurt lounged on the side of the boat, giving interviews to sports reporters. When Michael emerged from the cabin a few minutes later, he steered me around to the side of the boat that wasn't facing the harbor, so that we could talk.

'Don't count on taking the guys back to the hotel; they already said they plan to stay around the yacht club for a few hours to get their land legs back,' Michael said. 'Frankly, I think they don't mind being showered with free drinks and adulation.'

'A little adulation is in order for the fastest finishers in your class.'

'We don't know yet if we're the fastest – and I don't really care, to tell the truth.'

'Come on.'

'I'm just glad I did the race, and it got me out here, with you. I have to say, though, that I'm more than ready to be on land and get a full night's sleep.'

Michael didn't just need sleep, he needed help walking. After the customs official finally cleared the boat, Michael hopped off, then nearly collapsed on the deck. Two men from the yacht club steadied him until I'd made my own precarious, high-heeled way off the boat and could walk him up to the yacht club, where I left him with his bags while I walked back to the mall for the car. I decided I didn't want to risk Michael collapsing as he crossed Ala Moana Boulevard.

'Once again, you're taking care of me,' Michael said as we continued by car from Ala Moana toward the Waikiki district. 'Though I can't say this vehicle has the Rei Shimura style to which I'm accustomed.'

'Yes, I know it. But what can I do? My new uncle chose it for us,' I said, more aware than ever of the shiny new vehicles around me, the tour buses, convertibles, and luxury sedans streaming with us toward Waikiki.

'No offense meant, but I'll see about renting my own car tomorrow. So, tell me about your newfound relatives. You were so nervous before you left.'

'Most of them are pleasant. But there's a complicated agenda – just like I expected.' I began telling the story in a more or less chronological fashion, with Michael listening quietly. It was complicated enough that by the time we'd parked in the garage around the corner from the Hale Koa hotel, I was only halfway through Uncle Yoshitsune's story, at the point where he'd been interned.

'I wonder if it's true about his tampering with military mail,' Michael said as we stepped up a curving stairway and then entered a large, breezy open air lobby, where ceiling fans whirred and a military population lounged on rattan furniture with crisply striped cushions.

'Apparently he was suspected, but never formally charged, which makes it seem quite unfair.'

Michael paused by the check-in desk, waving a family with four small children to go ahead of him. 'We'll have to pick up on this conversation later, but should I look for corroborating records at the Pearl Harbor archives? You could probably get in yourself with the Freedom of Information Act, but it'd take longer.'

'That would be great.' I shouldn't have been so happily surprised by his interest, but I was, especially since he must have been exhausted. 'And another thing – I hope to see Harue and Yoshitsune's old cottage, which can be reached by a road that runs through the old Barbers Point naval air station. If I give you the address, can you look up the route to get there?'

'Sure, and once I get a military access sticker, we can drive there together.' Michael leaned on the counter, and I wondered if he was suffering a balance problem again, or just exhaustion. Probably both. Now I was thinking I'd requested too much.

'That's awfully generous of you, and I don't expect you to do a bit more, honestly. It's your week off, and you have Kurt, Parker and Eric to gad about with, and sailing honors to accept—'

'Twelve days and eleven nights are about all I can take of that crew.' Michael reached over with his free hand and squeezed mine with it. 'Come on, Rei, let me help you with your family research. It'll give us more time together.'

# Fourteen

M ichael was a man of routine. Before he even opened the door to his room, he'd located a laundry and had dumped almost the entire contents of his duffel bag into a coin-operated washer. After that we went up to his room, which was quite small, but functional, with two double beds, a dresser, and a closet-sized bathroom.

'Maybe I should wait in the lobby to give you some privacy,' I said as Michael unzipped a small case containing clean, non-sailing clothes and toiletries.

'No, no. Just kick back for a few minutes. I'll be really fast,' Michael promised.

He wasn't fast at all – and I could understand why, not having had a hot shower for a week. But after a while he came out with a towel wrapped around his waist, got some shaving supplies out of his duffel, and set himself up in a narrow galley space with a fluorescent light and a sink, just outside the bathroom.

I spent a pleasant minute looking at his hard chest, lightly furred with hair that had turned more silvery from the time at sea. Michael glanced back at me, in the mirror, and nicked his neck.

'You cut yourself, and it's my fault because I distracted you.' I went closer to examine him.

'No, it's just that I can barely keep my eyes open to see what I'm doing.'

'Let me do it then.' I rinsed the razor, and pressed a hot, wet facecloth to his neck and face, holding it there for a half-minute.

'This could be dangerous,' Michael said.

'It's a bit tricky, when you have this much growth,' I said while lathering his face and neck with Barbasol. I shaved his neck first, and then seated myself on the edge of the vanity to be closer to his face. He closed his eyes, and they stayed closed as I finished and pressed a warm cloth across his face again.

'You're an excellent barber,' Michael said, opening his eyes and turning to the mirror to survey the results. 'I wish you could do this on a regular basis.'

'I'm afraid that's not part of my job description.' I spoke lightly, thinking to myself about how I wished I didn't work for him. How nice it would have been if I could have met Michael as just a guy in another office at the State Department or the Pentagon. If he'd never hired me, we could have done whatever we wanted, from the start.

'Rei,' Michael said, stroking the curve of my neck with his finger, mimicking what I'd done to him with the razor. 'At sea there's plenty of time just to stand and think. I'm starting to conclude that . . . well . . . perhaps we've been making things more complicated than necessary.'

'What do you mean?' There was so little space between us, with me up on the sink just a few inches from his chest. My fingers longed to press themselves against him, but I held off.

'You don't work for me right now. Your current OCI contract closed out seven weeks ago.' Michael took a deep breath. 'To make things even more above board, I'm on vacation for the next seven days. We're not involved in company business at all.'

'Remember what the agency psychiatrist said.' I couldn't look at him.

'It was such nonsense that I've put it all out of my head.'

'He pointed out that we have this problem because we're defining ourselves by gender. If we were two guys, we wouldn't be in this wretched position to begin with—'

'I like our position just the way it is,' Michael said, looking down at our bodies pressed up against each other. 'And I'm so glad you're not a guy. Come on, Rei, tell me what you really feel. Not what you think you should say.'

'I want more. I don't know what exactly,' I said slowly. 'The thing is, I made a personal pledge to myself to focus on my helping my father recover. I can't trust you right now. You're overcome by fatigue, and you've told me that your hormones go blotto when you're tired.'

'Stop,' said Michael, and he pulled me against him, hard, so there was no more space, and then we were kissing each other, the kind of kiss that I'd wanted on the boat, but couldn't have because of all the people. Michael kissed me again and again, tasting of lime and toothpaste, and I drowned in it, thinking that maybe things had changed after all.

Michael's fingers traveled over my bare back, then slipped under the edges of my dress. As my own hands began moving over Michael's bare chest, I felt something buzz between our hips.

Michael laughed, and I swore and reached into my dress pocket to haul out my small Nokia with my father's telephone number staring up at me from the window.

'Hi, Otoosan,' I said, but in fact it was Uncle Hiroshi. 'You?' I answered, so startled that I spoke in English. 'Did something happen to Otoosan?'

'No, he's fine, and watching the news. Tell me, are you driving home now?'

'Not just yet,' I said, feeling Michael lift himself away from me. He went to the duffel bag with clean clothes and began sorting through it.

'The fire that started yesterday has spread across the mountains,' Uncle Hiroshi continued. 'Edwin and his family came to us early because they heard the Farrington Highway is going to be closed in one hour. You must return home now.'

'I'm in Waikiki, but of course I'll start driving. See you soon.' I glanced at my watch. It was four fifteen, which meant rush hour had already started, plus there would be even more cars traveling, because of the imminent road closure.

I clicked the phone off, and looked at Michael, who had gotten his jeans on, somehow, without my seeing anything.

'You have a pressing appointment, it seems?'

'My uncle called to tell me there's a big fire on the Leeward Side, and the highway I'll take home will shut down in an hour.'

'What? You mean you're going to try to race a fire during rush hour?' Michael shook his head. 'Just stay with me till it's over. I'll make it worth your while, I promise.'

'No, you don't understand,' I said. 'I'm supposed to serve dinner to nine people tonight. I promised them I could manage dinner, even if I came out to meet you.'

Michael shook his head. 'That's a crazy thing to worry about, in the current situation. Aren't they concerned for your safety?'

'Michael, I think the road's still OK.'

Michael gave me a long look, then said, 'Let's see if we stand a chance.' He flipped channels on the television until we reached a local news channel covering the fire live. A map flashed on the screen, showing exactly where the road closure was scheduled.

'A few miles past our resort,' I said, tracing the screen with my finger. 'If we leave now – I mean, if I leave now – I'll definitely make it.'

'Of course we'll go together,' Michael said. "You can't drive into a fire by yourself.'

'But we should go now – like, within two minutes.'

Michael offered to drive, but I refused; he wasn't on the car-rental policy, and he was sleep-deprived. He acquiesced, staying awake only to help me find the Piikoi Street entrance to H-1 West. Because of my companion, I could use the HOV lane, where I pushed the van to seventy-five. There were solo drivers in the HOV lane tonight and, luckily for them, no motorcycle police to catch them. The expressions on the faces of the drivers of the battered trucks and vans surging westward were tense, as if everyone was thinking the same thing: get me home, before the road closes.

The miles ticked by, and in about thirty minutes I'd reached the place where the lychee truck usually stood. The sky had turned from blue to a brownish-gray, and it smelled as if I were on the verge of a bonfire. The fire was finally visible to me, a long jagged line twisting through the mountains, and down to the Pierce fields. Firefighters with tense, dirty faces trudged the land lugging hoses; their trucks were parked every fifty yards or so along the H-1 shoulder.

Michael coughed himself awake. 'Why did you let me fall asleep?'

'You needed it,' I said. 'And your being awake won't help anything. I know the way, and we're really close now.'

'The air in here is . . .' Michael coughed.

'A lot like a mesquite barbecue. I already took care of that,' I said as he reached for the dashboard's air-recycle button.

He drew back his hand, then placed it over my right, which had the steering wheel in a sweaty death grip. 'Hey, I recognize this place. I once swam at a beach around the bend – oh, Christ.'

'What do you see?' I asked anxiously.

'It's nothing, just that there's a high-voltage power plant just across the street.'

'They wouldn't let us through if the fire was too close,' I said. I slowed, because the traffic ahead of me had slowed mightily, and eventually we were side by side with the power plant, though I could barely make it out because of the smoke and many fire engines surrounding it. The old plantation village and Kainoa's coffee shop were close. I wondered if they had survived.

A mile past the plant, it became very difficult to see anything except for the crisp line of flames on my right. Smoke billowed across the road, traffic slowed to five miles an hour, and a line of smoke rose from the earth to my left. I looked again, and saw what I'd feared – there was fire on both sides of the road. We and the other cars were traveling on the firebreak itself. It was hard to feel calm and collected, driving a few feet from a fire in a minivan containing almost twenty gallons of gas. And even if the worst happened, and we had a chance to jump out of the van, there would be nowhere we could breathe. You could run from fire, but not from the smoke.

'Flames on both sides of the road now,' I said to Michael in a low voice.

'I guess the fire must have traveled through tree root systems to the other side.' Michael powered down his window and called out to the firemen, 'How far ahead is the closing?'

Someone shouted something back, and Michael rolled up the window again. 'I could barely understand him, but I think he just said try to go through.'

'Try? What kind of advice is that, to drive through a fire?'

'They wouldn't leave it open if we couldn't make it,' Michael said.

'This is a hell of a first date.'

'Let's not count tonight. We'll start fresh tomorrow – that is, if we live until tomorrow,' Michael added grimly.

During the time we'd been talking, the smoke had become lighter. I could see clearly again, and while there was fire on the right side of the road, it seemed to be spreading right back up the mountain. Had the wind changed?

'You did it!' Michael said as Kainani's hibiscus hedge appeared. As I took the Kainani exit, a short bridge over the highway into the resort, my heart rate slowed to normal. There was no fire here on the emerald green lawns, where the in-ground sprinklers were going full-blast. The guard booths had been abandoned, and the gate was up, so we went straight through.

'Look!' Michael pointed at the golf course, where five lean golden animals streaked swiftly across the green. They looked like wild dogs, and I guessed they were a family because there was a range of sizes.

I slowed at the turn so the dogs could get across the street bisecting the golf course. I imagined they'd left their mountain home in desperation, but what would there be for them here? I kept my foot on the brake until the dogs had passed, then drove the remaining block to the Pineapple Plantation gate, where I stopped again. We'd made it.

After a half-minute, Michael asked, 'Do you need to call the house to get someone to buzz you through?'

I shook my head. 'My keychain has a microchip that acti-
vates the gate, but I'd rather not hurry through.'

'Why?'

I turned to him, and took both of his hands in mine.
'Michael, I'm not sure I should have brought you. I didn't
prep you about what might happen. I don't know if you can
endure it.'

'Come off it!' Michael laughed lightly. 'What could be so
terrible after all we've just passed through?'

I took a deep breath and said simply, 'My family.'


# Fifteen


Tom was in the garden with his back to us, busy filming
the fire ravaging the mountains. At the sound of our
approach, he spun around. 'You returned safely. We were so
worried.'

'It was quite a drive,' I said, preparing to introduce Michael.

'You must tell me about what you saw, along the road. And
have you brought with you the Four Guys on the Edge?'

'Just the one,' Michael said, smiling and stepping forward
to shake hands with Tom. 'My name is Michael Hendricks.
Are you the infamous Tsutomu?'

'Tom. I always prefer Americans to call me Tom.'

'Michael drove back with me because of the fire,' I said.
'And he'll join us for dinner.'

Tom took his hand back from Michael and nodded at me.
'Everyone's waiting for you to prepare the meal, but the television was exciting enough to distract them. Come in, both
of you.'

'The gauntlet's not as bad as you led me to believe,' Michael
whispered to me as we followed Tom into the house. When
he saw the interior, his voice rose. 'Wow, this place certainly
beats my hotel room, doesn't it?'

'I *wasn't* in your hotel room – and remember, shoes!' I hissed at him because he seemed ready to stride with his weathered Topsiders into the living room. Everyone had turned from the television to inspect the two of us: Edwin, Margaret, Courtney and Yoshitsune on one side, my father, Hiroshi, and Calvin Morita on the other.

'This is my friend Michael Hendricks – he helped me drive here, because of the fire.' I went on to introduce everyone to Michael.

'How kind of you to accompany Rei,' my father said formally, when it was his turn. 'I'm Rei's father, Toshiro Shimura. I have to ask, though, how will you return to your hotel, now that the road is closing?'

'If the road hasn't re-opened in a few hours, I'll stay in the hotel we passed on the way in,' Michael said. 'And I apologize for intruding on your family. I now understand my arrival this afternoon placed Rei in a dangerous place at the wrong time. I'm sorry for that as well.'

'Eh, these fires, we must drive in and out of them – no other way to survive!' Uncle Edwin said. 'Our way of life. When was the last time we had a really big fire, Margaret? Six years past?'

'It was three years ago,' Calvin corrected him. 'I know, because I'd just started in my position. Michael, let me introduce myself. I'm Dr Calvin Morita, a neighbor here in Pineapple Plantation.'

'Yah, the fire was 2005,' Uncle Yoshitsune chimed in. 'I remember that some neighbors dredged the water out of my pond to wet down the firebreak. Three of my fish died.'

'That's terrible about your fish, Uncle Yosh. Hopefully the fire won't get close enough to Honokai Hale for that to happen tonight,' I said, trying to be jocular in order to drag attention away from Michael.

'Nobody there to throw water; the police made everybody leave,' Yosh said.

'Hey, will you join me in a drink? So I won't be the only one?' Calvin invited Michael.

'No thanks, I think it would just put me to sleep,' Michael said. 'What about you, Rei? Since you're not driving any more tonight?'

'No, thank you. Where's Braden?' I finally realized who was missing.

'He's gone upstairs to watch the FX channel,' said Tom.

'I'll call him down. Braden, you get your behind down here!' Margaret stood at the foot of the stairs and hollered up.

'So, you a sailor, huh?' Edwin said to Michael, as Braden eventually dragged himself down the stairs. 'Been stationed at Pearl Harbor for long?'

'Well, I'm actually based in Washington, DC, although I did live at Pearl during my teen years. This time around, I'm here because of a sailing race.'

'For a guy your age, it's a long time to be enlisted,' said Edwin, who clearly still misunderstood the situation. 'You going try for promotion or get out?'

'Both are possibilities. Depending on my luck.' A twitch at the side of Michael's mouth told me he was trying not to laugh. And I suddenly understood why he was letting Edwin believe he was a Navy sailor – he was creating a cover close enough to a semi-truth without actually lying. My father's expression was closed, but Uncle Hiroshi was frowning, and Tom was looking at Michael with a considerably less friendly expression than before. Braden, who'd trailed downstairs, gave Michael a sarcastic salute before flopping down next to his sister and staring with a bored expression at the television news.

The situation seemed to worsen after Margaret asked Michael where in Hawaii he had attended high school. Michael mentioned a place called Punahou; I'd never heard of it, but it obviously meant something of significance because Braden hooted, and Courtney looked up from her book with an expression on her face that almost looked like envy.

'You were a Punahou graduate, and then you enlisted in the Navy?' Edwin sounded incredulous.

'I didn't graduate from Punahou; I was actually there less than a year.'

Braden whistled, then said, 'You flunk out or something?'

'Actually, they asked me to leave.' Michael's voice was short.

I heard a collective intake of breath around the room.

'Most people try so hard to get into Punahou, they want to stay.' Edwin said.

Everyone, including me, was waiting for an explanation, but none came. I put my head down and went back to cooking.

Oddly enough, Braden seemed interested in conversation, and he began peppering Michael with questions about wave heights and nautical miles. Michael answered him easily, and I saw my father appraising Michael as if he was trying to reconcile all the discordant elements: the crisp New England accent, the private school expulsion, and all the sailing knowledge.

'Why don't you sit down with the others?' I said to Michael when he left Braden for a minute and came over to watch me chop ginger and garlic to go into the spinach sauté.

'Nobody's helping you,' Michael said *sotto voce*. 'Surely I can do something.'

That would have made me even more nervous, so I shook my head and said to the people who were watching us, 'Michael should tell you all about the fire we drove through. We saw some incredible animals fleeing.'

'What kind of animals?' Courtney looked up from her book.

'We spotted dozens and dozens of large, fluffy white birds with their heads tucked under their wings. There was a whole flock of them gathered on the bushes that border the resort. I guess they'd given themselves an evacuation notice, from wherever they normally live.'

'How cute,' Courtney said. 'I bet they were waiting there for their friends to join them!'

'Maybe so,' Michael answered. 'We also saw a beautiful family of wild dogs running across the golf course when we drove in.'

'You couldn't have – there are no wild dogs in Hawaii,' Edwin said.

'True,' Calvin added. 'There's such a fear of rabies here that the numbers of dogs are kept really low and there's a ridiculous quarantine for dogs coming in from the outside – six months! The Kikuchis have a Maltese they wanted to bring over for Jiro, but gave up because of the difficulty.'

'You're both wrong,' Braden interjected. 'Wild dogs live in the mountains. Scary yellow buggahs, make good watch dogs if only they could be trained.'

'Well, if these supposed wild creatures keep running *makai*, they might wind up on our little bit of seaside property and take shelter,' Edwin said with a false smile. 'Which reminds me, we need to talk about our land.'

*Edwin has no idea of timing*, I thought while exchanging glances with my father and Uncle Hiroshi and Tom. Calvin raised an eyebrow, but to hell if I was going to enlighten him.

'Please don't worry,' Uncle Hiroshi said. 'We will definitely help. We're just not sure how we can best assist you.'

'Yes,' my father chimed in, 'that's the problem. We must lend a hand, but how?'

Edwin smiled as if to reassure him. 'It's not you that's gonna do any work, it's the lawyer. A trained expert. That's what I mentioned before. If it's a matter of you wanting to make sure you get your share of the house price, I'll put it in writing.'

'No, no, it's not about the money,' my father said. 'We don't want to take any portion of what belongs to you. But the question is whether anything could be proven. Preparing a good case takes considerable time.'

'Before you know it, his time will run out.' Edwin pointed dramatically at Uncle Yoshitsune.

'Enough,' Yosh said, leaning forward with his eyes blazing at his son. 'I don't want this again. All we get this time is family embarrassment, all over again.'

As if to punctuate his comment, the oven buzzer rang. I opened the door, and looked at my trio of beautifully sizzling whole *weke ulua*.

What was the word for dinner time? I struggled for a few seconds, and then remembered.

'*Kau kau!*'

Dinner briefly interrupted the conversation. Everyone ate heartily; the *hiyashi chuka* noodles were properly creamy, tangy and nutty, the warm spinach was terrific with its ginger, soy and *mirin* dressing, the long beans were marveled at, and the fish were quickly reduced to skeletons. The fruit trifle was such a success that Braden, who had a thing against fruit, actually ate it: Margaret asked me for the trifle recipe, which I gladly gave her. Michael ate steadily, from time to time looking at me with the same mix of awe and pleasure that had been on his face the first time he'd realized that I could whip him at chess.

I offered to make both decaffeinated and real Kona coffee,

but nobody wanted any except for Michael and Braden, who was forbidden by his parents to taste it because of his age. The others and I all took green tea. We moved outside to sit on the *lanai* for a better view of the fire. The winds had changed, blowing so much smoke that we were driven back inside after about five minutes.

By midnight, the newscasters seemed as weary as Michael, who had lost the battle to keep his eyes open and was asleep, upright, at a dining table chair. I watched the television, hating it for the monotony – how many times could the news people say that the fire was still burning and Farrington Highway was closed?

Michael awoke and asked me for a telephone directory. I gave it to him, and from the phone in the kitchen he called the Kainani Cove Inn to make a reservation. I waited in vain for someone in my family to offer him a chance to lie down upstairs, but the offer never came.

Around one o'clock the winds shifted and the fire was no longer spreading along Farrington Highway. The Honolulu fire chief came onscreen and declared that the danger had passed, and all evacuated neighborhoods were clear. However, the fire had burned over ninety thousand acres of Pierce lands. Ten firefighters had gone to the hospital because of smoke inhalation, and an unknown amount of cattle and horses had been lost.

'Thank God,' Margaret said. 'I'm truly grateful. And sorry we were here so long – you all must be very tired. Michael, you go to your hotel now. There's no more need for anyone to watch the news.'

To my dismay, Michael canceled his hotel reservation and ordered a taxi back to Waikiki. I walked outside with him to wait, while the Hawaii Shimuras loaded up in Edwin's Nissan to head back to Honokai Hale.

'Why go back now when you really should go straight to bed?' I put my arm around Michael, after they'd driven off. 'You heard how expensive a taxi to Waikiki is. You should sleep in the hotel here, and I'll drive you home tomorrow.'

'A night at the resort hotel costs about three times what a cab would,' Michael said dryly. 'Besides, the guys are expecting me. We have early-morning surfing plans, and then I want to find a car rental place.'

Calvin walked past us, calling a loud goodbye just as Michael's taxi arrived. I waved off both of them and went right into the kitchen to wash the wineglasses; Michael had loaded everything else in the dishwasher hours ago.

Tom followed me into the kitchen and picked up a dish towel.

'Thank you!' I said, realizing that perhaps Michael had set a good example.

'I noticed your friend Michael is quite happy in the kitchen. Maybe that was his duty on the ship?' Tom asked.

'Oh, he doesn't talk much about his past.'

'So, did you meet him at a bar – or was it on the street?'

'Actually, it was at a museum,' I said, as if I didn't understand Tom's insinuation.

'A museum! That's good, he's broadening his horizons. But as for Washington, is he attached to a ship there? I wasn't aware Washington DC was a seaport.'

Now he was insinuating that Michael was lying. Swiftly I said, 'He's not working on ships anymore, and I don't care for all these nosy questions. Please, Tom!'

'This Michael seems to be pleasant and friendly, but when I think about his way of life, I worry for you. He probably earns even less money than Edwin. Calvin Morita, on the other hand, has a very good situation and seems so interested in you – yet you unkindly ignore him.'

'Calvin's a nanny with muscles,' I shot back. 'You know the kind of men I've gone out with. Calvin's nowhere in the ball park.'

'I disagree. He is a good-looking fellow, and he's also in the same specialty as your father. In Japan, we think it's a good thing to marry someone like your own family – not these foreign Shimuras, of course, but your own family.'

I paused to digest my cousin's xenophobic words. Then, in my mildest voice, I asked, 'Have you ever thought, Tom, what would have happened if Harue Shimura hadn't been the one sent off to Hawaii?'

'No. What do you mean by that?'

'Since we've been here, I've been thinking a lot about how we're stamped by who our ancestors were. Here in Hawaii, most Japanese, Chinese and Filipinos descend from ancestors who worked terrible, back-breaking jobs on the plantation.'

'Ah, there you exaggerate. I doubt many backs were broken, though I'm sure there were some strained muscles and herniated discs!'

'Just think, after all these sugar workers did to survive in Hawaii, they would never return to their homelands, although some would live long enough to be looked down on by wealthy tourists from Japan who'd never shucked anything tougher than an ear of corn.'

'How can you say that about me and my father?' Tom interrupted. 'You're forgetting all that we suffered. The war! Starvation! Bombing!'

'Tom, your father was born in MacArthur Japan, and you didn't come along till the seventies. All you know is life in the richest country on earth.'

Tom gaped at me. 'What is happening to you? Since you arrived here, you're not the same.'

I nodded, because he was right. I couldn't put myself on one side or the other anymore; maybe I never would. I was mixed up somewhere in the middle of the Pacific, like the islands of Hawaii itself.

# Sixteen

I pried my eyes open, then shut them fast. The sun told me I'd slept past my usual five thirty wake-up time. It was almost eight, I discovered when I could finally adjust my eyes to the light and read my watch.

When I trailed out of my room, I found that I was the last to rise. Dirty dishes in the sink told me that everyone had eaten, and the quiet told me they'd left the house. I saw the minivan was gone; perhaps it was a pre-emptive strike to keep me from seeing Michael. They might be shopping, or on a fire-damage sightseeing tour.

I drank a glass of mixed passion and orange juices while I unloaded the dishwasher, then refilled it with what was left in the sink and finally stepped outside. The flames were gone, leaving behind a blackened mountain range. The sky was as bright and beautiful as that in the beach scene posters sold at Kainoa's coffee shop.

The fate of the coffee shop and old plantation village had been in my mind ever since I'd woken up. I stretched on the *lanai*, drank some water, and set out on my usual route through the resort, and into the fields. The dry, slightly scorched fields near Kainani gave way to a flat landscape as black as the mountains, punctuated only by small, smoldering piles of brush. Ironically, without any vegetation I ran faster, though the dust I kicked up made the experience more like running in a city than the countryside.

As I'd feared, the plantation village had been burned to the ground. Only some tin mailboxes had survived, and when I saw a name I remembered, I knew the orientation for the coffee shop.

Here, the devastation was just as bad. The asphalt parking lot had survived, but the building was like the plantation cottages – charred wreckage of fallen beams. Here and there some metal things had survived, such as the espresso machine and a sink.

A well-built brown man in a tank top and shorts was leaning over one such pile. He turned round when he heard me approaching. As I'd expected, the man was Kainoa. His face and clothes were smeared with ash, and his eyes were red.

'You shouldn't be here.' Kainoa's voice broke, and his shoulders sagged.

'I'm sorry . . .' I began, but he cut me off.

'This is a fire scene. It's dangerous and none of your business.'

'When I heard where the fire was headed last night, I started to worry. I didn't know for sure, so I came over. I had to know what happened.'

'Shit happens,' Kainoa said, pronouncing each word precisely in a mainland accent. 'Everyone knew, it seemed, that the local yokel couldn't run and save his own business any more than he could save his own ass.'

'It isn't necessarily over,' I said. 'Fight for it. You can rebuild.'

'No, I can't. I wasn't insured.'

'But that's impossible.'

'I bought insurance for construction, which costs me an arm and a leg, and thought it would cover everything I owned. It turned out I was wrong.' Kainoa sighed heavily. 'I was here for a while yesterday, trying to hold it off, build a fire break. But then the village started to burn and I got the hell out.'

Kainoa sank down on a pile of scorched wood, his head bowed. Without taking time to think anything through, I went over and put my arms around him. I couldn't smell pleasant after my run, but Kainoa was in about the same state. He held on for a minute and then released me. He shook his head. 'The whole thing, it was the worst mistake of my life.'

'What do you mean?'

'Let me give you a ride back to your place,' Kainoa said. 'You shouldn't run across that field again without having water.'

Kainoa's dirty white Toyota Tacoma trunk was packed to overflowing with files and boxes of things he'd saved from the shop. I caught a glimpse of the espresso maker on its side, deflated beach toys, and lots of balled-up clothes – bikinis like the one I'd bought, and board shorts in the same pattern that Braden wore.

Kainoa dug around and found a lone Fiji water for me and a Budweiser for himself. It was pretty early to be drinking, not to mention drinking while driving. But I didn't say anything until we were heading toward the border of the old sugar cane field and were about to turn on to Farrington Highway.

'Do you want to get rid of the bottle?' I said, shifting uneasily on the seat's bright floral cotton cover.

Kainoa looked at me as if I were insane. 'I can't throw a bottle out of this car.'

'I'm not suggesting littering, but you don't want to have to explain what you're doing if you get pulled over by a cop.'

'Well, if he sees the bottle and connects it to me, it's arson, baby.'

We heard the sound of a vehicle at that time; fortunately, it wasn't a police car, but a black truck turning off Farrington

Highway and heading in our direction, kicking up ash as it traveled. Kainoa seemed to stiffen, and threw the empty bottle into the backseat and told me to throw something over it. I did, and my nervousness accelerated.

'Who could that be, driving across Pierce lands?' I asked.

'The obvious. Albert Rivera, the guy I told you about.'

The dreaded land manager. My stomach dropped when the black truck began honking, then cut squarely across our path and stopped. A tall middle-aged man in jeans jumped out of the truck. Kainoa rolled down his window, hung out his head and beckoned for the man to come toward him.

'*Aloha*, Albert,' he called out in the boisterous, happy-go-lucky tone I'd heard him use often in the coffee shop. But Kainoa's right hand remained in a death grip on the steering wheel, as if he was ready to take off at any second. 'You cleaning up after the fire, too?'

The *luna* wore a baseball cap, so I couldn't see his hair, but his flinty eyes had an Asian crease, which could make him anything. But Rivera probably had some Portuguese blood, because of his name. In pidgin as thick as Great-Uncle Yoshitsune's, he roared, 'Kainoa Stevens, what you think you doing? And who's in there with you this time?'

'My name is Rei Shimura. I'm staying at Kainani,' I added, because I was on the verge of concocting an excuse about being a lost tourist who Kainoa was helping home.

He snapped his fingers. 'The running chick. You went across the field the last couple mornings. So, Kainoa, you got an explanation for this trespass or what?'

'Just trying to get a lost runner out. You got a problem with me helping this girl?'

'I went out to the coffee shop, and he's bringing me home,' I said, my heart starting to thud. I'd noticed an ominous bulge under the thin woven shirt that Albert Rivera wore.

'Pierce Holdings don't like vehicles carving up their land. You know that, Kainoa.'

'This land's in pretty bad shape to even think about my truck making an impact,' Kainoa said. 'Anyway, the Pierces got no trouble carving it up for Kikuchi.'

'You watch what you say,' Albert said. 'Mr Kikuchi's in the truck. I'm giving him a tour of the damage.'

I'd been nervously focused on Alberto Rivera, so I hadn't

noticed a passenger in the truck. But now I saw a silhouetted figure in the passenger seat.

'Just a minute,' Kainoa said to me, putting the truck in park and swinging down. He strode over to the red truck's passenger side window and stood there until the man inside rolled it down.

Albert stared at the two of them, and then stomped over to join the gathering. Feeling left out, I slid out of my seat and followed, figuring that I might employ my Japanese to smooth things over.

The passenger door opened now, and Mitsuo Kikuchi stepped down, with a hand from Alberto Rivera. He needed it; he was a very small man, about five feet tall, with thin white hair and wrinkles. Despite his age, Mr Kikuchi wore surprisingly childlike clothes – a pink golf shirt, and pink and orange checked Madras cotton shorts. He wore his glasses on a red string around his neck, and soft white loafers were turning gray around the edges from the ashy field.

'Welcome to Hawaii,' I said in Japanese. When Mitsuo Kikuchi remained stern, I made a deep bow and began my personal introduction, which quickly segued into thanking him for building such a beautiful resort where I was staying with my family. It was all polite nonsense, the kind of thing that was de rigueur when you met somebody in Japan.

'Do you live there all year?' Mr Kikuchi's voice was polite, and he spoke English without much of an accent. It was a clear signal to switch languages.

'Just a month this time, although I'm sure I'll be back. It's such a nice community. I already met your son and his physician.'

'My son is the resort CEO.' Mr Kikuchi had noticeably stiffened.

'Yes, I've heard that. I saw him at the pool on my first morning.'

'He rarely leaves his office; you must be mistaken,' Kikuchi said, turning his attention to Kainoa. 'Have we met?'

'Yeah. My name is Kainoa Stevens. You visited my coffee shop to talk last February.'

'Oh, yes, Mr Stevens. You own the place made out of an old general store. I hope it's all right after the fire?' Mr Kikuchi's voice lowered to a suitable, pitying level.

'The whole plantation village burned and that coffee shop with it,' Albert Rivera put in. 'All the old tings gone.'

'I guess it looks more likely that I'll consider selling.' Kainoa spoke in a firm voice, but his eyes were on the ashes, not any of us.

'Is it true, then? Your building is destroyed?' Kikuchi pressed.

'Everything except the espresso machine.'

'I'm afraid I must make a new price. Now that there is damage, it means more work for my company. When you count in the plantation village, it's really a tragedy, all those important historic buildings gone.'

'But you were planning to tear down the village! Everyone knows that.' Kainoa sounded testy.

'You are almost correct. I wasn't going to use those buildings for my project, but I had been told by the government that the buildings are important, so I planned to transport them. These days, you can make a small hotel village from old cottages.' Mr Kikuchi shook his head. 'Your coffee place was a very nice, authentic plantation general store. That could have been a centerpiece building for a historic resort somewhere else, like Molokai.'

'What? How would an old plantation store from Leeward Oahu fit on a neighbor island with its own buildings?' Kainoa sounded both angry and incredulous.

'I'm quite sorry about your loss.' Kikuchi's slight smile belied his words. 'If you are honestly ready to cooperate, Mr Stevens, call my office tomorrow. It will be your last chance, so think carefully. Right now, I must resume my tour of the Pierce property.'

I couldn't bring myself to look at Kainoa after the red truck had disappeared in a cloud of choking black smoke. It was just too depressing. Kainoa hadn't said much to me, just fished another couple of bottles of Budweiser out of the back of his truck. I'd shaken my head at the beer that he offered me, so he drank one bottle after the next as he drove off the Pierce lands and on to Farrington Highway.

At Kainani's gatehouse, he didn't pause to let me identify myself but drove straight through, leaving a trio of anxious-looking teenage security guards in his wake. As we passed the hotel, I started to tell him where to turn for the Pineapple Plantation, but he interrupted.

'I know where it is. You gonna open the gate for me?'

'It's OK, you can just drop me now. You've done so much already—'

'You don't want the family to see you with a *moke* like me, yah?'

'Of course not.' I handed him the fob with the gate entrance chip and told him how to swipe it. Slowly, the gates parted and I directed Kainoa how to drive on. Looking around at the emerald lawns still being sprinkled, I felt embarrassed. 'I'm staying in the third house on the left – oops, did I miss it?' I was confused, because although I recognized the breadfruit tree by the walkway, a different vehicle was in the driveway – a white Chrysler Sebring convertible with the top down. But then I saw the shoe rack by the door, with my relatives' sandals. It was definitely our house.

'OK, I'll just get out here,' I said, waving my hand toward a tree just past the driveway. If I craned my head, I could see beyond the trees into the fenced pool area. There were a lot of children, nannies and parents, but the only Japanese man I could see was Jiro Kikuchi, lying on a chair like a flabby beached whale, with Calvin Morita at his side, both of them directly in the line of vision of two teenage girls splashing in the pool. So much for another hard day in the office.

Kainoa turned off the ignition. 'I got a lot of trouble to take care of. Don't think I'll see you again.'

'You know, I'm here another three and a half weeks. I'd like to stay in touch as things progress. Where can I find you?' I was more worried about his situation with Mitsuo Kikuchi than I was about the Shimura land.

'I stay in Makaha. You already got my card, but just in case . . .' Kainoa fished a takeout restaurant menu out of the glove compartment and scrawled a number on it. 'It's OK if you don't call. I got a lot of shit going down, as you saw.'

'I understand.' I broke off because I caught a flash of movement in the passenger side mirror. Michael Hendricks, wearing khaki shorts, a rusty-red polo shirt and his Topsiders, was heading straight for us.

# Seventeen

'I was beginning to wonder where everyone had gone.' Michael's gaze slid from me to Kainoa.

'Michael, this is Kainoa Stevens. He owns the coffee shop I told you about.'

Kainoa looked at Michael as if perplexed. 'I thought your cousin was Japanese.'

'Hey, I was born on the Japanese island of Kyushu.' Michael grinned at him. 'Can't you tell?'

I burst out laughing, because this was something I had no idea about, but could very well be true, since Michael's father had been in the Navy. I said, 'Michael's an old friend. He lived here for a while, and arrived last night for Transpac.'

'Oh, the hot-shot boat race,' Kainoa said in the same exaggerated accent. 'Or should I say regatta? What do *haoles* call it?'

'Call it whatever you want. I don't really care.' The warmth in Michael's tone had evaporated.

'Used to live here, huh? Where did you go to high school?' Kainoa asked.

'Near Manoa Valley,' Michael answered.

'Punahou?'

'Don't tell me you're also a graduate?' Michael returned the volley.

'No way, man. I'm a proud graduate of Kamehameha – you know, the school for Hawaiian people.'

'Everyone in Hawaii seems very interested in high school.' I tried to lighten the mood. 'I hated mine, so I put those years behind me as fast as I could. Well, thanks for the ride back, Kainoa. I really appreciate it.'

'Sure. And remember, don't be a stranger – you've got my number!' Kainoa swaggered back to his truck, made a U-turn, and burned rubber heading out of the cul-de-sac.

'Well, it was awfully nice of him to give me a ride,' I said to Michael. 'Though it wasn't very nice of him to call you a *haole*. About the phone number, I'll gladly explain . . .'

'You don't need to explain anything. I know you have a vast network of friends. But I had really hoped that this week you were planning on dating *me*. But now I learn I'm just an old friend.'

'What else could I say? And I'm not dating Kainoa. He's a recent acquaintance.'

'I see.' Michael shook his head, looking at me. 'From the way he looked, and the state of your clothes, I wonder what you were doing: climbing all over him!'

I glanced down at my tank top, once red and white, and now covered with black ash. 'Obviously some of the ash is from running through burned fields and yes, I hugged Kainoa briefly when I found him, because he was so upset. He lost everything in the fire.'

'I'm sorry for anyone hurt by the fire,' Michael said. 'But something tells me it's not a good thing that you've made this acquaintance.'

'Really? Give me one good reason.'

Michael shrugged. 'Can't really explain. It's my gut.'

Gut instinct was everything – in antiques or spying – so I tried to sound reasonable in my protest. 'I appreciate your concern, Michael, but I've learned a lot about the island from Kainoa. And his connections are helpful. Today, as we were driving across the Pierce fields, we ran into the Pierce family's lands manager chauffeuring Mitsuo Kikuchi, the Japanese investor who's trying to buy and develop more beachfront property from Josiah Pierce. It was an incredible stroke of luck, meeting Kikuchi in advance of Josiah Pierce; I'll have something interesting to tell him.'

'Maybe I slept through you telling me about a Josiah Pierce meeting last night,' Michael said. 'When and where is it?'

'One o'clock, at his home on Tantalus Road. It's north of Honolulu.'

'I know where Tantalus is. It's a beautiful historic neighborhood built on a mountain – rather remote, but the residents like it that way.'

'What's your schedule this afternoon? Can you go with me?' I asked impulsively.

'Of course. But you're so independent; why would you want me tagging along?'

'Oh, just to clue me in on your gut instincts.'

'Well, I'd better tell you that I may be a liability, in this case. In my class at Punahou there was a boy named Will Pierce, who might be related to your Pierce. His father's name was like a girl's name, Lindy or something . . .'

'Lindsay,' I said. 'Lindsay Pierce is the younger brother of Josiah Pierce the Second. And don't be so pessimistic; maybe this Punahou thing will finally play in your favor.'

'It won't be a good thing. Will and I had a series of fights the year I was in school. Our fathers talked, if you could call it that.'

'Is this the reason you were expelled?' I caught my breath.

'Partially. I was a pretty troubled kid, but I'll tell you about that some other time.'

'You're right. It's already almost eleven. There's not a lot of time for me to eat something, shower and get dressed for the interview.'

'How long will your grooming take? Do I need to apply extra sunscreen?'

'About ten minutes – and yes, you do need more sunscreen. Whether you like it or not, you're a white guy.' I blew him a kiss and went inside.

# Eighteen

Michael looked taken aback when, nine minutes later, I emerged, scented with jasmine and wearing a chrysanthemum-patterned wrap dress.

'That was quick.'

'I want to make sure we have time to get there.' I'd been hoping for more of a compliment than quick, because the dress fit beautifully and its pattern reminded me of a vintage Japanese textile. But I wore no make-up except for lipgloss, and I'd slicked my wet hair back with a leave-in conditioner instead of drying it.

'We're in very good shape, although wouldn't you know, I'm low on sunscreen. On the way to Tantalus, can we swing by my favorite store? I don't think it'll take more than twenty-five minutes.'

'We could go to Long's Drug in Kapolei.'

'I'm sure my store has better prices.' Michael combated my annoyed expression with a sly grin. 'You told me yourself that I'm the cheapest man in America. I've decided to embrace my nature.'

Michael's special store turned out to be military – a super-sized, double-floored Navy Exchange located in the section of Pearl Harbor that was unguarded and more or less open to the public. Still, I could only enter the Exchange escorted by Michael, who had decided to dress down his image and only show his State Department I.D.

'By the way, I'm the only one who can actually purchase things. So if you want something, let me know. Don't attempt to buy it yourself, or you'll get in trouble.'

Michael selected two tubes of Neutrogena Sport, and then led me downstairs via an escalator. 'Why don't we stop in jewelry for a minute? I had a brainstorm that we should wear wedding rings to your interview with Josiah Pierce.'

'That's overkill, don't you think?'

'Sssh.' Michael looked around. 'It'll make me seem more legitimate. Unless you've already told him I'm your old friend.'

'I didn't mention you when I spoke to him . . .'

'Superb. That makes me your husband. You can explain that you didn't mention I'd be along earlier because you didn't know when my sailboat was arriving.'

'Michael, I can do that, but I think you're trouble-shooting to an extreme degree. Sometimes telling the truth is easier than lying. Have you ever thought of that?'

'Too much.' Michael smiled at me. 'Come on, let's shop.'

At least I wasn't paying out of my own pocket for this nonsense, I thought as we were fussed over by many friendly Filipina sales clerks at the jewelry counter. Apparently we were on the old side for prospective newlyweds – much was made of Michael's silvery hair, which he seemed to enjoy. I concentrated on selecting comfortable golden bands for the

two of us, after which Michael declared I needed an engagement ring, too, and we went to the counter with diamonds
and cubic zirconium rings. I pointed to another gold band
with an oversized cubic zirconium solitaire surrounded by tiny
fragments of the artificial crystal. It looked properly bridal,
but Michael didn't seem pleased.

'Is that really your taste?'

'Not exactly.' I shrugged. 'But it looks like what every girl
wants, doesn't it? And it's on sale.'

'No,' said Michael. 'It'll blow your cover, big time. Look
at how low-key and tasteful you always are, especially today
in your dress. On your hand, that ring looks misplaced and
fake.'

Since when did he work for the Style Network? I grumbled, but went back to looking. In the end, Michael located
a simple, square-cut solitaire. On my hand with its neatly
trimmed, clear-polished nails, it looked like it belonged.

'Can you return the rings?' I asked Michael after we left
twenty minutes later with all the jewelry tucked casually in
the same bag as the sunscreen.

'I'm almost certain, but I didn't ask the ladies for fear of
being slaughtered. Hey, shifting gears for a minute, I have to
tell you about what I did earlier this morning.'

'OK.' I'd put on my rings, and settled back in the passenger
seat.

'The guys decided to sleep in this morning, so I got the
convertible and drove to Pearl Harbor to see if I could get
into the wartime archives. I located Uncle Yosh's arrest
warrant.'

'You did?' I found myself feeling strangely worried. Here
at last would be the truth about Uncle Yoshitsune – at least
as the wartime government saw it.

'Yes. He was detained on suspicion of espionage and held
at Sand Harbor for two months starting in April 1942. Other
papers in his file described how he was transferred to Camp
Minedoka in Idaho. There was yet another paper detailing his
release to work overseas with the troops as a Japanese language
translator.'

'So the story's exactly as he said. I can trust Uncle Yosh,'
I said with a flood of relief.

'It looks that way. But while I was in there I reviewed

many files of other Japanese-American civilians arrested right after the attack on Pearl Harbor, and I noticed something. There were no witness reports of Yoshitsune Shimura doing anything out of the ordinary. None of his co-workers reported him.'

'You're wondering how they reeled him in, then – and why?'

'This is speculation, but we do know that the government was forcing Japanese nationals out of their homes, if the individual family's home was located in an area convenient for espionage. Usually this meant near the ocean or a military base. Perhaps the cottage location, plus the ease at which he could handle all mail coming into Oahu, was just too much for them to handle.'

'It's so unfair. Did you bring copies of these documents for me to read?'

'I didn't make photocopies because I didn't want to raise red flags. There was enough curiosity about why a suit from Washington wanted to get into their archive without a prior appointment or even an actual suit. I don't ever like to play on my father's name, but here I was forced to.'

'I suppose it's impossible to know everything about Yoshitsune and Harue's past.' I sighed heavily.

Michael squeezed my hand. 'I'm not as pessimistic as that. It's just that we've only seen your family's movie one way. I wonder how the screenplay would read as written by the Chinese family who moved into the house.'

'Or by the Pierces,' I said. 'If we put all three together, we'll have *Rashomon*.'

'Hey, did you see the tiled-roof estate we just passed? Tantalus must have the most beautiful group of old houses on this island.'

I had been noticing the houses, but they'd blurred together in my mind. Older mansions tucked away behind protective old stucco or rock walls overgrown with vines, not just the typical bougainvillea but rarer things. And there were flowers from Europe and North America, hydrangeas and roses the missionary wives must have propagated to remind them of home. I said, 'Wealthy colonials always seem to gravitate toward hill country. I guess it's the combination of cooler temperatures and great views.'

'Not to mention moisture,' Michael said. 'It's perfect here. This Hawaii just doesn't look like where your family's staying.'

'Do you want to know why?' I felt a need to defend my side of the island. 'The early developers channeled the water that was naturally in the mountains to the cane plantations by building artesian wells. That's one of the reasons the leeward mountains are so eroded and parched.'

'It can't all be man's doing. There's a different weather pattern here. The proof is that we've gone through three rain clouds in the last fifteen minutes, and I bet if we called Kainoa, he'd tell us it hasn't rained a drop.'

'Would you want to live up here, if you could?' I asked, keeping my eyes on the view as we climbed the switchback that was Tantalus Road. We'd already been on it for fifteen minutes, which seemed interminable to someone with motion sickness.

'Oh, I don't think so. I'm one of the hoi polloi who think the ultimate is to live next to water. Speaking of which, later today, are you up for a sail? I'd love to take you out on *Four Guys on the Edge*.'

'I thought you knew I don't sail.' I could barely get the words out because this was a tough drive for me, up a narrow pitted street that zigzagged back and forth like a switchback train track.

'What I remember you saying is that you haven't *tried* sailing,' Michael said mildly.

'Well, if I get motion sickness on planes, trains and in cars, I'm not likely to be much of a sailor.'

'You may surprise yourself. Hey, what's the house number again?'

'Twenty-seven,' I said, reading from the directions I'd written down when talking to Josiah Pierce Jr. the day before. 'He said we'd notice it because of the roses.'

I could hardly believe the mountain road could wind any higher, but it did. On the last stretch to the top, we found the house. The sign was ancient and almost too small to see, but the rock wall surrounding the house was low, and I could see it clearly – a well-kept white stucco house with well-finished brown woodwork and a beautiful old green slate roof. The house looked like it had been built before 1920, but the condition was excellent, as were the grounds, which were beautifully landscaped, but this time with local flowers like hibiscus and ginger.

'Here we are,' I said, glad the car had stopped. I took a sip of water from the bottle and began to feel my stomach settle.

'Are you OK?' Michael looked at me with concern.

'I'm fine now the car's stopped.' I took a few deep breaths and said, 'All systems go. I hope I don't put my foot in my mouth too badly . . .'

'I feel just the same,' Michael said. 'If I start to screw up, just call me honey.'

'Got it,' I said. 'The code word is honey.'

# Nineteen

A dark stone path overgrown with moss led up to the teak front door, which opened before we reached the threshold. Standing at attention was a very old man with silver hair and a chestnut-brown complexion as weathered as that of the resort gardeners. But this man wore a crisply ironed white shirt tucked into cream linen trousers, and his thick head of silver hair was uncovered.

I was confused. Was this a butler? He seemed very well dressed. My unspoken question was answered when the man nodded at us and spoke in the same well-bred voice I'd heard on the telephone.

'So glad you didn't have trouble finding me. The road up the mountain can be confusing, and there's constant construction.'

Josiah Pierce was *hapa* – just like me. As I drew closer, I examined his face carefully; there was nothing Asian about his eyelids, or his nose. No, I decided, he looked more Hawaiian, with an echo of Caucasian ancestry.

'Mr Pierce,' I said, smiling. 'I'm Rei Shimura. And I enjoyed every minute of the drive.'

'You may call me JP, if you like. And who is your companion?'

'Michael came in yesterday with the Transpac race.' I didn't have the gall to lie and call him my husband. 'I'm sorry I didn't mention him yesterday. He asked to come along, because he has fond memories of this part of Honolulu.'

'So you know Tantalus? Please come in.'

'I've never been up this high, sir, but I did know people farther down. I went to Punahou around the same time your nephew was there,' Michael said, holding out his hand. 'My name is Michael Hendricks.'

'Hendricks, Hendricks.' JP was still for a moment, and then his eyes sharpened. 'The Army brat!'

'Navy juniors, or so the parents like to call us,' Michael said wryly.

'There was bad blood between you and William, wasn't there? I can remember my brother Lindsay wanted to set the Chinese mafia on you after you broke his boy's nose.'

I gasped, and Michael's face flushed.

'He needed it, frankly; the boy actually stopped beating up his sister once he knew what it felt like to be beaten to a pulp. Anyway, William's fine and healthy in Los Angeles, though he's regrettably on his third divorce.'

'I'm sorry to hear about that, and I assure you my behavior's improved since then. Mostly,' Michael added with a glance at me.

JP laughed. 'If you two aren't newlyweds, I'm not eighty-five years old. Come inside. Midori is just preparing our lunch, and I'll have her set another place on the *lanai*.'

I was being charmed, I realized with a sinking feeling, as the old gentleman ushered us through a grand hall with a Carrera marble floor. Aged stucco walls were decorated with many dour portraits of old white men, groups of stiff-looking children, and a lovely young Hawaiian woman looking stifled by her high-necked Edwardian blouse. The woman looked familiar, and I wondered if I'd seen another picture of her in the Bishop Museum. Princess Something-with-an-E. I would have liked to linger to figure it out, but we were being steered out of the darkness to a sunny outdoor *lanai* overlooking the spectacular rose gardens and a view of Honolulu's skyscrapers.

An Asian maid in a powder-blue uniform was adding a third place setting to an old teak table. It was already laid for lunch, with antique rose-patterned china and scrolled silver. Sliced mango and papaya were fanned across ice-packed silver bowls; there was also a salad of tomatoes and herbs, a basket of fragrant bread rolls, and a platter of sliced pork tenderloin. Pretty fancy, I thought, when I'd just called yesterday afternoon, and there had been no mention of any food.

Actually, I reflected, the genteel setting reminded me of the east coast. There hadn't even been an indication that we should take off our shoes – in fact, JP wore soft beige leather loafers. Everything was different here, in Josiah Pierce Junior's home; I half-expected to see the *New York Times* or the *Washington Post* on the side table, but the papers that were there were local, and folded over to show he'd been reading the stories about the fire.

The maid was sweeping the floor as we sat down, and I realized she was after some errant hibiscus blooms that had fallen off the trellises.

'This is really much more than I expected,' I said. 'This lunch – it's lovely, but we didn't imagine you'd do so much for us.'

'I live by my own rules – or, I should say, the old Hawaiian rules of hospitality. When someone visits, you enjoy food together.' JP looked over the table at us. 'And frankly, with the bad news about the fire, I'd rather put off my misery for a while and enjoy some unexpected company.'

'It's nice for us, too,' Michael said.

'Well, when I heard your wife's dulcet tones on the telephone, I was intrigued. Mainland accent, but a Japanese name, even after marriage. Tell me, what are your plans for the children's surnames?'

I tried hard not to look at Michael, because this was a bit of back story we hadn't dreamed would come up. I said, 'No children yet, so I guess we haven't had to deal with that challenge.'

'Don't wait too long.'

'No, sir, I won't,' Michael said, taking my hand.

'It likely isn't a matter of *you*, but rather a matter of *her*. That's usually how these things work.' JP's eyes twinkled. 'Though you can't have scored any points in the fertility game wasting two weeks at sea for Transpac.'

'Do you sail yourself, Mr Pierce?' Michael asked, after we had all finished laughing.

'Goodness, no. When I was young, I was too busy working on the plantation to have time to play at sea with a bunch of prep school boys. I was my father's firstborn, you see. After Punahou I went straight to work, and there was no mother to spoil me or interfere.'

'You mother – may I ask what happened to her?'

'She died when I was six. That was her portrait you passed in the hallway; her name was Evelyn. Here, this is passion-fruit jelly that Midori makes from our own harvest. You must try it with the bread roll.'

'Delicious,' said Michael, smearing it across his roll.

'Do you mean the Princess Evelyn?' I asked and, after a pause, he nodded. I put together the genealogy: Josiah Pierce the First had married a princess, and she'd borne JP Junior, the man we were having lunch with. After his wife's death, Josiah Senior had remarried a Caucasian woman who had fathered Lindsay Pierce. This was how Lindsay Pierce could be WASP blond, while his older half-brother was as brown as many Hawaiians.

'The blond woman in the other hallway portrait is my step-mother, Natalie Talbot Pierce,' JP said, as if following my train of thought. 'She was originally from California, and immediately after my father's death, she relocated to Los Angeles. She's happier there, and now Will's there with his children, her life is perfect.'

'Did you grow up in this house?' I asked.

'No. It dates from the 1910s, and my father did build it, but I didn't move in until ten years after the war ended because I was involved in round-the-clock management of the plantation. Before H-1, a drive from Honolulu to the Leeward Side took half a day.'

'It still does, practically, when it's rush hour,' Michael said.

'How do you know that? Aren't you staying in Waikiki?'

'Actually we're at the Kainani resort,' I said.

'Ah yes, Kainani was built on land we sold to Mitsuo Kikuchi. The fire was quite close to you yesterday, then.'

'Yes.' Michael took up the conversation easily. 'We had to drive through it just before the road closed, and there was a stretch of road with fire on both sides of us.'

'We have damage on over ninety thousand acres, and the ranchers using our lands lost almost a hundred head of horses. Still, it could have been worse,' Josiah said.

'I was out jogging through the fire-damaged areas this morning, and I saw Mr Kikuchi and your land manager, Mr Rivera. I told them I was sad to see that old plantation village was gone, and the coffee shop as well.'

'Actually, the coffee shop's not my loss; the half-acre it stands on we sold about thirty years ago. But the old plantation village that's gone was part of Pierce Holdings.'

'I feel fortunate to have seen it before it burned,' I said. 'The village was like a perfect, lost little world.'

'You liked the cottages?' He smiled wistfully. 'They're almost universally deplored by people now, but they were better than most housing in Hawaii at that time. A commission in the thirties established rules for the construction of plantation cottages. Depending on family size, our workers had multiple bedrooms, kitchens, and the crowing glory: indoor plumbing.'

'Well, I suppose that now that the land is cleared of brush, it will be easier for Mr Kikuchi's development plans, although I imagine he'll try and drop the price he's willing to pay you, citing the unfortunate damage to historic structures.'

JP's expression seemed to have changed from open to guarded in an instant. 'You said you had a question about land, but I didn't realize you were one of the anti-Kikuchi agitators. Who pays your salary, Honolulu Heritage? Or do you do it as a volunteer?'

'Honey,' Michael said softly.

'We're not preservationists, I swear, although I really do like old places, and old things.' JP didn't look any more relaxed, so I added, 'I work out of the home so I'm afraid I don't have a business card. Michael, why don't you give JP your card?'

Michael's State Department card was impressive-looking, and only slightly fake. Josiah Pierce looked it over carefully then said, 'Last fellow I know with a job like this wound up with a bad case of blowfish poisoning.'

'I'm glad we're not having sushi for lunch, then,' Michael said, smiling rather faintly.

'What are you really here for?' JP's voice was cold.

'As I said over the phone, I'm trying to put family history in order. Some of my relatives worked at the plantation from the twenties through the forties.'

'Shimura,' said Josiah Pierce, his sharp eyes fixing on me. 'You're not using Hendricks as your last name, but Shimura. Are you one of the family with the failed lawsuit?'

'Sort of,' I began. 'I didn't know about the lawsuit until recently, and the Hawaiian Shimuras are technically my third cousins.'

'The Circuit Court dismissed Edwin Shimura's case for lack of evidence. How could he have thought he could claim land without a deed?'

'I understand your point. It's just that, when I hear my great-uncle's account – I'm talking about Yoshitsune Shimura, who was a child on the plantation – I believe he's being as honest as he can be.'

'Can be?' Mr Pierce sounded markedly sarcastic.

'He's eighty-nine years old. There are things he remembers, and things he has no idea about, because his mother, Harue Shimura, didn't tell him everything and she died while he was away in a Japanese-American internment camp on the mainland. What my great-uncle told me was that he saw a letter signed by your father in his mother's chest of drawers. The letter described the gift of a seaside cottage to her. I should probably mention that he found this at the time he was living within the seaside cottage, so he assumed all was well and normal.'

'What else did he tell you?'

'Yoshitsune lived there with his widowed mother until he was sent to an internment camp on suspicion of espionage. He wound up leaving the camp to serve as a translator with the OSS, and when the war was over, he returned to Hawaii and found the house had been taken over by a family called Liang. Your father had passed away, so he asked your mother about it, and she said she didn't know anything about the matter.'

'Natalie was my *stepmother*, remember that, and she really didn't know anything, because to her, the plantation was a hot, dirty place she didn't like to visit. It's a shame he didn't come to me, because I have an idea what might have happened.'

'You do? Well, why didn't you say anything at the trial?' I asked.

'Maybe because there was no trial,' Michael suggested.

'That's right, and I think if things had been handled personally between us, with more *aloha*, I would have said something. But I'm not sure I should tell you, because my guess is you'll get the lawyers revved up again, causing me legal and PR trouble at a time when I have my hands full just dealing with my ranchers who are going to want all kinds of compensation and favors because their horses burnt to death in my fields.'

I bit my lip, thinking how I'd misjudged the man, and the situation. Things were deteriorating as fast as I was shredding my bread roll. I put my hands on my lap, to control them.

'Mr Pierce, I'm very sorry we disturbed you,' Michael said to fill the awkward silence.

'You think I'm just like the Big Five, don't you? Big, bad landowners, abusers of the masses?'

'I don't think it's as simple as that,' I said.

'Drive farther along the coast, and you'll come to Maile Beach, and see hundreds of tents on the grass. It's an impromptu housing development for the homeless, who come from all over the island because they can't afford a roof over their head. Hawaii wasn't like that in sugar plantation days.'

'I have to agree,' Michael said. 'When I was here in school, and there were still a few sugar plantations going, there weren't many homeless, unless you count drunks in Chinatown.'

'We had flophouses then,' JP said, seeming to relax slightly. 'Now they're fancy boutiques and restaurants.'

'I think we're getting away from the topic,' I said. 'Look, I know my relatives in Hawaii will not get that acre and a half they're dreaming of. All I really hope for is a better idea of what your father was doing when he visited Harue Shimura in her house one evening, when Yoshitsune was a boy.'

Josiah Pierce looked at me for a long moment, and then said, 'Do you know what year that was?'

'Uncle Yoshitsune was in his mid-teens. He'd finished high school and had started at the post office.'

'There was a fire on the plantation in 1938, a regular burn that we'd scheduled for a field that needed rest. Unfortunately, the wind changed. A spark jumped to the mill, and it was ablaze before anyone noticed. Not everyone escaped.'

Michael and I sat in silence, waiting for more.

'Some people said it was the *luna*'s mistake for going ahead with a scheduled burn on a day with wind. Others said it was my father's fault for wanting to have every field perfect when the demand for Hawaiian sugar was dropping. Who knows? It was a bad fire, an unlucky wind, and nine men died.' He looked from the distance back at us. 'All of the men who died had wives and children. These are the women my father visited personally to give condolences, and offered help with housing outside the village, if they chose to leave.'

'Kind of like death compensation?' Michael said.

'We didn't have fancy union terminology in those days. We just called it doing the right thing.'

'That couldn't have been the reason Harue was given a house,' I said. 'You see, her husband, Ken Shimura, wasn't working at the mill in 1938. He'd left for the Big Island by 1926. He worked on another Pierce plantation there, and I guess passed away there, because Yoshitsune never saw him again.'

'You don't say.' JP's words came slowly, and he seemed to be studying me as sternly as when I'd casually said the words about Mitsuo Kikuchi that had sent him into a fury.

'What can you tell me about the Liangs, the family to whom the house is still leased?'

Michael cleared his throat. 'Honey, this has all gotten a bit awkward, especially after Mr Pierce – JP – has been so generous as to give us lunch.'

'I have no problem telling you what I know, but it's not much. Winston Liang was the son of a good Chinese worker who'd already retired and moved into Waipahu, running a laundry. Winston asked my father if he could lease the cottage and land around it. It was as simple as that, and you know, all things considered, it was a good move; from the fishing business he started there, he made enough money to buy a house in town, and then another – and lo and behold, today he's gone, had a heart attack over-eating at Zippy's, but his surviving heir is one of the biggest Chinese property owners on Oahu.'

'Do you think it's possible that Winston Liang assumed control of the property with all Harue Shimura's possessions still inside?'

'Sure. You have to understand, she died in her garden – dropped from a stroke, the doctor told us. No relatives or friends came to clean up anything. In situations like this, the new tenant's wife keeps what she wants and throws out the rest.'

I was about to say that it certainly would have been in the Liang family's interest to throw out any deeds of ownership they found, but the maid returned, a cordless telephone in hand. In her soft voice she said, 'Your brother wants to speak to you. Shall I tell him later?'

'No, I'd better take it.' He looked at us. 'Sorry for cutting things short. Lindsay must want to know the extent of the fire damage.'

'Oh, we understand, and although we didn't mention it before, we're very sorry about your losses because of the fire,' Michael said, getting to his feet. 'Thank you for the delicious lunch, your time, and your patience.'

Belatedly, I echoed his thanks, thinking to myself that I wished I could whip out the same kind of boarding school manners that Michael had. I was just too blunt.

'Nothing to thank me for. I don't think I particularly helped anything,' Josiah Pierce answered.

But as Michael and I said goodbye, I thought that he had helped, and perhaps it was better that he didn't know it.

# Twenty

I took the wheel on the way down Tantalus Road, because driving is easier than being a passenger when it comes to carsickness. Part of it was avoiding a replay of my earlier nausea, but I was also feeling frustrated and tired of sitting on my hands. Driving at least gave me power.

'The deed of sale, if it ever existed, is gone,' I said glumly. 'The Liangs probably got rid of it, either accidentally or intentionally.'

'That's what he wants you to think,' Michael said. 'He was quite warm and seemingly open, but that could be disingenuous. I'd meant to catch him off-guard with the mention of Will, but his memory was sharp – maybe too sharp.'

'I want to find Winston Liang's son. I wish I'd asked his name.'

The Sebring's top was down, and a gust of wind flared a bit of my dress upward. Michael put his hand on my thigh, and I felt the hard wedding band against my skin. Now I felt desire mixed with sadness that it had all been a ridiculous game.

'Don't forget to take off the ring,' I said, lifting his hand and fixing the dress. It was a rather complicated maneuver, with the hairpin Tantalus turns.

'Can't wait to be divorced from me, huh?' Michael sighed heavily, slipped off his gold band, and dropped it into one of the car's two empty cup-holders.

I looked straight ahead, not wanting to meet his gaze. 'It's just that I don't want you to embarrass yourself by forgetting to take the ring off. Earlier today you mentioned that we should stop in at the yacht club, and I'd hate for you to walk in and have your friends think you'd just, boom, had a quick marriage.'

'I don't care what anyone thinks – you should know that by now. But there is something I'm starting to get mad about.'

'What?' I asked cautiously.

'You haven't kissed me yet today. It's like what happened between us yesterday has been absolutely buried and forgotten! Hello, there. We're officially dating.'

'It's a two-way street,' I said, unable to suppress a smile. And when we reached the stop sign at the bottom of the hill, and I was trying to remember which way to turn for Ala Moana, he took advantage of the lull, and he kissed me with such a mixture of passion and yearning that I knew he must have felt the same way.

We left the car at the shopping center again – I was starting to feel vaguely guilty, like I should step in and buy something there, sooner or later. It felt nice to stroll hand-in-hand to the yacht club, and nicer still to see Michael warmly welcomed by fellow racers, who had grown in number since the previous day. Three more sailboats had arrived, and we were both coaxed into sitting down. A quick meet-and-greet, Michael said, before he dropped me back at the resort.

'Mike!' Kurt called out, his fingers forming a mock-gun the way little boys liked to do.

'Rei, I'm sorry we didn't know about you! I would have ordered you a T-shirt too.' A fair-skinned redhead wearing shorts and a white T-shirt with a photo of *Four Guys on the Edge* greeted me. She was sitting next to a pretty black woman about ten years my senior, with stylishly upswept black hair. She was also wearing the T-shirt, but with floral patterned capris.

'That's OK. I run, so I have too many T-shirts already.'

'What you don't have is a drink. You look like a mai tai girl.' Kurt appraised me as if it were the first time he was seeing me.

'I don't know about that—'

'We don't have time for a drink at all,' Michael said. 'We really just stopped in to say hello.'

'Why are you always leaving? You missed out on a chance to be interviewed by both papers yesterday,' Parker said.

'I'd rather not be in the papers. So what's your plan for the rest of the day? Beach and then a good dinner?' Michael stood up, and from his posture, I could see he was about to bolt.

'Just wait a minute! You've been so rude, Michael, not

properly introducing Rei to Jody and me. I'm Karen, Parker's wife.' The woman in Pucci extended a hand with long, scarlet nails toward me, making me regret my own manicure's lack of color. 'You're joining us for dinner tonight at Alan Wong, aren't you? We booked a table for seven at seven. Easy to remember that way.'

I was about to say I'd like to, but I should check with my family first, but Michael was already shaking his head. 'I hate to miss catching up with you, Karen – and Jody, too – but Rei and I have another plan tonight. We'll all eat together at the Transpac banquet, though.'

'Weren't you being a little rude, Michael?' I asked as we waited to cross Ala Moana Boulevard a minute later. 'Or is there a reason you don't want me to know your friends?'

'I'm . . . I'm a little bit nervous, yes,' Michael said. 'The guys at least were spinning crazy fantasies about why I didn't get home until two in the morning. They're too happy about your existence, Rei. It makes me nervous.'

As I started to tell him to relax, my mobile phone buzzed against my hip.

'Not again,' Michael said.

I fished the phone out of my dress pocket and looked at the number in the window. 'Oh-oh, a Tokyo exchange. That means my cousin Tom, most likely.' I clicked the phone on and greeted Tom coolly; it was the first time we'd spoken since our argument the previous evening.

'Where are you, Rei-chan? We tried to reach you earlier, and your phone just rang.'

'Sorry, I turned it off during a meeting,' I said. 'Is my father all right?'

'Yes, but you must return immediately. Edwin has requested our help.'

'Of course he needs our help,' I interrupted. 'He's been saying that for days.'

'No, no, Rei-chan, this time it's different. The police have arrested Braden.'

'What on earth . . .?'

'He's at the police station in Kapolei. This is very bad for your father! I told him not to go, despite his wish to help. My father, I worry, won't make a good impression because of the language barrier. I could go alone, but I'd rather we did it together—'

'Actually, Tom, I think it's best if you stay with our fathers. I have Michael and his car, so we can go directly to the station. But tell me one thing – why was he arrested?'

'Edwin didn't say. He just needs a family member to sign a paper and pick Braden up as soon as possible.'

The Kapolei police station didn't look like a place for bad guys. It was far too pretty, built of new, golden brick, in the same neo-colonial style as the rest of the planned community. Inside there was a soaring atrium with tall windows. It looked like a place to hold a choral recital, not arrest and detain people.

Behind the desk was an attractive local man in his twenties, slimmer than Kainoa, and more south-east Asian in appearance. He wore a green and yellow print cotton aloha shirt and khaki shorts. I would never have guessed he was a cop if I hadn't seen the tag around his neck identifying him as James Than, Community Liaison Officer.

'You guys lost, yah? Just hang a right out on Farrington Highway, and that'll take you back to H-1, and make sure you go east. You don't want to visit the western beaches, trust me.' Officer Than smiled briefly, then went back to the comic he was reading.

He'd mistaken us for tourists, but I was too stressed out to be offended. I said, 'Actually, I'm here to pick up a family member, my nephew Braden Shimura.' I'd decided, a split-second before coming in, that aunt sounded a lot more mature than cousin.

'Oh, Braden Shimura.' He paused, looking me over with new interest. 'That's right, his old man said another relative would be picking him up. Too busy to come in and face the sad truth!'

'What is the truth? Why was he arrested?' I asked.

'Before we get into it, I'll need to see your government-issued photo ID.'

Feeling flustered, I slapped my driver's license down on the counter. He read it, then inclined his head toward Michael. 'And who's he?'

'I have a government ID as well.' Michael placed his CIA identification card on the desk.

Than's eyes widened, and he lowered his voice. 'The kid wanted for terrorism, too?'

'No,' Michael answered shortly. 'I'm a friend of the Shimura family's who'll be driving Rei and Braden home. But I'd like to get back to Braden's situation in – what's the charge?'

After a moment of indecision, Officer Than slid a small packet of papers across the desk toward us. In my state, it was unintelligible. I handed it to Michael, then looked back at Than and asked for a translation.

'Right now, your nephew's being charged with one count of arson. And there might be some other charges, too – a body was found, and right now, the coroner's trying to determine if it was an accident or foul play.'

'But he was with his family during the fire, including me . . .' But as I said it, I was thinking. The fire had started the day before, and Braden was out of school and unsupervised.

'This morning, he was caught on Pierce lands out toward Nanakuli with a wheelbarrow full of rocks. He dropped the barrow and ran when we told him to stop. Still had his lighter in his pocket.'

I was about to say that lots of innocent people ran on the Pierce lands – myself included – but thought better of it. I asked instead, 'What can you tell me about the body?'

'Like the way you phrase that. I can't tell you anything. Watch the news. You'll hear, sooner or later.'

'OK, that I understand. But if you didn't catch him setting the fire, how can you charge him with arson?' Michael asked.

'He may have set the fire just to get the rocks – that was the arson investigator's original thought,' Than said. 'But you never know who's gonna be caught in the midst of things when a fire gets raging.'

'With such serious charges, I'm surprised you're letting him out,' I said.

'He's a juvenile. Kids stay with their parents until the trial – although with his prior arrests, I gotta wonder why's he's getting another chance.'

'Prior arrests?' I asked.

'You don't know your nephew got caught before on petty theft, vandalism, and loitering?' Than shook his head. 'So, where is he going to stay – with you, or his parents? Don't want him skipping to California.'

'He'll be going to his home on Laaloa Street. I came to get him because, as you know, his mother and father are working right now,' I answered.

'Well, let me warn you, don't drop the boy at his house without his parents there. He might bolt.' He pointed a finger at me 'You are legally responsible for his whereabouts. You hang on to him until you hand him over to the parents, yah?'

# Twenty-One

Only after Officer Than had walked behind a door to fetch Braden did I reach for Michael. I kept my face against his polo shirt, because the warmth of his body was the only thing that felt secure and real at the moment.

'Ironic how I checked Edwin and Yoshitsune's police records, but not the kid's,' Michael said, wrapping both arms around me. 'Sorry about that.'

'I never mentioned him to you. Never in my wildest dreams would I have imagined my teenaged cousin three times removed would have a rap sheet as long as his hair. This is like a bad dream. Wake me up, please.'

'I think we should take him for a private talk, Rei, before we jump to conclusions. I played good cop last time, when we were talking to Josiah Pierce. Let's reverse roles this time.'

'Of course.' I was trying to think of something else to add – how sorry I was that Michael's short time in Honolulu was being smashed to pieces by Shimura family troubles – when my cell phone rang.

'Did you meet Braden yet?' It was Tom.

'Not quite. Michael and I are waiting for him to be brought out to us at the police station. And the situation is quite serious.' I told him about the arson and manslaughter charges, and about Braden's police record.

'Have they hired a lawyer yet?' Tom asked.

'Nope, but I'd say that's what he needs. And just watch; Edwin will need us to pay the retainer.'

'It's a good thing we didn't hire anyone yet for the land troubles,' Tom said. 'And Rei-chan, I must apologize for what I said about Michael yesterday. I'm grateful that he's helping today. I should be there, I know.'

'Thank you, Tom,' I said. 'And if anybody wants to know where we are, tell them we're hanging on to Braden until at least one of his parents is home.'

An arrest is a sobering event for most people, but I was shocked to see Braden moving toward us with more than just an anxious expression. He was limping, and there was a gash on one side of his face.

Had the police roughed him up? I wondered, looking at the seemingly mellow Officer Than. The cop was saying something to us. It sounded like 'Goodbye, and good luck.'

I murmured back something even I couldn't understand.

'We should go.' Michael put a hand on my arm, realizing how distraught I'd become. 'Thanks a lot.'

'No problem, Mike.' Officer Than gave Michael the *shaka* sign as we walked out of the station.

I was momentarily blinded by the sun, but when I oriented myself I saw two neatly dressed men in their twenties, one carrying a video camera, the other a wireless microphone. They seemed headed for the station itself, but when they saw our group, the two of them conferred and begin hurrying toward us.

'Hmmm. Wonder why they're here,' Michael said.

'My guess is to interview the police about something.'

But the cameraman started his camcorder, and the reporter, smiling a big, fake smile, was headed straight for Braden.

'I'm a juvenile. They're not supposed to know who I am!' Braden said, grabbing my straw handbag and using it to cover his face.

'Either you watch a lot of reality TV, or you've been through this before,' I said as the distance shortened between us and the men.

'Hey kid, you the one charged in the fire?' a reporter shouted loudly enough for pedestrians just going by on the sidewalk to turn around.

'Let me bring the car around,' Michael said. 'It'll be an easier get-away.'

As Michael loped away, the journalists closed in. 'Is this the youth who set the fire?'

'I never set no fire,' Braden said from behind the handbag before I could stop him from convicting himself with double negatives.

'Say it again in the microphone, OK?' entreated the first reporter, an oily looking young man with a goatee.

'No!' I squawked, waving away the microphone that had been shoved in my face. 'He has no comment, and neither do I.'

'You his lawyer?'

I shook my head miserably.

'Then who are you? You look too young to be his mama.' Another reporter had shown up, and his cameraman was bringing up the rear.

'No comment.'

'That man who just ran away, is he the lawyer?'

'No comment.' Where the hell was Michael? How could he have left me to the lions like this? Then I heard the sound of the car, and it swept up to us, scattering the men like water bugs after a light goes on.

'No comment, no comment, no comment! Please leave us alone,' I said.

'Ninety thousand acres burned yesterday. You got nothing to say about it? Not even when a person dies?' the second reporter called after us as we piled into the car, Braden in the backseat and me next to Michael.

I closed my door as Michael put the car in gear and we sped out of the parking lot, making a left turn only to be caught in a traffic jam. I'd half-expected the reporters to follow us, but instead, they just trained their cameras on the car and its license plate. Nice finish, as any enterprising person could check it back to the car rental agency, and acquire Michael's name.

'I'm starving.' A snide voice came from the back seat. 'Can we get something to eat?'

Michael fished in the glove compartment and took out two granola bars. He gave one to me, and threw the other one into the back seat.

'I meant real food, from a restaurant like Zippy's,' Braden said in a louder voice as the stoplight finally went green and Michael zipped over to the left lane.

'Be thankful for what you've got,' Michael said. 'And eat fast, because you have a lot of talking to do.'

'Rei taught me to say no comment.'

'Braden! If you don't start explaining what happened to us, the people who saved you, I'm going to have Michael drive you right back to the station.'

'There is no connection. I just was in the mountains, wrong place at the wrong time, and they busted me . . . Hey, why you going on H-1 East? You supposed to take me home.'

'There's a chance the media may be waiting there,' Michael said. 'Therefore, we're going to one of the few places they can't follow us.'

'Where's that?' Braden sounded dubious.

'Pearl Harbor. They won't be able to get on without permission from public relations. And I still have my day pass from this morning.'

'This is bullshit,' Braden muttered.

'Actually, I think the proper term is *custody*,' I said.

Braden didn't speak again until Michael exited H-1 for Pearl Harbor. Ahead of us was a short line of cars and a checkpoint with at least half a dozen armed sentries. 'You sure you're not taking me to another jail?'

'Michael, how are you going to explain us? I don't have much ID with me—'

'Since you were so keen to take off your rings, you are simply my girlfriend, and he's simply your cousin – please don't go into the three times removed business, that'll only give them a headache. We're going to the Morale, Welfare and Recreation office to buy reduced-price admission tickets for the glass boat ride at the Pearl Harbor Memorial.'

'I never did that. Can we?' Braden said from behind, where he was craning his head to get a look at the State Department ID that Michael was readying for inspection. The card worked; the guards largely ignored us, but saluted Michael through, wishing him a good visit at Pearl Harbor. I looked back at Braden, who had a funny expression on his face. I could only imagine what he'd think if he'd seen the CIA card.

I'd heard that Pearl Harbor was the largest US navy base in the world, and that seemed entirely believable. We took a circular road down by the docks, which were dominated by hulking gray aircraft carriers and warships.

'I used to live there,' Michael said, indicating a row of large, colonial-style villas seemingly besieged by a circle of traffic whizzing around.

'I'm all for historic preservation, but what was it like to live in the middle of a traffic circle?' I asked.

'It wasn't this manic twenty years ago.'

'You lived there? Who are you anyway?' Braden burst out.

'We can have an information trade, Braden. You talk first, then I will.' Michael continued the loop past more ships, a tiny group of stores, and giant housing towers. At last, he stopped at a desolate gas station, where there were a few pumping bays, but no vehicles. He pulled off to a corner of the asphalt and turned off the ignition. Then Michael began the talk that he'd probably been composing ever since we'd picked up Braden. He told Braden he knew what it was like, to be a foot away from falling off a cliff, which was where Braden was now, with the pending charges. Braden could either volunteer the story to us in his words, or sit back and just answer our questions. Either way, we weren't leaving until he talked.

Braden said nothing, and Michael and I exchanged glances. The interrogation would begin.

'This morning, the cops found you in the mountains of Nanakuli. What were you doing up there?' I asked.

Braden shook his head, and remained mute.

'Braden.' Turning around, Michael fixed him with a gimlet gaze that I'd always found particularly spooky. 'If you don't tell us what really happened, how's the lawyer going to figure out a way to save your sorry ass?'

'OK, I was working. I don't like to talk about it, because my dad doesn't want me to work. That's why I was over there. I can't work at Safeway or somewhere oblivious like that.'

*Obvious*, I thought. He doesn't even know the word obvious. I felt a new surge of annoyance with both him and Edwin. 'Tell me about the job. What is it, exactly?'

'It's like landscaping.'

'Excuse me?' I had a vision of the gnarled old men at Kainani, who always worked with heavy cloth headdresses on, to shield them from the elements. Braden, in his board shorts and skin-tight Quiksilver T-shirt, did not seem a likely gardener.

'We work after the fires, because that's when you sometimes find lava rock.'

'Lava rock?' Michael asked, and I explained that Oahu was studded with volcanoes that had erupted long ago, and that lava had hardened into amazing rock, each piece one of a kind. I'd seen lava rock in garden shops in San Francisco for exorbitant costs. It was said that since lava rock was holy, anyone who removed it from Hawaii would be cursed with terrible events; the only solution was to bring the rock back to where it belonged. I wasn't sure how fate worked for people who stole lava rock and just took it a few miles away.

'So you're finding and loading up lava rock for a contractor?' Michael continued. 'Were you paid for what you did today?'

'Nope, the police came round before I finished. Had to leave everything lying.'

'Large rocks can be heavy,' I said, trying to follow his story. 'Do you carry by hand, or use something?'

'When my buddy picked me up today, I used an old wheelbarrow of Jii-chan's. Actually, it tipped over when I was trying to make a getaway; that's how I bashed my foot and cut my face.'

'OK, so you were using Uncle Yosh's wheelbarrow, bringing the rocks to . . . where? Somebody's truck? Where was your friend when this was all happening?'

'He went to work another area. I'd pile up whatever rocks I find, then get a ride back home around three, either from him or the boss. I'd get the wheelbarrow back in the yard before my mom or dad came home. Nobody had an idea I had a job.'

'Did you tell the police about your job and the boss?'

'No, I didn't tell them squat. Like you said, no comment.'

'You talked about the rocks,' Michael said. 'But what about the cigarette lighter in your pocket?'

'There was a lighter in my pocket, but that's because I smoke every now and then. The police got it now.'

'The thing about fire is, when it sweeps through an area and burns brush, it's easier to see what lies underneath,' Michael said. 'Do you think it's possible that the people behind your rock-gathering business might have set the fire a couple of days ago, in anticipation of you doing a little work for them?'

'I never heard nothing like that.' But Braden looked uncomfortable.

'Well, when did you get the call to work today?' I asked.

'An hour before I left this morning. See, it couldn't have been planned. They didn't know I could work.'

'Whether the fire was accidental or arson, it would be helpful if your boss would come forward to explain that you were just out gathering rocks because he'd told you to do that,' I suggested.

'He's not gonna come forward.' Braden pressed his lips together. 'No way.'

'Then we've got to *make* him come forward,' I persisted. 'I mean, not us literally, but your lawyer could subpoena this person.'

'I can't tell the name to you or any lawyer either.'

'Why?'

'Because the boss said to me once that if I ever say who's behind this, I won't live to see eighteen.'

# Twenty-Two

Someone must have been watching out for us, because the door to Edwin's house swung open without our having to knock. Feeling uncertain, I surveyed the stranger who stood guard – a solidly built, middle-aged Asian-Hawaiian man in a red aloha shirt. I introduced myself and Michael, while

Braden squeezed past, kicked off his sandals and went upstairs.

'I'm Wally Nishimura, a neighbor they asked to come over and help. Thanks for bringing Braden home. Does the family know him?' Wally spoke about Michael as if he wasn't even there.

'Yes, they do. And if Michael hadn't been with me, we wouldn't have been able to pick up Braden.' I felt I needed Michael with me at this time. I had already caught a glimpse into the living room. Edwin sitting there, staring blankly into space. A glass with golden liquid rested on a bamboo-legged table in front of him. Edwin wasn't a drinker, so things had to be pretty bad. And he'd come home from his internet auction early.

'Thought you'd be back a while ago. I was getting worried,' he said, after he'd noticed our presence.

'We wanted to talk to him about what happened, and the best place to do it was a few miles away,' I explained. 'The case against him seems rather weak, but it's a lawyer who'll really be able to come up with a strategy.'

'I was just telling him about my cousin, Lisa Ping,' Wally said. 'She's a partner in a big firm in Honolulu, and she's willing to come out to meet Braden.'

'Is that P-I-N-G?' Michael had already taken a BlackBerry out of his pocket, and I imagined he was going to try to search the name.

'Yes, that's it,' Wally said. 'She's a partner with Martin and Funabashi on Queen Street.'

'Wally, I don't know if a girl lawyer can save my boy,' Edwin interrupted. 'I left a voice mail on Bobby Yamaguchi's number.'

Margaret came into the room with a telephone in her hand. 'Bobby said he's sorry, but he can't take it. He'd be happy to refer you to someone.'

'Never mind.' Edwin waved Margaret away and then grumbled, as if to nobody in particular, 'Too bad somebody who had a good lawyer in her pocket traded him for a sailor.'

'That's enough,' I snapped at Edwin before glancing apologetically toward Michael. He was busy with his BlackBerry, as if he hadn't even heard the comment, but I knew better.

'Don't worry another moment; Lisa's on her way in. Meet her, and see what you think.' Wally's voice was reassuring.

'What's her rate, Wally?' Edwin asked. 'Do you think she could take it on pro bono?'

'I thought you'd ask that. Lisa told me she's normally two-fifty, but she'll give you credit,' Wally said. 'As long as there's a guarantor, somebody to promise to pay for you if you can't.'

'I'll guarantee the defense,' Michael said, looking up from the BlackBerry. 'From just a quick search, it looks as if Lisa Ping is a past president of the Honolulu Bar Association, and she's qualified to argue before the Supreme Court. Criminal law is one of her specialties.'

'My cousin!' Wally said, smiling.

I wondered if Michael was reacting to Edwin's sailor comment, because his offer was simply too rash. I'd told Michael all about Edwin's past bankruptcy; in fact, we were standing in Edwin's father's home because Edwin hadn't re-covered enough to buy or rent his own house.

'Hey, it's Braden's turn now on the TV!' said Courtney, who'd been silently sitting on a cushion in the corner since we'd entered. 'Someone get Mom!'

I poked my head into the kitchen and saw Margaret slumped at the kitchen table, head in hands, seemingly unaware that one of her elbows was resting on an empty Styrofoam takeout tray.

'I don't want to see my kid on the news,' she said in a monotone. 'You go out there, but don't tell me if it's real bad.'

I returned to the living room, where my two-word encounter with the press outside the police station was replayed, followed by a clip of our getaway car. A newscaster intoned gravely about the burned body of a woman near the coffee shop; her identification had been released. Charisse De La Cruz was eighteen and had worked part-time at the coffee shop.

'Charisse!' I said, remembering the pigtailed barista at the coffee shop. Kainoa had complained about her inefficiency, but what stayed in my mind was her guileless curiosity about new people, and her warmth. She was hardly a woman, having just turned legal age, and now she was gone.

'Did you know her?' Michael was watching me closely.

'Not very well. She made me coffee once.'

'That fire been blazing for days,' Edwin said. 'Who's *lolo* enough to hang around a coffee shop in a fire zone?'

'She worked there. Obviously, she must have been there to work, and not evacuated in time.' My thoughts were flying wildly as I remembered Kainoa's emotional collapse. Maybe he hadn't just been crying about his coffee shop; maybe he'd found Charisse's corpse.

I came back to the present, seeing Michael's mouth moving.

'Sorry, what was that?' I asked.

'It's your aunt. She wants you to go to her.' He gestured toward the kitchen. Still feeling disconnected, I returned to the kitchen, where for the first time I noticed my ancestor Harue Shimura's framed face looking down from a small Buddhist altar crammed over the door. A saucer with the offering of a tangerine sat on the shelf in front of the picture with a line of ants crawling up the wall toward it. I looked away from the picture and toward Margaret, who was hugging herself as if the room was not in the high seventies, but freezing.

'I should have picked up Braden from the station,' Margaret said. 'Thanks for what you and Michael did.'

I looked at her tired face. 'You couldn't get away early, I know.'

'I didn't even try to see if I could leave. I've had to leave work early so many times because of Braden. This time I wanted just a few more hours' peace before I saw him.' She looked down, then into my eyes. 'I could hear some of the talk out there, and we don't need Michael's money. I got money of my own, in a 401K. I can take it out early, and it should be enough – if the trial's short.' She blinked her eyes, and I saw that she was starting to cry.

'Aunt Margaret, I know Braden's had trouble in the past, but this time around, the basis for the charge is so weak. And it turns out he has an alibi for being in the mountains; he gathers rocks for somebody. It's illegal, I know, but a misdemeanor's a lot easier to face than a felony.'

'It's my fault,' Margaret moaned softly. 'If I stayed home, Braden couldn't be going around with those people who keep getting him into trouble. I never heard of him working for anybody. He's not supposed to have a job!'

'Braden mentioned that someone phoned this morning and asked him to work. Can we check the phone to figure out the caller?'

'Our phones don't do that,' Margaret said. 'Edwin said that it's better to invest in the computer. Can't you just ask Braden?'

She wanted me to do it. Clearly, Margaret had little authority over her son. 'Unfortunately, Braden wouldn't tell us. He said the boss threatened his life, if he said who was behind the operation.'

'That doesn't sound like the kind from around here.' Margaret's face was sorrowful. 'But you know, things in Hawaii have changed.'

'Why don't you and Edwin allow Braden to get a regular part-time job?'

Margaret sighed. 'It may sound strange, but he wants the kids to break the mold of people here, to go farther than we did. To Edwin, that means stay away from hamburger shops and hotels and all the places that keep the local people down. Courtney's a good girl, she uses her time at home to study or read, but Braden's always out. All this time, I thought he was at the beach. It figures he was making money, because he sure couldn't afford all the surfing gear just on his allowance. So . . . I guess I want you to tell me . . . what did they say about him on TV?'

'Not much – certainly not his name. But they released the identity of the woman who died. It was Charisse De La Cruz.'

'Charisse De La Cruz? Oh my God, I've known her mother since my own small-kid time.'

'I met Charisse once at the coffee shop. I liked her.'

'You did, huh? Very pretty girl, but not very *akamai*.'

'*Akamai?*' The word sounded Japanese, but I didn't know what it meant.

'Means smart in Hawaiian. Charisse, she loved to chatter, ever since she was a tiny girl. She goes with any person who smiles at her – some people say she's easy, but I just thought she's not too smart.'

'Her body was found near the coffee shop where she works. It's not as if she ran off with someone.'

'What could Kainoa have been thinking, letting Charisse

stay at the coffee shop during a fire?' Margaret shook his head.

'I don't know that he did. He mentioned that he was there that afternoon, trying to build a firebreak. He didn't mention that anyone was helping him.'

'Excuse me.' I turned at the sound of Michael's voice. 'I didn't mean to interrupt, but the lawyer's here Mrs Shimura, would you like to meet her?'

'Margaret, please. Yes, I'll see her. And I want to tell you something first: don't worry about guaranteeing our payment to the lawyer. I have the money.'

'That's good to hear,' Michael said, a trifle uncertainly. 'But the offer stands. The other thing I was wondering, Margaret, was whether you know Kainoa Stevens?'

'Of course. He and his family used to live close to Honokai Hale, but I think they're in the homesteads now, more toward Makaha. He's a good boy, used to take Braden surfing when he was just learning. Why?'

'He owns the coffee shop that burned.'

'Sure, I know that, but Kainoa wouldn't have anything to do with setting a fire,' Margaret said. 'Why would he destroy his own business?'

'The insurance . . .' Michael began.

'He's not insured,' I said.

'How do you know that?' Margaret asked.

'I went running this morning over the Pierce fields to see what happened to the shop. I found Kainoa there, pretty upset.'

'Girl, that was stupid!' Margaret sucked in her breath. 'Embers live a long time. A fire could have flashed up and trapped you.'

'I was perfectly OK. The only problem I encountered was when the land manager saw us.'

'Albert Rivera's a bastard. You ask me, he's the likeliest one set a fire.'

'Really? What's wrong with him?' I asked my aunt, but Wally Nishimura came in and basically ordered Margaret out to meet the lawyer. We followed but, to my regret, Lisa Ping, an efficient-looking woman about a decade older than I, banned us from the conversation. It was just going to be Edwin, Margaret, and Braden. A privileged conversation, or whatever it was called.

As Michael and I were driving out of the neighborhood on

Waialua Street, I looked at the digital clock on the dashboard. It was almost seven.

'Hungry?' Michael asked.

'I'm too depressed to eat anything. I'll sit with you if you want to eat something, though.'

We cruised Farrington Highway into the heart of Kapolei, and Michael selected a seedy-looking fast food shop called L&L. Confidently, he ordered a starter of Spam *musube*, which turned out to be a sushi-like concoction of sticky rice and a thick slab of spam bound together by a narrow band of seaweed. Only in Hawaii, I thought to myself, as he followed that with a five-scoop plate: rice, chilli, macaroni salad, shrimp tempura and a deep-fried pork cutlet.

'Something's missing there,' I said, sipping my water as I watched him sip enthusiastically from a Yoo-Hoo chocolate drink. 'I know – fruits and veggies.'

'There are beans in the chilli, and doesn't the seaweed count?'

'I meant fresh fruits and vegetables,' I chided.

'How about coconut cake? I remember the best version was at Zippy's. We could walk over there now – could I tempt you to share a piece?'

'No thanks.'

When we left L&L, the evening air had cooled to a perfect temperature. The trade wind was blowing, making me think of how nice it would be to lie in bed with all the windows open.

'I'll skip Zippy's if I can have something else,' Michael said as we settled into the car.

'What?' I asked absently, and then he moved close to kiss me. Thinking about all that I could never really have, I pulled back.

'Is it the chilli?'

'No, it's you and me.' As Michael's face fell, I said, 'Come on, think about it. What are we doing? This playing at dating is pointless. You don't have the kind of life where you can even have a real girlfriend, let alone a contract employee-slash-girlfriend.'

'You don't want to try dating, then?' Michael's voice was flat.

'There's too much on my mind. Braden, his parents, my

father's health, and a fire that killed a young woman and
almost burned us out of Kainani.'

'I'll take you home,' Michael said, and without another
word, he did.

# Twenty-Three

I'd been hoping for a quiet evening, but when I arrived at
the house I found Calvin Morita was there, lounging at the
dining table with Uncle Hiroshi and Tom.

'What's going on?' I asked as I slipped off my sandals.

'Calvin took us to a very good sushi restaurant,' my father
said from the kitchen, where he was making tea. 'We brought
some back. You must try it; it's delicious.'

'I can't eat right now,' I said, not even trying to sound
apologetic. 'So much has happened today. I think I'll just
say goodnight.'

'But we must know what happened with Braden,' my father
said.

I raised my eyebrows at him, trying to give him the message
that the last person I wanted to overhear our family conversation was Calvin, but he didn't seem to notice.

'Yes, Rei-chan. We want to know why you were gone so
long, and why you didn't explain yourself better on television,'
Uncle Hiroshi said.

'It sounds as if you know everything that I do,' I said.

'What I want to know is have you eaten supper at all?'
Calvin asked.

'Not really,' I admitted.

'You're under stress and this will keep you from crashing.'
Calvin strode into our kitchen as if he owned it, opening up
the refrigerator and removing a Styrofoam box, which he set
on the dining table. 'We still have an assortment of *tai,* eel,
tuna and abalone. Sound good?'

I grunted my assent, because I had a feeling he wouldn't leave until I'd taken at least one.

'I wouldn't use so much *wasabi* if I were you. This fish is top-notch,' Calvin said.

'I like *wasabi*,' I said, digging into the little container that had come with the sushi. It was the real stuff, made from freshly grated horseradish root, without the golf-ball-green color.

'That's not how the Japanese do it.' Calvin folded his arms across his chest and looked at me. 'The Kikuchis take their sushi and sashimi absolutely plain. Only a drizzle of soy sauce.'

'I'm not sure the Kikuchis are representative of most Japanese,' I said, biting into it and relishing the fiery rush from my nose to skull.

'Can you at least tell us what happened after you picked up Braden?' Tom asked.

'Michael and I took Braden to Pearl Harbor.' I took my time chewing, so I could concoct the right answer. 'We took Braden home, and a lawyer arrived.'

'Ah, very good,' my father said. 'I worried we'd have to find one ourselves. What does the lawyer say about the case?'

'I don't know. Once she learned that Michael and I weren't immediate family, we were sent off.' I chose my words carefully, because anything related to the fire would be an interesting topic for Calvin to bring to Mitsuo Kikuchi. I asked, 'So, Calvin, how's Jiro doing?'

'What do you mean?' Calvin was being cagey too.

'I thought you were his twenty-four-hour psychiatrist.'

Calvin smiled. 'Even shrinks get a break, now and then. Tonight Jiro is dining with his father at a nice restaurant called Roy's. You should try it, there's one nearby at the Ko Olina golf club.'

'Golf?' inquired Uncle Hiroshi, who'd been looking dazed at all the English that had been flying about.

Calvin switched to Japanese and, as I'd expected for someone who worked for a Japanese family, his Japanese was good and swift, though slightly American-accented.

'I hope that you're not upset about this news,' I murmured to my father, remembering his condition.

'Well, I'm certainly concerned. But it's natural, don't you agree?'

'I think I'd like to check your blood pressure.' Tom rose from the couch and went upstairs, presumably for his medical supplies.

'It's really not necessary,' my father protested to those of us who remained.

'Of course it is! You must drink some more water,' said Uncle Hiroshi, heading to the fridge.

'Don't worry about me so much, Rei,' my father said to me. 'I'm not the one in danger; Braden is. The boy misbehaves to attract attention from his parents, but this latest act, if in fact he did it, will change his life, as it changed the lives of the poor family who lost their daughter.'

'It's very sad, yes. I think Braden understands how serious things are.' I spoke in an undertone, because Calvin was still hovering near us.

'It's been a while since I've been involved in forensic psychiatry, but I would like to talk to the boy,' my father said, as Tom returned and began wrapping the cuff around his upper arm. As I'd feared, Calvin volunteered his services. 'Your family is working much too hard, taking care of your relatives' troubles. Wouldn't it be less of a conflict of interest if I did the interview with Braden? And, you know, I could advise his family on finding a psychiatrist who may be willing to testify in court that the boy has some pathological issues.'

'You mean, the insanity defense?' I shook my head. 'Let's stop this conversation here and now. Especially if we're trying to keep my father's blood pressure from rising.'

'The reading is one-forty-five over one-hundred; I'm not thrilled with it,' Tom said. 'Ojiisan, you're going to need to relax if you want us to include you in tomorrow's trip to Hanama Bay.'

'I don't know if that's a smart idea,' Calvin began.

'Sure it is. I'll go, too,' I said. The timing was right, because Michael and I had decided to spend the day apart. I'd been unable to explain to him how frustrating his show of interest in me was, and how restraining myself felt like torture. So I'd let him feel a little bit hurt when we'd said goodnight, because it got me off the hook. And now I was going to spend the next day with my family, which was where I really belonged.

\*     \*     \*

Calvin was right about one thing; it was not a good idea to commit to the next day's plan. In the middle of the night I awoke drenched in sweat. My stomach pitched and heaved, and a sickening flow inched up my esophagus.

Trying to turn on the bedside lamp, I knocked it to the ground. I heard the sound of a bulb breaking, and a few seconds later, felt a shard pierce the palm of my hand as I crawled to the door. I couldn't get to my feet; it was impossible. I hadn't felt this sick in years, not since I'd been poisoned by gas in Japan. I reached the doorknob, wrenched it open, and then crawled into the cool marble hallway and toward the bathroom door, where a nightlight glowed softly, leading me on.

I made it just in time to lose my supper and a good bit more. When I'd finally stopped, I blearily noticed someone had entered the bathroom. My eyes traveled upward from a pair of short, broad bare feet to see Uncle Hiroshi standing in his blue and white striped pajamas, patiently holding a glass of water. It was only because of the pajamas I recognized him; I felt so sick that his face was just a blur.

'The others,' I whispered, because I'd lost my voice along with my dinner. 'Are they sick?'

'No, just sleeping. You poor child,' he said, and put the glass to my lips. I drank gratefully, but in a few seconds the water sliding down my throat came right up, so I spun around to the toilet again. When I was through, he offered me another glass of water, and I waved it away.

'I can't take it,' I said weakly. 'I'll go back to bed now.'

'What's wrong? Why are you ill?'

'I don't know—'

'Maybe it's a virus,' he said. 'I could wake Tsutomu and get him to take your temperature. I'd rather not bother your father, if that's all right with you.'

'Don't get Tom either,' I said, noticing for the first time that my hands were trembling. 'I'm sure in the morning, I'll be fine.'

But I wasn't fine. Between episodes of vomiting and diarrhea, I tried to recall everything I'd eaten, which was a challenge, given my light-headedness. Sushi seemed obvious, but I'd been feeling sick earlier in the day, on the road up to Tantalus. Maybe it hadn't been just motion sickness, but a reaction to the mainland-shipped yogurt I'd had in the morning. I could also have become ill from food at Josiah Pierce's home. This was much more sinister, given that I'd confessed my agenda to Josiah Pierce over lunch. But we'd already been eating when I dropped my bomb. He had no idea of my motivation when I'd called him the previous day, or so I hoped.

I wanted to talk to Michael. When there was enough light in the room, I made it to the desk where I'd left my cell phone to charge. My call rang straight into his voicemail. Maybe he was still asleep, and the phone was recharging. The other less pleasant idea was that Michael was suffering his own bout of illness. I whispered something about not feeling well and asking him to call me when he had a chance.

I clicked the phone off and fell into a sickly slumber, waking to an odd, clanking sound and midday sun. I rubbed my eyes and saw a man on his hands and knees behind the bed.

I screamed.

'The next time you fall ill, you should wake me to help.' My father's tone was as reproving as his words.

'Sorry, I . . . I didn't see that was you, and Uncle Hiroshi did all that anyone could. Otoosan, you don't have to pick up the broken lamp. Don't lean down. I'll clean it up myself—' I struggled upward and, hit by a new wave of nausea, fell back.

'I checked your temperature, and there's no fever. I suspect you're suffering from food poisoning.'

'I don't know,' I said warily. 'My vision's all blurred.'

'Really?' My father leaned close to me, and suddenly, I was flat-out terrified. 'No, please, no,' I heard myself saying. Or rather, screaming.

There were more people in the room then, Tom and Uncle Hiroshi. Tom was trying to take my temperature and read my blood pressure and I was fighting him. Couldn't any of them understand they were frightening me? In the midst of all this, I heard my cell phone ringing.

'Let me talk!' I cried in vain, but nobody did. The next thing I knew, they were bundling me into the third row of the minivan. Between vomiting and crying, my aching head exploded with panicked thoughts. I couldn't go on, but how would I get out? The window? But the windows were locked, and my father and uncle were staring at me, listening to my every thought. Where was Michael? He'd save me from this, if only he knew.

They took me to Queen's Medical Center, unloading me fast, and suddenly I was surrounded by more blurry people who rolled me on to a stretcher. A needle shot something into my arm, and within minutes, everything slowed, even the fear. The last thing I remembered was the sound of my father arguing with somebody about whether I needed a pregnancy test, and then everything went black.

# Twenty-Four

I woke up, no longer nauseated, but feeling quite uncomfortable. An IV line snaked into the top of my left hand, and another one attached to the intersection of my shoulder and neck. A line even ran between my legs, where I should have had underwear. But I had no panties, and I had no regular clothes, either; just a dismal cotton gown, and underneath it, electrical patches sticking to my chest, with more lines connecting to a piece of equipment that I recognized from my father's hospital stay as a heart monitor. Oh God, had I turned into my father?

No, I realized with relief, my fingernails still had the same ballet-pink nail polish I'd applied at the start of the Hawaii trip. And my father was sitting on an uncomfortable chair in the hospital room across from me.

I could see him; I could see my father. My vision was back. My stomach still hurt, though, and my throat was sore.

I croaked aloud, 'I see!'

'It's about time,' my father said, breaking his chain of movements to come to the bed and embrace me.

'I'm feeling better, too – oh my God, so much better. I don't like to remember . . .'

'You had a drug overdose. That's why you were ill.' My father's words came slowly.

'Otoosan, I didn't take drugs, I swear it. All I remember was getting sick in the middle of the night. I thought it was food poisoning . . .' I broke off. 'What about Michael? Do you know, did this happen to him, too?'

'Michael's in the waiting room. Now that you're conscious, I'm sure they'll allow him to see you.'

'You mean, he's been out there for . . . how long?'

'You arrived here yesterday. We've all come and gone, staying for blocks of time. It was a very serious situation, Rei. You could have died, if they hadn't treated you in time.'

'Thank you for bringing me here,' I said. 'I don't know what got into me; I barely remember anything but . . . terror.'

'You were in a state of psychosis,' my father said. 'I've seen it many times before. The mechanism of your brain had simply gone haywire; despite your best intentions, you couldn't have done anything other than what you did.'

At least I hadn't killed anyone. I asked, 'What kind of drug was in me? Heroin, crack, crystal meth? Am I addicted now?'

'Of course not. Your system was full of Lithium mixed with Motrin, one of the most highly toxic combinations of legal drugs that exists. If you had died, the medical examiner might have tried to classify it as suicide.'

I glanced at my father, wondering if he was trying to ask me a hard question. I forced my dry lips into a smile. 'You know I'm not suicidal. The drugs must have been chopped up and added to something I ate or drank yesterday.'

'Michael suggested the same thing. As the situation stands, you will have to take very good care of your thyroid and kidneys for a while.' I could hear the relief in my father's voice.

'Does that mean a special diet?'

'No, just avoiding certain irritants. You should try to consume very little alcohol, citrus, and caffeine. And stay away from most over-the-counter painkillers and get your thyroid checked regularly, for a while.'

'Will do.' I breathed deeply, glad to be alive. 'Otoosan, will you do something for me?'

'Yes. What do you need?'

'Michael. Could you bring him to me?'

\*　　\*　　\*

'I hope you'll never see me look this bad as this again,' I said to Michael, when he rushed into the room a few minutes later. There were rings under his eyes, his face was unshaven and he looked as if he'd slept in his clothes. He was carrying a large brown paper bag with an oily stain, which he set down on my tray. All in all, he looked more disreputable than I'd ever seen him – but utterly glorious.

'I don't care, Rei. I'm just glad to see your eyes open.' Michael took the hand that didn't have a tube coming out of it, and held it tightly.

'I'll just go downstairs and get a decaf,' my father said, and the door closed behind him.

'That was nice of him,' Michael said. 'Giving us some privacy.'

I sighed. 'I apologize in advance for anything that my family might have done, while I was out of commission.'

'Oh, there's nothing to apologize for. We talked a bit in the waiting room, and your cousin Tom was good enough to let me know what was going on by finding my number on your cell phone. I'm so sorry that I missed that first call you made. My phone was recharging, and by the time I got the message and called you back, it was too late.'

'I heard the call come in, but it's hard to pick up when you're in a state of psychosis,' I said wryly. 'You heard about the drugs in my system, I'm sure. Looking at you, I'm guessing the same thing didn't happen to you.'

'No, it didn't. Since we ate lunch together, it's unlikely that you picked up the poison at Josiah Pierce's, unless he was extremely devious and sprinkled the drugs in your water glass – though if that were the case," Michael added, 'the powdered tablets would just sink to the bottom and not affect you much at all.'

'The maid poured for everyone out of the same pitcher,' I said, 'and my water tasted fine. My suspicions are leaning toward the fellow we know who can write a prescription for any controlled substance he wants. Calvin Morita was fixated on my eating this sushi he'd brought back from a restaurant . . .'

'I heard that from your father, yes. But regarding Calvin – yes, he's a creep, but the fact is that anyone with bipolar disorder could have lithium prescribed to them, or borrow or steal someone else's. We have to think about *everything* you ate or drank in the last few days. There's a concession stand at the resort pool; did you order something and leave it while you swam? What about all those lattes you've been consuming at Kainoa's coffee shop?'

'Are the police treating this as a criminal case?' I asked.

'Not until they've interviewed you. And maybe, now that you're better, that can happen. Are you hungry? One of the nurses clued me in on a street nearby that's full of amazing cheap Korean restaurants. I took away a container of black noodles. It's a phenomenal dish that I haven't had since I was last in Seoul.'

'Not just yet. How much longer will I be here?' I couldn't hide the waver in my voice, as I thought how I'd already lost two days of Michael's precious week in Hawaii.

'Maybe you'll get out tomorrow, or the day after; that's the best case scenario.' Michael reached into the bag and pulled out a can of cold barley tea and poured it into two glasses. 'I heard about your liver, and this has no caffeine. Enjoy.'

I took a sip from the glass that he held to my mouth, and it tasted better than any wine I'd ever had. 'You're sure I can drink this?'

'Positive.' He put the glass in my hand, and continued talking. 'Let me tell you what's been going on. Everyone's been so worried; Edwin and Margaret and Uncle Yosh visited the hospital in turns, because somebody had to stay behind with Braden. The best thing for the kid is that his grandfather has taken over his care – can you believe he's making him spend two hours each day digging an extension to the koi pond? I heard Yosh say to Braden if he's man enough to carry big rocks, he's man enough to dig a bigger home for the fish.'

'Has a mutiny occurred?'

'No. I think Braden realizes that every day at home could be his last. The threat of a manslaughter charge really hit him hard, and Yosh told me there's a threat the ranchers who lost horses may sue whoever's found to have set the fire. Who knows, Pierce Holdings could sue as well.'

All the troubles of the past flooded back to me. 'I can't understand why Braden won't give up the name of the person who could save him.'

'I agree, but who knows what Lisa Ping's got up her sleeve?' Michael cleared his throat. 'Now for the other bit of news.'

'Yes. I'm hoping that you're going to tell me you're taking an extra week in Hawaii . . .'

'Sorry.' Michael looked rueful. 'There's another thing that I have to tell you, relating to the cottage address you asked me to locate for you.'

'Great. Did you find it?'

'Well, I didn't want to waste too much time away from you, so instead of exploring the land I just went to Pearl Harbor for a couple of hours to examine maps. Hawaii land maps are quite complicated to figure out, because you're dealing with state land, privately held land, and military land. There's also this weird unit of land measurement called an *alapaa* which is basically a strip that goes all the way down from a point on a mountain to the sea.' He reached into his backpack and withdrew a thick folio.

'So you found these maps at Pearl Harbor.'

'Yes. I had access to military maps, which are better re-solution and more accurate. Anyway, I had to do all this because the street name you mentioned didn't seem to exist on the military maps, which was strange. Finally, using the aerial maps and geographical coordinates, I was able to locate the Harue's old house squarely on military land.'

'But I thought it was on Pierce land.'

'It's not. The land was seized by the military during the war, and at one point it was clearly marked by fencing – see?' He showed me a map, which looked meaningless, followed by a photocopy of an old black and white photo-graph of the coastline, with the edge of a shack protruding into one corner.

'The fencing came down later, but that doesn't mean it isn't still owned by the Navy – and I doubt they'd be inclined to sell it to a Japanese developer. If anything, the military is likely to sit on it, to please the local population agitating for preserving unspoiled Hawaiian coastline.'

'How can you be so sure about this?' I asked.

'I double-checked the maps and got extra paperwork from a military lawyer in the JAG office at Pearl. Apparently, the

military isn't always the best at keeping track of its holdings, especially if the area hasn't been developed, or is being
planned for development. But this sure woke up the sleepers,
the fact that somebody was attempting to sell government
land.'

'We have to tell Josiah Pierce,' I said slowly.

'Navy Legal will be in touch with him. And it's better to
have the information coming from them than from us.'

'Before I leave Hawaii, I want to see the house and land,'
I said. 'And I think Uncle Yosh and his family should be there,
too. Obviously that ban on Edwin being near the house can't
stand up in court anymore.'

'I made my own map, since the ones I saw were still classified, though they shouldn't necessarily be, after all this
time.'

'Maybe that's the reason nobody in the military caught on
that Josiah Pierce had retaken the rights to that land – the
map was misplaced or forgotten,' I thought aloud.

'It's easy to see how that could happen. The thirty-eight-
and-one-half acres surrounding this little piece are in a
completely undeveloped area that's open to the public.'

Undeveloped, but considered by one and all to be Pierce
land. 'Do you know whether the fire touched this land
parcel?'

'I don't know, Rei. I didn't drive out there yet.'

'I'll go,' I said.

'You'll need to feel better very fast, if that's going to happen.'

I gave him my first real smile. 'Just watch.'

# Twenty-Five

I slept well that night, the best night's sleep since my arrival night in Hawaii. Maybe it was from whatever was in the IV drips the doctors had given me, or the Korean tea, but I suspected it was because the drugs had finally left me, as had my worries about needing to fight for Harue's land.

Uncle Edwin wouldn't get the land, but nobody else would, either. And chances were that the military would leave it alone in a wild and natural state.

Looking out my hospital window at a vivid rainbow, I knew that the sooner Uncle Edwin gave up on his dreams of land wealth, the better for everyone. What mattered was Braden and his future.

I thought about all of this again a few hours later, when I was released from the hospital, as I'd predicted to Michael. Tom was driving, with Uncle Hiroshi at his side. My father sat in the back seat next to me. He fussed over our non-functioning seat belts, and swept cracker crumbs off the back seat.

'Hey, these crumbs are new. Who's been eating *sembei* in the car?' I teased.

'Souvenirs from the trip to the beach,' Uncle Hiroshi said. 'Your father didn't eat any. The criminals are simply Tsutomu and myself.'

'Is that true?' I asked, peering at my father.

He sighed. 'I tried something Hawaiian – crack seed. And I also ate a container of pineapple while we were in traffic yesterday. Does that pass inspection?'

'Oh, leftover pineapple is what I'm smelling. Great.'

'What can we say? We need you to keep us neat and clean, Rei-chan,' Tom said from the front, chuckling. 'But take a rest today.'

'I will rest, but I would like for us to take a short excursion later today or tomorrow. Hopefully, Uncle Yosh and anyone else can come along, too.'

'We can fit seven people in the van,' my father said. 'Eight, if Courtney's one of them. But where do you want to go?'

To my surprise, Uncle Edwin's car was parked in front of the townhouse when we pulled in. Without us home to open the Pineapple Plantation gate, he must have convinced another driver to let him in.

'Welcome home!' He emerged from his sedan as we piled out of the minivan. 'Are you really sure you're ready to come home? You gave us a scare!'

I murmured politely that yes, I was fine, all the while thinking, *Did he want me to be in the hospital?* His greeting was strange. I had never considered that Edwin would want me incapacitated, but I had been a major stumbling block in his efforts to get my family involved in his land scheme. And I'd been at his house only hours before I fell ill, though I couldn't remember eating or drinking anything.

I was distracted by Courtney, who bounded out of the back seat and thrust forward a fancy shopping bag. Packed in it were a variety of gifts – a bouquet of torch ginger and heliconia from their garden, a plastic container of the famous Okinawa donuts, and Courtney's own dog-eared Harry Potter book, plus a copy of *Hawaii Brides*.

'I'm finished with both of them. You can keep them after you're done,' she said.

'That's sweet of you, because I just finished the mystery I was reading.' I reached out to hug Courtney, and she relaxed into my arms with a happy sigh. I finally understood why she was always reading bridal magazines and Harry Potter novels; she lived for fantasy, because nobody seemed to notice her. The reality of always playing second fiddle to a troublemaker had taken its toll.

Braden and Yoshitsune had emerged from the car, too. To my surprise, Braden was holding his grandfather's arm. Uncle Hiroshi, my father, and Tom all looked at him approvingly. This was good Confucian behavior, indeed.

'Braden been doing so much with the pond, I decided to go for broke and help him with that last bit of shoveling. Like a fool, I twisted my ankle,' Yosh said, as if sensing everyone's attention.

There was a flurry of questions and Tom went to examine the old man's ankle, which he pronounced, in the end, was fortunately just a minor strain.

'And how are you, Braden?' I asked.

'Hanging in there.'

'I'm glad you're all here, because I've got some big news. Perhaps we can all sit down on the *lanai* together, with a drink, and talk over what it means . . .'

'I have news, too!' Edwin said. 'Hey, Courtney, you run inside with your cousin Tom and get everyone fixed up with drinks.'

'Did you find out who poisoned you?' Braden asked.

'Not yet, but apparently the health department is making the rounds,' I said.

The winds were blowing hard, so we used our drinking glasses on the corners of the photocopied maps and documents to keep them from blowing away. I thought that showing Edwin the signed military orders announcing the takeover of a portion of Pierce land in 1943 first, and then showing the series of maps, with and without government chain link fencing, would be stronger evidence than any words I could offer.

'So it's not Pierce land. This is the proof,' Edwin said, as his finger traced a military boundary on an old map.

'The executives at Pierce Holdings may think that these thirty-seven acres along the water belong to them, but they don't. And the beauty of the situation is that you don't have to hire a lawyer to prove anything. The military's got their own legal team who are alerted and apparently eager to save the land from development.'

'But will they give it back to us?' Yosh asked.

I searched for words to comfort my great-uncle, but there were none. 'Even if we had a letter or deed, it wouldn't help. Michael explained to me that in times of national emergency, the military can seize property—'

'Or seize people.' Yosh's voice was bitter.

'I'm so sorry, Uncle Yosh. If it's any consolation, Mitsuo Kikuchi won't be able to profit by building a restaurant complex in the special place where you lived – and I wonder whether the military might be agreeable to letting you move the actual cottage. I could help you renovate it as a little garden house. Maybe there's room near your pond . . .'

'Enough.' Edwin's voice came quick and hard. 'That place isn't ours, it seems. Time to put away all thoughts of it, and who cares about making garden houses when my boy's facing jail time?'

'Yes, certainly, there are much more serious things to discuss,' my father said, his voice consoling. 'Please tell us how we can help, in this regard.'

'Well, I did what I should have done days ago, and fired the lawyer,' Edwin said. 'Last night I told Lisa Ping that I expected her to go to the police to try get the case dismissed. She said we need witnesses, sworn testimony, this that and the other. So I said thanks, and goodbye.'

'You shouldn't have fired her!' I cried out. 'Good lawyers don't grow on trees.'

'She's a lawyer who wouldn't even *try*,' Edwin said. 'That's not the right attitude, you know? We need a real pro who's a fighter.'

'Edwin, if Lisa Ping told you she can't get the case dismissed before trial, it might be for legal reasons, not for lack of fight. After all, it's a felony case—'

Edwin cut me off. 'Oh, don't worry about my business anymore. I'll be getting an expert opinion quite soon.'

'Whose?' my father asked politely.

'Mr Hugh Glendenning himself,' Edwin said, looking defiantly at me.

'Hugh Glendenning?' I repeated dumbly.

'Yes, Hugh. This is the big news I came over to tell! I made a call to Tokyo and reached his office, and he took the call personally. He was very worried when he heard you were lying in the hospital maybe dying from poison.'

'You said *what* to him?' I'd been feeling well, but now my stomach was cramping.

'At the time, I didn't know if you were going to live or die, so I thought he better know. He said he would fly out as fast as he could. You're the main reason he's coming, but I'm sure he wouldn't mind listening to the situation with Braden while he's out here.'

Uncle Hiroshi, my father, and Tom only stared; I was sure they were as shocked as I was.

'I don't believe it,' I said. 'How could you do such a thing? You've tricked Hugh into helping you, just like you tricked us with your father's birthday!'

'Rei-chan, please don't make yourself sick again.' My father put a restraining hand on my arm, as if he thought I might strike Edwin.

'You *can't* afford Hugh's help; none of us can! He's even more expensive than Lisa Ping, and I'm almost positive he's not licensed to practice law in Hawaii.'

'Whatever the case, he's flying in on JAL this afternoon. I offered to give him a ride from the airport to the hospital, but he said he'd already booked a driver. Gonna have to reach him somehow, tell him you're not at Queen's anymore.' Edwin pulled a mobile phone out of his pocket.

'Take care of yourself, Rei! Please don't get sick again!' Courtney called after me as I got to my feet and unsteadily walked into the house.

In my bathroom, I locked the door and leaned against it, ready to fight off anyone who might come after me. I put the lid down on the toilet and sat there with my head in my hands, unable to stop crying. This was nothing to get upset about – a comedy of errors, really. I'd apologize to Hugh as soon as he arrived.

There was a knock at the door, followed by my father's voice. 'You are justified in being upset with Edwin. But, please, look at the bright side of the situation.'

'How can there be a bright side to this . . . embarrassment?' I couldn't find a word to express the horror that loomed.

'You were once engaged to Hugh, and separated under unhappy terms. Now is a chance for closure. Rei, please let me in.'

I reached out and turned the doorknob, allowing my father in. He caught sight of my tear-streaked face, and his concerned expression grew. He beckoned me into his arms and I finally went.

'I'm just not ready for this to happen now,' I said into his shoulder. 'I obviously have to see Hugh because he's flown all the way here, but I feel really bad about it. He's married and happy, and I'm still alone. It's all so awkward.'

'This family would much rather have you alive and temporarily unhappy than to have you dead, with your pride intact. I'm sure Hugh will feel similarly.'

'Thanks for the kind thought,' I said sarcastically.

'I have many more of these thoughts, Rei-chan. Hugh is on an airplane right now, traveling to hold the hand of someone he fears is dying. Imagine his happiness and relief upon arrival, to hear from Edwin that you have recovered enough to leave the hospital. And what if the words you offer him are generous – go happily with the woman you love, for I am happy in my new life, too?'

I rolled my eyes. 'Otoosan, that's not the way I would speak to anyone.'

'Use your own words, then.'

I struggled for a minute. 'I could say that I'm happy, because I finally realize how much I have: my family, my friends, and the chance of living almost anywhere in the world. You know that I don't have to worry about a mortgage or car payments. Some people might say I have a net worth of zero, but the reality is I have zero responsibilities. That's liberating.'

'Turn your statement around,' my father said quietly. 'Could it be that because you have no responsibilities, you hunger for them? Is this the reason you labor mightily to take on everyone's troubles as your own?'

'That's not quite true, Otoosan. You're the one who asked me to look into the business about Harue's house, when I was ready to spend my days here swimming and reading.'

'It's not the only thing you've done. You also helped your great-uncle by compassionately listening to his stories of the past, and you are helping your cousin Braden as much as anyone can, in this difficult circumstance.'

'Actually, I'd say Michael is the one who's really done a lot of that work. I won't take credit.'

'And why is it that Michael has done so much for the Shimura family?' My father's voice was soft.

'Loyalty to me,' I said, without hesitation.

'And what have you done for him?'

'Excuse me?' I looked at my father suspiciously.

'Maybe the only responsibility you are shirking is the one you have to Michael.'

'But you don't think he's suitable,' I reminded him.

'I never used those words,' my father said. 'I'll admit to you that I disliked the way he allowed everyone to initially believe he was someone he wasn't, but now I understand. You see, when we were all waiting in the hospital for news, and learned about the poisoning, Michael became extremely . . . agitated. He questioned the doctors and exhibited an unusual knowledge of toxicology.'

'He would know about drugs,' I said. 'But it doesn't mean he uses them, Dad, he's the straightest arrow I know.'

'When I confronted Michael about this behavior, he asked me to walk outside for a shaved ice. As we drank our ices, he explained about his work, and yours. He was concerned that you might never have a chance to tell me. I'm not happy about the risks involved in the work, but I understand the work you did with him had great meaning for the future of this country – and its relationship with Japan.'

'OCI is all in the past,' I said. 'All I ever wanted to do is work with Japanese antiques. After this vacation, I'm getting back on track. For real,' I added, then laughed. I was picking up Hawaiian slang.

'I shall leave you to rest now, but I think more of Michael for telling me what he did. He's a good man, Rei, and I regret giving you any other impression.'

'Oh?' This was magnanimous of my father, to say he'd been wrong about something.

'Yes, I was wrong. And you're thirty years old now, my dear. Behave within reason, but don't be afraid to follow your heart.'

# Twenty-Six

I was sorting through the few remaining clean dresses in my closet, wondering what I should wear to confront my own past and future, when my cellphone rang with a call from Michael.

'Brooks,' I said, relief flooding through me like a gentle anesthetic. As awkward as things might be in a few hours time with Hugh, I would step into the Sebring at seven o'clock for my long-anticipated dinner date with Michael. I'd tell him everything, and he'd help me get over it. And then we'd have fun.

'I'm glad you answered – I was having trouble with reception earlier, because I'm on the North Shore. Are they going to let you out of Queen's today?'

'Oh, I'm sorry – I didn't have time to call you before I left the hospital.'

'Left the hospital?' Michael interrupted. 'Where are you now?'

'Home! You caught me in my room, figuring out what to wear tonight; that is if you're still interested in dinner.'

'Of course. The reservation is on the late side, though. Do you think you can stay up till nine? Are you truly feeling fine?'

'Yes and no. My body's more or less back to normal, but I'm a bit anxious about something.'

'And why's that, honey?'

He used the endearment without any strategic reason – just affection, which made my revelation all the harder. 'A visitor I never expected is coming to see me today. I'm not really in the mood to face him.'

'Kainoa?'

'Actually, it's someone flying in from Tokyo. Hugh.'

'Who?'

'Hugh! You know, my ex-boyfriend. Edwin conned him into flying over here from Japan, saying I was deathly ill. I think it was all a way to get another person working on Braden's legal defense.'

'If you didn't invite him, then why would you see him?' Michael's voice was tight.

I was speechless for a moment, then said, 'Of course I'll see him. I must explain about what Edwin did and make some apologies, at least.'

Michael was so quiet that I half-worried that our connection had broken. At last he spoke. 'If you see Hugh, it's over.'

'What's over?' I asked.

'This thing we have.'

Now I was angry. 'Michael, you and I have never gotten past first base, so you're a fine one to talk about having any kind of relationship, and I'm not hoping to rekindle anything with Hugh. He's happily married to a beautiful actress and flew here intending to absolve me of all my past sins, or something like that, at my bedside as I lie dying—'

'He flew out here because he's still in love with you, Rei.' Michael's voice was somber. 'When he finds out you're OK, he's not going to be content at the side of your bed, either.'

'I'm not going to be in bed, I'm up and well and walking around,' I protested. 'Come on, Michael. I didn't have to tell you this at all, but I did it because—'

'Because why?' Michael interrupted. 'Because it's a handy way to cement the running-away-from-me scenario you started, just before you became ill?'

'You're over-reacting, Michael. Just stop.'

'You have to decide what matters, Rei. Who you really want.' And with that, Michael Hendricks hung up on me.

I stood still, absorbing the shock. After a while, I clicked off the phone – after all, Michael wasn't going to be able to phone back and apologize if the line was busy. And he *would* apologize; it was out of character for him to give me an ultimatum. Sure, he was jealous, but he'd calm down after a while. All men did.

I put off my thoughts about glamour gear for the evening and slipped into a clean T-shirt and shorts. I had to sit down on the edge of the bed to put on my socks, because I didn't trust my balance.

The doorbell rang, and I started. It was too far from Waikiki to be Michael already, and I doubted it was Hugh, either. I waited for my father or somebody to open the door, but nothing happened, so I went myself.

'Rei!' Calvin Morita moved as if he intended to embrace me, so I stepped back, crossing my arms over my chest.

'Please don't. I just woke up and was sick again,' I lied.

'Let's sit down, then.' Calvin urged me over to the couch. 'I'll get you a glass of water, Rei. Ice?'

The last thing I wanted was Calvin Morita to hand me anything to eat or drink.

'Nothing right now, thanks,' I said, but he didn't close the fridge door until he'd pulled out a bottle of mineral water for himself. Cracking off its top, he sat down across from me.

'Where's Jiro?' I asked.

'Ah, the question you always ask me! He's taking an afternoon nap. I took advantage of the lull to come over and welcome you home from the hospital. I saw your father, uncle and Tom at the pool.'

'I wonder why they didn't tell me they saw you,' I said.

'Well, you were sleeping, weren't you? I did have a chance to chat with them, and your father said you were the victim of food poisoning. If it turns out that it was the sushi, I'll feel awful.'

'Why? I mean, why would you think it was the sushi?'

'You vomited, right? Did they talk to you about salmonella?'

'I'm sure the restaurant sushi was safe. Everyone else who ate it that night was fine.' I wanted Calvin out of the house; my gut was clenching and wrenching overtime, just being alone with him.

'Yes, and I was fine, too. I don't understand. Your cousin told me that you actually ate at the home of Josiah Pierce earlier on the same day.' Calvin gave me a tell-me-more look.

'Yes, Michael and I were there. Mr Pierce is cooperating with the health department, too.'

'How did you get invited over there?' Calvin blurted, as if no longer able to contain himself.

'He's the uncle of one of Michael's former classmates.'

'Oh, right. The Punahou connection!' Calvin seemed to

relax slightly. 'Well, I wouldn't think you'd get sick at a place like a multi-millionaire's Tantalus estate. That house is really nice, for an old place.'

'Have you been there?' I asked.

'Sure. I've dropped off Jiro's father there a few times. They have a business relationship, as you might have guessed.'

'Really.' I stood up. 'Calvin, it was very nice of you to stop in. I appreciate you keeping the heat on the health department, as well.'

Calvin stood up too, as if understanding his time was over. 'I was wondering – did your doctor at Queen's give you any medicines to take home?'

'No. The prescription was just rest and relaxation.'

'I hope that's enough. Let me know if you have any symptoms like nausea that continue to trouble you.'

'My medical care's all taken care of by Otoosan and Tom,' I said dismissively. 'I couldn't be more fortunate to have them in-house.'

'But they can't write prescriptions in Hawaii, and you're clearly under a lot of stress,' Calvin said. 'I can see from your slight pallor, and the darkness under your eyes, that you aren't sleeping well. You might benefit from a temporary course of Valium.'

'Valium?' I asked incredulously.

'If you tried Valium once and didn't react well, perhaps the dosage was wrong. It's a matter of weight. What are you, about one hundred ten?'

Struggling to keep control, I answered him. 'Calvin, thanks for your concern, but my weight is none of your business. I'd prefer not to be your patient, period.'

'That's OK.' Calvin gave me a wave and headed for the door. 'Just let me know if you change your mind.'

I located my relatives shortly after Calvin left; all three of them were at the swimming pool, having just eaten plate lunches purchased at its concessions stand. They hadn't seen Calvin knock at the door, and agreed that I'd done well to reject a Valium prescription. I went back to the house to put on a bathing suit while the concessions stand prepared a special mini-meal for me, at Tom's insistence. It was a two-scoop lunch, just fruit salad and rice.

After the meal, I submerged my body in the shallow end, while my father swam laps, if you could call the short distance from one side of the pool to the other that. I wondered how things had gone so crazy, so fast.

The sun moved and suddenly the pool was cold. I got out and lay on a chaise with the last Juanita Sheridan novel, and the last Harry Potter. My father had brought them out along with a water bottle and the cell phone, which he pointed out was showing an icon signifying that a message was waiting. Michael, I thought with relief, pushing buttons until I could find the number of the person who'd just called. I recognized it as that of Uncle Edwin's household. Reluctantly, I dialed back.

'You feel better now?' Yosh asked in his rough voice.

'Yes. It's just . . . everything was a bit overwhelming. I hope my outburst didn't upset you.'

'I seen a lot worse yelling in our house. Hey, I want to tell you, I think it's a nice idea you had, to visit the cottage.'

'Now that I have the maps, it will be easy to find our way via Barbers Point,' I said, glad I had something positive to think about. 'When would you like to go?'

'Tomorrow. I'll take Braden along, because Edwin's got a sales conference. The boy say he don't want to go, but he should see the place. It's part of who he is, yah?'

'And what about Courtney?' I asked, mindful of the one who always was ignored.

'Well, she got school tomorrow, but she can go if we wait till two-thirty.'

'Fine. I'll bring the minivan.' I wasn't going to ask Michael to come with us after all.

Evening was approaching; the sun had moved around the pool, and the little children and their parents were dragging their water toys behind them on the way home, while the young officers were arriving, hefting coolers and staking out grills. It was time for all of us to leave too – my father for tai-chi practice, and Tom and Hiroshi to pick up pizza in Kapolei.

I showered and pulled out the garment I'd selected earlier, a rose silk charmeuse dress that skimmed my body like a wave. Somewhere in me, I harbored the hope that Michael would drive over with roses and an apology. In the meantime,

I might as well look nice for my meeting with Hugh, who'd last seen me looking very depressed in dirty gym clothes.

As I dried off and rubbed a plumeria-scented cream on my arms and legs, I slipped into matching lace underwear, also pink. I leaned before the bathroom mirror to apply my usual evening make-up: a tinted moisturizer, plum color for the lids, and a smoky gray liner. It was a kind of meditation, the strokes of the mascara wand, the etching of the lip liner. Here were the outlines: crisp edges distracting from the inward mess.

My face finished, I sat on the *lanai*, watching the sun slip farther down, and feeling the air cool against my skin. The sound of a car slowing down cut into my thoughts. I looked up and saw a long black Lincoln town car stop at the driveway.

It would be impolite not to meet him. As he emerged from the car, I started toward him, my bare foot squashing something soft. The lithe green lizard scuttled away, but not before I'd screamed.

'Darling, are you all right?' Hugh steadied me. I shook off his hands and took him in, handsome as ever in slim-cut khaki trousers and a white linen shirt that was only slightly wrinkled.

'I just stepped on a lizard.' I made a face.

'Are you sure it wasn't a snake?' Hugh looked warily at the clipped lawn around us.

'There are no snakes in these islands. It's one of the fun facts about Hawaii.'

Hugh turned back toward his limousine, carefully shielding his eyes from the sun. 'May the driver stay where he's parked? I don't intend to keep you long, since you've just gotten out of hospital, but I did hope for a real visit.'

'It's no problem. Uncle Hiroshi and Tom took our minivan to Kapolei to get some extra provisions. They won't be back for a while, I'm sure.'

'I would have liked to see them. And where's your father?' He gazed toward the house.

'He's at tai-chi.'

'You must have made a miraculous recovery for them to leave you on your own, the first day out of hospital?' Hugh's green eyes were looking at me with the skepticism I'd anticipated.

'I wouldn't call it miraculous. In fact, I have some explaining to do. Tea?'

'Never thought I'd ask for this, but do you have any iced?' He pushed back a lock of damp blond hair from his brow.

I smiled my answer, and he followed me into the kitchen, where I took out the chilled ginger rooibos tea my father had made a few hours earlier. I chopped some mint and squeezed a quarter of a lemon between his glass and mine.

'Delicious,' Hugh said after a sip. 'Thank you.'

'I'm just happy that you didn't ask me for one of your favorite whiskies,' I said as we walked back outside.

'Oh, my drinking days are over.'

'Marriage will do that to you, I guess,' I said.

'What are you talking about?'

'Well, I gather that you're married.' He looked at me blankly, so I confessed. 'I Googled you a while back. I saw pictures of you at an engagement party with a beautiful Hong Kong ingénue.'

Hugh winced. 'Ming prefers to be called an actor, thank you very much, and she actually broke off the engagement a while back, so I'm once again the extra man.'

My face flushed, and I stilled the urge to put my hands to my cheeks. Hugh must not think I was excited about this turn of events. I was flustered, though.

'But tell me, Rei. I thought you were at death's door, from what your uncle told me, but you look . . .' He paused. 'A bit thin, but spectacularly alive.'

'I wish I could have talked to you before you decided to fly here. I was very ill for a short while, but never in critical condition. My fourth cousin Edwin used a ruse to get you to come here. He did a similar maneuver to get my family to Hawaii, you know.'

'Hold on. Weren't you in the hospital? And wasn't it your last wish to speak to me?'

'I was in the hospital, yes. But I never said anything about last wishes because I was unconscious for a while, and when I woke up, everyone told me I was going to recover. Hugh, I feel wretched about this imposition on you,' I said, watching his expression darken. 'I'd offer to reimburse the cost of your flight, but I suspect you flew first class.'

Hugh laughed. 'Don't worry about it for a minute, Rei. I used my frequent flyer miles, as usual.'

'But the hotel – you're surely staying overnight in a hotel?'

'Actually, I booked the Royal Hawaiian for three nights. I could use the R and R, to be frank. But I won't quite relax until I understand what led your fourth cousin to his rather bizarre interest in me.'

I explained about the fire, and about Braden's arrest. As I'd expected, Hugh wanted to know what Braden had been doing in the mountains, the day after the fire.

'He was collecting large, loose rocks; the kind that formed when volcanoes erupted here millions of years ago. Lava rock can be gorgeous, so it's sought after for landscaping and building stone walls. The rocks are much easier to find and remove in areas where fire has burned away the brush.'

'Is it OK to do that here – just pick up lava rock where you find it?'

'It's legal if the rocks are on your property. Braden was trespassing on land owned by one of the wealthiest landowners in Leeward Oahu, Josiah Pierce the Second. Mr Pierce is planning to sell a portion of land to a Japanese developer, and now the developer doesn't want to pay as much for it, because of the fire damage.'

'Who's the developer?' Hugh eased a legal pad and pen out of his briefcase.

'Mitsuo Kikuchi. Maybe you've heard of him? He's based in Tokyo.'

Hugh looked startled. 'I know him very slightly, but what you're saying about his bargaining strategy doesn't surprise me. Kikuchi's as tough as they come.'

'This isn't even the worst of it,' I said glumly. 'After the fire was extinguished, the police discovered the body of a young woman who worked at a coffee shop that was destroyed in the fire—'

'Hang on.' Hugh pointed at me with his fountain pen. 'Are you saying the Starbucks or whatever didn't evacuate its employees even when threatened by fire? That would be negligence on the part of management—'

'It wasn't a Starbucks. It was a little place called Aloha Morning that's owned by a local man, Kainoa Stevens. Kainoa was there the afternoon of the fire, trying to create a fire-break.'

'I should jump in now, I think,' Hugh said. 'Here's the main problem. I'm not qualified to argue cases in the courts here.'

'I expected that. It's what I've been telling Edwin constantly.'

Taking in Hugh's puzzled expression, I gave him the short version of Uncle Yosh and Edwin's dreams of regaining Harue's cottage and land. 'Edwin had the mistaken impression, before he invited my father and me to come here, that you and I were still an item, which to him meant you'd be happy to help him win his battle for the land. His hope is to get hold of it before the Pierces sell their land to Mitsuo Kikuchi, and thereby be able to exact a high price. The reality is the military has owned the land since the war.'

'I see. Now another red flag is waving itself at me. I can't do anything that might possibly work against Mitsuo Kikuchi's interests, even to the point of giving your uncle advice. My hands are tied because Kikuchi was involved in some real-estate work for Sendai, where you know I once worked.' Hugh looked around, as if suddenly paranoid. 'He's not on the island now, is he?'

'Actually, he is, but I doubt he'll be walking by this house. His own is in a remote section by itself, right on the water. Anyway, as I said before, I really never expected you to help. These are my problems, and I'll face them as best I can.'

'No, it's not *your* problem; it is Edwin's problem, or his son's problem, but certainly not yours.' Hugh sounded almost angry.

'But . . . they're family. Like them or not, they're family.'

'Asian family obligation syndrome,' Hugh said. 'The only Asian I've met who doesn't constantly worry about her family is Ming. She didn't even care that her mother went to the cardiologist for her broken-heart syndrome after the cancelled wedding.'

I smiled at Hugh and said, 'It's very hard to believe that Ming broke your engagement.'

'Oh, I knew she'd had an affair in the past with another

actor, and as the wedding approached, he began to remind her of the good old days.'

'I'm sorry that happened to you. It hurts to be left.' I spoke slowly, thinking that Hugh was still charming and sexy, and I was touched that he'd still cared enough to fly from Japan to be with me. But that was it; I could hardly believe that this was the man who'd broken my heart three times running. Perhaps, finally, my heart had healed.

'Well, it's all water under the bridge. Or how do the Japanese put it?' Hugh broke into my thoughts.

'Water washes everything away.'

'Yes, I think that Mitsuo Kikuchi is reputed to have said that about his son's dealings.'

'Oh, are you talking about Jiro?'

'I don't know his name, but he would be in his late twenties, I think, and a bit off, mentally?'

'That's the one! What do you know about him?'

'Jiro was in the news – or rather, was deliberately kept out of the news – about five years ago, when he was in his early twenties. Jiro became too aggressive with a hotel waitress or maid. Because she was a foreign worker, she was convinced not to press rape charges in exchange for a cash settlement and help securing a permanent visa.'

'Mitsuo Kikuchi arranged all this?'

'That's the rumor, and it's an old one, which is why I'm unfortunately fuzzy on the details. And keep quiet about it, please. If it ever gets out that I slandered him or his son, Kikuchi would probably send goons after me.'

'I won't talk about it. But God, my instincts were right! I knew there was something creepy about Jiro when he came up to me in the swimming pool. And Kainoa Stevens thought Jiro was trying to date Charisse. I wonder . . .'

'You went swimming with Jiro?' Hugh sounded aghast. 'How close to these people are you?'

'Don't worry so much! The house is about a half-mile away, and Jiro lives with a round-the-clock psychiatrist. They have a private pool, but the two of them occasionally visit our community's pool for some reason.'

'I can imagine the reason.' Hugh shook his head. 'Damn it, Rei, you've landed in about the most unsafe location in

all of Hawaii, walking distance from a suspected rapist.
Please tell me that you'll move into my suite at the Royal
Hawaiian!'

I laughed shakily. 'You've got to be joking. At the moment
I'm living with three valiant family defenders.'

'None of whom is home.' Hugh frowned. 'Please come with
me to Waikiki, just for the evening. We can eat something,
and then I'll have the driver bring you back here, once you're
certain that somebody's home.'

'Come on, Hugh. I'm not your girlfriend anymore! There's
no need to be so protective.' But all the while I was thinking
that it would be nice to have a ride into town. After Hugh and
I had finished our meal, I could track down Michael at the
Hale Koa and try to make amends.

'I know that. We're friends now, Rei, which is the way it
always should have been. And your keeping me company
over supper would give me a chance to . . . well, apologize
for the way I ran off to South America, and my other
misdeeds.'

I looked at him, thinking that what Michael had predicted
would happen, was starting to happen. The ending would be
different, though; I'd make sure of that.

# Twenty-Seven

The Royal Hawaiian was almost as pink as my dress, and
pleasingly old. We ate outdoors on the *lanai* – grilled tuna
for Hugh and a small green salad for me. I wasn't hungry; it
was too distracting, being outdoors in Waikiki, sitting with
Hugh while Michael was somewhere nearby. When twilight
fell and Hugh started yawning, I pressed upon him our house
phone number, as well as Tom's mobile, in the event that a
golf date could be arranged between the two of them the next
day.

I asked Hugh's driver to stop at the edge of the green

parkland of Fort DeRussey, the military-owned land that surrounded the Hale Koa. But as I began walking to the hotel, I noticed a significant number of people heading toward the Alai Wai Canal. Michael still wasn't answering his phone, so I decided to follow the crowd.

'Is there a festival?' I asked a local woman at the edge of the crosswalk, before I made the commitment to crossing Kuhio Avenue.

'It's the end of *o-bon* season. People start at a Buddhist temple, where they light candles and send them down their canal in memory of their ancestors. The tradition stopped for some years, but it's come back.'

The green banks of the Alai Wai were lined several people thick, but so many of them were short that it was easy for me to get a good view. The lights blinked and bobbed and slowly traveled along with the current; as I squinted westward down the canal, I could see no end to the lights. If I'd known about this earlier, I would have found my way to the temple to light candles for Harue and Ken Shimura. Instead, I selected two of the most brilliant lights and pretended these belonged to them.

Someone brushed against my back, and I took an extra step to regain my balance. The local crowd was starting to evaporate, and tourists from the bars, having gotten a glimpse of the lights, were pressing in. Drunken-sounding laughter made me realize that it was time to return to the brighter lights along Kalakaua Avenue.

Ten minutes later I walked the curving steps up to the Hale Koa, thinking about the rest of my night. My father, Uncle Hiroshi and Tom were at home; I'd confirmed this with a quick phone call after I'd parted with Hugh. But I'd refused to let Tom pick me up right away as he'd suggested. It was still early in the evening, and I was dead set on finding Michael.

I walked through the Hale Koa's wide, open-air lobby toward the elevators. I remembered Michael and Kurt's room number, and knew that the two rooms to the left of it had been reserved by Parker Drummond and Eric Levine. I tried Michael's door first, with no luck, then tried the other two. The last door was opened by Karen Drummond, wearing a short silk bathrobe.

'Oh, I'm sorry to catch you dressing.' At least, that's all

that I hoped was happening. 'I was wondering if you knew where Michael was.'

'It's no problem.' Karen opened the door wider, and ushered me in. 'How wonderful to see you! We were all so worried when we heard you were in the hospital. I'm sorry but we're getting dressed to go out. We've got a dinner reservation in, what, an hour?'

'Forty-five minutes!' came an answering call from behind the bathroom door.

I dutifully followed Karen inside, but felt too uncomfortable to sit down on the corner of the rumpled bed she offered, while she in turn went to a sink in a galley that was a twin to the one in Michael's room and started brushing her teeth.

'He should be back from sailing any time now. He's been out for hours,' Parker said from behind the bathroom door.

'Did he take your boat?' I asked.

'No, no, no – it takes at least two to handle her. He went out on a little catamaran,' Parker added as he emerged from the bathroom, buttoning the top few buttons of a mauve and turquoise print aloha shirt. When I looked uncomprehending, he said, 'It's a small sailboat. He checked it out at the yacht club a few hours ago.'

'Well, he hasn't been answering his phone.'

'He may not have taken his phone on the water because of the risk of capsizing. Those little boats go over easy.'

'Really?' I said, feeling a prickle of unease. 'Do you think he wore a life jacket?'

'So you *do* care about him.' Karen gave me a speculative look, then passed her husband in the narrow area outside the bathroom where there was a sink and mirror. She opened a make-up bag, and began extracting a top-quality arsenal that put my collection to shame.

'He's an excellent swimmer and seaman, Rei,' Parker said, coming over to sit down next to me. 'Don't worry. If the two of you had plans tonight, I'm sure he'll make it back.'

'We didn't have plans. I mean, we had them and then he cancelled.'

'No date with you tonight, when he's flying out in forty-eight hours?' Parker's forehead wrinkled. 'What is with that boy?'

'Maybe he's just trying to be on the careful side and give

Rei time to rest,' Karen said. 'After all, she was just released from the hospital.'

'I'm sure that it's something I said.' I was regretting what I'd blurted out to Michael about Hugh arriving on the island. I'd thought it was important to be honest, but what I'd said had clearly dashed what faint progress the two of us had made.

I wrote a short note telling Michael that I wanted to talk to him, and slipped it under his door before I took the elevator downstairs again. Against my better judgment, I checked my phone for any voice messages, and came up with zip. Sickened by the prospect of paying over $100 for a cab ride back to our house, I asked the bell captain if there was a cheaper way to get to the Leeward Side.

I was pondering a sheaf of bus schedules when I caught a glimpse of a bedraggled lean man in wet shorts, T-shirt and Topsiders walking purposefully toward the elevator. I paused, wondering if I should wait to let him read the note. No, I decided, there was too high a risk he'd avoid me. I hadn't come all this way to be meek.

I took off after him, and as my heels clattered against the granite floor, he turned abruptly. His voice was guarded. 'How did you get here? This is a surprise.'

'If Mohammed won't come to the mountain . . .' I shrugged.

'You look good, Rei. I know I'm a mess.' He ran a hand through his hair.

'With sailing, that's par for the course, isn't it?'

'Not exactly.' Michael smiled. 'You're mixing your sports metaphors, but yes, people do get messed up when they're out in a catamaran by themselves and are distracted enough to capsize.'

'I knew it!' I exclaimed. 'I had a bad feeling about you going sailing at night.'

'You worried about me tipping over in a catamaran?' Michael shook his head. 'Well, you shouldn't. It's the easiest kind of vessel to right; kids do it all the time. Why are you even here?'

'We have unfinished business, don't you think?'

'OK then. I'll just clean up first,' Michael said easily, as if our heated argument of a few hours earlier had never happened.

'Good!' I moved to follow him toward the elevator.

'You'd be better off waiting down here.'

'If you prefer.' I watched the elevator doors close after him and a half-dozen other hotel guests.

As the lights on the band above the elevators showed the car traveling upward, I tried to think of why he didn't want me in the room. Maybe he feared I'd once again be moved by his semi-clothed body and attack. How ironic that the undergarment that I was wearing beneath my dress was sometimes referred to as a merry widow, because Michael was the opposite: an unhappy widower.

After about ten minutes in the lobby, watching children skip about, my cell phone vibrated, surprising me.

'Miss Shimura, this is Josiah Pierce.'

'Oh, hello.' Even though I was standing in a breezy, open-air lobby, I felt pinpoints of moisture form on my face.

'I heard you became violently ill the day after our meeting. Are you still in the hospital?'

'No, I was released this morning. Thanks for your concern.' My mind raced. How much did he know about my poisoning, and had the Navy reached him yet to tell him about the land?

'I apologize if something in the meal may have sickened you. Have you learned what kind of food poisoning it was?' JP continued in his well-bred tone. 'Midori and I are mortified that anything we served might have been off.'

'The verdict's still out on what made me sick. That's the reason the authorities are visiting everyone I ate with that day, plus examining our own refrigerator's contents.'

'Well, no doubt they're operating on Hawaii time, which will mean you'll find out later rather than sooner. I was wondering if you could stop by again, because I have something to discuss with you, and as you mentioned, these things are sometimes better done in person.'

Now my heart was thudding. The man who might have poisoned me, inviting me to return to his house? 'I'm without a car at the moment, but I can't stand suspense. Can you please tell me over the phone what you know?'

'Very well then.' He'd caught the reserve in my voice, and now sounded different, too. 'Actually, the chief reason I'm telephoning is that I did the research, as I promised you I would, on Harue Shimura's situation.'

'Did you find out something about ownership of the cottage?' I could barely breathe, I was so excited.

'As you know, I inherited my father's house, and I use his old office as my own,' JP began. 'He had two file cabinets relating to the plantation, which Midori's been after me to dump for years, but I haven't. I guess I had it in my mind that someday a historian might be interested in an account of this long-ago time. Anyway, once I opened the files, I found hundreds of papers relating to the plantation. It was just a matter of looking through folders until I found the employment records for Keijin Watanabe, who later became Ken Shimura.'

'Do you have the originals?'

'Yes, and I'll have my lawyers send you copies, if you'd like. But to summarize, Keijin came to us from Okinawa in 1910, having signed a contract promising a minimum of five years' employment. He started at one of our sugar plantations on the Big Island. He was described as an average worker – which meant a very hard worker, in terms of how we look at productivity in retrospect. However, he had a number of citations for drunkenness and fighting with other workers. There was a particularly bad fight with another worker, a well-liked Filipino boy, who wound up losing his sight in one eye. The solution the plantation manager came up with was to move Keijin from that plantation, get him married, and convince him to change his name to avoid having his reputation follow him.'

'So he came to Oahu,' I said.

'Yes, and within the same month of his arrival, Harue Shimura came to Hawaii. My father spotted Harue when she arrived at the docks in Honolulu by herself, without a sponsoring fiancé to meet her. She asked him for a job, in good English. In his diary for that day, he had a notation: "Hired Harue Shimura, well-bred young lady originating from Yokohama, near-fluent in English, both spoken and written. Agreed to salary of $10 per month and marriage to another worker."'

'It sounds almost like a slave being sold at auction block, doesn't it?' I thought aloud.

'I'm sure my father thought she was a willing participant because, after all, she'd traveled here alone, and there were plenty of women emigrating in search of husbands that for one reason or other they couldn't find in Japan. After the wedding – at which Keijin changed his first and last names – an employment record was also opened for Harue. She began work shucking cane in the fields, but her production was lower than other women's; she was weaker, not coming from peasant stock, the *luna* noted numerous times. The camp medical record notes that she miscarried her first pregnancy. After she became pregnant again, she was reassigned from the field to teach in the plantation school. Her baby was born full-term, a boy named Yoshitsune. A few months after the birth, she resumed work as a teacher.'

'So she never had to carry her baby to the fields,' I said.

'Yes. This was the 1920s, and we'd made significant improvements to the conditions for families, which meant more jobs for women in places other than the fields. You already know what the housing of this period was like, and there were schools at our plantations and most others. Before long, those schools became obsolete as the plantation children began attending regular public schools in Honolulu.'

'Steps toward a normal life?'

'And with that, trouble for your family. The Japanese workers, I'm not proud to admit, were paid less than the other ethnic groups, and Ken Shimura was among the chief agitators for wage parity. There was a strike and, when it finally settled, Ken was reassigned to Maui. Harue and Yoshitsune did not go with him. I can only imagine that my father's managers didn't want her to leave the school. Thus the offer of the house, which was recorded in my father's diary as, "Harue Shimura agrees to remain teaching, and will pay $10 for house on Kalama."'

'It made sense for her to take the house,' I said, thinking about how she must have thought here was a home that would be her property, no longer subject to the whims of management.

'What happened next is unclear,' JP said. 'I'm guessing that neither side recorded the transaction with the state, which left nothing for our company to use as evidence to handle both Yoshitsune Shimura's complaint, and the Liangs' request for a lease. At this point, there's little that can be done; obviously, my father's intent was to give the land to Harue Shimura, but it doesn't make sense to give that portion to Yoshitsune Shimura, because Mitsuo Kikuchi will do more with that land, for the people of the Leeward Side, than Edwin could.'

'But you can't give him the land, even if you wanted to.' There, I'd said it; Michael had thought I should wait for the lawyers, but the level of frankness that JP had employed with me made me feel he deserved the truth too. As carefully as I could explain without having the pictures and maps in hand, I described the evidence of the military's takeover of forty acres of land bordering the ocean. At the end, I said, 'You can, of course, sue the military for taking your land.'

'I don't doubt your story,' Josiah Pierce said, after a short silence. 'It was the war, and we'd been bombed – the military had good reason to have such powers. And we were willing to give them concessions, too, because they left us the means to stay financially solvent. Because the government gave us a break, though, we never protested when the military ran roughshod over Oahu, seizing whatever land they wanted in the name of defense.'

'As you said, the island had been bombed. There was a reason for securing areas.'

'Just as there is now,' Josiah Pierce said. 'I'm torn, because I know that on the Leeward Side, in the areas where I and other people have granted thousands of acres to Hawaiians, the people aren't doing well, in terms of employment. The restaurant complex made sense to me – both from a financial and social viewpoint.'

'There are two sides to every problem, aren't there?'

'I hope you don't mind that I end our conversation now, Rei.'

'No, not at all.' Had I said too much?

'This is a shock to me; there's no doubt about it. And you too will need to think over the information that you now possess.'

# Twenty-Eight

'I'm sorry that you had to hunt me down,' I said when Michael found me, a few minutes later, sitting in the hotel's lower garden underneath a massive banyan tree.

'I'm trained to hunt,' Michael said, smiling slightly. 'Well, at least you had something to occupy you. I know I took a good while longer than nine minutes.'

'But you look wonderful,' I said. Michael was wearing what looked like raw-silk trousers with a green and brown patterned aloha shirt – the first Hawaiian gear in which I'd seen him.

'You were here for the phone reception, I'm guessing?' Michael's eyes went to the telephone still in my hand.

'Josiah Pierce called me. It was quite a conversation.'

'Let me guess: he wants to see you to discuss something he's found out about the land deal? When you were in the hospital, he phoned me, using the state department number. He asked me for your phone number because, as he said, he didn't want the truth to be inadvertently filtered.'

'He really does trust me, then,' I said.

'Yes. And I'm dying to hear everything, but we'd better get on our way to the restaurant first.'

We drove slowly out of Waikiki, sandwiched in long double lines of luxury cars and tour buses. I would have felt claustrophobic if it weren't for the canal on our right, where a few golden lights still floated in the darkened water.

'Do you know anything about that?' Michael inclined his head toward the water.

I explained what I'd learned about Hawaii's Japanese population marking the end of the *obon* season, offering the lighted boats to lead their ancestors' spirits home. 'I was regretting not having had the chance to send lights for Harue and Ken, but now I realize a candle was lit tonight, because JP found something in his father's diary.' And this was the perfect time to begin with the sad story of Ken and Harue, with all its twists and disappointments.

'So Harue rehabilitated a guy with problems,' Michael said at the end of everything, when we were pulling into the garage at Restaurant Row. 'That sounds familiar, doesn't it?'

'She turned a stranger with a penchant for drinking and fighting into a family man and labor activist. But they died separated, which is what's unusual – and so sad.'

Michael shut off the car and looked at me closely. 'Now that you and Josiah Pierce are so chummy, do you think he's off the list of suspect poisoners?'

'I don't like to think I'd change my opinion based on a conversation,' I said slowly. 'However, I like him, and I don't think my brain would allow that to happen without some kind of intuition. I'd like to see him in a few days to look at the documents he found.'

'Rei, I'll be gone by then. I still can't help feeling anxious about him, after your poisoning. I'm still dreaming at night that I've lost you.'

'Maybe I've lost you,' I said. 'I saw Hugh this afternoon, and I talked to him. Does your ultimatum still stand?'

'Of course not!' Michael exclaimed. 'I regretted the words the instant I hung up. But you know how I am: I run away when I think I'm at risk.'

'Hugh had a driver bring him to the townhouse mid-afternoon. We talked a little bit about the land deal and Braden. He told me that Sendai, his old employer in Japan, collaborated with Mitsuo Kikuchi for some real-estate purchase.'

'Really? Does he know him?' Michael pressed the button to pull up the convertible's whiny-sounding roof.

'By reputation only. He said Mitsuo Kikuchi was a hard bargainer, which we already know. It's what Hugh told me about Kikuchi's son, Jiro, that's creepy. Hugh says there was a rumor a few years back that Jiro assaulted a woman. That's why he's here, tucked away at Pineapple Plantation. Hugh tried to scare me about him, but as you know, I'm already steering a wide berth.'

'You and your sailing metaphors,' Michael said, taking my hand. 'I regret never having the chance to get you on *Four Guys on the Edge*.'

'I don't regret it,' I said. 'I don't regret anything about this visit, even having to face Hugh. He was kind enough to give me a ride into town, and we had a light bite at his hotel and said a pleasant goodbye. It's really over, Michael. Nobody kissed or even cried.'

We walked out of the shadow of the garage and on to the street. A mix of emotions passed over Michael's face, and finally he said, 'I've been so stupid.'

'I would never say that about someone I love.' The words came quickly, before I could take them back. And now, under the streetlight, I could see that Michael's face was as flushed as mine.

'Rei.' Michael's voice cracked slightly, and then he kissed me, a long, sweet kiss that I'd been waiting for, all day long. After we broke apart, I waited for the words I wanted to hear him say, but he remained quiet. Still, I felt like a weight had been lifted, having finally had the courage to express what had been plaguing me for months.

The restaurant's atmosphere only seemed to heighten my feeling of having crossed into a new world. Michael held the door for me as I stepped into the first of a series of high-ceilinged rooms painted a deep blue-green.

I'd eaten so little with Hugh that I was hungry again. And, after reading the menu, I decided that if I didn't eat seafood soon, I might develop a phobia. I ordered carefully, choosing butterfish grilled with *miso*. Michael shared with me a more delicate fish called *moi*, which floated in an intense broth made from fresh local tomatoes and the Japanese seaweed, *hijiki*. For dessert, we shared a pot of jasmine-flavored green tea and sparred over a single bowl of *haupia* lemongrass crème brûlée.

The drive back to Waikiki was quick, since it was after eleven, and after we parked at the Hale Koa's garage, it seemed only natural to walk for a while. As we walked along Lewers Street, the trade winds blew fiercely, whipping my dress.

'Too bad I can't drink, because that looks like the perfect place for a fancy cocktail,' I said, inclining my head toward a small hotel that looked like a white jewel box surrounded by all the high rises.

'There's always coffee, tea or me,' Michael said, and I

smiled at him as we walked up a few steps into the Halekulani, admiring its small emerald-green courtyard lawn before finding a bar called the Lewers Lounge. It was a shadowy, art-deco paradise, with one empty table for two in a corner. I decided tea wouldn't cut it, so I ordered an alcohol-free version of the passion fruit and ginger cosmopolitan.

'This is the best night I've had since I've been here,' I said, marveling at how everything had turned out; that I was having cocktails with Michael, cuddled in a cozy banquette, listening to romantic jazz standards.

'I still feel terrible for what I said to you; for forcing you to chase me down, for this to happen. The more I think about it, you put yourself at risk for me – how were you going to get back to the Leeward Side, anyway?'

'Maybe I would have taken the bus, or paid for a night's stay at one of the cheaper hotels around the corner. My father would have understood if I stayed out – as long as I called.'

'Would he?' Michael looked at me intently. 'Would he understand if you called him at this hour and said you weren't coming home tonight?'

'But . . .' I was taken aback. 'You share a room with Kurt. How could we?'

'I was thinking about this hotel, not the Hale Koa. I'll go out to the lobby right now and ask if they have a room, but only if you're willing to stay the whole night – and tomorrow morning, as well.'

'Are you sure?' I asked carefully, my heart thumping under my dress.

'Of course I'm sure. But your response makes me wonder if I'm rushing you?'

'No. It's just that this seems like a very expensive hotel. I didn't lure you in because I expected to stay overnight.'

'But after what you said to me on Restaurant Row, don't you want to?'

I was glad the darkness hid the color that rose on my cheeks. 'The thing I noticed was what you *didn't* say to me in return.'

'Rei.' Michael's voice softened. 'If you don't realize that I love you too, you're truly in the wrong line of work.'

'What?' The world just seemed to have shifted ten degrees on its axis.

'I've loved you *forever*,' Michael went on, taking my hand again and drawing me close to him on the banquette. 'But there are so many reasons why I've thought this is the world's most impossible romance. There's the matter of professionalism, but even if that wasn't a factor, I'm just a simple American guy.'

'It's true that I've never dated an American,' I admitted. 'But that doesn't mean I wouldn't try, and you aren't simple, you're complex! Don't you realize how sexy spying is?'

'I'm not James Bond; it's clear from my lack of an English accent and my less than glamorous drink.' Michael tapped the Bud Light he'd insisted on drinking from the bottle.

'I was trying not to notice.'

Michael laughed. 'I am insane about you, Rei. Will you reform me, the way Harue did for Keijin?'

'No, I won't reform you. I want you just the way you are.'

Michael gave my hand one last squeeze, stood up, and headed out of the lounge.

I knew what he was about to do. And in the meantime, there was a very difficult phone call that I needed to make.

# Twenty-Nine

From past experience, I know that it's pretty embarrassing to take a hotel room without luggage. At the Halekulani there was no need for me to give my name – Michael's was enough – but to my chagrin, the registration actually took place in the hotel room. This meant that a young Asian woman in a trim blue suit escorted us upstairs and did the formalities at a small desk with Michael, while I stared out the window of our deluxe room at a lit-up round pool seventeen floors below us. Only when the desk clerk had left did I turn back to examine the soft cream and tan room, with a watercolor by a Japanese artist above the queen-sized bed.

'Small but perfect,' Michael said, walking into the bathroom. 'This reminds me of a really good hotel in Japan.'

'Well, this place is Japanese-owned,' I pointed out. 'It's interesting how much of Hawaii is owned by Japanese, but it doesn't really seem to bother people. So different from when we were young – remember the outcry when Sony bought the Rockefeller Center?'

'Ever since I've become Japanese-owned, I've been happier.' Michael turned and wrapped me in his arms.

'That's a terrible joke.' I kissed him. 'And I don't own you.'

'Oh, you've owned me ever since I conducted your background check.' Michael was slipping my dress straps off my shoulders, trying to figure out how to get it off. I started thinking about what was underneath, whether my underwear was going to be too dramatic – and then I remembered something even more important.

'Michael, I don't have anything with me. You know.'

'I have a three-pack,' he said, pulling a foil package from his pocket. 'But I must warn you, it's been a very long time. And you're so gorgeous, I'm just . . . afraid.'

Michael Hendricks, afraid? I pulled him down on the bed and said, 'Don't worry so much. It's been a while for me, too.'

This was right, I thought as we were finally naked, and our fingers blazed their first trails across each other's bodies. I was thrilled by the idea of playing teacher to someone who'd forgotten how to make love. But Michael didn't need to offer a disclaimer. He'd been married for almost a decade, and in that time he seemed to have learned many ways to please a woman.

We rolled together, the once-pristine bed now an utter shambles. Michael moved into me, and my legs wrapped around his waist. As we kissed, I tasted the exotic dessert we'd shared at dinner overlaid with our past: the gray streets we'd jogged, the long mornings reading dull reports, the text messages. I breathed deeply, feeling my body confidently follow where my mind was going, and then I was no longer able to postpone the inevitable.

'Yes,' I murmured, moving against him hard. I felt myself rising as high as Diamond Head outside the window – hidden by darkness now, but still there.

'Marry me,' Michael said, as everything erupted.

'Yes,' I sighed, my lips against his throat. 'Yes.'

When I woke up, Michael was curled around my back, kissing my spine.

'What time is it?' I murmured, reaching behind me to stroke him.

'Time to rise and shine.' He folded himself around me, and I opened my eyes to the bright sky and ocean outside the bedroom window. We'd forgotten to draw the curtains last night. And there was something else troubling me that I couldn't remember. The problem lay in the back of my mind, just as Michael lay against my back now, warming me in the chilly, air-conditioned room.

I grabbed the bathroom first, cleaning my teeth vigorously with the brush and toothpaste that I'd kept in my purse as a precaution ever since my illness began. Then I stepped into the shower, and let the warm water rain down on me. Slowly, I began to relax. I lathered up my calves with shaving cream and was just starting in on them when Michael slid into the room.

'Share your toothbrush with me?' he held up my brush.

'Why not? I've shared everything else.' I waved him toward the sink. 'Don't mind me, I'm just doing a quick bit of grooming.'

'You're going to a lot of trouble.' Michael was stark naked, but looked utterly comfortable as he lounged against the wall, brushing his teeth.

'I thought I should be prepared,' I said, as I turned from him and bent over my left calf again. 'In case we have a half-hour for the pool this morning. I could look for a swimsuit in the gift shops downstairs.'

'Shopping is not a priority right now.'

When I looked again, I saw this was true. I smiled and said, 'Good morning to both of you.'

Michael didn't answer, just opened the shower door, and gently lifted me against him. Before I could react, he'd carried me back to the bed, suds and all.

'I shouldn't be doing this,' Michael said as he began kissing his way down my body. 'I should get dressed, take you down to breakfast and then to your home, where I'll declare my intentions to your father.'

'Mmm,' I said, savoring his tongue, until the words he'd

spoken with it had connected with my brain. I sat straight up. 'What are you talking about?'

'Last night, I asked you to marry me. Surely you haven't blacked that out?'

'I remember you interrupting me, and my not being able to answer.'

'What? You said yes. Several times, in fact . . .'

'If I said yes, it's because I was in the throes of passion. It's not actually fair to ask someone a thing like that, when she's halfway out of her mind.'

'Come on, Rei. Your guard was down, and you said yes to marrying me.'

'Michael, have you forgotten our original intention?' I stared at him. 'We would try dating. Last night was our first official date, and I'd say it went extremely well. We could have another date, tonight.'

'But I've decided I don't want to date you.' Michael had risen from the bed and was pulling on a bathrobe. 'If we keep dating, you'll walk away. I'm afraid that's your *modus operandi*. Look at what happened with Hugh and Takeo.'

'That's not true. It was only after Hugh and I became engaged that things went to hell, and Takeo never asked.'

'But you'd lived with him, just as you'd lived with Hugh. You don't do well with live-in boyfriends. I refuse to join the chain.'

Was Michael laughing at me? Rather huffily, I answered, 'I'm not asking you to live with me.'

'Of course you aren't. Living together is playing, and so is dating, at our ages. Come on, Rei. Agree to the deal and when I return to work, I'll immediately ask Len about my getting shifted off the Japan desk.'

'But you live and breathe for that job. You can't leave it.'

'You're wrong about that, Rei. I live and breathe for you. Even if you just want me for one thing.' And with that, Michael went out to the balcony and stared intently at the sea – so intently that I got the message, got dressed, and went downstairs, where I cruised the gift shops and bought an overpriced pair of yoga pants and a Hawaii-themed T-shirt, because I couldn't bear to go home in the clothes I'd worn the night before.

I was relieved that he joined me for breakfast. We didn't

share many words, but we did share a basket of warm popovers and massive amounts of tropical fruit. There was a hole in the popover the waiter served me, and as I bit into it metal clinked against my teeth. I extracted a square-cut diamond solitaire ring.

'Sorry. I arranged for this to happen yesterday evening, when I booked the room. But I can probably take the ring back.' He sounded glum.

'Is it the ring from the Exchange?' I asked as the waiter who'd served us hovered on the periphery, beaming.

'I returned there when you were sick and swapped it for a real one.'

I held the diamond ring in my palm and looked at it, thinking of the beautiful vintage emerald I'd flung back at Hugh, and the ring that had never come from Takeo. Was I about to throw away the best thing I'd ever had?

'Michael, I feel all choked up. I want to cry.' I laid the ring on the table, still studying it. I imagined all the happiness the ring could bring me, if I were brave enough to take it.

'Please don't. We've already attracted enough attention.'

'Marriage is a lifetime, Michael. Won't you give me time to think about this?'

'Of course I will. But I'm telling you now, when I drop you back at the resort today, I'm going to investigate whether it's possible to book one of the wedding chapels. Half your relatives are here already, and it won't be hard to get mine to turn out on short notice. They'll be ecstatic.'

'You're leaving in one day, Michael.' As I spoke, I remembered that I'd almost gotten married in Hawaii once, to Hugh. Perhaps this meant that I was actually fated to marry here, just like my ancestor Harue.

'Yes, and it's unfortunate. So we won't get married today or tomorrow, but I think within ten to fourteen days is reasonable. I can get things done quickly.'

'Not everything quickly,' I reminded him, and was rewarded with a look so fond and knowing that I threw caution to the wind. 'Michael, we still have our room until noon, and I don't have to be home until around two.'

'You drive a hard bargain, Rei,' Michael said. 'This morning, I will bow to your wishes. But the next time will have to be within this hotel's wedding suite. Do you read me?'

'Roger that.'

# Thirty

W e made the most of every last moment to love each other, then drove back to the Leeward Side, holding hands most of the way. When I arrived home, my father greeted us cordially, and did not say a word about the missing night. I was grateful for Japanese discretion – the art of ignoring the obvious, and for letting water wash everything away.

I swung into dutiful-daughter mode, preparing a luncheon salad of local cucumbers, tomatoes, and lettuce. As I started chopping, my father invited Michael to stay to eat with us, but he begged off because of a lunch appointment at Pearl Harbor. It was probably just as well because right after he left, my father dropped the information that Uncle Hiroshi and Tom would meet Hugh for a round of golf at Turtle Bay on the North Shore.

'Otoosan, I guess you're the only one who'll be able to come with me to see Harue's cottage,' I said ruefully. 'That is, if we can still go. Won't Hiroshi and Tom need the minivan?'

'We can drop them off, and then use the car ourselves. And thank you for including me, Rei. After all the research we've done, I'd very much like to see the house.'

As we washed dishes, I relayed what Josiah Pierce had told me about Harue's brave and painful family history, and how he'd found confirmation of the sale of the house – a sale that could never have been legally made because of the military maps that included the house.

'When are you going to tell Yoshitsune?' my father asked at the end.

'I thought I'd wait until I had the written documents,' I said. 'Then, Yoshitsune will have as much of the story as exists and can draw his own conclusions. This afternoon I just hope the house visit will allow him a bit of closure.'

\* \* \*

Courtney was feeding the fish in the koi pond when we pulled up in the minivan, a few minutes before the time Uncle Yosh had suggested. She cocked her head and looked me up and down.

'You look good for someone who's been sick. It's like your face is pinker, but it's not sunburn.'

'Thank you, Courtney.' I wasn't about to tell a teenage girl my personal recipe for glowing skin. I felt different inside, too, thanks to an extra two hours in bed with Michael.

'You want to try?' Courtney asked, handing my father the box of fish flakes.

He shook a few in the water, and we all laughed as the patterned orange and cream fish swarmed to him. It was fun to watch them, and sent me back to memories of similar ponds in Japan. I said to Courtney, 'I can't tell where the extension is that Braden's digging.'

'That's because it's finished! Look over there – he did nothing but dig the last several days. Dig, and cry.'

'Oh, Courtney. He's really worried about his future, isn't he?'

'He doesn't show it to people. But when he's alone, I see it. He's very scared.'

When Braden and Yoshitsune came outside, I left the fish and opened up the Odyssey, requesting that Braden sit next to me and read the map. I explained, 'These maps are really complex, and I don't want to strain the older gentlemen's eyes.'

'I could do it, too!' Courtney piped up, from the very rear of the minivan, where she was sitting with Tom.

'I know that, Courtney. You may navigate for us on the way back.' Truth be told, I was going to use the handheld GPS once I arrived there, and mark the point as a way station. I would bring Michael back to see the place at sunset that evening, perhaps with a bottle of champagne.

'OK.' Braden shrugged, and took the first map I gave him. 'So we go into Barbers Point, huh? That's simple. The guard booths are always empty.'

Braden knew his way around Barbers Point better than Uncle Yoshitsune, because in his day it had been closed. Yosh told us, 'Planes taking off there, day and night. Never know exactly what's going on.'

'Who was Barber, some famous American Navy pilot?' I asked, looking around at the ink-black, burned fields.

'No, no,' Uncle Yosh said. 'He was a very bad sailor.'

'Like a pirate?' Courtney asked.

'No. I mean he was an English captain who tried to land ashore in bad weather. Everyone on the ship told him, don't even try, too dangerous, but he was in a hurry and wound up wrecking his ship here. Everybody died.'

As I was thinking, *how could anyone know what the people aboard told the captain, if they'd all died?*, Courtney asked, 'Do you think we can find bones, Jii-chan?'

'No, Courtney. It was long-ago times, maybe 1600s. Bones all gone by now.'

*Don't let the house be gone, too*, I thought. The picture that Edwin had taken to an appraiser had been about ten years old, and the place had been a wreck then. Winds could have finished it off.

'I don't think we can go any farther,' Braden said, pointing to a Pierce Holdings sign about fifty feet ahead, with NO TRESPASSING written underneath.

'Sure we can,' I said.

'The boy has a point. We could get in trouble.' Uncle Yoshitsune sounded regretful.

'Will you let me see the map?' I stopped the car and put it in park, so I could make myself comfortable while I looked. 'Yes, just as I thought. We're definitely on military land; Pierce Holdings' sign is incorrect.'

'But that's not what Pierce Holdings thinks,' Braden said. 'Albert Rivera's got video cameras everywhere, and field glasses.'

'If I'm prosecuted, I can win the case in court, based on these maps. Besides, I don't think Josiah Pierce would do anything to us.'

'Turn left,' Braden interrupted as we came to a crossing of dirt roads.

I wasn't sure about that, but I followed the directions and drove for a few minutes with blackened fields on either side, until I saw cars whizzing by on H-1.

'We're supposed to be driving toward the water,' I said.

'Just following the map,' Braden said brightly. 'You still want me to navigate, or what?'

'Whatever fool map you're following is wrong,' Yoshitsune said. 'I remember now, turn back and go the other way at the crossing.'

'We shouldn't have come out here,' Braden mumbled. 'I'm in enough trouble already; you want to pile on some more?'

'This is perfectly legal,' I said, and as we drove on, I was pleased to see the fields and trees appeared only singed, not burned to the ground. So the fire had petered out; this boded well for the house.

'I'm excited,' my father said, from the back seat with Courtney. 'And look, Uncle Hiroshi's camcorder is still in its case here, though I'm not sure I know how to use it.'

Courtney begged my father to let her use the camcorder, and soon she had her window down and was recording the sights with her own commentary on the side.

I glanced sideways at Braden, who was looking grimmer than I'd seen him since we'd left the police station. 'I'm sorry if you didn't want to come. It's just that you must be with a family member at all times—'

'Yeah, yeah. OK, the map says a left at the fork in the road—'

'No!' Uncle Yoshitsune called from the back. 'I know this place. Stay straight.'

I followed Uncle Yoshitsune's advice, driving slowly and taking in the surroundings. Clearly this area hadn't been used to grow sugar, because the grasses were so long and there were many old trees, the scraggly wili-wili in addition to the usual kiawe, and flowers that looked native. A showering of passion fruit lay on the path before us, and I steered around it, planning to pick up the unexpected bounty on the way back.

'On the way back, let's gather any good fruit that's fallen. I'm sure the Navy won't mind,' I said.

'*If* we get back,' Braden said ominously.

'There, there I see it! A small house,' my father cried, and everyone turned to look out the left windows where, in front of the brilliant Pacific, stood a weathered gray cottage listing slightly to one side.

'No, that can't be it,' Braden said. 'Keep on.'

'I'm not sure,' Yoshitsune's voice was low. 'My house, it was white, not gray like that.'

'Time takes its toll,' I said, slowing to a stop, to allow him a chance to look. After a few moments, he responded. 'That's the mango tree Kaa-chan planted. Hey, still bearing mangoes, after all these years.'

'Well, we've seen it, now let's head back. There's a TV show at three I want to catch,' Braden said.

I ignored Braden and proceeded the last few yards to the house, where I put the car in park and set the waypoint, before turning off the ignition. 'Come on, everyone. Let's get out and take a good look. Courtney, bring that camcorder, OK?'

I pressed the button to roll back the side doors, and my father and Uncle Yosh disembarked.

'Don't step on the porch, it looks like you could fall straight through,' I warned.

'Yes, yes,' my father soothed. 'Don't worry so much, Rei-chan. Come out and see for yourself.'

'I'm not going,' Braden said, after I got out of my side and walked around the car to his.

'Fine. That's your choice.' I gave him one last pitying look, then walked toward where my family had gathered on the straggly weeds outside the front of the house. 'See, here are the flowers my mother planted,' Yoshitsune said, pointing to a twisted little hibiscus plant that had somehow survived. Hibiscus: a lovely imported but hardy flower, like Harue herself.

'And if you continue round the house, you'll see our old vegetable garden.' Uncle Yoshitsune was leading the tour, and we all followed him around to the back, paralleling rutted tire tracks that seemed to end at the back, and an opening where a door must once have been.

'Oh dear,' said my father. 'It looks like the door was broken, and someone has made a terrible mess inside.'

We stood there gaping at piles of rock, in varying shades of gold and brown, and sizes ranging from plate-sized to doorstop. The piles were roughly grouped by color.

'The lava rock,' I said at the same time I heard the minivan's engine. I bolted around the corner of the house, only to see Braden reversing the Odyssey, turning sharply, and driving off in a cloud of dust.

'Where's he going?' Uncle Yosh yelled. 'Who that boy think he is, driving alone? He only got a learner's permit.'

Courtney followed the progress of her brother with the camera. 'Wow. He's going to get it, when Dad gets home!'

How were any of us going to get home? That was the question. All thoughts of spending a leisurely few hours on Yoshitsune's old property were gone. It was hot, and we had two elderly people with health risks facing a trek of almost an hour to the gas station in the developed section of Barbers Point. If I were in better shape, and with the proper shoes, I could have run the distance to get help, but I imagined that I was as likely to wind up with heat exhaustion as anyone else in the group.

'Do you know the number for a taxi service around here?' I asked Uncle Yosh, relieved that at least my cell phone was with me, although the battery was low after my long conversation with Josiah Pierce the evening before.

'Nobody gonna find their way here,' Yosh said. 'And even if they might, drivers know better than to come in to a place marked no trespass. They don't have that same kind of map that Braden got with him in the minivan, yah?'

Now I thought of Albert Rivera, with the field glasses and surveillance cameras that Braden had mentioned. If he came upon us, we wouldn't have the maps to explain anything. I doubted that Rivera would shoot a group of unarmed visitors, but he could be nasty enough to give my father high blood pressure, or worse.

I knew Michael would have wanted me to call him. But I also knew that at this moment he was having lunch with his JAG friend, and the last thing I wanted to do was alert the Navy's legal division that Michael had given us maps of their land. And even if Michael tried to find us, he didn't have the maps either, to follow our route, and his convertible could only take three passengers.

It was all such a mess, but I could see why Braden had taken off. Here was the thing that had gotten him in trouble, staring him straight in the face. He ran the risk of being caught red-handed, looking as if he was up to trouble again.

The sound of a loud engine drew near, breaking into my rambling, panicked thoughts. It could be Braden returning, or Alberto Rivera, maybe even with Mitsuo Kikuchi on board.

'Let's go by the rocks. Nobody see us there,' Uncle Yosh said, as if reading my thoughts.

'Yes, you do that; take everyone over, and I'll check who's there, and if they look OK I'll ask for help,' I said. I didn't want to be too far away, if it turned out the driver was just a local passing through who might prove perfectly willing to help.

'No, Rei-chan, that's not a good idea. You go with Courtney and your great-uncle,' my father said.

'But Otoosan, I know the man who manages this land, and the one who owns it, too. Regardless of who shows up, I can explain.'

I couldn't convince my father to leave me, though, even as the sound of the motor grew louder, and Uncle Yosh and Courtney had gone toward the craggy rocks at the water's edge. They'd just taken cover when, through a cloud of dust, a dirty white truck appeared. It followed the thick, rutted tire trail that wound around to the back of the house and, sensing the driver's intent, I gestured for my father to follow me from the back of the house to the long side where the bedrooms must have been. The truck stopped, and I heard the sound of feet crunching on the ground, then the slam of the truck door. Then the person stepped up easily inside the house, moving into the old kitchen crammed with rocks. We couldn't see him, but I peeked around the corner, trying to get a look at the man.

He was too far into the house; I couldn't see him at all. But I did get a better view of the truck – a Toyota Tacoma, its two seats slip-covered in blue and white floral cotton, and its back window marked with a Kamehameha School decal. The last time I'd seen the back of this truck, it had been crammed with the surviving items from Aloha Morning. Now the payload was empty save for several folded white tarpaulins, which I imagined would be used to cover up the lava rock once Kainoa Stevens had loaded what he needed.

# Thirty-One

Iknew enough not to show myself – too much was at risk. I remembered Braden's words about dying, if he snitched. And now I felt anger build in me, as I remembered what Kainoa had said, and how he'd effortlessly gathered intelligence on my family's futile quest. Everything was starting to fall into place: Kainoa's mention of a sideline construction operation, and the nervousness he had shown about Albert Rivera, who must have seen him on Pierce lands before and suspected something.

It took Kainoa almost half an hour to carry the rocks he needed out of the house, and the worst part about waiting was knowing that I could have been recording it all with the camcorder, if Courtney didn't have that with her down by the shore. *Don't show yourselves*, I prayed silently to her and Uncle Yosh, who surely must have been wondering what was happening, for such a long time.

Finally, Kainoa's heavy breathing and grunting stopped, and I heard a tarpaulin being whisked over the payload. The truck drove off, slower than it had come, no doubt because of the weight. When the truck had disappeared, I ran out from the side of the house and gestured for Uncle Yosh and Courtney to join me.

'It was the rock man,' Uncle Yosh said. 'The bastard who get Braden in trouble, and won't tell nobody the truth about it! I peeped around the rock and caught a glimpse – very big guy. Hawaiian or Samoan, for real.'

'Yes, it's Kainoa Stevens. The guy who owned the coffee shop that burned down.' Now I was remembering Kainoa's tear-stained face the morning after the fire. Just how bad was he? Was he grieving for Charisse – not just because he'd found her, but because he had some culpability in her death, too?

I was caught unaware by the sound of wheels on a rutted path. Oh God, he'd come back, and we weren't in a position to get to the water in time. I saw the fear on my relatives' faces as well, but the cloud of dust revealed a surprising sight: our battered Honda Odyssey. Braden had returned. He drove slowly all the way over to Uncle Yoshitsune and my father, and then stopped. He made no move to open the passenger door, so I pulled it open for us.

'I got lost.' Braden looked sheepish. 'I couldn't read the map and drive at the same time, and the damn GPS sent me in a circle back to this place. Then I got to thinking, I really should come back for you.'

'I'd say so, fool!' Uncle Yosh sputtered. 'You leave us out there to . . . what, sweat to death?'

'It's OK,' I said, helping Uncle Yosh and my father board into the blessedly cool car. I shot a glance at the dashboard; Braden had burned a lot of gas driving through the fields. Hopefully, we'd have enough to get back home. 'Courtney, can you get some water bottles for everyone out of the very back?'

'I'm . . . I'm sorry,' Braden said. 'It's just, when I saw where we were going, I didn't know who we'd meet there.'

'Well, you were right to be wary. We met him,' I said, and as Braden's eyes popped, I clarified, 'I mean, we *saw* Kainoa. He didn't see us and wound up leaving with a load of lava rock about five minutes before you returned.'

'A tremendously lucky circumstance,' my father said.

'Well, it's my *beiju*,' Uncle Yoshitsune said. 'A lucky year.'

But not for everyone. As I showed Braden the way home, I thought about how the first thing I would do, once I got back to civilization, would be to make Kainoa Stevens pay for what he'd done.

But it wasn't that easy. Later that evening, sitting in the Kapolei police station with my father, Uncle Yosh, and Michael, a Kapolei police detective called Bill Vang told us he was interested, but needed much more to arrest Kainoa. They even pointed out that I hadn't even seen his face, but was identifying him on the basis of the truck and Courtney and Yosh's physical description.

'Can't you just put out a call to all police on the island to look out for his truck, and once they stop it, check under the tarps?'

'It's five hours since you saw him. He probably already unloaded it at whatever construction site he's working at,' said Lieutenant Vang. 'And if there's rock dust in his truck's payload, well, that's no big deal. On the Leeward Side, there's dust from rock and ashes from fire and red earth everywhere you look and touch. Of course that payload's gonna be dirty. My truck's dirty, too.'

'What about a wire?' Michael suggested.

'Huh?' Vang responded.

'I could confront Kainoa, wearing a wire, and get him to admit he was the one who ordered Braden to work.'

'You think he's going to talk about all of this to a *haole*? He's either gonna think you're a cop, or stupid. Better for the kid to face him, and get the direct instructions to hush up, or whatever. Yeah, tell you what, Braden wears a wire, and it turns out there is truth to this business about Kainoa Stevens' sideline, I'll talk to the arson investigator about it.'

'It's too dangerous for him,' Michael answered shortly, as Uncle Yosh, my father and I all nodded in agreement. He continued, 'Braden was too scared to come with us to see you this evening. How's he going to be effective with Kainoa and successfully hide the fact he's recording their conversation? You need someone with experience doing that kind of thing.'

'I could do it,' I volunteered, because the thought had come to me a few minutes earlier. 'It makes perfect sense. Kainoa considers me a friend. He gave me his card, and wrote down his phone number another time. Obviously, he'll meet me if I call him.'

'Rei, that's nice of you to want to help your cousin, but like Mike said, there's a lot to this kind of operation.' Vang sounded patronizing.

'I not only know how to wear a wire, I can set up a listening station,' I protested. 'Tell them, Michael!'

In a few minutes, Michael had laid out my few accomplishments at OCI in a way that left my father looking dazed and Uncle Yosh quite approving.

'You willing to do something, then, day after tomorrow maybe?' Vang asked.

'Tomorrow,' Michael said firmly. 'It has to be tomorrow.

I'm leaving the day after that, and I want to be part of this operation.'

But back at Pineapple Plantation that evening, I learned that my job was harder than I anticipated. My father was distraught and had to be reassured constantly that the police would be waiting moments away, ready to take over at the slightest indication of trouble. He enlisted Tom and Uncle Hiroshi in the effort to get me to change my mind, but I knew what I had to do.

'I couldn't do squat for our family, in regards to the cottage property,' I said. 'But you know, this is more important. How can I not try to save their child?'

After a while I left Michael to talk to them, and I went into my bedroom, where after fifteen minutes of scavenging through my messy underwear drawer I came up with the card with Kainoa's various phone numbers. I rang every number, and either got no response, or a chipper voicemail message: 'It's Kainoa. Leave it at the beep, brah.'

He might be fast asleep in bed, but I doubted it. I left messages on the phones that allowed me the chance. My request was simple – and, I hoped, intriguingly vague. I wanted him to call me back because I wanted to see him before leaving the island.

Michael retreated to the Hale Koa by midnight and we all went to bed, but I barely slept, turning over thoughts of how the operation would work and how I could best lead Kainoa into an incriminating conversation – that is, if I could locate him. In the wee hours of the morning, I remembered the second time Kainoa had given me a phone number; it was on a takeout menu, tucked into the pocket of some running shorts. I located the shorts lying neat, clean and folded, with an empty pocket, in my drawers. As soon as I judged it late enough in the morning not to disturb anyone, I went upstairs to the washing machine and dryer, and found the takeout menu crumpled in the wastebasket there. Tom must have tossed it when he was washing the clothes during my illness, I thought, looking with gratitude at the number. Maybe, just maybe, this would work.

I waited until seven to call, and it was answered by a young woman.

'Who's calling?' she demanded after I asked for Kainoa Stevens.

'This is Rei, a friend. I had a question about a building project.' I decided I had to say something, in case I was speaking with a girlfriend or wife.

'I'm Kainoa's cousin, Leila. I could take a message for him.'

'Oh, are you the one who makes the crocheted bikinis?'

'Yah. Why?'

'Your work is amazing.'

'For real?' She sounded warmer. 'Kainoa left for work around six this morning. Probably won't be back till dinner. He works a lot now, you know, because he lost everything in the fire.'

'Yes, it's terrible about Aloha Morning, not to mention Charisse. Could you tell Kainoa to call me?' I gave both my local number and the cell phone.

'I'll do that, but like I said, he isn't really a building expert. He helps my brother–in-law Gerry with labor sometimes, is all.'

'Oh, do you think I should talk to Gerry, then – is he based in Waikiki?'

'Gerry doesn't have a lot of time for talk. And no, he doesn't live in Waikiki. He's lives in Lanikai and got an office in Chinatown. Unless he's on site, that's where you'll find him'

'Lanikai the island?' I was trying to recall the geography of the Hawaiian chain.

'No, not Lanai! Lanikai is a neighborhood near Kailua. Where you from?'

'California. And what was Gerry's last name again?' I asked, although she'd never said it in the first place.

'Liang. They're Chinese. My sister Randy married a Chinese guy called Chin, and his sister Millie married Gerry. That's the connection.'

It was almost too much to follow, but there was one thing I had to verify. 'Is that Liang with an i?'

'Yep. How did you guess?'

The wire and microphone were undetectable, once I'd gotten it all inside the strapless bra I was wearing under a sundress with a tightly smocked bodice. I had friendly, hands-on assistance from Michael in a police station ladies' room with Vang and another police officer, Jose Fujioka, standing outside. I also had a tiny speaker in my ear that would permit all of them to secretly communicate with me in the duration of the time I was talking with Kainoa. But the first step was tracking him down, and since he still wasn't answering his cell phone, it seemed the likeliest place to start was with Gerald Liang.

Lanikai, the town that Leila had told me about, was on the windward side of the island – the green, picture-postcard Hawaii. I drove Michael's Sebring by myself through Kailua, a charming small town with huge old trees hanging over streets lined with simple, mostly 1950s houses; Lanikai was smaller, a neighborhood, really. As I drove along, Vang and the others were in a police van two blocks behind, but never seemed far, keeping up a steady travelogue in my ear. Apparently Lanikai had once been as unpretentious as Kailua, but now, the rich had torn down the old bungalows and replaced them with the elegant mansions that sat cheek-to-jowl. Almost every Lanikai home was surrounded by a wall and had a fancy gate, many of them crafted out of copper, just like the Kikuchi mansion back at Kainani. The wall around Gerald Liang's house had been built beautifully out of irregularly shaped green, gold and gray rocks. Lieutenant Vang confirmed my suspicion that this was a lava rock wall. I parked, watching their Escalade go by and take a left on the next street, where they'd wait for me.

I waited for two teenagers carrying surfboards to disappear into the neighbor's garden before I emerged from the convertible. Belatedly, I realized I'd left the top down, so I went back to the car to close it. It was sunny for the moment, but I knew that on the windward side, rain showers dropped by like uninvited guests.

I walked slowly toward Mr Liang's fancy copper gate decorated with dolphins – no, I realized with some distress, they were hammerhead sharks. I located a buzzer and pressed it, thinking what a shame it was I couldn't just go to the front door, where it was harder to be turned away.

'Yes?' a woman's voice yelled out of the speaker, making me jump.

'Hi, this is Rei Shimura,' I stammered. 'I'm a friend of Kainoa's; I came to see him—'

'Why you think he be here? My husband doesn't run a boarding house.'

I was guessing that this was Millie Liang. Her accent sounded local – local and pissed off. I asked, 'Oh, is Mr Liang on site somewhere? Maybe I could track him down there. It's kind of important,' I said.

'Oh, yeah? You pulled me out of the bathtub for this, and I was doing my ginseng mask. Now it cracked!'

'Your ginseng mask cracked? I'm so sorry!' As I spoke, I could hear Vang chuckling in the receiver I wore in my ear and fervently hoped the sound wouldn't pick up.

'Yah, it done crack, and I'm gonna get off now before my face is ruined.'

'Will you tell them I stopped by?' I asked, desperate to come away from the house with something.

'Don't repeat your name.' Vang's voice came in my ear.

I spoke again, before she could answer. 'Oh, thanks, then! Bye.' I stepped back, and walked back to my car, got in, and started it up, not bothering to take the time to lower my roof before I peeled off.

'If he's on site, it's not going to be too improbable for Rei to show up there,' I overheard Michael saying, at his location a block away.

Once I was back in Michael's car, I asked Vang why he'd told me not to repeat my last name.

'The less information that's left behind, the better,' he answered. 'You don't want Gerry Liang or Kainoa Stevens to feel stalked, especially as this search is turning out to be ongoing, and there are some things about Liang that could be trouble.'

'What kind of trouble?' I asked.

'Well, there are some rumors about gangs,' Vang said. 'Gangs and construction go hand in hand in a lot of places.'

'You know, we should try Chinatown,' said Fujioka. 'Liang's got a building on Smith Street.'

'I saw the name on a building, but it was so faded I didn't think anyone was there anymore,' I said.

'They are still there – I know, because they were cited for a fire code violation last year,' Fujioka replied, as I parked my car behind their Escalade, got out, and went to its driver's door to talk to them. 'It's a big shop, and they got all kinds of construction odds and ends below, and the office up top.'

'OK, to Chinatown then,' said Vang, 'Though I think the chances are slim. Liang is probably out working, and Stevens is probably hiding out somewhere.'

'So you guys will be around the corner again, listening?'

'Yah,' Vang said, grinning. 'And maybe while we wait, Mike can pick up some *manapua* from Char Hung Sut.'

I'd thought Michael would flatly refuse to leave the listening station when he thought I might be in danger, but instead, he eagerly started asking about other kinds of *char siu* pork dumplings sold, and whether they carried half-moon cakes. Perhaps he assumed that this stop would be a failure, like the one before.

But I had a hunch that something would happen. Maybe it was because this section of Smith, once I'd reached it, looked even shabbier than I'd remembered: a succession of attached twenties and thirties storefronts marred by peeling paint and grit. The only people on this particular block were a pair of lost Italian tourists and a veteran panhandler heading determinedly their way.

'What about you, Rei? Are you there?' Michael asked, while I was parking my car in front of the Liang Building.

'I just parked in front of the building. Can't you guys see me?'

'No, but we can hear you, and that's good enough,' Michael said. 'Before you go in, tell me what I can pick up for your lunch.'

'I don't know, Michael.' I was too distracted to think about food. 'Maybe something with tofu.'

'Tofu, are you kidding?' Vang laughed in the background.

'Hey, if nothing happens here, I want a sit-down lunch at Little Village. OK?'

The glass door was stamped Liang and Sons, in faded gold print that looked pre-war. I pulled at the grimy door handle, expecting it to be locked, but it opened to a narrow, terrazzo-tiled foyer lit by an exposed light bulb. My eyes passed over a listing of floor numbers and names. Horace Liang,

Doctor of Chinese Medicine, was supposedly on the third floor. Liang and Liang real estate was on the second, and Gerald Liang, construction, on the floor where I was standing.

'First floor, construction,' I said aloud, as if I were talking to myself, though of course I wasn't. The Escalade was parked blocks away, and I wanted Vang and Fujioka to know exactly where, within the building, I planned to be.

The obvious way into the construction office was through a different glass door which had brown paper taped over it, the way businesses do before they open to the public. Interesting, this place looked as if it had been around for a long time. I tried the door lightly and found it to be locked.

'Yah?' A rough male voice answered my knock. I thought it sounded like Kainoa, but I couldn't be sure.

'I can't hear you,' I called back. 'Can you let me in?'

I'd taken a gamble, but the door jerked open. I remained in place, but found myself looking at Kainoa. If he'd looked bad the morning of the fire, he looked worse now, with the kind of facial stubble that reminded me of the villain in old Popeye cartoons.

'Hi, there,' I said, and from the way his eyes studied me, it seemed as if he knew why I had come. Still, he kept the door open. Beyond the bulwark of Kainoa's massive body I saw the edges of a dusty room packed to overflowing with cardboard boxes, pipes and other construction materials.

'How d'you figure to find me here?' Kainoa's voice was still borderline unfriendly, but he stepped back into the room, allowing me to enter.

'So how long have you been working here in Chinatown?' I was scanning the room, looking for something, I just didn't know what.

'Just got here this morning, to help Ger— my boss get some shit together. I need something full-time, and this is going to be it for a while. As I was asking, how did you find me?'

'Your cousin Leila told me – I spoke to her on the phone this morning,' I added, when I saw Kainoa's shaggy eyebrows rise 'And she said you were the middleman for Gerald Liang on his construction projects.'

'Might be doing more, now that the shop's gone.'

'Was it just labor you sub-contracted for him before?' I was trying to phrase my questions carefully, the way the cops had suggested.

'Yah. How you know that?'

I was going to get nowhere, if I didn't reveal some of my hand. 'I know about the rocks you've been stockpiling in my family's old cottage.'

'That what Braden told you?' Kainoa's voice remained calm, but his expression was deadly.

'No, I drove out and saw the rocks myself. Braden didn't say anything; he was too scared, said the boss would kill him if he gave him away.'

'He said that about me?' Kainoa's voice cracked. 'What a liar – and you, too. I thought you were here out of compassion, or some bullshit thing like that.'

'Kainoa, just tell me what happened. You could save my cousin, if you'd just admit you sent him to get the rocks that morning.'

'But I didn't! I mean, not exactly.'

I wondered if 'not exactly' was going to be enough to satisfy the cops – somehow, I doubted it. I tried again. 'It was a case of bad timing, wasn't it?'

'Who's the girl?' A new voice cut through my concentration, and I saw Kainoa was no longer focused on me, but somebody else.

I turned and saw a short, scowling Asian man in his early forties. He wore a baggy green and white print aloha shirt and black shorts that revealed solid, muscular legs with tattoos like Kainoa had. But while Kainoa's tattoos were geometric Polynesian designs, Liang's were quite different; one leg was marked by the *kanji* characters for moon, power, and aggression, and the other bore the emblem of a Sino-Japanese mafia group, the Night Runners, which I recognized from a book of Michael's.

'My name is Rei Shimura,' I said. 'Are you Gerald Liang?'

'See if you can get him on the record,' Vang whispered into my ear.

*No way*, I said to myself. After reading the fine print on Liang's legs, I intended to separate from him as fast as possible.

'Yes, I'm Mr Liang. Has Kainoa been talking about his friends?'

'Not at all, Mr Liang,' Kainoa said hastily.

My mind was working overtime as the men exchanged tense looks. The cottage with the rocks piled up was still rented by the Liangs, according to Josiah Pierce. Maybe my original assumption that Kainoa had seized a forgotten property for his own purposes was wrong. Gerald Liang might have known about the cottage's uses for storage of illegally gathered lava rock – in fact, he might have been the one to decide to use the abandoned cottage to warehouse rock.

Belatedly, I realized both men were looking at me. I said, 'I was just catching up with Kainoa before I left the island.'

'You know how the mainland chicks are, Gerry.'

I glanced at Kainoa, who seemed to be trying to help with my cover. Why? Was Gerald Liang that dangerous? *Yes*, I thought, and perhaps he, and not Kainoa, was the actual big boss that Braden feared.

'You work for me a long time, Kainoa. You should understand by now to keep your social life off this jobsite.' Now Liang was scowling at Kainoa.

'Got it, boss. You go, babe. But first, this.' Kainoa grabbed me at an awkward angle for a hug that filled my nose filled with his musky body scent and my ear with his hot breath. As he kissed my mouth, and then moved to my ear, he whispered one word: 'Careful.'

And as I pulled apart from him, shocked by both the intimate touch and the warning, my earpiece dislodged. It bounced off my shoulder and landed on the floor with a soft click. Kainoa glanced at the earpiece lying between us, but, instead of picking up the tiny, peach-colored piece of plastic, he moved his foot over it. His eyes held mine for a second, as if to intensify his warning.

# Thirty-Two

Without my earpiece, I had no idea what Vang and Fujoika and even Michael might be advising me to do. I could only hope they'd shut up, because if voices started coming from the floor, it would surely alert Gerald Liang.

My instinct told me to leave. Fortunately, Gerald Liang seemed to think the same, because he grabbed me by my right elbow and started walking me to the door.

'How kind of you to walk me out, Mr Liang,' I said as we passed through the papered-over door into the grimy vestibule I'd entered only five minutes earlier.

Hawaii was a place of courtesy, so I thought my words would ease things, but Liang reached for my other arm. Instinctively, I brought one elbow up to free myself, hitting his nose on the way.

'I'm sorry,' I lied, turning toward the grimy glass door that was the only barrier between the building and the street. I was doing my best not to sound scared in front of Gerald Liang.

'You're not one of Kainoa's girls.'

I looked toward the brown-papered door and considered raising my voice to call for help. But I doubted Kainoa would be suicidal enough to battle his gang-member boss.

'I heard you, when I came into the room the back way.' Liang's voice was silky, and dangerous. 'You're trying to incriminate me.'

'What do you mean?' Resolutely, I turned away from the door. Now that it appeared he might say something worthy of the wire, I couldn't duck out.

'Well, you may not know that the penalty for taking lava rock is maybe a thousand bucks – chump change. I also gotta let you know that kind of charge would never be made.'

'Why?'

'The Pierces and I go way back.'

'Really? I just know one of them – Josiah Pierce, Junior. Is he the one who's your pal?'

'What's your interest in me?' His breath, so close to my face I could feel its warmth, smelled of tobacco and booze.

I shrugged, as if none of this was rattling me. 'It's not you; it's that my teenage cousin Braden was charged with arson, when we both know he was only out in the mountains gathering lava rock for you.'

He shook his head. 'You're not related to that boy. In fact, if you're not a mainlander, I'm not Chinese.'

'I'm a mainlander, yes, but my relatives live here. My cousin is Braden Shimura, the kid who's going to be charged with setting the fire, and everything bad that came out of it. Imagine what you'd feel like if your own child was in the wrong place doing a part-time job at the order of adults, and wound up getting railroaded for arson.'

'My kid don't work. I won't let him; he's on honor roll at Punahou.' He shook his head at me. 'So, who you thinking should be blamed for the fire?'

Remembering the wire on me, I decided to go for broke, as Uncle Yoshitsune might say. 'Well, I suppose some people might think the fire was ordered by you.'

'I go back with the Pierces, remember.' He tapped my forehead with a hard finger. 'Why would I set fire to their property?'

'The same reason you'd take rocks from it.'

He shook his head. 'You know nothing about this island, the way things work.'

'Tell me then.'

'Nobody gives Gerry Liang orders. But I'm warning you, Rei Shimura, I got a closet in a room upstairs for people who talk too much. It's kind of like a holding site until two of my boys can swing by, and you know, drop you off at a work site where we might be laying cement . . .'

'I don't want to go upstairs,' I said for the benefit of my colleagues, who were feeling awfully distant at that moment. 'I have a lunch appointment a few blocks downtown, and I need to get on the road.'

'Three o'clock?' he scoffed. 'This is Honolulu. Nobody eats lunch at three.'

'Early dinner?' My back was against the glass door, but unfortunately it wasn't the kind that simply pushed out. There was no easy escape.

'Get moving.' He slapped my face then, so hard that I was too stunned for a few seconds to do anything. But then, I maneuvered my free hand behind my back to turn the doorknob. To my horror, it didn't move.

He'd locked me in.

'Did you know the door's locked?' I asked, for the benefit of my hidden listeners, all the while striving to sound non-chalant.

He laughed and reached his other hand into a pants pocket to extricate a key ring. But instead of opening the door for me to get out, he unlocked the door to the upstairs floors. He fished into his pocket again and pointed a small, black gun straight at my face.

*Never go anywhere that the guy with the gun tells you to go.* This rule of life, drilled into me ever since I was a child in San Francisco, came to me now. As adrenaline surged, I yelled and I kicked as hard as I could at his groin.

The door to the room where I'd left Kainoa had opened, but through my grappling with Liang, it was pushed shut again. I heard glass shatter behind me, felt shards bounce on my bare shoulders like hail. Now I was being pulled back-wards, the left shoulder strap of my sundress breaking. From the crack in the other doorway, Kainoa stared as I tripped backwards out of the opened front door into the muggy, welcoming Chinatown air. And from the familiar smell, and the wiry strength of the arms and body, I knew who'd gotten hold of me: Michael.

'Stay there,' Michael snapped at Kainoa, who stepped back a pace and nodded.

'He's not the bad guy,' I said to Michael, my heart still jack-hammering.

'I know,' Michael said to me, and as Vang and Fujioka crowded into the foyer, he said to his colleagues in a voice as relaxed as if he was continuing the restaurant discussion, 'Liang's gone upstairs, and he's armed.'

Now that I was safe, I was flooded with feelings: relief at being in Michael's arms and not upstairs with Liang, anxiety for Kainoa, and some embarrassment that I'd had to be rescued.

I said to Michael in a low voice, 'I didn't mean to blow my cover. It just sort of happened.'

'Don't worry about that. What I want to know is why you didn't follow our instructions to vacate immediately when Liang walked into the room?' Michael demanded.

'I never heard it because my earpiece fell off.' The rest of what Michael was saying was drowned out by the sirens of three arriving police cars. At Michael's urging, Kainoa explained the layout of the building, including a back exit. Two men headed to the back of the building and the others went up the stairs to join their colleagues.

By now, a curious crowd of people had assembled – a few panhandlers, Asian merchants, and tourists with their camcorders. I tried to ignore the spectacle as best I could, but imagined I was going to wind up in a few home movies, broken dress strap and all.

'But this is so fast. Don't they need a warrant to go in?' I asked Michael.

'Honey, we all witnessed an attempted armed kidnapping. There's plenty of reason to go after the bastard.'

'I suppose so. But that's completely different from the reason I went in there – to get him to say something about Braden.' I turned, and spoke directly to Kainoa. 'I just wanted you to tell the truth.'

'If Liang wants the judge to knock a few years off his sentence, he's going to have to talk about his operation, sending minors out to steal rocks,' Michael said.

'You really think Liang's going down? He's got a lot of power behind him, if you catch my meaning,' Kainoa said. He no longer looked shaken; the mask of island cool was back.

'He'll go down for what just happened to Rei,' Michael said. 'Anything else you can help the cops with would be much appreciated. And it would help you, too.'

Michael and I drove back to the Leeward Side of the island with the Sebring's top down, a hot, dry wind whipping my hair across my face. I consciously avoided staring at the blackened fields on either side of us, focusing instead on the ocean shimmering in the mid-afternoon sun. My exultation at having completed the operation with success beyond our expectations was fading. I glanced at Michael, silently counting how many hours we had left before he flew to Washington that night.

I could have a lot more time with him, if we got married. But could it work? I knew what I loved about Michael, but I wasn't sure if he had a realistic picture of me. Would he wake up one morning, realize I wasn't going to be around forever, and feel the need to run?

Work was another problem. Michael had blithely mentioned giving up OCI, his life's passion, to avoid impropriety and give me a chance to continue. On the other hand, I was just a freelance contractor to the Japan Bureau, and while there were things about spy work I enjoyed, I couldn't see myself growing old taping wires in my lingerie.

'I don't know what to do,' I said aloud.

'I don't either,' Michael said. 'Do you think we should go to Braden's family first, or your own?'

'My father was pretty worried about the operation, so I want to see him first,' I said firmly.

'Let's not forget about Braden, though,' Michael said. 'Think how relieved he'll be to know Liang is in custody. Maybe this is all he needs to step forward and tell the truth about what was happening with the rocks.'

'Braden was scared of retaliation. He still might be, because of Liang's gang ties.'

Michael was silent for a moment, and then said, 'If it's all right with Edwin and Margaret, and the judge, Braden could come back with me to the mainland. There's a boys' boarding school in central Virginia I have in mind.'

'A surfer at an east-coast prep school?' I shook my head. 'Braden would hate it, and they'd never admit him anyway!'

'They're used to wild boys, Rei; it's their specialty, and I know there are generous scholarships for under-represented minorities.'

'Why do you know so much about this place?'

'I'm a trustee.' Michael shrugged, as if this was the most normal thing in the world.

'It just might work,' I said, wheels turning. 'If he agreed to go, and you did all the paperwork.'

'Everything will work out. I've got a gut feeling about this.' Michael slowed the car to stop at the traffic light and turned

to me. I put my head on his shoulder for a minute, until the
car beyond us honked, letting me know the light had
changed.

When we pulled up to the townhouse, we were met by the
now familiar sight of Edwin's car in our driveway. Well, maybe
it was all for the better: I could tell them that Braden's terrible
boss was now behind bars.

But when I got inside, nothing was what I expected. Edwin
and Margaret were crouched next to the sofa, where someone
lay motionless, with a blanket over him.

My father.

# Thirty-Three

'**Y**ou here at last!' Edwin shot a glare at me, filled with
what looked like a mixture of relief and anger. 'Your
dad's not feeling good at all.'

'How long has this been going on?' I was already at the
couch, looking at my father's closed eyes and sweating forehead, despite the full-force air-conditioning. He was alive,
but he needed a doctor. 'Has Tom examined him?' 'Tom and
Hiroshi are still playing golf on the other side of the island,
we think,' Margaret said. 'We think we got Tom's voicemail, but we're not positive, because the message was in
Japanese.'

'Yeah, fat lot of good your lawyer's done, taking away the
family doctor when we need him. I sent Braden and Courtney
to get that Calvin who lives with the Kikuchis,' Edwin said.

My father's eyes flickered open as I leaned over him. I
whispered, 'What's going on?'

My father's eyes remained closed, but he muttered,
'Headache. The worst I've ever had.'

The night before, I'd worried that my working with the
police might raise my father's blood pressure. Now I knew
that the worry had been valid, and blood pressure was the

least of it. I held my father tightly, willing him to live as I prayed. *No. Don't let this happen. It's not fair!*

'We should call an ambulance.' Michael's voice cut through my desperate prayers.

'Ambulance ride around here starts at six hundred dollars,' Edwin said. 'If you don't call the insurance first, they won't pay. And you better find out if the hospital's pre-approved.'

'Enough,' Michael snapped; he'd already made it to the kitchen, and the telephone on the counter.

The ambulance came within fifteen minutes, the slowest quarter of an hour that I'd ever passed. But in this time, I learned from Margaret that about thirty minutes had passed since my father had telephoned them, asking if they'd heard from me and then admitting he had a headache he was worried about. Now, I calculated, it would be around forty minutes to Queen's Medical Center, even in an ambulance speeding along the shoulder. And that could be too long, from what I'd read in all my stroke books.

Honolulu was too distant, but there was another option. I remembered Michael mentioning an emergency clinic in the other direction, up the coast.

'Can they treat stroke at the Waianae Comprehensive Health Care Center? And how far is it?' I asked the lead paramedic as they shifted my father from the couch to a gurney.

'Sure they can treat it. And it's ten miles away, a third of the distance to Queen's.'

'Well, that's where my father's going, then.' I said.

I rode along in the ambulance, an experience in itself with all the paraphernalia on the walls of the small van – tubes, canisters, pumps and paddles – all the things that could continue life. My father had an oxygen mask over his face and a paramedic at his side monitoring blood pressure and heartbeat.

The ambulance made a sharp right and began climbing a curving road up to the clinic. The land around the clinic was scrubby and rocky, and its small parking lot was filled with a mix of late-model cars and shabby older vehicles, some of them with surfboards strapped on top.

As the paramedics started unloading my father on his stretcher, Michael pulled up in the Sebring. He handed me my father's wallet. 'I found this. It's got his insurance card in it.'

'Thanks.' I hugged him for a long moment, thinking how odd it was that responsibility, and sexiness, seemed to be part of Michael in equal measures.

Michael kept his arm around me as I filled out my father's paperwork in the waiting room, and a few minutes after I'd handed it back to the nurse at the desk, the attending physician, Dr Yamashiro, emerged to get me. I waved to Michael and went off, shoulders squared and preparing for the worst.

'You are his daughter, right?'

I nodded.

'It's not another stroke. His brain looks good. Heart, too. But did your father have . . . psychiatric problems?'

'No, he didn't. Why do you ask that?'

'He's overdosed on lithium. We asked him for his list of regular medications and he didn't mention it, but sometimes, people are ashamed—'

'He was poisoned. I know for sure, because the same thing happened to me.'

'What do you mean?' The doctor looked at me with concern.

'Someone tampered with my food, sticking in a mixture of Lithium and Motrin. I had more than my dad, because it sent me into a kind of psychosis. I had to undergo haemodialysis at Queen's.'

'You mean . . . you didn't accidentally take these medicines together?' the doctor pushed.

Sometimes people were really slow. 'No. I was poisoned. Call the people at Queen's, compare what happened to me to what's going on with him.'

'Yes, you can release your medical records to us, if you'd like.' The doctor was already signaling to the nurse. 'Did you ever find the substance containing the drugs?'

'No. But if you let me talk to my father, maybe I will finally be able to find it.'


My father had two IV lines running in his arm, but was sitting up on the gurney when I was allowed back behind the curtains. I embraced him, and told him what a scare he'd given everyone. He told me that the doctors had already spoken to him about the treatment, and he was prepared to undergo two days of what I'd been through.

'The good thing is you never went as nuts as I did – and you can help me figure out what you ate that did this.'

'I have an idea, but I'm afraid to tell you.' My father's voice was weak. 'The last time I went to Safeway, to buy new food to replace that which was taken for examination, I bought a few Japanese-brand instant noodle bowls. Today, I couldn't resist the temptation.'

'It couldn't be the noodles. What did you drink today?'

'I made one cup of green tea with a new tea bag, and drank water the rest of the day. Bottled water, the Fiji brand.'

'You had nothing extra? You didn't add anything to the noodle bowl?'

'I chopped green onions and stirred them in to make it a little healthier.' He shook his head. 'You know, I feel bad about preparing the noodles, because I felt quite fine until about an hour after eating. Now I understand that kind of processed food isn't nearly as good as homemade.'

My father's propensity to tinker made me think he might not have stopped at green onions. I asked, 'Was there anything else you added to the noodle soup?'

'Well, I would have liked to add Sriracha sauce, but we don't have the bottle anymore, so I used a pinch of *wasabi*.' He made a pinching gesture with his finger.

'*Wasabi*? Did you order sushi for dinner last night?' By the time Michael and I had arrived home, the kitchen had all been cleaned up; I had no idea what they'd eaten.

'No, I grilled an *ahi* tuna and ears of corn. Tom steamed brown rice, too.'

'But where did the *wasabi* come from?'

'The fridge – a small container.' At my shocked expression, he said, 'I believe it must be something that Hiroshi and Tom brought back from the pool concession stand. They serve sushi there, you know. I found it in a corner of the refrigerator's door.'

'What did the *wasabi* look like?' I asked.

'Quite pale; it's the fresh *wasabi* without an artificial color. It came in a small, covered plastic cup.'

'That sounds like the condiment Calvin brought along with the restaurant sushi, earlier in the week.' My thoughts were racing faster than the words could come out. 'I must have taken the *wasabi* container out of the sushi box, when I was fixing my own plate, and put it down somewhere else in the fridge, where it was missed by the police inspectors.'

'I can't believe it.' My father sounded as dazed as I felt.

'Why would Calvin do it?' I asked, then moved on to something more important. 'Dad, what did you do with the *wasabi* container after you were finished seasoning the soup?'

'I returned it to the refrigerator, but this time on the top shelf.'

I recalled Calvin's most recent, annoying visit. Uninvited, he'd opened our fridge to get himself a drink. Perhaps that had been his intent; to check that the *wasabi* was gone – or had he intended to add more poison to it?

'Dad, if it's OK with you, I'm going home for a while. I have to find that *wasabi*.' I stood up.

'Just wait. I'm thinking, Rei-chan,' my father said. 'Don't jump to conclusions about Calvin's behavior. There's a chance he's suffering an illness.'

'What do you mean?'

'To behave like this makes me think of one disease in particular: Munchausen's-by-proxy.'

'I don't think so. He's super-fit; he didn't look like he had any kind of disease, let alone a German-sounding one.'

'Munchausen's is a psychiatric disorder, named for a German doctor who studied a woman who intentionally made herself very ill, repeatedly, because she craved the attention of a physician. In Munchausen's-by-proxy, some people – often the parents of helpless children – intentionally sicken or disable someone.'

'Weird,' I said. 'Very weird.' But I could see my father's point, because ever since we'd arrived at Kainani, Calvin had been overly interested in our family. Perhaps he thought that if one of us became quite ill, he could become indispensable.

'I can understand that a few people out of every ten thousand or so might have this problem, but a psychiatrist with a great job in Oahu?' I couldn't hide my skepticism.

'Maybe he chose to work with a private patient because he had trouble in a hospital setting,' my father said. 'Another reason is that a percentage of people are attracted to psychiatry or psychology careers to find answers to their own problems. Not everyone succeeds.'

'I hope to God that somebody remembered to lock our house.' I'd been the first one out, following my father to the ambulance, with Michael right after me. Edwin and Margaret were still at the resort, trying to find Courtney and Braden. I hadn't thought to leave them my key to lock the door.

'Rei-chan, please relax. I'm so relieved the cause was found quickly, and . . .' Looking bilious, my father cut himself off. I looked wildly around until I spotted a bedpan. Afterward, my father's voice was barely a whisper. 'The more I get out, the better.'

'I'll stay longer,' I said.

My father shook his head. 'I'm in good hands here, so please do what you need to – check the house lock. But not alone, go with your . . . with Michael.'

After the nurse I'd summoned had arrived to help my father clean up, I said goodbye and went to the waiting room, where I found Michael had been joined by Edwin and Margaret.

'My father's stable,' I said. 'He's sick to his stomach and still has the headache, but it turned out he was poisoned. It wasn't another stroke.'

Michael sat bolt upright, and looked ready to say something, but Edwin spoke first.

'Food poisoning can come from shopping at chains stocking mainland food. You should have shopped at the Kapolei farmer's market. Your Uncle Yosh will take you there next time.'

'I know where the poison was: in the *wasabi*, which was leftover from sushi that Calvin brought for me. It must have fallen into a place in the refrigerator where the health inspector missed it, but unfortunately, my father found it today and ate some.'

'But why?' Margaret sounded incredulous.

'He may have been concerned I was going to muck up the land deal for his boss. Perhaps they talked about it privately, and it was decided that Calvin needed to make me sick enough, at least, to stop pursuing the matter,' I said.

'I'm sorry.' Edwin's voice came slowly, and there was a

tone to it that I hadn't heard before. 'I invited you to visit Hawaii, thinking many good things could come out of it. I never dreamed . . . this. But it's my fault, I guess, just like everything that happened with Braden.'

'Edwin, it's not your fault,' I said, and was surprised to realize that I meant this wholeheartedly.

'It's Calvin's fault,' Michael said crisply. 'And we're going to do something about it, as soon as possible.'

'Braden and Courtney went to find him,' Margaret said. 'Thank God they didn't, and we brought them with us—'

'Before you left, did you lock the door?'

Edwin and Margaret exchanged glances, and shook their heads. 'Sorry,' Edwin said again. 'Here in Hawaii, we don't always think of that.'

'It's OK. If you'd wait here, I'm sure you can see my father in a bit. Michael and I will go back and take care of locking up.'

'Say something to Courtney and Braden on the way out. They're waiting outside the clinic,' Margaret said.

Michael and I walked out of the clinic together, and found Braden lounging on a low retaining wall, smoking. At the sight of us, he dropped the cigarette in the scrubby area on the other side of the wall.

'That's how fires start, Braden. Put it out.' Michael's voice was tight, and I realized he was very angry.

'I did, man.'

Michael picked up the cigarette and stuck the ashy butt right between Braden's lips. He yelped, and then spit it out on the cement.

'Always extinguish it with something wet,' Michael said. 'Now throw it away.'

'How's Uncle Toshiro?' Courtney sounded anxious.

I answered, 'He's going to be just fine, but I want to ask you both what happened when you went to look for Calvin Morita.'

'We went all the way to the Kikuchi house and rang the doorbell, but nobody answered,' Braden said. 'A person came by and said he thought the Kikuchis went to Maui. He saw Calvin out around the resort, jogging.'

'Thanks, Braden. We better get moving. You're flying out tonight, remember?' I pulled on Michael's hand.

'I'm not flying anywhere tonight. Rei, isn't there some-thing you want to tell Braden?' Michael asked. 'About the cops taking in Gerry Liang?'

'Oh, of course.' I told Braden that Gerry Liang had been recorded admitting that he contracted underlings to dig up rocks all over the island, and that was his smallest problem, given that he'd been booked for attempted assault and kidnap-ping.

'Is Kainoa going to go to jail, too?' Braden asked at the end of it.

'He'll probably get some fine or minor punishment for being a middleman in the business, but the more he talks about Gerald Liang's business practices, the easier things will be for him,' Michael said.

I was impressed that Braden had asked about Kainoa first, rather than whether he, himself, was out of trouble. I wasn't sure of the reason, though. 'Braden, I wanted to ask you some-thing you couldn't answer before. It's about the guy who threatened to kill you – was it really Kainoa?'

Braden looked around as if to make sure there really were no other listeners before he answered. 'No, Kainoa's OK. It was Gerry Liang. He said that to Kainoa, in front of me. If a guy as big as Kainoa looked like he was about to shit bricks, it taught me to look the other way, and keep the mouth shut.'

'Things will work better for you, Braden, from now on.' Michael's voice was warm. 'But I want you to think about what kind of man you want to become, now that you won't be charged with arson.'

'Whaddya mean, I won't be charged?'

'No, the arson investigator is definitely dropping charges, but the police expect you to testify in the case they're building against Liang.'

'Michael, he still needs professional legal help, if he's going to talk to anyone,' I pointed out.

'He's got that.' Michael grinned at me. 'Hugh talked to Edwin and convinced him to apologize to Lisa Ping and rehire her. It was a good decision, because she's the one who called with the news about the legal break that's opened for Braden, if he's strong enough to take it.'

As Michael spoke, a range of emotions passed across

Braden's face – disbelief followed by apprehension. Finally, he asked, 'Why did you do this for me?'

'You know why,' Michael said. 'I remember what it's like to stand at the edge of a cliff. I stepped back, and look where I am today.'

'It's a little different for me,' I said, looking warmly at both Braden and Courtney. 'I never had any brothers and sisters, and I thought I'd have a child by now, but I don't. You two are the only kids in my life. That's why I don't want you in reform school or jail, OK?'

'We're going back to the house now.' Michael clapped Braden on the shoulder, and ruffled Courtney's hair. To her, he said, 'You're the one who puts up with nonsense all the time, aren't you? We need to think of something special to do for you, before we all leave.'

# Thirty-Four

Moments later, Michael and I were driving ten miles above the speed limit back to the resort. Because I was in a convertible instead of the closed-in ambulance, I could see out, and realized we were passing the Hawaiian Homesteads that Josiah Pierce had been talking about. The soaring Waianae mountains were beautiful, but their foothills were marked by shanties and trailers around which wandered children, chickens and dogs. A fierce wind was blowing the laundry hanging on outdoor lines almost horizontal to the ground.

I was starting to feel like a gawker, so I looked fixedly at the ocean on my right. But soon we came to a long, sandy beach which was marred by hundreds of tents and a few cars and trucks that had seen harder times. Was it a camper's convention? I wondered, until I saw a weather-beaten baby swing blowing from a tree branch. Hawaiians walked between tents, visiting with each other. Some stirred a bonfire, apparently cooking. So this was an even harsher homeland, for the home-less.

I tried to bring my attention back from this sorrow to the present, but I was feeling pessimistic. I said, 'Braden threw the cigarette in the grass like he did that kind of thing all the time.'

'Are you thinking he still might have been the one to start the fire?'

I nodded.

'Well, I don't even care about what Braden did or didn't do anymore.' Michael's voice was fierce. 'I just want to get my hands around that bastard's throat.'

'Calvin?'

Michael made an exasperated sound in his throat. 'Obviously. He almost murdered you, and if that wasn't enough, your father too. He's not going to get away with it.'

'My dad thinks it's a mental disorder, that he might have something called Munchausen's-by-proxy where you intentionally make people sick, but it's really out of the perpetrator's control.'

Michael shook his head. 'Your dad's a very nice guy. Buddhist, right? His gentle philosophy shows, but I don't buy it for a second.'

'Once I find the *wasabi* container we can call the police. Or maybe it should be the health inspector first?' I waited for Michael's opinion, but it didn't come, and that made me nervous.

We arrived at Kainani with the sun at its late-afternoon peak. A hot, rough wind raced through the trees and plants around the house. A newspaper from another house's *lanai* whipped across me as I emerged from the convertible.

'The door's locked. That's good,' I said, testing the handle. I'd been unable to shake my worry that Calvin had entered the townhouse and removed the only evidence that could connect him with the poisonings.

After I unlocked the door, I kicked off my sandals and headed toward the fridge. My father had said he'd returned the *wasabi* container to the second shelf of the fridge, where it would be easy to see. I began scanning for it, but among the many groceries there, it wasn't obvious.

'Rei-chan! Once we were driving home and checked the telephone, we heard your father was ill. Where is he?' Tom's voice came from upstairs.

'We had an ambulance take him to the emergency room at Waianae. But it's all right, I just came from there.' I spoke distractedly as I continued to search the fridge with no luck.

'Oh, no.' Tom clattered down the steps in fresh shorts and T-shirt. His hair was wet, as if he'd just taken a shower. When he saw Michael, he nodded shortly. Tom had been the one who'd answered the phone when I'd called the previous night to say I wouldn't be home.

'Hello,' Michael said.

'Hello,' Tom answered him shortly. 'Why not Queen's in Honolulu? They know him there.'

'The first sixty minutes after a stroke are the golden hour,' I said. 'I thought he needed care as fast as possible.'

Tom nodded. 'Yes, of course. That was the proper decision. Sorry for my haste. And was it . . . I mean, is it . . . a stroke?'

'He had an MRI and his brain's fine, and they also checked for heart attack. They think he has a case of lithium poisoning. And I think I know where it came from: the *wasabi* that Calvin offered me with my sushi, the night before I became sick.'

Tom interrupted me. 'How could any *wasabi* be in the fridge? I've not seen it, and I know a food inspector took everything away.'

'This small container must have been missed. Dad said he found it in a corner of the fridge door. He was so eager to add spice to his bowl of ramen that he just scooped some out of the container without thinking about whether it was old or new.'

Tom's words came slowly. 'If the *wasabi* was poisoned with drugs, that means Calvin is the likeliest person to be the poisoner.'

'Yes; Calvin's goal was to murder Rei,' Michael said. 'We're thinking that the poison was left behind accidentally, and it was taken by Dr Shimura.'

'But Calvin was just here!' Tom's voice rose in alarm.

'What?' I exclaimed.

'My father and I came in from golf and went upstairs to take our showers. Otoosan dressed first, and when he went downstairs, he saw Calvin had arrived. Apparently he came to say hello, because he'd heard our young cousins, Braden and Courtney, had been looking for him. Father offered him a glass of juice, and the two had a short chat, during which time I came down, and then the two of them – my father and Calvin – went out for a walk.'

'Where's Uncle Hiroshi now?' I'd finished taking everything out of the fridge in my fruitless search. 'Let's hear from him exactly what happened.'

'As I said, he left the house with Calvin. He was planning to walk to the hotel gift shop to pick up a Japanese newspaper.'

'How long ago did this all happen?' Michael asked.

'I'm not sure,' Tom answered. 'About forty minutes, maybe? Just before the big winds started to blow.'

'Was Calvin going to go to the hotel with Uncle Hiroshi?' I asked.

'I don't think so – let me call my father. He might have the cell phone with him.' Tom punched the number into his own phone, and then had a brief conversation with his father in Japanese. To us, he said, 'Calvin turned after the gate for our development to go to his house, and as I thought, my father continued on to the hotel. Father said Calvin told him that he would be home this evening listening to some music while the Kikuchis are away in Maui. He extended an invitation to us to please visit, if we have the time.'

By now, I was digging through the top of the kitchen trash: mango remnants, old paper, empty water bottles, but nothing that looked like a *wasabi* container. Where else could he have put it? I ran to the little waste can in the hallway bathroom. Nothing there either.

'Don't run water down the kitchen sink,' Michael said to Tom. 'There's a chance there's residue there. But Rei and I are going to head out to try to find this container.'

'How can you do that?' Tom raised his hands helplessly. 'It's probably floating out in the Pacific right now. I mean, his house is right on the beach.'

'Not so fast,' Michael said. 'We'll start by checking trash cans along the route they took. You can help us, if you like.'

I interrupted, 'There won't be any trash cans anywhere. Trash collection isn't until Monday, and there's a prohibition against putting out the cans until that morning.'

'Should we call the police?' Tom said.

'I can tell you right now there isn't enough for a warrant,' Michael said.

'How can you be so sure of everything?' Tom's voice was sharp.

'If he told you, he'd have to kill you,' I said to Tom, smiling as I parroted the old joke, but still giving him a significant look.

'All I ask is that you give me a chance,' Michael said, looking straight at my cousin, who nodded very slightly.

'I want to help,' Tom said. 'Rei may have forgotten to mention that I was in the kendo club at Keio. I may not be able to kill a man with my bare hands, but I can hold my own quite well with a stick, bat or club.'

Michael smiled. 'OK, then. Rei, is Tom's number programmed into your phone?'

'Yes. What are you proposing we do?'

'I want to make a visit with Calvin, and have a conversation.'

'Oh, yes, I'd like to tell him something,' Tom said.

'All in good time.' Michael's voice was soothing. 'We'll call you when to come, Tom. In the meantime, I think you should stay here in case anybody telephones on the landline. Maybe your father can get to the clinic to check on Dr Shimura. Rei and I have to go shopping for a few supplies.'

'Exactly what is your intention?' I asked Michael, when we were driving to the shopping center in Kapolei. 'I can guess you're going to wire yourself, or me, but you can't imagine Calvin's going to confess if we go right over there.'

Michael shook his head. 'No, I'll go there at dusk, and will probably come by water.'

'Why do it the hard way?' I glanced to my right at the roiling Pacific. It was rough tonight; the radio announcer had said the waves would swell four to six feet.

'The waters and beaches are legally open to every man, woman and child in Hawaii. If we show up on the sandy beach on the other side of the mansion, technically we're not trespassing. And as Courtney mentioned, there's a camera at the regular entrance to the house.'

'There might be a camera in back too, Michael, and in any

case, why can't we just...' I broke off, remembering the answer to why we couldn't walk along the beach. Huge rocks had been turned up from the ocean floor, in order to create the sandy swimming lagoons. These rocks were mounded between the public areas of Kainani, and the private area where the Kikuchi house lay, creating an insurmountable boundary.

'Approaching by water will be a cinch. I'll line up Kurt and Parker to sail with me, and you can wait with Tom at your house, and if and when the timing is right, we'll call you to join us.'

'It's my family problem, just in case you haven't noticed,' I said sharply. 'You can't do it without me. You have no right.'

Michael was silent for a while, then said, 'I love you, Rei. It's not that I think you're too weak for this. I just would prefer you not to see me behaving in a way that you haven't before.'

'Oh, come off it, Michael. You're going to have a conversation, not a Guantanamo Bay interrogation. And I know more about Calvin than you do. I should be there the whole time.'

Michael looked at me for a long moment. 'All right, then. But don't say I didn't warn you.'

# Thirty-Five

The sun was going down in a glorious, painted-velvet kind of a sunset when we cast off from the Waikiki Yacht Club. The crew for *Four Guys on the Edge* was a full one, since Karen had insisted on joining Michael, Kurt and Parker. Eric and Jody Levine had already flown home, or they would have probably helped.

'I can't believe I'm supposed to fit in this,' I said, as I tried to pull a snug wetsuit top and shorts on, inside the boat's cabin. Despite the warmth of the ocean, I had to wear the wetsuit, because it was the only way to both conceal and keep dry the tape-recording equipment Michael had bought.

'Vaseline helps,' said Michael, who was just wearing swim trunks and a polo shirt. It was very nice being rubbed down – in fact, I wished that the experience would lead to something other than a night sail across roiling seas to an unwelcoming place. But, as Michael had said to Tom, our detective friends from the Kapolei Police Department wouldn't want to jump off to an unrelated mission at the same time they were booking Gerald Liang. Time was short, and we would have to act for ourselves.

The trip to Kainani was about twenty nautical miles, and with the winds as high as they were, the ride could be swift. The plan was to drop anchor several hundred feet down the beach from the Kikuchi mansion, and use a dinghy to get to shore. Kurt, Michael and I would use a walkie-talkie to stay in touch with Parker and Karen, who would stay on the boat and help us up when we returned with the dinghy.

I'd expected to be given a job on the boat, but I was advised to sit in the cockpit as Michael and the three others carefully guided *Four Guys on the Edge* out to sea. I'd thought the slow departure from the yacht club harbor would be the easy part, but there were so many obstacles to watch for – dozens of bobbing boats tied up on either side of the narrow channel as we were leaving, and moving boats either returning to the club or making their way out.

Once we were free of heavy boat traffic and sailing leeward, everyone relaxed, except for me. The boat pitched and dove in the choppy Pacific, and incomprehensible instructions flew back and forth between Michael and his friends.

'Did anyone check the forecast?' I asked when there was a lull in the shouting.

'Of course,' said Karen kindly. 'It's a beautiful night and we've got good sailing winds. No storms on the horizon.'

'Actually, it feels kind of stormy to me.' The winds were so strong, I would have considered it the best idea of all to abort the mission and return to Waikiki.

'Rei, you can stay aboard with Parker and me if you're nervous about anything.'

'I'm not nervous.' I gulped, because in the last few minutes, my seasickness had started.

'Karen's right. You can bail if you want,' Michael added.

'You mean bail right now?' Some water had sloshed over the side of the boat nearest me.

'Don't worry about that!' Michael chuckled. 'It's all part of the experience. But if you're not feeling well, go below deck for a little bit.'

'There is a bathroom there, right?' I asked as I half-crawled toward the stairs.

'It's just ahead. And don't throw up in it, OK?' Kurt said.

I started down the steep staircase just as the boat pitched and I fell forward on my hands and knees and face.

'That's the other thing,' Kurt called after me, laughing. 'Always take the ladder backwards.'

As I dabbed my scraped face with antiseptic from a first-aid kit Michael brought me, I thought to myself, if there was one person we didn't need along, it was Kurt. But Michael had insisted and I'd remembered how in Japan, he always liked to have backup in case things became dangerous.

The cabin was tastefully fitted in teak and brass, and there was even a neatly made bunk where I could lie. But the air was hot and stagnant, and after ten minutes below, I felt the need for air. I climbed the ladder, facing the right way this time, and emerged just as the boat swung to one side, nearly shooting me across the deck. But I kept my balance this time and crept back to the cockpit, gulping the salt air.

As we approached Barbers Point, the winds changed and almost seemed to swirl in circles. Kurt and Michael were furiously working to release lines from cleats, and Parker was shouting from the helm while Karen cranked the winch. All I could think about was how much longer would it be to Kainani – and whether I'd make it without being sick.

I realized after a few minutes that Michael was calling for me to join him. 'Is this the house, Rei?'

I crawled over, took Kurt's night-vision binoculars, and started to rise. Michael put his arm around me to help steady me, and slowly I took in what I'd never seen before: the resort from the water. Here was the twenty-story Kainani

Cove Inn, the row of wedding chapels, and the time-share tower. And there, past a heavy border of volcanic rocks and shrubbery, was the white Kikuchi mansion, with a few lights on.

Karen dropped anchor at a spot that seemed to me was quite far from shore, although Kurt opined that the position was too close. Michael said firmly, 'It's perfect.' Then to me, 'One last chance to decide what you're doing, Rei. I won't love you any less if you decide to stay aboard, but once we're in the water, there's no going back.'

'You can't do it without me,' I said. 'Let's go.'

The crash of the dinghy dropping into the water cut through the sound of the wild winds. Michael and Kurt dropped in first; I handed down a waterproof box containing the walkie-talkie and other supplies, which Michael strapped to himself in a waterproof equipment belt. At last, I climbed down a small ladder on the side of the sailboat and joined them.

I'd never been this far out in an ocean before, and certainly never been tossed about on such waves. As Michael and Kurt rowed, I recalled the sharks in Gerald Liang's gate design. If we capsized, my lifejacket could save me from going under, but not from sharks.

'There's something I want to ask you,' I shouted to Michael. 'What exactly are you planning to do to Calvin, as I'm getting his confession on tape?'

'It depends on how much he cooperates!' Michael leaned in so I could hear him over the wind and waves. 'I should ask what you're going to say.'

'I could tell him that I was bodysurfing at the hotel beach and got pushed along his way by the current.'

'It's pretty dark to be bodysurfing.'

'Oh. Maybe I was washed up along that horrible pile of rocks earlier, and was trying to find my way across them, and his house was closer than the rest of the resort?'

'Now you're talking . . . What is it, Kurt?'

On the other end of the dinghy, Kurt was shouting something about rocks.

'We don't want to hit the rocks, so we're going to drop anchor here,' Michael translated. 'We're going to have to swim or wade in the rest of the way.'

'No way!' To me, it looked like we were at least three hundred feet from the shore. It was going to be a challenge for me to get in, given the darkness and size of the waves, and I wasn't sure how we were going to get out, either.

Michael leaned over to kiss me, and spoke in my ear. 'Look how close the lights of the house are now. You can hang on to the strap of my lifejacket, if things get rough.'

After the rowboat was secured, Kurt slipped into the water and started walking, using a series of hand signals to indicate to us where the rocks were. Michael and I followed, and I was grateful for the buoyancy the life vest gave me. The hardest thing was not swallowing water from the giant waves and their spray. Kurt reached the beach in what seemed like five minutes, while Michael and I continued to struggle.

'It looks as if Kurt's started the reconnaissance,' Michael called out to me. 'Notice how he's creeping into shore – typical Navy Seal.'

I didn't answer because a massive wave was building, starting to pull me into its undertow. I wouldn't be able to fight it, but would it separate me from Michael?

I grabbed the strap on his life vest with both hands, and we were flung about like a toy, knocking against each other painfully.

'You're pushing me down,' Michael said, when we came out of it. 'Can you relax a little?'

'Yes, I'll just pretend I'm in the Kainani pool,' I said as I loosened my hold. 'Someone will be coming around with a low-glycemic index mango smoothie for me any minute.'

'Make mine strawberry, with extra sugar.'

That made me laugh. 'Michael, I've decided something.'

'Mmm?'

'If we make it in, and I recover from my injuries, I'll definitely marry you.'

Michael didn't answer, and suddenly, the wind was awfully loud. There was now a different feel to the water – not of power building behind, but something underneath. Michael finally spoke between hard breaths. 'It's a rip tide, and it's going to move us. Just let me hold you.'

The water pushed us again, and when I opened my eyes, I couldn't see Kurt on the beach anymore.

'Damn, I lost my belt. Did you see it?' Michael asked.
I shook my head.

'Well, at least we've got you.'

Michael's hold seemed to be stronger, as if he were pulling me in on both sides of my body, not just my left. In confusion I looked to the other side, and saw Kurt's face.

'Need a hand?'

'Thanks,' said Michael shortly, loosening his hold of me as the new, massive arms encircled me.

'Took me a while to catch up with you, but I saw where the current was heading,' Kurt said. As he powered me to shore, I relaxed in relief, unable to do anything but breathe.

'What the hell happened here? Mikey forgot how to swim?' Kurt asked as the shore grew closer.

'Kurt, give us a hand getting Rei to shore. I've got to find my belt, which ripped off in the waves.'

As Michael searched the water, I lay on the beach, catching my breath. It was dark, and there seemed to be only giant globs of seaweed and a discarded potato-chips bag nearby. The prospect of abandoning the mission, because we'd lost our equipment, seemed almost tempting. But then I thought about what Calvin had done to my father and me, and knew, as Michael had said, there could be no going back.

# Thirty-Six

'That was close,' Michael said to Kurt, when he finally swam back in, nothing in hand. 'Thanks a lot.'

'Yes, thank you,' I echoed.

Kurt shrugged his hulking shoulders. 'You two could have made it, but I was getting bored just hanging by myself.'

'I can't believe I lost my belt.' Michael sounded grim. 'Now Karen and Parker won't know what's going on.'

'Do you want me to look for it?' Kurt asked.

'I don't think there's any point. We can get him on tape; all that equipment's inside Rei's wetsuit.'

'Yes, I'm wearing everything we really need. I think we should just get it over with,' I said in a voice that was braver than I felt.

'Remember, I don't want you going inside the house. It's important for your safety,' Michael said.

'OK. But I'll have to connect with Calvin, and that could mean knocking on the door, stepping in the kitchen for a moment—'

'Enough chatter,' Kurt said. 'When I was checking the house out, I saw an Asian guy through the downstairs windows, in a huge room – I guess you could call it a home theater, or entertainment center. I'd like one just like it, only there's the problem of my military salary.'

'So Calvin really was planning to listen to music.' I told them what Tom had said to me.

'I don't know if there's music on because the windows were closed. All I can tell you is he was dancing like a fool,' Kurt said. 'Check out that second-floor balcony. Beautiful entry point.'

Michael cleared his throat. 'Ordinarily, Kurt, I'd say have fun, but there is no need for a home invasion. Calvin will answer the door when Rei calls on him, and we'll just back her up as needed.'

Kurt looked ticked off, so I smiled at him and said, 'There are jobs for everyone. Michael, will you please help me turn on the recorder inside my wetsuit? When that's fixed, Kurt can give us a tour around the house and explain what else he noticed. We'll go from there.'

Kurt had spotted a lot of interesting details, including which windows were locked and where the house alarms were, but he'd missed one crucial detail which I was to discover myself: the front door had no buzzer, bell or knocker. I knocked, and there was no response. I realized that probably nobody ever came to the front door, because all visitors would use the buzzer at the gate.

I silently rehearsed my cover story about the body surfing, and thought about what I'd do if I'd washed up at a house like this and felt desperate. I trekked around the house, heading for the big ground-floor *lanai*, a tropical fantasy veranda with its own pool and an elegant bar. Beyond that were ground-to-ceiling sliding glass doors leading to the entertainment room, lit up to reveal a massive flat screen television playing VH1 and low chairs upholstered in what looked like black velvet. On the wall, I spotted a few Haruki Murukami paintings. The object of my pursuit, Calvin Morita, was not in there.

I continued around the house and finally saw him illuminated through the window of a stainless steel and marble luxury kitchen. Calvin was mixing himself a cocktail, with blue and yellow liquids. I rapped on the door here, which had a glass window, and called his name. Clearly startled at first, he identified me, smiled, and moved toward the kitchen door.

'Rei! This is quite a surprise.' He opened the door wide, and stepped back to allow me entrance.

'For me, too.' I was breathing audibly, because I was nervous; I hoped he took that as a sign that I'd just come out of the water. 'I was body surfing around sunset, and the waves carried me right past the hotel beach. I started climbing my way back to land over the rocks, but it got so dark I didn't know if I'd make it . . . I hope you don't mind me coming this way!'

'What were you doing exerting yourself so soon after hospitalization? By the way, have you heard from the health department yet?'

'No. I assume they're operating on *aloha* time.'

'Well, I'll take you back to your house right away. Let me get my keys.'

This wasn't the way it was supposed to go; I couldn't leave Michael and Kurt on the beach, wondering.

'Actually, Calvin, could I have a drink first? I would love to sit outside with a simple glass of tap water.'

'Of course. I should have thought of that.' Calvin reached into a cabinet for a glass and filled it at a sink set into the kitchen island. I watched it unblinkingly; nothing was dropped in, so I took a sip. 'But why are you out, anyway? Don't you know your father's in the hospital?'

I thought quickly. He could suspect that my father was

poisoned, but he wouldn't know for sure. 'Yes, I took my father in hours ago, but he's fine – just a migraine headache. The MRI didn't indicate a stroke or anything like that. I got out of the house because he likes to lie in absolute dark and stillness; Tom is there with him, anyway.'

'Headaches can be a sign of trouble,' Calvin mused. 'Maybe he's got something else, a kind of influenza, perhaps.'

'I don't know. How I wish you'd been here earlier, when we sent my cousins to look for you. You would have known exactly what to do.'

'This is a change of direction for you.' Calvin smiled at me, as if pleasantly surprised. 'When we met, you wouldn't give me the time of day!'

'Calvin . . .' I paused, trying to look humble. 'I'm sorry that it took my father's sudden illness and the fact that Tom and Uncle Hiroshi can't always be there to realize how much we've all grown to depend on you. Ever since you've arrived, you've only wanted to help us. Why, you're practically part of the family.'

'Well, that's a relief. Are you sure you don't want a real drink to take outside? Oops, I just remembered that you shouldn't. It's not good for your recovery.'

I dropped my gaze, thinking how glad I was the recorder was on. He'd just given an indication he knew that what had poisoned me was a serious drug, rather than overgrown food bacteria. I needed more to get a warrant for his arrest, but if he was this loose already, and continuing to drink, our interview should be a snap.

Calvin stepped outdoors with a fresh drink for himself, and we retreated to the ocean-facing *lanai*.

'I just can't get enough of the ocean,' I said, angling myself so I was facing the direction away from the part of shoreline where Michael and Kurt were presumably hiding.

'Yes, I know what you mean,' he said, following my gaze. 'That's why, despite the unrelenting hours, I'm still with the Kikuchis after three years. The whole environment here is just so gorgeous that I really enjoy times like these all the more.'

'The stone underfoot is really nice,' I said. 'Is it lava rock?'

Calvin glanced down, and must have caught a glimpse of

more than the pavers, because he said, 'Whoa! What happened to your feet?'

'I must have gotten cut on the rocks.' My alibi was solid, thanks to the fact that I really had suffered some cuts and scratches coming in from the ocean. I'd been too stressed to notice when it was actually happening.

'I'll say. We need to go right back in and clean that. You might want to take a Vicodin for the pain. There's a vial of it in Jiro's bathroom.'

'I don't take painkillers. I'm kind of a health nut that way.'

'But I noticed . . . yes, you are limping! You must at least clean the cuts and bandage them.'

'I'm really not that badly off,' I protested, thinking that perhaps my father really had been correct about Calvin having Munchausen's-by-proxy.

'You've got to clean the cuts!' Calvin's voice was rising, probably loud enough for Michael and Kurt to hear. And based on that, I made my decision.

'OK, then. I'll clean them up myself in the powder room, and then I'll come out again and we can chat.'

'Excellent. And while you're in there, I'll look for a pair of flip-flops, or as they call them here, slippers.' He laughed.

I left the kitchen door open as I followed Calvin in and up the stairs.

'I'm going to let you use Jiro's bathroom; it was just cleaned. You'll see that as well as a deep bath with a handspray, there's a Toto toilet with the built-in-bidet. We get a lot of raves about that from the ladies.'

'I bet,' I said faintly. 'Isn't there a powder room downstairs?'

'Yes, but it doesn't have any first-aid supplies or painkillers. And like I said, the bath is perfect for cleaning your feet. Don't worry about using it; the cleaning lady will be in tomorrow morning.'

I locked the bathroom door and looked around for hidden cameras; when I found none, I relaxed. The bathroom truly was beautiful, with a large window facing the ocean, through which I could make out the lighted outline of *Four Guys on the Edge*. There were Japanese antiques and modern glass everywhere, including a massive Dale Chihuly vase with a single spray of helicona.

I turned on the hot water in the tub, and opened the sink's

mirrored medicine cabinet to look for band-aids. There was a pharmacy's worth of drugs inside: everyday painkillers and the Vicodin that Calvin had mentioned. My eyes lingered on the other vials – Zoloft and Paxil and Rohypnol, which I knew was a sedative sometimes used by rapists.

I wished I knew some trade names for Lithium, but I didn't, so I decided to tuck one of each pill in a toilet-paper wrapped bundle, which I inserted into my wetsuit top. I'd have all the pills evaluated later on by my father and Tom.

'Are you OK in there, Rei?' Calvin's voice, a few feet away, made me jump.

'Sure. I just decided to follow your recommendation and soak my feet a few minutes.'

'Of course. I brought you a robe, too, in case you want to slip into something more comfortable.'

Struggling to look pleased, I unlocked the door and took the classic blue and white *yukata* and slippers that he handed me.

'You found the band-aids all right? There's also a triple-antibiotic ointment.'

'I did. Thank you so much.'

'I'll be downstairs, cutie.' He winked at me.

The things I had to put up with in the name of investigation! I shut and relocked the door and settled back down at the edge of the tub. This was also a Japanese import; a special kind of tub with a stainless steel lining, and a control on the outside that could heat the water to a spa-like temperature. But the regular tap water was hot enough for my purposes, and I planned to be out soon.

The tub had already filled about five inches, and as I settled my feet in with gratitude and moved to turn off the faucets, I heard a knock at the door. Maybe Calvin had brought me a face cloth. I opened the door to find Michael standing there.

'I got in through the open kitchen door, after we'd made sure you'd both gone upstairs. We thought everything was happening *outside* the house, cutie.' Michael's whisper was clearly sarcastic.

'I was. But I did need to clean my feet and . . .' I pointed downstairs in horror. 'He's down there, Michael! How are you going to get away?'

'We know where he is. Kurt's hiding downstairs while I'll stay up here in the bedroom area.'

'We could change the questioning to here, then!'

'Not a good idea from a legal perspective. Get back out to the beach and we'll join you when we're done.'

'OK, don't get yourself worked up. I'm on my way out.'

'I'll only leave after you both are outside.' Michael slipped down a bedroom hallway just before Calvin's voice floated up from downstairs.

'Rei? Are you finished?'

'No, the water's just so soothing. I'll be out in a few more minutes.'

As I locked the door again, I put my feet back in the tub and began opening a band-aid, and I noticed something red floating up from the drain. I leaned closer, trying to figure out what it was. It looked like a piece of fabric – no, it was a band. A terry-covered hair band, the kind girls used to secure ponytails or braids.

Braids. A picture flashed into my mind of Charisse, the last time I'd seen her, with swinging braids tied in red. The band I was looking at was soaked, so it was a little darker than the one I'd seen her wear, but I was willing to bet that once it dried, it would be the same tomato hue.

# Thirty-Seven

The red hair band bobbed in the water before me, and like a sad echo, I remembered what Hugh had said about Jiro's unprosecuted crime in Japan.

As I stared at the band, my own memories surfaced too. I remembered the black Mercedes S-class speeding out of Kainani the morning I took my first run, with two men in front and a woman in back. Charisse was late to the coffee shop that morning. And I also recalled Kainoa complaining that Jiro and Calvin sometimes came to the coffee shop, angling to pick up Charisse.

*I've been to Kainani. I have a friend there.* Charisse had

smiled when she'd told me this, that very morning. A day later, she'd been absent from work, and the fire had flared out of control. The next day, arson investigators found her burned body.

Without thinking, I reached out to touch the hair band and discovered that some of its fibers were tangled in the underside of the trap. Maybe the trap had also caught some of Charisse's hair.

I knew that I shouldn't move the band, but nor could I allow it to be washed away. Still, I had to empty the tub. I carefully turned the stopper on the drain so the water didn't rush out too quickly. My intent was to let the band settle back down in its hiding place, protected until the police could come.

After two minutes all the water was gone, and my feet were clean and bandaged. Still, there was sand on the bottom of the tub, and I worried about the cleaning lady working hard the next morning to get rid of it. I wet a towel and carefully wiped the surface until it was spotless, then dried it. As I worked, I heard a thud and a dragging sound. I was on instant alert, thinking about Kurt. Had he moved against Calvin?

I dropped the wet towels in a hamper made from an old Japanese basket and stepped out of the bathroom on to the soft, white carpet. I glanced down the hallway where Michael had gone and saw an unmistakable trail of sand. I couldn't allow it to stay, no matter what might be unfolding downstairs.

I turned back to the bathroom to pick up another towel, dampened it, and began to clean up the sand.

'What are you doing?'

I jumped because Calvin was standing right behind me; apparently he'd walked up the carpeted stairs without making a sound.

'My . . . the sand.' He'd caught me off guard, and my words came out before my thoughts were aligned. 'I'm sorry that I dropped some sand.'

'All the way *there*?' He pointed toward the bedrooms, where I'd last seen Michael go. 'Where were you going, and why haven't you showered and dressed in the *yukata* I brought you?'

He sounded like a bossy little boy; I would have rolled my

eyes and snickered if we'd been by the pool. But I couldn't do that here, so I turned my lips into a smile that I hoped looked helpless and endearing.

Calvin shook a finger at me. 'Rei, I told you before, it's time to take off that wetsuit. I brought you that robe to wear.'

'Calvin, that's not . . . that's not proper! You know how old-fashioned my father is!'

I'd barely gotten the words out before Calvin slammed me against the wall. Now I was regretting how I'd joked about his muscles, because I'd underestimated his capabilities. I wondered how long Michael would hide before he came to my aid.

'Your father doesn't know you're here – anyway, he's still at Waianae Clinic,' Calvin said. 'When I telephoned Tom just now to double-check, that's what he told me. And that's where he was going, because apparently there's a complication.'

'A complication?' I caught my breath, hoping either Tom or Calvin was bluffing. But if there had been a real complication . . . No, I told myself. My father is in a safe place, with a good doctor.

'Tom said he thought you were out swimming and was quite worried you didn't come back,' Calvin said. 'He has no idea you're in this house. Nobody else does, either.'

He was smiling an odd smile, and now my heart was working overtime. Tom knew I was here, but I remembered how I'd drilled him not to do anything until he got the call to come. Perhaps he thought I was still on the boat. Who knew what he thought; it was just unfortunate I had no way to contact him. Michael could; that was the only hope, but then Michael wasn't about to leave the house until I did.

'Calvin, I'm so sorry about the sand. May I borrow your vacuum?' I tried to wiggle my shoulders away from his hands. I had to get an excuse to get away from him.

'The game's up, Rei.'

'What game?' I spoke loudly. 'It sounds as if you're threatening me.'

'You're completely alone now.'

'Of course I am.' I was measuring distances – eight steps down the hall to the stairs, but his short, solid body to get past. Ten steps in the other direction, to the bedroom where Michael had gone.

'I've taken care of your boyfriend. And the other one, too, the guy with no hair. It amazes me how many fellows these days want to look like chemotherapy patients.'

'How . . .?' I was unable to finish the sentence. Despite Kurt's strength, I couldn't believe he could have physically triumphed over Michael or Kurt, let alone both. Had he forced them to poison themselves or shot them with silencers? Or was he bluffing?

'Do you want to know what happened to them?'

'Calvin, I'm afraid I don't know—' I switched tactics midstream. 'Yes, I was swimming with Michael and one of his friends before the riptide carried me out, and if they've come to find me, that makes sense, doesn't it? I'm sorry if they entered without ringing the bell . . .'

'They certainly didn't.'

'Well, I suppose you better tell me what you did with them, then!' I spoke up for the benefit of the mini tape-recorder. Maybe it would be the only way to tell the story . . . But no, I couldn't think like that.

'Jiro ran into the bald one in the entertainment center, and got him under control with one of his toys. After we got him bound and put away, we got Michael.'

'What kind of toys are you talking about?' I asked.

Calvin released one hand to reach into his cargo shorts and pull out a black rectangular object that looked like a slightly large razor. Not a razor – a stun gun, the weapon that was easy to buy, and legal almost everywhere.

'Did you use that on Charisse, too?' I asked.

'Didn't need to. That was, well, an accident after a good time was had by all. A shame, but nobody would ever have thought anything more about it if it wasn't for you.'

'An accident, maybe, but you chose to move her body and burn it.' I kept my eyes on the stun gun. Was he going to use it on me, too? I wondered if the wetsuit would offer me any degree of protection.

'What do you think we should do, call the ambulance and say our favorite stupid girlfriend got hurt?' Calvin answered sarcastically. 'Hey, as you know, I'm under orders to keep Jiro calm and out of trouble.'

'First, do no harm. Isn't that the first line in the Hippocratic Oath? I should know; my father has it framed in his office.'

I saw a strange expression cross Calvin's face – a mixture of anger and shame. I'd broken through, reminded him of what he'd once hoped to be. In that moment I brought up my free hand and smashed his nose, sending him rearing backward as I broke out of his weakened, one-handed grip.

I ran the three steps to the bathroom, but Calvin had recovered and was on my heels in no time. As I struggled with the flimsy lock, he pushed his way in and I was left with no recourse but to jump atop the toilet, reach toward the towel cabinet where I grabbed up the Chihuly vase and flung it straight at his forehead.

Calvin collapsed on the bathroom floor as blood spurted everywhere.

'Calvin-san? *Daijoubu?*' A high-pitched male voice called from downstairs, asking Calvin if he was alright. Jiro! Now I remembered what Kurt had said about seeing an Asian man in the house. Maybe it had been Jiro, whom I'd thought was on Maui, but really had never gone. And now I think I understood why Calvin wanted me out of the wetsuit and into a robe: I'd be Jiro's entertainment, before they bumped me off.

Calvin was knocked out, but my problems were far from over. I locked the bathroom door and dragged Calvin's limp body in front of it, to make a barrier that would delay Jiro a few minutes longer.

Sliding the bathroom window open to the second-floor *lanai*, I saw the waiting sailboat again. How I'd hated the boat, but now I longed to be on it. I wondered if Parker or Karen had the binoculars trained on the house. Probably, but since I was inside, they couldn't know what was happening.

Well, there was one thing I knew about sailing. I reached back through the window to the light switch near the bath, which controlled an overhead chandelier. I flashed it on and off in three rhythmic sets of three pulses, the set in the middle longer to form an old-fashioned SOS signal.

I still had to evacuate, and going down the *lanai* seemed a good choice, although there was no waterspout or trellis to serve as a support. *Come on*, I told myself, *commandos do this kind of thing all the time.* But as Kurt had implied, I couldn't carry my weight; I was as soft as the towels I'd used to dry my feet.

The towels! I went back to the floor and grabbed up the heap of clean towels that had scattered when I'd thrown the urn. As I square-knotted the towels together, I noticed they were bamboo, not cotton, and could only hope they would be more flexible and strong than cotton. Soon I'd crafted a rope about twenty feet long; it wouldn't get me all the way down to the ground, but close enough to make the jump safer. I used the same square knot to tie one end of the towel-rope securely around the *lanai* railing and had just climbed over when I heard the bathroom door crash open. I glanced toward the lush garden below me and, seeing nobody waiting there, slid.

My landing was good, with knees bent and feet and hands straight on the ground. I came out of the crouch fast and collected the last two towels, which had torn off the bottom of the rope when I'd jumped.

I melted against the side of the house, knowing that in seconds Jiro might look out the window for me. What would he think, that I'd run for the beach, or the main road?

The reality was that I had to find Michael and Kurt, as quietly and quickly as possible. I tried the kitchen door and found it had been locked. I hurried around the house, debating whether I should cut and run, coming back with the police for Michael and Kurt, but I couldn't imagine them deserting me. I'd find them, and then we'd leave.

As I rounded the side of the house by the driveway, a slight sound caught my ear – it sounded like the purring of an engine. The main garage door was locked shut, but when I ran around the structure I found a second doorway sized for people, not cars. This door was unlocked.

As I'd feared, the dark garage was filled with poisonous fumes, and lit only by the running lights of the Mercedes, which was parked and running. In the hazy gloom, I could make out two men sprawled on the floor, their heads pressed against the crack between the garage door and the floor. I fumbled along the wall in the dark, pressing every button I could find; the light went on finally and then the main door groaned upwards.

As the fresh, life-giving air rushed in, Michael and Kurt's bodies rolled forward. They had been gagged with socks and had their wrists and ankles bound with sharp plastic ties, the kind the police used now instead of handcuffs.

I grabbed a small pair of sharp Japanese gardening shears that I saw hanging on the garage wall and cut Michael's ties. As his arms fell free, Michael's eyelids flickered open. 'Getting out,' he rasped.

'Yes, I'm getting you out.' I would have covered him with kisses, if there had been time.

'Getting out . . . of this . . . business.'

'I keep saying that too.' I cut Kurt's ties, but Kurt's eyes didn't open quickly like Michael's had. I pressed my fingers to his pulse, and thought I felt something, although I wasn't sure.

'How long have you been in here?' I asked Michael, trying to stifle the horror inside me.

'Not as long as him,' he said, getting on his hands and knees and looking at Kurt with sorrow.

It was clear that neither man was well enough to escape on foot. But if I could haul them both into the Mercedes, I could back out of the opened garage door, and get us all to safety. I made the decision quickly and as I opened the rear passenger door, Michael staggered upward.

'Get in the car,' I said, as I heard the sound of the doorknob to the small garage door being twisted. That was locked, but the wide door meant for cars was open. As if he understood what I was thinking, Michael turned from the car and ran a few drunken-looking steps to the switch on the wall which sent the large door creaking down.

As Jiro, dressed in black shorts and matching tank top, came speeding barefoot around the corner, he slowed to get through the decreasing space. The garage door responded to the presence of an obstacle, and stopped.

Jiro seemed stunned, and in the time he paused, as if making sure the door had really halted, I'd grabbed the gardening shears from the floor where they lay beside Kurt and, without stopping to think, drove them into Jiro's face. This was a day for surprises; I'd never been as rough on anybody before, but when I thought about what Jiro and Calvin had done to Charisse, and almost done to Kurt and Michael, I felt desperate, and justified.

Jiro fell to the ground with a cry, covering his face, and as he did so, the stun gun clattered to the floor. I grabbed it and held it ready to use, although Jiro showed no signs of being able to do anything but cower and cry, the hands covering his face turning red from blood.

Now, for the first time, I felt sick about the violence I'd committed, but Michael had in the meantime pushed Kurt into the car, and was calling for me. I pressed the garage door all the way open, jumped into the driver's seat and backed straight out, assiduously avoiding running Jiro over, because now a corner of my brain was telling me that I'd seriously messed with the son of a billionaire, and there could be consequences.

Out on the lava rock driveway, I made a three-point turn and headed out to face the property's gate. To my surprise, the gate didn't automatically open; nor did any of the buttons set into the driver's side visor work. *Key chain*, I thought frantically, and fumbled until I found a device with six buttons. The first one I pressed set the house alarm going, but the next opened the gate.

Out we sped, surprising a mother coaching a toddler on a tricycle, then past a lush grove where my father's friends were practicing tai-chi. I was going so fast that I almost missed Tom, whom Michael pointed out was running behind the car with a baseball bat. I slowed down and he jumped into the unlocked back row.

'Where are you going? Tom asked, between hard breaths.

'To the clinic in Waianae,' I said. 'Kurt's had carbon monoxide exposure . . .'

'I see that – and Michael doesn't look good either.' Tom spoke crossly, as he took Kurt's pulse. 'Why didn't you call me for help earlier? You said you would do that.'

'Sorry. We lost our supply bag with Michael's phone, our walkie-talkie and other equipment in the ocean.'

'OK then. When I received a telephone call from Calvin, I was confused, but tried to keep calm. Then, when Michael's friend from the boat telephoned, I realized you must be at the Kikuchi house, despite what Calvin had said, and I was quite worried.'

'Parker called you?' I was stunned.

'You apparently left your mobile telephone aboard, and Parker scanned the numbers stored within and started calling all the ones with Hawaii exchanges. It took a few calls before he tried our landline, and reached me.'

'I told Parker about Tom as a back-up,' Michael said in his slowed-down, weak voice.

'He thought you three were signaling trouble from the house. Some lights!'

'There was no signal,' Michael said ruefully. 'Calvin knocked me out too fast.'

'I did it when I was upstairs,' I said, then was distracted by the sight of Tom, who had angled Kurt under him and was now performing CPR.

We were fast approaching the Kainani gatehouse, and while I knew it would probably look incriminating for me to stop there in the car everyone knew was the Kikuchis', I knew that to avoid stopping would be worse. In a few clear sentences, I told the startled teenage attendant to call an ambulance to the guardbooth to take Michael and Kurt to the Waianae Clinic.

'Please go with them, Tom,' I said. 'And when you get there, please tell my father I'm absolutely fine.'

'Where will you be?' Tom gasped on his up-breath.

'I'm staying here to meet the police. They have to know what happened, before they find two mashed-up guys at the Kikuchi mansion, notice the stolen car, and come to a different conclusion.'

'It could be bad for you, Rei,' Michael said groggily. 'Did you get anything good?'

'I hope so, because I kept my wetsuit on and the tape recorder running the whole time. I found a bit of evidence in the bathroom that's more than we ever dreamed of, too.'

'The poison?' Michael murmured.

'Maybe. There were plenty of drugs, but also Charisse's hair band, which I pray to God is still trapped in the bathtub where I saw it.'

# Thirty-Eight

I don't know if it was because of everyone's prayers or swift medical care, but Kurt survived, albeit with some changes. His words came more slowly, and what he said was a bit nicer. Still, the military doctors at Tripler, where he was transferred, were sure he was fit enough to stay with the SEALs. I was also relieved that he didn't resent me for what happened, but rather credited me for sticking around in a dangerous place long enough to save his life.

A number of other good things happened, too. Charisse's hairband, which I'd worried so much about moving, was still inside the bath drain cover along with a few strands of her hair. The tape-recorder I'd worn had functioned and recorded all the damning words that Calvin had said. As a result, both Jiro and Calvin had been charged in the murder of Charisse. Additionally, Calvin faced charges of arson, and various counts of attempted murder regarding Michael, Kurt, my father, and myself.

Over the phone from Tokyo, Hugh had said the way that things played out was sheer luck – that a hairband in a bath drain alone probably couldn't have sent Jiro and Calvin to jail, and Michael, Kurt and I might have been charged with home invasion if Calvin and Jiro hadn't so clearly attempted to murder us.

'I miss you, Rei, but I don't miss all your high drama and danger,' Hugh had said at the end of our conversation. I'd hung up and thought about his comment. For me, events in the month had been remarkable; I'd come to believe that Hawaii was a place where miracles could, and did, happen. After all, my father had gotten better, and so had I. And, in my case, healing meant more than a recovery from poisoning; it was a recovery from chronic loneliness, the discovery that not only was I able to live with other people, I loved it. Taking care of my father, uncle and cousin had been the opening act; now I could commit myself to Michael with an open heart and confidence. And while I would probably always love Uncle Yosh and Courtney more than the rest of the Hawaii Shimura clan, I felt Edwin had learned something from knowing us, and I fully accepted my role in his particular tribe.

Edwin had finally made some money on an internet auction, and he'd undertaken a new job to keep himself busy: family wedding planner, although Aunt Margaret was the one who actually secured a sunset wedding on the hotel lawn, with just five days' notice. Braden was dutifully filling out his application for the James School with the help of my father, Uncle Hiroshi and Tom, who all had a different take on the essay question 'Tell Us about Yourself!'

Courtney and Uncle Yosh had been my shopping companions at every bridal boutique in Honolulu, and helped me decide on a long, bias-cut, creamy silk gown tinged with just a bit of yellow on the bottom. 'Look like plumeria,' Uncle Yosh had said, and Courtney had promised to make both Michael and me wedding leis that were rich with my favorite Hawaiian flowers.

Michael returned to D.C. the day after Jiro and Calvin were arrested. That morning, he'd come Leeward one last time to ask my father, who was still in the hospital, permission to marry me. Of course, my father granted it, and Michael and I drove back to Waikiki to pick up his luggage and walk the Alai Wai Canal one last time.

'There's something we need to talk about,' Michael said.

I shot a glance at him, because he sounded so sober. Surely he wasn't changing his mind?

'The other night, you made a crack about there being some kind of James Bond attraction.'

'Yes, I did say that, although of course, I don't really want to marry a celluloid man. I want to marry you.'

'When you rescued me, I told you I was getting out of the business. I mean to do it. No more spying.'

'Oh, well. At least I'll have my memories.' I squeezed his hand.

'Actually, when I was meeting with my old friend at Pearl Harbor – I didn't mention it before, but that lunch was more like a job interview.'

'Do you want to join the Navy again?' I felt something inside me drop. Sure, the Navy was safer work than OCI, but he'd be away from me for months at a time every year. It would be like being single again.

'I wouldn't reactivate, no. But there's a center for Pacific Rim intelligence based right here. The pay's OK, and . . . well, we could live here, in Hawaii.'

'You'd want to live here?' He'd hinted at it before, and of course I loved Hawaii, but I hadn't imagined it could ever happen. I was used to hardship and suffering, not the prospect of life on a tropical island.

'After I get Braden squared away at the James School and some projects are tied up at OCI, I'd love to come back. The sailing is unbelievable, and this mix of Asian and Western culture makes it the perfect place for us to raise children. They won't be singled out for being half-anything; they'll just be like everyone else.'

'I see your point,' I said slowly.

'And it's not just for our kids; it's the state itself. We're halfway between Japan and the US, the perfect neutral ground for both of us. You can continue with OCI, and there'll be no conflict of interest if I'm working for the federal government at Pearl Harbor.'

I imagined myself in Japan, overworked, alone and exhausted in OCI's luxurious apartment in Hiroo. Then I flashed to myself queuing at Narita airport every second weekend for the flight that would take me to join Michael in the sun for two or three days at a time. I shook my head firmly. 'No. Forget OCI; the only reason I kept my ties to that place was to be with you. I don't want to live away from you, or have you worry about me. I don't exactly know what I'll wind up doing here, but jobs have a way of finding me, don't you think?'

'Trouble has a way of finding you,' Michael had said, and then he kissed me, as if we were the only two people alongside the canal. By the time we'd broken apart, the ring that I'd thought he'd returned had transitioned from his pocket to my finger, and now all I had left to do was convince my fiancé that in Hawaii, not only brides wore white, but their grooms did too.

\*　　\*　　\*

'Will you come to my wedding?' I asked Josiah Pierce, when I'd accepted his invitation to tea in the garden of his Tantalus home.

It was the afternoon of the day after Michael had left for the mainland and, as if in protest, the weather was bad. The sky had opened right at the start of Mr Pierce's exhaustive garden tour, so we traversed the garden under the protection of a golf umbrella. Standing close to him, I wondered how I could ever have been afraid. His courtesy, and thoughtful attention to old manners, reminded me of my Japanese mentor, Mr Ishida. Of course I would want Mr Pierce at my wedding, where he could meet Mr Ishida and the rest of the handful or so of very close Japanese friends and relatives who could come to Hawaii on short notice.

'What do you mean, wedding? Are you leaving the husband you have?' Josiah Pierce's wry question brought me back to the present, and I remembered my long-ago fib.

'I'm not leaving Michael. I must admit to you, with some embarrassment, that we're marrying. For the first time.'

'You didn't want me to know you lived together? My, you are an old-fashioned girl.'

'No, that wasn't our situation. It's actually a rather new romance. I'm sorry we weren't honest at the start, when we met you. Michael thought . . .' I trailed off. It was impossible to explain.

'Well, I can only imagine that Michael said these things because he wanted the situation to be different. I think that's an indication he's likely to be a devoted husband.' Josiah Pierce sat down on an aged iron garden settee, and indicated that I should join him.

'I used to question whether I . . . whether I could commit to anyone,' I said. 'But those fears are gone now. Permanently.'

'What changed for you, then?'

'I credit it to spending time with my father, day in and out. I just got used to living with someone I cared about, and having more family around. And I think it's better that way. You know, Michael and I are in the midst of deciding whether to permanently relocate here. It seems crazy to give up our past lives, but awfully tempting.'

'Yes, lots of people want to live in paradise, but when they really settle in, they get something we call Rock Fever – an insatiable desire to get off this island and go somewhere larger and more interesting.'

'Don't you think we could make it here? We can't help speaking with mainland accents, so maybe we'll never escape being *malihini.*'

JP smiled. 'Oh, don't worry about that. This is not only the best place on earth to raise children, but also to grow old. But before the children come, what will you do to stay busy?'

He meant well, so I decided to ignore my slight irritation at his assumption that I would stop working forever if we had a child. 'Well, I will concentrate on finding us a place to live first, which I gather is no easy feat on Oahu, and at the same time try to arrange some job interviews, maybe at the museums. I have more or less the right training and experience for museum work, but I always seem to be getting distracted.'

'Back up a moment. You're talking about buying or renting a place before you've got the two salaries in place, and one of them will be at a non-profit? This island is expensive, if you haven't noticed.'

'There are small apartments in the urban areas that aren't that bad . . . but Michael and I really have become fond of the Leeward Side. It's cheaper, sunnier, and it's where the real people live.'

'I like the Leeward Side too, but you've got to remember to call it what we do: Ewa. And you may want to hold on to the mainland condominium. The more real estate you can afford to hold close, the better.'

'Spoken like a true robber baron,' I teased.

JP laughed. 'I don't drive much anymore, Rei, but if you have time this afternoon, I have a hankering to go Ewa.'

'Do you want to see the burned village?' I asked, not wanting to revisit the destruction Calvin had caused on this particular beautiful day.

'Actually, I don't want to make myself sad on such an afternoon of good news. There's a place I'd been thinking of showing you, but then you fell ill and I didn't think you'd want to go anywhere alone with me. Now we can visit this place, but only if you aren't in a rush.'

'Sure.' I thought for a minute, and then took the plunge.

'And maybe – on the way back – we can stop and say hello to my Great-Uncle Yoshitsune. I think you should meet each other.'

JP nodded. 'Yes, I'd like to see him, if he'll see me. I agree that a conversation is long overdue.'

We departed the congestion of Honolulu freeways to H-1 West, where the dark skies gave way to a giant rainbow, and then plenty of sun – so much that I gave up on the ailing air-conditioner and asked Mr Pierce if he didn't mind my rolling down the windows. From the Ewa Beach exit, Mr Pierce directed me to a smooth, limited-access road, bordered by housing developments, gas stations, and strip malls. Then we left the highway for a spur road that led to a narrow quiet street overhung with old, lush trees. On the right side was a one-story church built in the long, simple form of a barn; it looked quite old, but was painted a fresh white and had a sign that indicated a community pre-school was operating within. Across the street from the church stood the abandoned sugar mill, a monument of rusted metal and broken glass.

'That was the last mill in operation on our island,' Josiah Pierce said softly. 'So many people cried when it closed.'

'Well, at least it's not a ghost town around here. It looks as if people are still living in this area. The church has a school.'

'Yes, and take a right on the next street. You'll see the village has residents, too.'

This was a plantation village? As I slowly drove the streets, I passed simple, box-shaped cottages similar to those I'd seen near Kainoa's coffee shop. But in this neighborhood, smoothly paved roads ran alongside freshly painted cottages, and the gardens were full of healthy fruit trees, flowers, and vegetables.

'You've brought me to old houses that are living happily ever after. What a wonderful gift!' I beamed at him.

JP looked at me with satisfaction. 'This neighborhood, Tenney Village, is a state-sponsored project – subsidized, so people of a certain income level were allowed to buy these 1920s plantation village homes at very reasonable rates.'

'It must have been difficult to get people to believe this could be done.'

'Yes, indeed. I was one of the naysayers, given the deplorable state of my own decrepit plantation villages, and the lack of interest from anyone except big money developers who wanted to raze them. But this village has something our older area by Kainani doesn't: it's close to the shopping in Waikele, and about twenty minutes from central Honolulu. Some people even commute by boat to their jobs at Pearl Harbor or downtown.'

I wanted to ask more questions about the development, but Josiah Pierce was looking at his watch and urging me back to the van. I got in again and said, 'To my uncle's house, then?'

'Yes. But there's another stop just five minutes away that I'd like you to see.'

With the van windows rolled down to bring in the gentle trade winds, I cruised back on to the limited-access highway, and then followed Mr Pierce's directions to make a couple of lefts. Passing a ramshackle supermarket and a series of worn-looking apartment buildings, we came to a rough path of gravel and that led to a vintage cottage with peeling paint, and then another just like it.

'Another plantation village,' I said.

'Yes, and this village still belongs to me and my brother, Lindsay. It used to house the workers for a pineapple-growing and canning operation that folded in the thirties, when Hawaiian fruit became too much of a luxury for main-landers.'

'Where's the pineapple field?' I was confused, because this tiny housing area seemed hemmed in by modern development.

'That supermarket you just saw, plus the strip mall, plus the apartments – there were the fields and plant buildings! Now, let's park and do some walking.'

I wandered a few paces behind my guide, spotting amid the tiny houses a longer plantation store building with faded lettering advertising groceries and beer. It was clearly vacant, with vines growing out of the glassless windows. A few of the houses in one cluster had trucks outside them, giving me the feeling someone was living there, perhaps illegally. *A step up from the outdoors*, I thought, remembering the homeless people I'd seen on Maile Beach.

These things didn't seem to faze Josiah Pierce, who was walking determinedly ahead, as if he had somewhere in particular to go. I picked up my pace, and when he rounded a corner, I saw a Beach Access sign, and a straight row of slightly larger cottages.

Beach access meant ocean. As we drew closer, I saw flashes of blue behind the houses. 'Great location,' I said. 'Who was housed in this row?'

'This is the Portuguese village, so basically any family in that community with enough children for two or three bedrooms. Swimming and lying on the beach weren't on the minds of many around here; they were too tired.'

He walked up to a door and tapped it lightly. It swung open, and he beckoned for me to follow him in.

'I don't know if we should walk through the houses,' I called out. 'The floors are likely to be rotten.'

'I'll take that risk.' He looked over his shoulder at me. 'If it's any reassurance, I was out here fairly recently with my property manager. This house is the soundest one.'

I stepped a few feet further into the empty entry hall, noticing now what I should have seen earlier, the footprints in the dust. Yes, this place had been recently explored, and if I stepped in the places where other feet had been, chances were I wasn't going through the floor.

To my left was a small, perfectly proportioned room that I imagined had been the parlor. To the right were two doorways leading to smaller rooms – bedrooms. There was a crumpled-up, ancient newspaper in a corner of one of them. I saw the date, 1938, but I couldn't read the Portuguese under it. The windows were large, and I saw traces of old electricity: the push-button light switches on the mottled walls, and old glass-shaded light fixtures and fans on the ceilings.

Proceeding to the rear of the house, I saw a small bathroom, all with the original porcelain fixtures, and a kitchen with a charming antique icebox, an apron sink, small table, and some old crockery on shelves. Josiah Pierce had opened the back door and was looking out.

'Big waves tonight,' he said.

I moved to stand next to him, and then went down the steps to explore a narrow stretch of overgrown garden, and a rough gravel path leading downward to a strip of sand and a broken wooden dock, and then the Pacific.

'This location is paradise,' I said. 'I'm very surprised you didn't sell it to Mitsuo Kikuchi or somebody earlier on.'

'Who wants to build a resort behind a downscale shopping center?'

'Well, you could tear it down. Couldn't you?'

'The commercial areas you saw aren't under my control. All I have in Ewa is this little portion of – as you put it – paradise.'

'I'm sure the local people would prefer a supermarket to another resort. This little area is such a haven, though. The area's convenient, and the water access is amazing.'

'Do you think this is the kind of place you might like to start your married life?'

'Sure.' I laughed shakily. 'The only problem is, each plot alone would be a million and more, wouldn't it?'

'If you knocked everything down to create a brand new housing development, perhaps. But that's not what I have in mind, so the price I was thinking of is somewhere around ten grand.' Before I could recover from the shock, he'd moved on. 'It's a low price because of all the renovation you'd have to pay for yourselves, according to your taste. That, and there would be an additional expectation.'

'Aha!' I smiled at him. 'I imagined some strings were attached.'

'You saw how Tenney Village was restored, and I'd like to do that, but I'm afraid I prefer not to have state involvement. I want someone to create aesthetic guidelines for the entire redevelopment and live onsite in a cottage that has been renovated to the highest standards. The homes are going to be reasonably priced and comfortable, but there will be development covenants, and ensuring buyers are agreeable to the covenants will take some finesse.'

'I understand.' I was afraid to ask the next question, because I wanted the job so badly, but I was afraid he'd think I was unqualified. 'The employee you mention – is he or she already working within Pierce Holdings, or are you getting an architect from outside?'

'I'm thinking of you, Rei. You may refine the title as you like, but the important thing is to remember that even though these cottages are small, you must think on a large scale.'

'I . . . I will!' I stammered, thinking that this really was a position I wasn't trained for, just like every other one I'd taken on in my life.

'There are things that only a person living here, day in and day out, could figure out, such as whether some unsalvageable or badly located cottages should be removed for open space. In the old days, we had lots of sports in the plantation villages, playing baseball in the evenings and so on.'

'That's a great idea, and you could also . . . make it a little more like a resort?' I knew I was throwing myself out on a limb, since he was so cautious about modern development.

'This is going to be housing for local people. In what way should we make it like a resort?' He sounded puzzled.

'There could be a communal barbecuing area, a small playground, and at least one swimming pool. And what about that empty plantation store? It's perfect for a coffee shop, which also could sell fishing and boating supplies.' I already had an idea who could run the place.

'I like those ideas.' Josiah Pierce's voice was firm. 'And I won't develop this village unless you agree to take the job. Of course, you may want to discuss it with Michael.'

But I was headstrong, so I had no intention of discussing it with Michael. Instead, I just married him. Only after a long day of hugging new relatives and old friends from Japan was the time finally right. We waved Michael's parents and mine off to dinner at Alan Wong, and boarded our white limousine, decorated in the gaudiest manner imaginable by Braden and Courtney. When we were safely en route to the Halekulani, I slid the glass partition separating us from the driver and instructed him to detour to the faded supermarket near Ewa Beach.

'Did you forget something?' Michael asked, looking at me with concern. 'If you really need it tonight, we can go to the supermarket, but I think we'll be a laughing stock, dressed like this.'

'Just wait,' I said, and continued with my directions to the old Pierce village. I remembered the little street, and had the driver stop, and ushered Michael out and up to my favorite cottage in the row.

'Let me guess – Josiah Pierce owns this area?' Michael asked as I led him up the short flight of steps and inside the empty old house.

'It's about to become mine – I mean, ours.' I laughed slightly, and leaned into him. It was going to take a while to get used to being married. As Michael listened, I explained Josiah Pierce's offer of a house, and an exciting new job for me. When I'd finished, he walked out to the back of the house, opened the door, and there was ocean.

'I could sail to work,' Michael said. 'This is . . . unbelievable.'

'Yes, and I haven't even told you how low the price is. You could keep your condo in Virginia, in case you – I mean, we – decide to go back.'

'There's no going back,' Michael said, slipping his arms around me, and burying his face in my hair for a moment.

'Hey, do you smell something?' I asked, finally noticing what had seemed different this time around.

'Just your skin. Is that plumeria body cream?'

'No, and I left my lei in the limousine. I think there's fresh plumeria nearby, and I swear it's not growing in the garden.' I broke away from Michael, and he wandered after me into the former parlor, which I'd pegged as our future bedroom.

I hadn't noticed anything before, but the room now held a small, weather-beaten card table, and on it was one of the old crocks from the kitchen filled with yellow hibiscus and white plumeria: the colors of my wedding gown. I inhaled sharply at the sight.

'You didn't arrange this to welcome me?' Michael said, leaning over and sniffing the lush bouquet.

I shook my head. 'No, and nobody knows this will be our cottage. I never told JP that I returned one afternoon, looked at all the houses, and decided this is the one I like best of all.'

Michael straightened up and slipped his hand into mine. 'Well, by the time we move in, we'll hopefully have an answer to this mystery.'

I smiled back at him, thinking to myself that it wasn't going to happen that way. I didn't need to know who'd brought flowers to the house; this was not a mystery either of us needed to solve. All we needed to do was to never forget the flowers, and let them scent our dreams.